Praise for the no

"This second chance story is ab
healing. I was utterly captivated
soul-rending yearning, could practically feel the bite of the misty
Scottish breeze on my cheeks through every page."
—Tarah DeWitt, *USA TODAY* bestselling author of *Savor It*,
on *Scot and Bothered*

"*Scot and Bothered* has that alchemic thing that makes me love
romance: gorgeous writing and atmospheric settings, unreal romantic
tension that would shatter the knife that tried to cut it, and characters
who feel like your mirror's reflection... This is a forever comfort read."
—Jessica Joyce, *USA TODAY* bestselling author of *You, with a View* and
The Ex Vows

"Passion, pining, a desperately hot Scot, only one tent—this delicious
slow-burn romance has it all. There's a reason Alexandra Kiley is one of
my favorite contemporary romance writers."
—Maggie North, author of *Rules for Second Chances*,
on *Scot and Bothered*

"Alexandra Kiley's sophomore novel is an absolute triumph! This is
second chance romance at its finest... Jack and Brooke will make
you believe in true love... With *Scot and Bothered*, Kiley proves she is a
writer to watch!"
—Falon Ballard, author of *Right on Cue*

"While readers will traverse the Skye Trail in rich detail, it's the journey
of romantic restoration that will leave readers breathless and
windswept."
—Livy Hart, author of *The Great Dating Fake Off*, on *Scot and Bothered*

"*Scot and Bothered* is as sexy and swoony as it is heartfelt and
thoughtful. Kiley deftly explores the stories we tell about our families,
our home, our careers, and more importantly, ourselves."
—Sarah T. Dubb, author of *Birding with Benefits*

"A deftly woven novel that's warmer than a shot of Highlands whisky.
Kiley explores ambition, forgiveness, and second chances, and
delivers a tale as fiercely beautiful as Scotland itself."
—Shaylin Gandhi, author of *When We Had Forever*,
on *Scot and Bothered*

"The Isle of Skye is famously beautiful, but the journey Alexandra Kiley
takes us on in *Scot and Bothered* might be even more so. I loved every
gorgeous step."
—Amanda Elliot, author of *Love You a Latke*

SCOT
and
BOTHERED

ALEXANDRA KILEY

CANARY STREET PRESS

CANARY
STREET
PRESS™

PLEASE RECYCLE

THIS PRODUCT IS RECYCLABLE

Recycling programs
for this product may
not exist in your area.

ISBN-13: 978-1-335-58008-5

Scot and Bothered

Copyright © 2025 by Alexandra Kiley

For questions and comments about the quality of this book, please contact us
at CustomerService@Harlequin.com.

TM is a trademark of Harlequin Enterprises ULC.

Canary Street Press
22 Adelaide St. West, 41st Floor
Toronto, Ontario M5H 4E3, Canada
CanaryStPress.com

Printed in U.S.A.

Also by Alexandra Kiley

Kilt Trip

Visit alexandrakiley.com for more details!

To the people who help us find the heartbeat of our own stories.

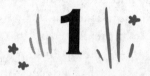

NOW

Brooke Sinclair had always dreamed of seeing her words in print. Only, she thought, as she picked up the book at the sign-in table, she hadn't pictured her client's name on the cover, her own name buried inside a legally binding gag order.

She ran her thumb over the raised text of the author's name and the letters singed her finger like they were cursed. *Maybe that's why they called it ghostwriting.*

"Better hurry in, Suzi's about to start the discussion."

Brooke gave the check-in woman a tight smile and skirted the D-shaped atrium of McEwan Hall at the University of Edinburgh—her almost–alma mater.

The front of the auditorium might've been a cathedral with a two-story gilded organ filling the space, capped off by a bridge of windows under a carved arch. The soaring dome rivaled St. Peter's Basilica, and three stories of balconies ringed the room. It felt like the type of place that would host a Shakespeare play instead of a signing for a book Brooke had written but could never mention.

The words that used to ricochet through her as she'd walked

these prestigious halls were *bestselling author* and *creative writing fellow*. But as she made her way to the back of the gathering, *try hard* clanged around in Brooke's mind.

She'd once thought she'd graduate in this room, even looked forward to sitting on an uncomfortable wooden chair so long as she was clad in a cap and gown. Surely seven years was enough time for the resentment to fade, but as she stared up at the blue-tinged rose window at the center of the ceiling, surrounded by ornately carved wooden embellishments and murals mimicking the Italian classics, that bitterness in her chest prickled as strongly as ever.

Usually, she swelled with pride when she attended her authors' events. She loved celebrating their stories and achievements from the audience. But there was something about being back on campus that prevented her from blocking out that voice that said these jobs were a far cry from what she'd set out to do. Like she'd left all her old dreams behind in these hallowed halls and they'd sucker punched her when she'd walked in the door.

It wasn't as if she hadn't attempted to write her own stories in the intervening years. But Brooke froze up. Choked. Wrote such absolute garbage, she was surprised her computer didn't self-destruct in an indignant display of disgust.

She'd been a shooting star who'd flamed out spectacularly. All that *potential* people had talked about her whole life…maybe it had never existed in the first place. It was easier to slip into someone else's story, someone else's voice, than to admit she'd lost her own.

Brooke made her way down the aisle, discreetly glancing around for her editor, Charlotte. Brooke only had enough bravado to make it through the signing, not to have one single conversation with anyone she'd known back then.

She'd overdone it with the makeup this morning, as if a heavy hand with a shimmery eye shadow stick could disguise her crumbled confidence. It didn't, and Brooke was reminded of that sad fact every time she had to raise her eyebrows to unstick the crease of her eyelids.

By the time Brooke spotted Charlotte in the second row, her flight reflex was in full-on hummingbird mode under her sternum. Or maybe a mockingbird. Mourning dove? Regardless, it was taking up her entire chest cavity and not leaving any space for her lungs. She clenched her hands to get some blood back into them.

Charlotte stood and waved to Brooke, the bangles on her wrist glinting in the low light. She was chic as always, her black hair styled in a wavy pixie with an undercut, wearing gold hoop earrings and an indigo floral midi dress.

Brooke moved down the row and slipped into the empty seat next to Charlotte, who ran a hand lovingly over the book Brooke held. "It turned out so nicely, didn't it?" she asked in her soothing Scottish accent.

"It's stunning." And it was. The colors were vibrant; the title was perfect. It was a cover anyone would be proud of. Brooke set the book on the ground, tilted against the wooden leg of the chair in front of her.

"How's Mhairi's draft coming?" Charlotte asked.

The thought of Mhairi—her old writing professor turned friend—brought a smile to Brooke's face.

"Great."

A research university demands publications and Mhairi loved teaching, running workshops, and inspiring students, so she'd hired Brooke for various academic projects over the years—including her first ghostwriting job after everything imploded. When Brooke had felt shell-shocked and aimless, not wanting to return to the States, but not sure where she fit in in Edinburgh, Mhairi had sat her down at her kitchen table and given Brooke a project, a direction, and a new dream.

But *this* project was different. Mhairi's memoir; the pinnacle of her publishing career.

And she'd given Brooke the single greatest thing anyone had ever offered her: a cowriting credit.

A second chance.

When Mhairi had first approached her, Brooke had blurted out, "You don't need my help!" Mhairi was a phenomenal author. But when she'd explained more about the story—founding the eighty-mile Skye Trail with a group of hikers through the Trotternish Ridge and the Cuillin Mountains on the Isle of Skye—Brooke had stopped objecting.

She wanted to live in Mhairi's memories, to get lost in her passion, in the way Mhairi reached for what she wanted and held on tight. Brooke remembered being that kind of wide-eyed dreamer, too, but while the world had slapped her down, Mhairi had thrived. She'd changed the world.

Getting to hear her story was a privilege, but *writing* it? That was an honor.

"I think we'll have a draft to you by the end of the week."

"I can't *wait* to read it." Charlotte clasped her hands together. "And as soon as you're done, I heard a juicy rumor this morning about a celebrity memoir opportunity. I can't share details yet, but I think you'd be the *perfect* ghostwriter for it."

Brooke tried to muster the same thrill that always coursed up her spine at Charlotte's faith in her, but like everything else today, it felt like a ghost of what it'd once been. "I would love to be considered. Thank you for thinking of me."

"You're the first person I'd call."

Charlotte turned to speak with the woman on her left and Brooke willed the chatter in the room to settle on her shoulders like a weighted blanket instead of burrowing under her skin as she stared up into the balconies.

The first time she'd been up there had been Fresher's Week ten years ago. Meant as an orientation for the University of Edinburgh, a time to get settled and buy books, Fresher's Week was, in reality, a five-day pub crawl. Brooke had been delighted that she could legally drink at eighteen while her high school friends were getting MIPs at frat parties back in the States.

That night, she'd come to the ceilidh and met Kieran and Chels. They'd twirled around to the sound of fiddles and stomping and when they'd been too sweaty to carry on, they'd retreated to the balcony to drink from Kieran's flask. He'd reclined in the maroon seats while Chels had heckled dancers from above and Brooke had had the sense she was falling in love, that she'd met her soulmates.

Another memory in that balcony floated to her, hidden in the dark, warm lips pressed close to her ear with whispered promises and stolen touches.

The pads of her fingertips caught in the seam of the wooden chair, as if her body was trying to physically hold her back from that particular memory lane. She wasn't thinking about Jack today.

The people in her aisle shifted while an older white man made his way to the empty seat next to Brooke. Charlotte leaned forward with a broad smile on her face. "So glad you could join us." She gestured for him to take the seat next to Brooke while Brooke's heart attempted to climb the balustrade and throw itself from the balcony.

The dean of the English Department.

She made a quick calculation of how easily she could hurdle over Charlotte's lap and how many steps it would take to reach the women's bathroom. She figured it was about thirty. Completely within dashing range.

But Brooke wasn't a coward. She rolled her shoulders back, ignoring the way her pulse had spread all the way down to her fingertips. She would show him she couldn't even remember the tiny dash of pity on his face, completely overshadowed by judgment, when Brooke had walked into his office seven years ago.

"Brooke Sinclair, this is my dear friend, Thomas Campbell."

Brooke dragged her eyes up to the dean's. He looked exactly

the same: white button-up and tie under his maroon sweater vest, full white beard, bushy eyebrows, wire glasses. He gave her a warm smile and reached out a hand. "Pleasure to meet you," he said in his low burr.

Brooke deflated like a popped bag of chips. He didn't even *recognize* her. As if that day didn't haunt his literal dreams like it did hers. As if his decision that'd caused an inflection point of catastrophic proportions in Brooke's life didn't weigh on him at all.

God, would she even recognize herself? She felt so far from the girl she'd been—so optimistic, so sure things would simply *work out* because she willed them to.

Brooke could only nod in response and shake his clammy hand. Where was Kieran's flask when she needed it?

"How do you two know each other?" Dean Campbell asked, ever the networker.

"She's one of my writers," Charlotte said before Brooke could fumble for an answer. "She's *fabulous*." Charlotte placed a comforting hand on Brooke's shoulder. She already loved Charlotte, but would now gladly give her a kidney for heaping praise on her in front of the dean.

"Oh, wonderful," Dean Campbell said with a broad grin. "Anything I've read?"

Brooke bristled at the question, clenching her teeth. Ghostwriting was a job of secrets—but not the fun kind like working for the CIA. She usually skirted this question, but she wanted to yell, *Yes, I wrote* this *book!* and wave it around under his nose. She wanted to revel in knowing that *he knew* how far she'd gone despite him. But she couldn't. Not with Charlotte sitting right next to her.

But there was one book she *could* talk about. "I'm cowriting Professor McCallister's memoir right now, actually." Brooke savored the way his eyebrows went up, in tandem with his stock in her.

Suzi walked onto the grand stage, her heels clicking until she made it to the plush rug and taupe armchair situated in the center. She set the copy of her travel memoir—a Costa Rican *Eat, Pray, Love*—on the little side table and tapped the microphone, the resulting feedback screeching through the room.

Brooke winced, partly from the noise and partly to brace herself against the words she was sure Suzi would throw around about *a labor of love* and *finding the right words* to tell her story, and Brooke would sit in the audience and no one would ever know about the painstaking effort and details she'd poured into those pages.

Oh, how the mighty had fallen.

THEN

Tripping over cobblestones, Brooke, Chels, and Kieran made their tipsy way across Edinburgh's lamplit old town. Kieran's older brother's house parties were legendary and they'd pregamed accordingly.

Kieran and Chels took almost nothing seriously, especially a costume party. He was in a red shirt with a sign around his neck reading Netflix and Chels wore athletic pants and a tank top with a matching Chill sign, even though they'd immediately part ways—Kieran to the beer pong table and Chels to the dance floor.

Chels hooked one arm around Brooke's neck. "I'm so glad you're coming with us," she squealed in her posh English accent, raising Kieran's flask in the air and bumping her fake glasses off kilter. Brooke snatched the flask before Chels spilled it and tossed back a burning swig.

"Classes haven't started yet. She's no excuse to miss it," Kieran said.

"You're making it sound like I lock myself in the library." Sure, Brooke was driven—she had a scholarship to maintain and the world to impress—but with friends like these two, there were always shenanigans going on in the periphery.

Kieran quirked an eyebrow at Brooke and she crossed her arms in indignation and also to combat the September wind cutting through her black hoodie, stealing away the warmth from her whisky-fueled alcohol jacket. "Not all of us can descend into a caffeine haze and learn an entire term's worth of material during revision week," Brooke defended.

Chels and Kieran always emerged as zombies from exams and proceeded to sleep for ten days straight. Brooke worked hard for her grades. And she wasn't graduating this spring and getting into the summer writing fellowship Professor McCallister— her favorite author and all-around idol—hosted by slacking off.

"That's literally what revision week is for. Why else would they give it to us?" Kieran asked, jumping over bike racks and hollering into the night. If he and his brother, Rohan, had been American, they'd be Philadelphia sports fans, for sure.

By the time they made it to Rohan's new flat, the party was in full swing. A heavy bass line reverberated in the stairwell and people spilled out onto the landing.

"Alright, overachiever." Kieran pulled his flask out of Brooke's hand midsip.

"Hey!" Brooke wiped away the whisky dribbling over her chin as she followed Chels into the humid living room—cleared of its furniture to make space for the crush of dancers, string lights hanging at the top of the tall ceiling. The electropop beat of Calvin Harris's "Summer" pulsed so loudly through the oversize speakers, Brooke was surprised the neighbors hadn't called in a noise violation yet. Rohan must've invited his football team, all their fans, *and* the entire building.

Chels punched her hand above her head to the rhythm, weaving through the crowd and towing Brooke behind her. She bumped against a guy dressed as Deadpool, a lumberjack, and a human piñata wrapped in fuchsia, yellow, and green fringed paper as they made their way toward the kitchen.

Crammed in with so many sweaty bodies, Brooke was sweltering. She pushed up the sleeves of her black hoodie and unzipped it so the low V of her black bra was almost showing. She felt bold tonight.

A loud pop sounded and silver confetti rained down to the screaming delight of the party. A beach ball bejeweled like a disco ball bounced around the room and Brooke reached up to hit it back into the air.

The night was awash with possibility. Like they might end up at the beach or climbing onto the roof, but either way, they'd have a story to tell.

Chels twirled her around and pulled Brooke in close, scream-whispering in her ear, "Jazz is here!" before heading into the middle of the dance floor toward her on-again crush.

Chels's peer pressure was the only thing keeping her dancing. As Brooke made to leave, she nearly collided with Rohan, dressed in a red-and-white-striped shirt, red ski hat, and glasses. At six foot two, it was the easiest *Where's Waldo?* she'd ever played.

"You made it!" he shouted over the noise in the room. He had all the dark-eyed beauty of his Indian mother and his Scottish father's penchant for mayhem; he and Kieran were a duo of charismatic menaces.

Rohan pulled Brooke into the kitchen and twirled her under his arm. "Meet my new flatmate." She spun and stumbled, hand landing against a frilly pirate shirt over a hard chest.

"This is Brooke."

She steadied herself and looked up at Rohan's roommate with a half-formed apology and a smile that got a bit lost when her eyes found his dark ones locked on her, framed with eyelashes that put her mascara to shame, a shadow under his full bottom lip.

He blinked twice, pulled off the skull-and-crossbones patch covering one lens of his tortoiseshell glasses, and slipped it into his pocket.

"Captain," Brooke said breathlessly.

A sexy half smile stretched across his face and spread through her like a vodka shot. He held out his hand. "I'm Jack."

"Sparrow?" She slipped her hand into his—warm, gentle, lingering.

"Sutherland."

"And here I thought you were the real deal," she teased.

Rohan placed a red cup in front of her and she dropped Jack's hand; she'd forgotten Rohan was there. Brooke hooked a thumb in his direction. "Bold move living with this one," she said to Jack, then tipped her head. "Or do you not know that yet?"

Rohan let out a full-throated laugh but Jack's was a low, rumbly thing that tugged at her stomach.

"I'm aware of the antics." His eyes didn't leave her face and she couldn't help tracking the bow of his lip and the curve of his glasses where they rested against his cheeks.

"We play footie together," Rohan added before turning to welcome a woman with a pink pixie cut dressed like Tinker Bell, wrapping her in a hug and lifting her off her feet.

It'd been a grave tactical error declining all of Rohan's invitations to his matches. If Jack was this good-looking as a pirate, he'd be devastating in joggers.

He tweaked the black felt ear safety-pinned on her hood. "And what are you supposed to be?"

"An I-Don't-Care Bear, clearly," she said, gesturing to the white circle in the middle of her stomach housing a pot leaf, a storm cloud, and a middle finger she'd drawn herself.

Jack broke into a full-fledged smile and the brightness was enough to turn her into an I-Care-A-Whole-Fucking-Lot Bear.

"Clever," he said, and in a lifetime of wanting to be the best, Brooke had never enjoyed hearing that quite so much.

A guy torpedoed in, wrapping Jack in a headlock and chanting, "Beer pong! Beer pong!"

Jack scuffled, attempting to knock the guy's feet out from under him, and Brooke took a step back. The other guy seemed to anticipate Jack's hook maneuver and remained upright. He held out his free hand to Brooke, his brown hair curling into his eyes, while Jack twisted uselessly under his arm. "I'm Logan."

Brooke looked to Jack who stilled and heaved out a defeated sigh. "My brother."

"Oh. Hi," Brooke said with a laugh and took Logan's hand.

Jack landed a heel on the top of Logan's foot; Logan yelped and released the hold. Jack's eyes were hot on her, as if he didn't like her attention on his brother, and it sent a thrill through her stomach.

"Where's Rohan?" Logan asked. Brooke scanned the busy kitchen and found him making out with the pink-haired girl sitting on the counter.

When Brooke turned back to Jack, he arched an eyebrow at her. "It looks as if I'm in need of a beer pong partner."

"Wait just a minute." Logan held his hand up between them. "How good are you?"

"There's a lot riding on this," Jack said, crossing his arms. "Two decades of competitive spirit and bragging rights." He lifted a hand to shield his mouth and mock-whispered, "Say 'Abysmal.'"

She bit back a smile and told Logan, "Totally average," when in fact, she was fantastic. She didn't do things she wasn't damn good at.

Logan eyed her skeptically, but she was pulled back to Jack's dark gaze.

"She's it," Jack said.

The heat flaring in her chest and spreading into her cheeks was better than any spark she'd read about in a book. Brooke smiled a too-wide smile as she followed Jack farther into the dimly lit kitchen, tracking the stretch of his shirt over his back muscles and noticing the way he cracked his knuckles down by his side.

A redheaded woman in sunglasses and a flamingo floaty racked cups on the far side next to Logan.

Jack handed Brooke a warm beer she immediately cracked and started pouring. He stood beside her, arm brushing hers as he poured his beer. Excitement fizzed in her like the bubbles inside the can.

"Now, you don't have to worry about Logan. He can't aim for shit when he's pissed," Jack explained, pouring the last of his beer into a red cup.

Logan threw a Ping-Pong ball at Jack that went wide and Jack caught it with a self-satisfied smirk. He turned around and leaned against the table, tipping his head in closer, as if it was of the utmost importance that he give Brooke every strategic advantage. "But Elyse, she gets better the more she drinks."

The red-haired girl curtsied, holding out an imaginary skirt.

"Unless she gets overconfident," Logan reminded her, making keep-your-eye-on-the-prize fingers at her.

Jack handed Brooke the Ping-Pong ball for her to start the game. With an easy flick of her wrist, she sank the first shot.

"Falsification!" Logan shouted.

Jack turned a crinkly-eyed smile on her. "Well, *you* appear to be perfect."

She glowed under his praise and gave a casual one-shoulder shrug. "I introduced Rohan to this game." She'd taught everyone in their first-year dorm, and like anything competitive and belligerent, Kieran and Rohan had immediately taken to it.

"Ah, so you're the American responsible for this preposterous kitchen table."

Brooke smiled. "You said you knew what you were getting into."

"I fear I'm not at all sure what I'm getting into," Jack said as Logan's Ping-Pong ball dropped into the beer. Jack picked up the cup, chugging, and slammed it back on the table with a devilish grin. "I have a new house rule," he said.

"You just moved in."

His eyes were bright and dancing. "For every ball we sink, we have to tell each other something about ourselves."

It was intoxicating, him wanting to know her. And she desperately wanted to know more about him, too.

"Aye, aye," she said with a pirate salute, and sank her next shot. She leaned against the table, studying the slight flush along the open neck of his shirt, while she thought of something interesting to tell him.

"I'm dying to know. Whatever you're going to say."

"I know how to gut a fish."

Jack's eyes twinkled as a smile bloomed across his face. "You're going to be full of surprises. I can tell already."

Jack sank his next ball and Brooke looked expectantly at him. He glanced up to the ceiling and his lips pushed to the side like he couldn't think of anything.

"Dig deep," she said, and his eyebrows furrowed dramatically.

He looked at her from under those long eyelashes. "I can play a rousing rendition of 'Kung Fu Fighting' on the piano."

Brooke broke out in a laugh, reveled in the glow that seemed to cling to the edges around them.

When Elyse sank the next ball, Brooke drank, wiping the

beer foam from her mouth with the back of her finger, and Jack's eyes followed the motion.

Brooke and Elyse were well matched in skill—and competitiveness—and a group of guys huddled around the table, cheering. A crowd usually elevated Brooke's performance, but it was hard to focus with Jack this close. There were too many people in the room, too much alcohol in the air, too much heat coming off his body. Her head felt lighter and lighter as they played and the music pulsed as if it emanated from inside her chest.

On Brooke's next turn, she made her shot and said, "I'm excellent at Balderdash. Using the right amount of detail to sound believable. I'm a writer," she added, volunteering more information than he'd asked for, her filter most likely lost on the walk over.

"It just so happens, I'm an excellent reader."

Earlier that night, while riffling through Brooke's closet for a costume, Chels had said, "When you're a famous author, sitting in your cottage by the sea, trying to write the next great American novel—from Scotland, of course—you're not going to have anything to write about if you don't *live*."

The image Chels had painted of that cottage Brooke absolutely coveted and the blinking black line in a blank document she deeply feared, had settled on her with the heft of a typewriter.

But now, looking at Jack as he ran his knuckles across his chin, his eyes soft and engaged, Brooke had to breathe through the lightness in her chest like there was simultaneously too much and too little oxygen in there. Like she could fill pages and pages with the sparks crackling between them.

He continued to brush against her arm as they played, holding her gaze while he tipped back cups, and cheering her on. He was a terrible player, but Logan was drunk and considerably worse.

When Brooke sank the last ball, Jack turned and gave her

a double high-five, his fingers slipping between hers, a bright smile lighting her up. He said something and she wasn't sure if she couldn't hear over the noise in the kitchen or because she was so distracted by the movement of his lips.

She leaned in closer. "What?"

He yelled something she couldn't make out. But she wanted to know more. Wanted to *live* more.

She yelled back, "Can we go someplace quieter?"

THEN

Jack's heart raced as he led the way down the hallway to his bedroom. He grabbed a pin from above the doorframe and slipped it into the knob to unlock it. Hand flat on the door, he pushed it open and gestured for Brooke to go ahead. She held his gaze as she walked past, and he held his breath. Cutting off the oxygen supply to his lungs didn't recalibrate his system like he'd hoped.

Jack closed the door and the noise from the party dampened. His ears rang, giving him that off-balance feeling like he was more buzzed than he'd thought. The lamp on his nightstand cast a yellow glow over the room, the mirror image reflected on the three-paned window on the far side. He scanned the floor for any discarded shirts, wished he'd made the bed this morning.

He wasn't exactly sure what to do now that Brooke was here, not sure what she wanted. Not sure what she'd make of all the clues about him in this room or if she'd even notice.

But he wanted her to. Wanted her to think of him as something more than one of the Sutherland brothers. Something special.

He liked her American confidence and the way her smile made him feel brighter, so different from the darkness that often dragged at him.

Brooke crossed to his dresser—ran her index finger over the spines of the books stacked there, the old guitar strings—and his pulse fluttered. She stilled when she saw the wall, strung up with his photographs, and his heart beat impossibly faster. Wanting her to see the things he loved. Dreading the potential dismissal, anything akin to the way his parents said, "That's nice, dear."

Brooke moved in closer, resting her hands on the pine wood dresser to get a better look. Most were pictures he'd taken prowling the city on lonely nights when he chafed against the expectations for his future. Jack had never quite taken to The Heart of the Highlands—the family tour guiding business— the way his brothers had. He loved exploring the land and sharing stories and the history of Scotland with tourists from all over the world, but being *on* all the time, leaving real life every weekend to join a vacation that wasn't his...it left him completely drained.

His family was energized by their trips—passionate in a way he truly couldn't identify with. He'd watched his brothers, how much they *loved* this, and all Jack felt was envy that this prede-termined life set before them was perfect for Logan and Reid, but not for him.

Jack didn't want to look too closely at how quick he'd been to jump at the prospect of business school—at the promise of lectures, office hours, and grading papers—instead of guiding at the weekends.

That familiar doubt swirled inside him. At least he had Rohan to go through the master's program with, despite a liv-ing arrangement that might be a tad wilder than he would've chosen. Jack took off the red pirate bandanna, ran his hands over the back of his head, then finger combed the front.

He watched the way Brooke's eyes tracked over the glossy images of neon lights staining the cobblestones pink, the sapphire blue of the night sky reflected in a puddle, the Forth Bridge lit in red in the darkness. The look on her face was almost reverent—too much for him to take in, so he cataloged the tiny earrings curving up the shell of her ear. Two hoops, a topaz stud, cuff in the middle, gold ring at the top.

"Did you take these?"

He nodded.

"They're incredible. You've captured everything I love about Scotland. The mystery around every corner. The minute I got here, it felt like home, this combination of welcoming and adventure and mystique. I could never get bored of it."

Even as his lungs ballooned at the praise, he said, "It's just a hobby."

How many times had he heard his dad say that? Maybe for some people who were talented and dedicated, but for Jack, this was simply a creative outlet to take the edge off when the world felt too heavy, his path so rigidly set in front of him.

She picked up his Nikon, cupping the telephoto lens in one hand. "This is hardly the camera of a hobbyist."

His stomach knotted at the casual way she held it.

"The distinguished poet of our generation, one Rohan Kelton, once said, 'You can't spend *all* your quid on whisky.'" He reached for the camera strap dangling by her hip. "But since I spent the rest of my money on *this*, do be careful."

He tugged the camera strap, raising it over her head, the backs of his fingers sliding over the ridge of her collarbone as he settled it. Her quick intake of breath made him pull away. The second he stepped back, he regretted it. Wished he was daring enough to hold her gaze, to see if it could lead to more. But he wasn't sure how to recreate the moment, not when Brooke had returned to studying the photos he'd taken of the city cast in shadows.

Jack cleared his throat, propping a hip on the edge of the dresser. "How'd you choose Edinburgh?"

"It's the world's first UNESCO City of Literature."

Jack's eyebrows lifted and a grin spread across his face. "Is that your real answer?"

Brooke cringed. "What I meant was, it's an English-speaking country that gave me a scholarship?" Her voice tipped up at the end like it was a question, like she was asking him to believe her.

He nodded in overblown agreement, but couldn't hide the smile breaking free from his lips.

She threw her hands out. "So I love books and think there's nothing greater than highlighting a syllabus, hole punching it, and clipping it into a binder with translucent, rainbow-colored dividers, okay?" Her eyes went soft and a bit wary. "I've had approximately three times too much to drink for impressing you."

He wanted to touch her cheeks and see if they were giving off the heat he felt under his skin. "I think I'd be a lost cause if you were sober."

As if he wasn't already.

She was open and driven and so very bright, where he was trapped and restless. He wished he was less concerned with what everyone thought of him. That he could voice the things he loved with such conviction.

Without blurting out that he admired the hell out of her for owning the things she loved, he still wanted to put her at ease. "Do you know Sir Walter Scott?" he asked.

"Personally? No."

He narrowed his eyes at her sarcasm about the two-hundred-year-old poet. "I know a secret about the Scott Monument. That only his biggest admirers know. I could show you sometime."

"Don't toy with me, Jack Sutherland."

"I would never."

Her eyes crinkled in the corners and her gaze clung to his,

so heavy his heart went achy under his breastbone. Her lips parted and he couldn't look away. Jack leaned his head close to hers, the smell of oranges wafting to him.

The bedroom door flew open and banged against the wall, the sounds of the party spilling in as he and Brooke jumped apart.

Rohan stood in the threshold, eyes wide. He grabbed the doorknob as the door swung back and gave Jack a guilty grimace. "Unfortunate news...the police are here."

4

NOW

For the second time in two weeks, Brooke found herself at the University of Edinburgh. She trailed her fingers over the rough-hewn stone wall of the bustling hallway, keeping her eyes out for anyone she might need to avoid—although nothing could be worse than running into the dean.

Typically, she met Mhairi in the yellow-painted coffee shop on Buccleuch Street, but Charlotte had requested an editorial meeting and Mhairi had suggested her office. Brooke wasn't expecting a revision letter so soon after sending in the first draft of Mhairi's memoir, and the unknown nature of this meeting sent coiling tendrils of anxiety through her stomach.

She found the office she wanted, the brass plaque on the wall inscribed with Professor Mhairi McCallister, Author in Residence. The thrill she'd felt seeing the inscription the first time she'd been on campus still sparked through her, but now it was mixed with a gratefulness for knowing Mhairi, not just knowing *of* her. Brooke knocked on the open door. "Good morning."

Mhairi looked up with her kind eyes and welcoming smile that made her the students' favorite. Her easy demeanor and gift for developing writing talent had everyone vying for spots in her workshops and fellowships. Her curly brown hair going gray at the temples was tied back in a red-and-purple bandeau and the sleeves of her silky shirt spread out like butterfly wings when she opened her arms to hug Brooke.

"Hello," Mhairi said, patting Brooke softly on the back.

Brooke gave her an extra squeeze and noticed Mhairi felt smaller than usual. "Have you been skipping lunch again?"

Mhairi waved the concern away. "Of course not."

"You sure?" Brooke perched on the arm of the leather guest chair and scanned the room, careful to flit right over the framed picture of Mhairi's family where Jack hooked his arms around his brothers, the sunlight glinting off his glasses. Those old barbs from memories of every other insignificant person had dulled with time, but Jack's still drew blood. Avoiding that picture—that beaming smile she used to bask in when she could draw it out of him—was half the reason she always asked Mhairi to meet off campus and never here.

Although, maybe she should have insisted—the office was in shambles: bookshelves were emptied, the books in stacks on the floor; boxes stuffed with papers littering the desk, tables, and the other chair. Brooke hadn't been here in years and while she remembered it being lived-in, she also remembered it being *livable*. This looked like an episode of *Hoarders*.

"What happened in here?" This seemed far more comprehensive than her impression of a professor's version of spring cleaning at the end of a term.

"Getting things in order…" Mhairi trailed off as she likewise observed the disaster of a room.

"Like all the things? At once?"

"I opened one filing cabinet and next thing I know…" Mhairi made an exploding gesture with her hands before digging through a box and pulling out a Sharpie and Suzi's book. "I have a favor to ask." She clutched them to her chest. "I'm a huge fan. Would you sign my book? Is that weird? You know what, never mind." Mhairi waved her hand in front of her face. "It's weird," she said with a teasing smirk.

Brooke laughed and took the Sharpie and book. "Never gonna let me live that down, huh?"

Brooke had said the exact same words to Mhairi on her first day in class seven years ago, fan-girling on the quad. Brooke uncapped the marker with a flourish, feigning exasperation, but she never minded the ribbing. Especially not today. Knowing Mhairi had bought the book for this exact purpose soothed the itchy-in-her-own-skin feeling Brooke had had all week.

Technically, telling Mhairi about her books was in breach of Brooke's confidentiality agreements, but moms never counted when spilling secrets in high school and she figured that logic applied to beloved mentors, too.

The Sharpie fumes filled the air and Brooke finished off her signature with an XOXO, her heart pinching with yearning for her signature to match the name on the title page one day. She handed the book back and Mhairi smiled her warm, eye-crinkling smile.

"For the Brooke Shelf," Mhairi said as she stood the book on the top shelf with the others Brooke had ghostwritten and paused to admire them. "It is truly an honor to hold your words, my dear."

Brooke's eyes welled up and she blinked rapidly. "Thank you." One day soon, Mhairi would hold their cowritten words in her hands and the thought was nearly too much for Brooke's heart to bear.

Charlotte knocked on the door and Brooke pulled in a breath to compose herself.

"Sorry I'm late." She moved a box from the second guest chair onto the floor as if this level of chaos was perfectly normal and said her hellos.

"How is campus life?" Charlotte asked Mhairi, fishing, as always, for humorous stories.

"Quiet now the students are gone for the summer, but I did have one roll an entire suitcase full of notebooks, extra pencils, a hoodie, and snacks into my one-hour final as if they were going to camp out for weeks in the lecture hall."

Charlotte laughed as she pulled out her overflowing legal pad of notes and Brooke's smile dimmed. She'd been counting on more time to watch TV and sit on park benches or whatever she was supposed to do to refill the well before jumping into a revision.

As Mhairi and Charlotte chitchatted, Brooke couldn't tear her eyes away from the yellow paper, trying to see how substantial the feedback might be. She struggled to keep the pressure in her chest under control, her fingers bouncing against her knee.

When Charlotte finally settled in, Mhairi pulled out a notebook and Brooke grabbed her laptop from her bag.

"I am almost always against a prologue, but in this case, I think it might be nice to show a little slice of Mhairi's childhood on Skye as a full chapter instead of the flashbacks we're getting early in the story, to show how Mhairi's love of the land and connection to the island started."

"I like that," Mhairi said.

Brooke typed out the note, her mind thinking through the flashback pieces she'd woven in as backstory and which would make the most compelling opening. "Maybe the story of when you got lost when you were eight? We can dig into the theme right away then of how much we trust nature to be unforgiving or nurturing and that bond you felt early on."

Mhairi spread her hands out. "Yes, I love that."

"I do, too," Charlotte said, her head tipping down to her notebook again, and she pushed her wavy hair off her forehead.

They went through page after page of Charlotte's notes about speeding up the pace in some places, slowing it down in others, adding more of the firsthand accounts from Mhairi's friends and colleagues who helped design and build the trail.

"I apologize, but this last note is not concrete." Charlotte tapped the tips of her fingers together in a guilty manner and Brooke's shoulders tightened.

"You're making me nervous."

"Oh, don't be. It's nothing we can't fix together." Charlotte waved her off, but the jingling of her bracelets sounded like a death knell. "The story is all here. It's structurally sound, but it doesn't feel...alive."

What did that make it? Dead? Brooke wasn't sure she could feel her feet.

Charlotte reached a hand out to the arm of Brooke's chair. "I know this is the worst kind of feedback, and you know how much I love your writing. We'll get there." Her encouragement felt like popped bubble wrap around those other, very sharp words that'd cut deep lacerations in Brooke's lungs. She couldn't even bring herself to look in Mhairi's direction.

She could handle feedback. Craved these two-hour sessions with Charlotte, decoding her sloppy legal pad of action items. But she'd never given Brooke something so amorphous that sounded an awful lot like, *You missed the mark.*

Brooke had spent weeks researching, listening to Mhairi's stories, looking through old documents, pictures, and journal entries. She'd been haunting the archives from open to close, waking in the night from fragmented dreams of Skye, broken storylines, and epiphanies. She'd thought this draft was some of her finest work. Something grand that her name would finally be attached to. But the soft look on Mhairi's face made all the blood rush from Brooke's head.

This was Mhairi's book, but Brooke had been doing the bulk of the writing, like most of her jobs. Brooke had taken Mhairi's preoccupation with her classes and students as a vote of confidence in her abilities, but clearly she couldn't be trusted left to her own devices. That relentless fear and self-doubt had crept into this work and she hadn't even noticed.

This is all my fault.

"Can you be a little more specific?" Brooke asked, her voice coming out squeaky.

"It's missing the details that make a memoir, well…memorable," Charlotte said gently. "I want to feel the wind on my face and taste the salt in the air and smell the boggy soil. I want to go on a journey."

"Okay, so the setting isn't coming through?" Brooke had spent countless hours watching videos of the Skye Trail to capture the details of Mhairi's story. But maybe seeing it wasn't the same as experiencing it.

Charlotte curled her lips inward before saying, "I don't think you've tapped into the heartbeat of this story quite yet."

A wave of hot shame pulsed through Brooke. She was sitting in front of a different mahogany desk, but it felt exactly like that day in the dean's office, watching everything she'd worked for snatched away. She could see it so clearly: Mhairi's disappointment that Brooke never lived up to her potential. A life of ghostwriting and sitting in the audience. Never holding a book with her name on the cover.

Charlotte stood and squeezed Brooke's shoulder. "Why don't you two take a couple of days to digest this. I hate to turn up the pressure, but I need the next draft back in four weeks to keep our publication timeline."

Brooke probably said goodbye when Charlotte left, but she couldn't be sure. She was too busy scanning her memory for any writer's craft book that would help her "find a heartbeat" in one month.

This memoir was supposed to be Brooke's second chance, the long-lost fellowship she'd never had, the key to launching her career. And she was blowing it.

Mhairi moved a towering stack of books from her desk to

the floor one by one. "I'm so sorry, Brooke. I clearly haven't communicated the stories well enough."

Sometimes clients had a picture in their mind of how their story would unfold and they hadn't quite translated that to Brooke. But this was different.

"No. Oh my gosh, no. This is on me."

Mhairi had the decency not to agree with her. She steepled her fingers under her chin. "I know you researched this. There's just something otherworldly about Skye. I think you need to experience it to really be able to write about it."

Brooke leaned forward on a rush of relief that Mhairi wasn't taking this project away from her. She knew Mhairi was swamped, but she'd take it as a sign that Mhairi hadn't lost all faith in her. "I totally agree. I need to see it."

She could take a train up to Inverness—that was about four hours—then another four-hour bus ride to Portree, the capital of the island. Stay in an Airbnb. Do a couple of little day hikes to really get a feel for the scenery.

"I trust Charlotte implicitly. It's key that we capture the essence of how transformative it is to be out there, connected to the Earth and the ghosts of the past and the hope for the future. I know it's a lot to ask. And I wouldn't, but this is my memoir. It's my *story*."

Brooke knew how important this project was, how personal. But of all clients—of all *people*—she'd do whatever she needed to give Mhairi the story that was worthy of her.

Brooke wouldn't jeopardize her second chance.

Sitting in Portree, fighting off gulls as she ate fish and chips on the harbor, and taking notes on the feel of the sea breeze wasn't going to be enough.

"I need to hike the trail."

Anxiety snaked through Brooke as she said the words. She'd never done a hike like that. Overnight backpacking trips, sure.

But the trail was eighty miles of brutal terrain—boggy, dangerous, and more or less for professional hikers only.

"Are you sure?" Mhairi asked.

Brooke nodded even though the queasiness in her stomach begged her to reconsider. "I want to get this right."

Mhairi's face absolutely glowed. She clasped her hands together. "Brooke, I would *love* for you to experience the trail. I worry about you sometimes. Your career has really taken off, but I wonder if you're feeding your soul."

Brooke had no concerns about the state of her soul—she got to do her dream for a living, but it would be worth it to do something important for Mhairi, to have a tangible connection to this trail she was so proud of—of course Brooke would go.

She mentally calculated the deadline on the book. The trail would take her over a week to complete. Transcribing notes when she got back would take two days. Heavy rewrites she'd have to do in two weeks to have time for a final read-through. In order to make it all happen and get the next draft to Charlotte in time, Brooke needed to leave for Skye this weekend.

It would be impossible for Chels to take off work on such short notice to go with her. And Kieran would die sleeping on an air pillow, not to mention the ground. But hiking by herself was out of the question. Just the idea of being alone with her own thoughts for seven days was enough to send her into a panic spiral.

"Would you want to come with me?" She and Mhairi climbed Arthur's Seat, the hill in the middle of Edinburgh, on days they needed to brainstorm. It would be a dream trip, actually. Spending time with Mhairi out in the wilderness, getting all of her stories in real time…

"I'm afraid the fellowship schedule won't allow it."

Brooke winced. The reminder of the fellowship still stung even after all this time. "Right, of course. When did you say the photographer was heading out?"

The publisher had hired someone to photograph the cover as well as images to match the important places in the narrative.

"Next week, I believe. In fact, he's supposed to be—"

"I could go with him." Hiking could be as social or solitary as they wanted. "Just so there's someone to, you know, make sure I don't die," Brooke said with as much humor as she could muster.

Mhairi's eyes darted across the room, then down to her shoes. "Brooke, I failed to mention…the photographer broke his leg and we've replaced him with my nephew." The careful way Mhairi said it made Brooke's stomach clench before she said, "Jack, that is."

The air rushed out of Brooke's lungs and spots littered her vision. She grabbed the armrests on her chair, thankful she'd been sitting or she'd surely be a puddle on the floor right now. She squeezed the cool leather.

Hiking with Jack Sutherland was absolutely out of the question.

She could do it alone. It was fine. This was fine.

"Ah."

"And that's all…history?" Mhairi asked gently, her eyes soft but still probing.

A wave of heat crashed over Brooke. Remnants of humiliation. Mhairi didn't need to know how much Brooke still thought about Jack. The what-ifs plagued her. Not *What if things had worked out between us?* but *What if Jack hadn't totally screwed me over?*

Brooke wanted Jack to stay exactly where she'd left him—in her past. "Ancient," she assured Mhairi.

"Wonderful. Because I'm expecting him any—"

A knock sounded and at the stricken look on Mhairi's face, Brooke turned to the man standing in the threshold.

Slate-gray slacks, white button-up shirt, his hand falling from the door, one knuckle still raised. Dark brown hair messy on top, tortoiseshell glasses, eyelashes for days.

"—minute."

Brooke's pulse scattered like leaves on a gusting Scottish wind.

Apparently this week *could* get worse.

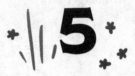

THEN

Jack Sutherland was a fraud. With his acceptance to a master's program came a requirement to teach a biweekly recitation—the mandatory small group classes paired with the three-hundred-person lectures taught by Professor McKinnon. As if Jack was qualified to teach students approximately twelve months his junior.

He'd been waiting—maybe his entire life—for something to *click*, to feel like the right path. He wanted business school to be the answer. His dad, Neil, certainly thought it was.

As Jack sat at the desk in the shared university office for teaching assistants, he pushed his glasses up, rubbing the bridge of his nose. Teaching would be a lot like guiding at his family's tour company, he reminded himself—it simply required getting into character.

As this was his first time teaching, he hoped the comparison was accurate.

Jack tried to breathe through the nerves sweeping through him like a brush fire; all he had to do today was attend the main lecture and stand in front of the lecture hall for recitation assignments. There was no reason to be this rattled.

A flurry in the hallway pulled him from his thoughts and he looked up to find his parents standing in the door, overblown innocence written all over their flushed faces.

"Oh, hello, Jack," his dad said with an air of surprise as if they'd bumped into each other at Tesco.

"We were just having tea with Mhairi," his mum rushed to add, gesturing to his aunt, who had appeared behind them in a familiar burst of billowing orange-and-purple fabric as if Neil and Gemma had given her the slip and she'd chased them down.

His aunt taught in the English Department—in an entirely different building. Resting her hand on the doorframe as if she was winded, Mhairi mouthed, "Sorry."

"We had no idea your office was so close by." His dad glanced around at the bare walls, his mustache jumping as if trying to keep a neutral expression.

"What a coincidence," Jack said. He loved his parents, but they were so *involved*, hovering so close he never felt he could trust his instincts because their opinions were so very loud.

They were not here for a casual tea with Mhairi. They were here to make sure Jack hadn't absconded on the last train out of the city. Which he *had* briefly considered before reminding himself that grad school might be the missing puzzle piece he'd been searching for. If he could run the operations—the finances and marketing and anything Agnes in HR wasn't responsible for—it could give Jack something besides tours and folklore to connect with his family over, to feel like he was truly a part of their legacy and not this hanger-on who didn't quite fit in.

And as much as he was annoyed that they were here checking up on him, never asking if this was what he really wanted, Jack felt some deep relief at the sight of Mhairi. He'd love nothing more than for her to hold his hand while he taught his first class, or—since that would truly undermine his authority—

at least sit in the front row and cast that encouraging smile on him for fifty minutes straight.

A decade younger than his mum, Mhairi had always been rebellious and brassy. In a family that constantly looked backward at history and tradition, she cared about the here and now.

She wrapped him up in a hug and Jack let himself be coddled, just for a moment. "You don't need to check up on me, you know," he said, more to his parents than to his aunt.

Mhairi waved a hand in front of her face as if swatting away bugs. "I only wanted to see my favorite nephew now that we're colleagues," she said, taking the blame he didn't for a minute believe was hers. "We'll be off, but I'd like a word with Jack."

Gemma and Neil gave him hugs like they were dropping him off at his first sleepaway before saying their goodbyes and heading out.

Mhairi's look turned serious, some mixture of affection and sorrow that made him believe she could see right through him. And maybe she'd always been able to. She was the black sheep and he was the wayward son. They'd forged an unbreakable bond on the outskirts of the family who loved them.

But the rare stillness that emanated from her echoed a summer morning on Skye when he'd been a boy. Standing on a bridge over a wide and languid river, Mhairi told him it was alright to not know what he wanted. Like she'd understood, even then, that he wasn't suited for this path. She'd turned and looked up past the deep valley into the Cuillin Mountains and said, "But when you find what you're looking for, don't let it go."

He'd finally found his path forward—grad school was the way to be what his parents wanted.

Mhairi squeezed his shoulder, her grip tight. "Live a little. Don't close yourself off to the possibility of something unexpected."

"I won't." Jack was completely open to the possibility this

year presented. In fact, he was counting on it to change everything with his family.

"That being said, stick to the textbook," she said with a mischievous wink.

With that facetious teaching advice and reminder of his present circumstance, he steered her from the office. "Goodbye, Auntie."

Over her shoulder, Mhairi gave him an amused grin and sauntered away.

Jack sank into his rolling chair and kicked his feet up on the desk. Ten more minutes before he needed to be in the lecture hall. Standing in front of one hundred students. *Deep breaths. In, one, two. Out, one, two.*

His relaxation was interrupted by the sound of footsteps outside the room. "One more thing, Jackie," Mhairi said from the doorframe. "Don't let the little buggers smell your fear."

"Off with you!"

Her laughter echoed down the hall.

Jack followed Rohan into the lecture hall. "You sure we don't want to bail. Move to Bali and live out our days on the beach?" Jack asked, his nerves flickering in his stomach.

Rohan laughed as if Jack was totally, completely joking. "The environment isn't going to save itself, Jackie. We got work to do."

The stairs of the lecture hall were painted the red of a warning flag for troubled water, but he followed them down to the first row and off to the side. Professor McKinnon wrote on the chalkboard and Jack had forgotten the way the screechy sound grated on the inside of his skull, underscoring the doubt swirling inside him the same way the professor underlined "Business for Non-Majors" in a broad white stroke.

Professor McKinnon was well respected, sometimes feared, not one to make a joke. "Good morning," he said, his loud voice projecting through the lecture hall without the aid of a microphone. "I am Professor McKinnon and this is one of the three classes you need to complete your Small Business Management Certificate—"

"Shite." A guy in a black button-up, tan vest, and jeans grabbed his knapsack and dashed up the steps.

A rumble of laughter went through the room as they watched him push through the door. Jack had never felt more jealous in his life.

"If no one else needs to flee the class just now, let us begin," Professor McKinnon said. "We'll focus this term on the basics of marketing strategy, financial planning, and sales strategies. You'll have one lecture per week and two recitations with your teaching assistant, who will go into more depth and conversation about the information we cover here." He projected a list of names on the screen. "If you haven't accessed the student portal yet, here are your recitation assignments. Will the teaching assistants please stand?"

Jack and Rohan stood and turned to face the students. Jack's palms were sweaty as his gaze skimmed over the lecture hall. The students were mostly looking at their phones under their desks, as if no one could tell what they were on about. The first set of eyes he met were summer sky blue. Jack's pulse tripped in recognition. *Brooke.*

She wore a plum-colored puffer vest over a white hoodie. Wisps of chestnut hair framed her face under a dusty blue ball cap with a buffalo patch ringing a mountain sunset. A bright smile curved her lips and then fell, the same way his heart did.

Fuck.

His eyes fluttered closed. She was a student.

Of course. Kieran's roommate, not Rohan's friend. Jack had clearly been too drunk and/or captivated to process that at the party.

Orientation for the teaching assistants had included very little detail on how to actually *teach* the students, but an extraordinary emphasis had been placed on absolutely not dating them.

Jack scanned the list of names on his class list, thankfully not finding hers, though it hardly mattered. He kept reading, finding her name under Rohan's recitation. *Brooke Sinclair.* As if he needed to collect any more details about her.

He looked back to Brooke and her eyes were still on him, a look of disappointment there. He hated the flush that spread over her skin. In another situation he'd want to know the exact shade of that color pink and exactly how to bring it to the surface.

But not with a power imbalance, not with university rules. He had too much riding on this year.

But *goddamn* he wished he didn't.

NOW

Jack slumped against the doorframe to the office, his lungs seizing up.

Brooke Sinclair sat in his aunt's guest chair.

Brooke Sinclair.

Same chestnut hair, same rosy lips—parting on a gasp—same earrings curving up her ear. But that look in her blue eyes—shock and pain and *fury* swirling like a hurricane—he'd only seen that look once before.

Jack's chest tightened, his legs urging him to get the hell out of there, but he was gripped in place by a deep longing to see that impish smile flit across her face. The one that preceded a flirtatious "Captain."

Everyone had a one-who-got-away, but Brooke had been *The One* and she'd absolutely vanished from his life.

Jack had imagined seeing her again a thousand times. Pictured bumping into her coming out of a coffee shop, or in the heart of Waterstones with her arms full of books, still so heartbreakingly beautiful.

He'd rehearsed what he'd say, if given the chance. How he

was the worst kind of bawbag, that he'd betrayed her trust, that he was so deeply sorry. Regret coiled in his chest like a dragon, scorching his sternum every time he thought of her.

But the surprise of seeing her in his aunt's office yanked any logical thought from his mind. Lightheaded, he stalled in the doorway, completely unsure of what to do next. Was he meant to shake Brooke's hand?

"You're early," Mhairi said, pulling Jack from his frozen stupor, and he redirected as much of his focus as he could to his aunt.

Jack moved into the room and tucked Mhairi into a gentle hug, holding her a bit longer than necessary and hating the way he couldn't keep from calculating how many more of these embraces they had left. When he stepped back, she gripped his shoulder in reassurance, as if *he* was the one in need of comforting.

And maybe he was, because the shock of seeing Brooke Sinclair had knocked his feet out from under him. She was just as stunning and all-consuming as she'd been the first time she'd walked into his flat.

Brooke wore cream-colored flowy trousers, cropped at the ankle, and a light pink T-shirt with a twist at the waist. Her necklaces were the same: the tiny gold-and-white beaded choker, the teardrop gem on a thin string, the longer simple gold chain. He'd traced them, twisted his fingers in them—

"You remember Brooke," his aunt prompted, and he realized he'd been standing there staring. Jack's mind was in a daze. Mhairi could've given him even a hint of warning—and based on the look on Brooke's face, she would've appreciated one, as well.

"Of course. Brooke. Hello," he said with a nod in her direction.

She stayed seated, hands balled in her lap. "Jack." The steel in her voice was of the slicing variety.

"We were just talking about the trail," Mhairi said and Jack's brain finally caught up.

Of course that was why she was here. Mhairi had told him Brooke was cowriting her memoir when she'd asked Jack to step in for the injured photographer her publisher had originally hired.

He'd agreed without thinking; he'd do anything for his aunt. She always supported his dreams, even now. Adding a memoir to his photography portfolio would be a ringing endorsement that might finally get his work into the galleries.

And if there was a world where he wasn't scraping by, wasn't addicted to his YouTube views or the affiliate link dashboard tracking paltry advertising pounds, he wanted in.

When Jack had agreed, he assumed he'd have no interaction with Brooke, only that he'd read her manuscript to match his photos to the story. He'd been avoiding it, truth be told; the thought of reading Brooke's words when she wasn't tucked up beside him in bed sent waves of anguish through him for all he'd lost.

"Brooke's decided to join you on your trip to Skye. While she gathers details for the memoir, she can help direct which photographs might be best."

Being in the same room as Brooke for the past eight minutes had sent Jack's system into overdrive to the point that he might pass out. Eight days with her sharp looks and silence might literally kill him.

"I didn't realize— We don't—" Brooke held her hands up. "I'm going by myself," she said, her voice somehow both flat and sharp, like a shovel she might use to knock him out before digging his grave.

It turned out Jack's stomach had not forgotten the feel of Brooke's disdain. It wasn't a particularly pleasant feeling, being turned inside out.

Of course Brooke wouldn't want to spend another second with him, not after what he'd done.

"You *can*…" Mhairi agreed. "Jack could read the manuscript and match his photographs to the important pieces. *But*—" Jack's stomach somersaulted over the word "—I'd worry about you alone out there. Anyone alone on that trail."

Mhairi hadn't protested *him* walking solo on the trail, so he assumed her concern was on Brooke's account.

"Brooke knows how to gut a fish," he said and immediately dragged a hand over his face.

Brooke stared at him like she couldn't for the life of her figure out why he would've dredged up that random bit of information, used it in this context, and truly, why he was still in this room.

"I mean to say, you would do just fine on a walk of that scale. You're capable and fit." He cleared his throat. "In shape, that is. Strong." Jack snapped his mouth shut.

"Be that as it may…" Mhairi drew out the words with a long look in Jack's direction. "Calamity has befallen plenty a hiker on this trail. The original photographer slipped on an escarpment, broke his leg, and waited five hours until another hiker found him. I would hate for something like that to happen to either of you. Safety in numbers and all that."

If Mhairi wanted them to hike this trail, would feel better knowing neither of them was alone, then he'd do it. The piece of Jack's heart that still called out to Brooke jumped at the chance to support her in this project—to make sure he never wrecked anything for her ever again.

A way to make amends, perhaps.

Brooke grabbed a binder clip from Mhairi's desk and snapped it onto a stack of printed papers Jack assumed was the manuscript before pressing it against his chest for him to take.

"I'll let you know," she said with a tight smile in Mhairi's direction before turning on her heel and all but sprinting from the room.

She wouldn't want to disappoint Mhairi, either. Mhairi had been Brooke's absolute idol in uni and the fact that she was writing Mhairi's memoir would be hugely personal to both of them. He needed to apologize. To try to fix whatever might still be salvageable between them and make this trip work.

For both their sakes.

Without thinking, he followed Brooke from the room.

"Jack," Mhairi called after him and he turned in the doorway, gripping the wooden frame. "Don't tell her about me."

Liquid mercury dashed through his veins. "You mean you haven't yet?"

Mhairi remained quiet.

"Auntie, the *last* thing I want is another secret from her."

She shook her head. "This one isn't yours to share."

Jack rubbed a hand across his face.

"I'll tell her when you're back. I want a memoir that's brimming with life, not a memorial. And that's how Brooke will write it if she knows. I don't want my prognosis to tarnish the story."

He could understand his aunt's hesitation, knew how much this memoir meant to her. Her legacy.

"And I want Brooke to experience the trail fully. Not to be grieving, but to be living. She deserves that." Mhairi's serious look cut through Jack's resistance. Brooke deserved the world.

"Alright." Jack let out a deep sigh. "But I don't like it," he said before running to catch up with Brooke.

7

NOW

Brooke dashed down the steps from Mhairi's office and into the warm, early-May air. The sun kissed her skin, the breeze ruffled her hair, the soft day so out of sorts with the darkness whirling inside her.

She might've blacked out when Jack walked in, the way he'd knocked on the doorframe with one knuckle. His jaw was more defined now, like he spent a lot of time clenching it. His dark hair was cut shorter than she remembered but she knew exactly how it felt between her fingers. His dreamer eyes were focused. Grounded. And he hadn't taken them off her.

Brooke used to light up under that kind of attention but she hadn't wanted him studying her now, noticing the struggle to mask her reaction to him. His glasses and the parting of his lips had been a wrecking ball to whatever composure she'd mustered around herself over the past seven years, laying bare those shattered pieces of her heart she'd never quite managed to sweep up.

She fled to The Meadows, the park next to campus. Cherry blossom trees flanked the central walkway, the pink flowers bursting with color and sweet perfume. She needed the open space and the tranquility out of the bustle of the city. Needed the fresh air to clear away the scent of his tea tree shampoo that'd pulled her back in time like the electropop beat of Calvin Harris's "Summer" on the radio.

"Brooke!"

She closed her eyes against the recognition of his voice, the stutter step of her heart. The way she used to crave the sound of her name in his brogue, low and rumbling.

She should've realized he'd know to find her here. How many times had they walked under these same trees on dark and snowy nights, gazing into the bare branches reaching for each other over their heads?

Brooke slowed but didn't turn. She sucked in oxygen to calm herself, to shore up her resistance.

Fingers brushed the inside of her elbow and her skin tingled long after they fell away. "Brooke."

She turned, her eyes stalling on the curve of Jack's shoulder in his white dress shirt like she might not be able to force her eyes to meet his. But she straightened her spine and pushed aside the discomfort and the fear that she might trip and fall back into those dark brown eyes.

A crease appeared between his eyebrows and a memory crashed into her—drunk, stumbling up the stairs, Jack sober and broody, her finger pressing into the soft skin there, saying, "Put those eyebrows away," hiccupping, his arm wrapping tightly around her waist, his head shaking with dry amusement behind it.

Her body remembered absolutely nothing about his deception. All it cared about was the way he'd made her feel. That one simple touch could spark fire in her veins. His attention had made her downright reckless.

But she wasn't twenty-one anymore. She'd learned enough times that giving second chances was for fools who wanted tarnished reputations and broken hearts they should've seen coming.

"I didn't realize you'd be here today. I'm sorry for surprising you. And I'm sorry…" He let out a heavy breath, his eyes pleading. "*Christ*, Brooke, I'm so sorry for everything I did back then."

As much as she'd longed to hear his apology—his *explanation*—she found she couldn't stomach it. She didn't want to be managed or handled or smoothed over. Couldn't bear to assuage whatever small amount of guilt he still carried.

"And the trail. I mean, this…" He gestured between them. "I know there's a lot of history here—"

Brooke raised her hand to stop him, not wanting to hear a single word about the wreckage left between them. "Mhairi wants your pictures and I want what she wants. This—" she made the same gesture "—is ancient history. I barely even remember it."

It was a blip on the radar she wished would vanish. Instead, it'd blossomed into a dark mark on her entire life. Brooke kept her chin tipped upward, defiant. Daring Jack to contradict her.

Something flickered in his eyes. It couldn't be hurt. She believed he might feel remorse. He'd utterly fucked up her life. But if he'd cared about her—even a fraction of the amount he'd let her believe—he wouldn't have turned her into a walking cliché of the young, dumb, ambitious student infatuated with the young, hot, off-limits teacher. He'd been the one person she'd trusted with her dreams and he'd single-handedly unraveled them.

"Alright, then. We'll leave this weekend? Saturday?"

She stared at him, at the light dusting of freckles under the glasses that *had* to be the same pair. He had once felt like forever and now eight days was impossibly long to spend in his presence.

"Does that work with your schedule?" he asked.

She would hike Mhairi's trail and find the heartbeat of the

story and do her best to ignore Jack. They would hike together for safety and the sake of the book. They weren't friends or anything else, either. She wouldn't give him the chance to derail her dreams a second time. "That's fine." Her words came out the opposite of confident.

Jack jammed his hands in his pockets. "I'll email you with logistics, then?" He leaned toward her like the curve of a question mark.

She stepped back, giving him a nod, her mouth tight from holding back all the furious words she'd rehearsed six hundred times while picturing this meeting, afraid that a choked sob would come out instead. A *How could you?* or *I loved you* or *You shattered me.*

"Alright," he said again, pausing like he might say more before turning to leave.

Rooted to the spot, Brooke watched him walk away as pink flower petals drifted down from their branches, one landing delicately on his shoulder before gently slipping off. She wished she'd let go of him as easily.

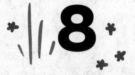

THEN

Brooke loved the university library with an adoration that bordered on fandom. Especially at this time of night. The daylight had slipped away hours ago, as had Kieran and Chels. The library was quiet now; only the sound of the radiators pinging interrupted the gentle scratching of Jack's pen from across the room.

He sat three tables away, facing her. Just like the past two weeks of classes, they'd gotten into a competitive game of eye contact, glancing up every so often to find the other already staring, and immediately looking away, making her stomach fluttery and her cheeks hot.

Realizing Jack was a TA for her class—and therefore completely off-limits—should have eradicated the fizzing in her chest. But that look of anguish on his face the day he stood up in front of the lecture hall said he'd felt everything she had that night at the party. And that pull, coupled with his moon-dark eyes, captured her entire imagination.

Brooke's writer brain wanted to fill in all the details of what could be—Jack's hair mussed, sleeping shirtless, the morning light spilling over his sculpted chest, the blankets bunched around his waist. The way he might look at her while tossing off his Jude-Law-in-*The-Holiday* glasses.

She wanted to know more about his favorite places in Edinburgh and what he hoped to do with an MBA and if he liked toasties with or without tomatoes. She wanted to know his stories.

It was a line they couldn't cross—she wasn't a practical rule follower for nothing—but thoughts of him consumed her every waking minute.

Brooke stretched her neck back and forth, working out the kink from sitting hunched over her computer for so long. She needed to focus. She'd written exactly 186 words of her first paper for Professor McCallister's class.

Brooke had been coveting a spot in Professor McCallister's fellowship since her first year here. A chance to work one-on-one with her favorite author, to perfect her craft? She'd be unstoppable. She wanted the Bachelor of Fine Arts, the fellowship, the MFA. Wanted to collect as many letters to add to her name as possible. She wanted it all.

But Professor McCallister's class was different than Brooke had expected. Harder. Maybe she'd been hoping for a checklist or at least a significant number of bullet points about how to become a fantastic writer. But—while holding class outside under the burnished tree leaves—Professor McCallister had told the class, "After this year, life will no longer have a syllabus, there will be no grades to measure your success. You will have to define that for yourself."

It'd sent a pang of anxiety through Brooke's chest. She loved the clear expectations of a syllabus.

The edges of Professor McCallister's poppy-printed wrap had fluttered in the breeze, and a few stray leaves tumbled by on the still-green grass as she'd said, "To be a truly excellent writer, you first have to experience the world. Dwell in the human emotions of living, of love and joy, of grief and strife. Collect stories, capture details, live presently through the feelings and experiences you encounter. Build your well of adventures and failures."

Brooke had scribbled down all these gems—but not the failure part. She had no intention of doing any of that.

The blinking cursor in her mostly blank document stared back at Brooke. She wasn't sure she knew anything about trying new things or taking risks. She couldn't say for sure that she'd ever experienced the euphoria Professor McCallister had described from doing something brave.

A pop of lightning flashed outside and thunder rumbled in the distance. A shiver raced down Brooke's spine. *Damn.* She'd been paying so much attention to Jack and fretting, she hadn't noticed the rain beating against the tall windows. Looked like she wasn't heading home soon.

But she didn't particularly want to wait it out alone…

She glanced across the empty room at Jack again, head bent, rolling a pen between his fingers.

They could be friends. Rohan was her *actual* TA and no one said they couldn't spend time together this term. What was it her mom always talked about? Exposure therapy? She could spend time with Jack and eventually his accent and dark eyes would lose their power over her. Maybe they'd just been drunk. Maybe she'd imagined their connection. They were in a completely public place. So what if she could spin vivid fantasies of him lifting her up and the feel of wrapping her legs around his waist as he pressed her against the stacks? She wasn't that bold anyway.

She stretched her arms above her head and let out an exaggerated yawn, the "aah" starting high and pitching lower as it went—too loud and too long. Jack's head snapped up at the sound.

"If we're staying, we're gonna need snacks," she said.

That grin that was always close to the surface but so hard to draw out pulled at Jack's lips. He hesitated, his eyes searching hers like he had the same instinct she'd pushed down. That this might be dangerous if it wasn't so innocent. "To the vending machines, then?" he asked.

Brooke nodded and couldn't deny that the feeling in her chest was much more than relief that he'd agreed to keep her company during a storm.

Jack trailed her as they made their way downstairs and Brooke leaned against the black side of the vending machine, crossing one foot in front of the other. "I'm buying," she said.

He looked at her skeptically, like 65p did not in any way alter the power imbalance between them. But it was a little hard to care when he wasn't *her* TA and seemed a lot more like Rohan's hot flatmate.

She slipped coins into the machine and ignored the way he rested a forearm on the glass and peered through. He punched in a number and crouched down to retrieve his Maltesers.

Jack's dark head was level with her hip and he looked up, bathed in the vending machine glow, that shadow playing underneath his bottom lip. Brooke's breath hitched and she wondered what his touch would feel like if he reached out and ran his hands up her thighs. If it would be rough and needy or soft like the worn pages of an old book.

She should not like Jack Sutherland on his knees in front of her quite so much.

Standing, he made a rough noise in the back of his throat as he took a giant step backward and gestured for her to make a selection. She tried to breathe through the tightness in her chest.

Brooke punched in a number, grabbed her chips, and headed for the stairs. If she walked behind him, she was going to break the most basic of rules: friends don't check out friends' asses.

"What are you working on so late tonight?" he asked.

"A paper for Professor McCallister's creative writing class."

"Mhairi? That's my aunt."

Brooke came to an abrupt stop on the stair above him and he nearly crashed into her. A flyer taped to the wall fluttered with their movement. "Your aunt? She's my absolute idol. Your *aunt*!" As if Brooke needed another reason to be intrigued by him. "Did you just sit at her feet growing up listening to her stories? Seriously, tell me everything. Spare no detail."

Mhairi wrote the most beautiful historical fiction novels, always set in Scotland, often with time slips and mysticism, her stories unwinding with a sense of mystery, historical plots, and romantic entanglements.

A slow smile spread across Jack's face, lifting his cheekbones and nudging his glasses. "Oh, you *love* her."

"Don't say anything. I'm trying to play it cool." She bit her thumbnail and when all his attention snagged on her mouth, she lingered just one second longer before dropping her hand. "I did ask her to sign my book on the first day of class. Do you think I gave myself away?"

"I'm sure she was honored." Jack's eyes danced. She could get addicted to that look.

Light flashed behind her, bright enough to reach her halfway up the stairs, and Brooke held her breath as she waited for the thunder cracking in the distance. She climbed the rest of the stairs and went toward the floor-to-ceiling windows in the back of the room, placing her palms on the glass, tracking the rain sliding down the other side of her hands to help steady her. To keep her in her body.

She was in the library, not out in the open.

"You alright?"

Brooke rubbed a hand over her arm and turned her back to the night, perching on the shallow windowsill that was more of a metal ledge between the top and bottom window. If she couldn't see into the night, maybe she could ignore those old memories. "Yeah."

If she could keep all her attention on Jack, she'd be just fine.

"So what's she like?" Brooke asked, opening her chip bag and crunching one loudly.

"Oh, Mhairi? Uh..." Jack leaned against a table, crossing one leg over the other. "Do you want to know about the summer she let me stay with her on Skye, or the time we took mushrooms last winter holiday?"

"Wow, I've never been more torn in my life," she said dryly.

"The summer, then. Of course."

Brooke threw a chip at him. He caught it, crushing it accidentally, and had no choice but to inelegantly shove the pieces in his mouth.

Brooke's laugh had him grinning in response. She pushed a rebellious strand of hair out of her face and when it fell right back, she set her chips down and pulled out her hair tie. Jack's eyes seemed to trip over her hair around her shoulders and the air suddenly felt thicker, his attention trained on her instead of in the periphery.

She retied the messy topknot, smoothing down the place that'd kept slipping free as Jack looked down at his shoes.

"Maybe another time, actually. I should head out."

She didn't have to question the retreat as much as she hated it. He was being smart, walking away before that spark caught again.

"Oh, okay." She couldn't keep the disappointment from her voice.

Lightning illuminated the room and the boom of the thunder cracked nearly simultaneously. Brooke squeaked, her hands balling into fists and crinkling her chip bag as she moved away from the window.

"Are you alright?"

"No. I hate storms," she said, her voice much higher than

normal. "That's why I'm still here—I don't want to go out in the lightning," she said, her eyes on the flashing clouds. "I got stuck in a bad storm once."

"I can stay with you."

"No, it's fine." She waved him off. "I'll just put on headphones and write."

Lightning flashed, a zigzagging threat across the sky. A clap of thunder rent the room, booming through the walls and vibrating across the floor.

The lights flickered before the room plunged into darkness.

Brooke's heartbeat roared in her ears, the thunder seeming to reverberate through her chest.

"Do we need to get under the table?" Jack asked. He might've been teasing her—it was ridiculous to be afraid of storms at twenty-one—but his voice was gentle.

She tried to scoff but it came out breathy. "I'm not hiding under the table," she said, but her knees made a liar out of her, going loose and wobbly. On second thought, going under a table would not be the worst thing. Certainly better than passing out.

"I won't lie—your face is a disturbing shade of green."

Brooke glanced up at the illuminated exit sign, the only light in the room. "You don't look so good yourself."

Another clap of thunder made her jump, her shoulders bunching and her insides curling in toward her spine.

"In that case…" Jack pushed two chairs away from the table, crouched down, and crawled underneath. "Better safe than sorry, I always say."

Hiding under a table was absurd, but on a scale from zero to panic, her body was responding the same way as when the emergency alert system came over the radio and advised you not to fuck around and find out.

Brooke climbed under after Jack. And since the space was particularly cramped, she had no other choice but to scooch in close. She pulled her knees up to her chest and wrapped her arms around them.

She kept her eyes on the flashing clouds, trying to guess where the next strike would blink. It was always like this, where she couldn't quite disassociate from the fear from that day. The lightning flashed again and the thunder rippled through the room and under her skin.

"Do you want to talk about it?" Jack asked, pulling her back from sinking into those memories.

"I got stuck above tree line once."

"Yeah?" Jack asked, his voice soft and encouraging.

Brooke's heartbeat fluttered underneath her breastbone. She took a deep breath through her nose. "I grew up hiking the fourteeners in Colorado."

"What's a fourteener?"

"A mountain over fourteen thousand feet high. We started doing the easier peaks when I was maybe ten and I got it in my head that I wanted to hike all of them by the time I graduated. I'm not sure my parents were really up for that level of summer excursions around the state, but they were always so supportive of everything I wanted to achieve."

She dropped her chin to the tops of her knees. "The day we hiked the last peak, everything was just off. My dad's knee was hurting. We got a late start. The parking lot was full. Everyone in Colorado knows you have to get off the big mountains by noon to avoid the summer storms but I kept pushing. I was so determined to finish this final peak."

As they watched the lightning flicker across the sky, she picked at the seam of her jeans until Jack wrapped his hand around hers. The touch might have sent fire through her veins under different circumstances, but right now it felt gentle and comforting. The thunder rumbled low and threatening, but she didn't flinch this time.

"My parents eventually realized we were screwed, but we

were too high above tree line to make a run for it. It started pouring and there was nowhere to hide. I can still feel the rain soaking into me, the electricity in the air that made my hair stand on end. We were absolutely the tallest thing on the mountain, and my dad was yelling at us over the noise of the rain to spread out, to crouch down, to only touch the ground with the soles of our shoes."

"Brooke, that sounds terrifying."

She took a deep breath and crossed her arms on top of her knees. "It was." But she didn't feel that terror on an instinctual level this time. In fact, she felt pretty damn calm. "How did you do that?" she asked Jack. "My brain feels quiet. My brain never feels quiet."

His quiet hum pressed against her skin. "I'm a really good listener."

Brooke's heart tripped at her vulnerable admission. As much as she liked this feeling, she wasn't sure she should tip her hand like that. "Well, enough about me," she said. "What are you going to do with your MBA?"

He rolled out his shoulders. "Take over the family tour company."

"You don't sound even a *little* excited about that."

She felt the weight of Jack's look on her in the dark, his breathing heavy. "You barely know me, but you've seen what my entire family has failed to notice for years." He let out a long sigh. "But my dad needs me. My brothers would have a conniption if we don't all run the business together. My life is mapped out before me."

"You're doing an entire graduate degree because your dad said so?"

Jack stiffened and then crossed his arm over his chest as he rubbed one shoulder. "I hadn't put it quite so bluntly to myself, but yes. I suppose that's exactly what I'm doing. My family's expectations feel crushing sometimes."

The darkness couldn't disguise his defensiveness. His retreat was slight, but Brooke felt the lack of his heat pressed against her leg.

"That's really hard," she said. "My parents are almost the opposite. They support me endlessly, but I feel the same way sometimes. This crushing fear of letting them down." The lightning stole Brooke's attention, pulling her gaze back to the window. "If no one had an opinion, what would you want?"

"I think I'd dedicate myself to the study of one Mhairi Mc-Callister," he joked. "Follow in your footsteps."

She nudged his shoulder. "Come on."

"I don't have the faintest clue. I'm not ignoring some deep desire in order to bend to my father's edict. Even back in school, they handed out aptitude tests like a pick-your-own-adventure, except none of them felt like an adventure and none of them felt like *me*. Everyone acts like you're supposed to know what you want to do with your life. I've been waiting for something to click into place, but nothing feels quite right. Not guiding. Not teaching. Not classes about financial statements and business plans." Jack rubbed the spot between his eyes where his glasses pushed down. "I don't have some great calling or passion."

Brooke tucked her knees up to her chin again just to keep from reaching for him, smothering this desire to tuck him against her shoulder and run her fingers through his hair. "I don't think most people really know what they want to do with their lives."

"*You* do."

"I'm just faking it since I failed chem."

"Really?"

"No. I'm great at school."

His faint laugh brushed over her skin.

She recalled the serious-looking camera she'd seen on his desk. "What about photography?"

"That's not a real job."

Brooke relaxed her grip on her knees, turning to face him in the dark. "That's absolutely a real job."

Jack shrugged. "Maybe for some people."

He'd said the same thing in his room even with unique and captivating photos strung up on his wall. But he didn't seem like he wanted to be pressed. "There's some freedom in not having a grand plan, you know?"

"I feel bound to a life I didn't pick. I have never felt free." The anguish in his voice broke her heart in two. And spoke to something she never felt allowed to voice.

Brooke shifted to sit cross-legged in front of him, her knee resting on top of his. "I don't feel free, either. I feel like I'm running this elaborate marathon sometimes, full of checklists and milestones. And I've got to keep my head down and push through if I want to make it to the finish line. I forget to look up every once in a while. Chels and Kieran are on some quest this term to keep me away from the library—"

"They're doing an extraordinary job."

She laughed, a low and listless thing. "I moved to Scotland for uni, for this grand adventure, and I haven't done anything but study. I've told everyone I've ever met about my big dreams of being an author. And what if I can't do it? Professor McCallister said to be a good writer, you have to go out and experience life, but I don't even know where to start."

"I know places. And I do loads of fucking about."

"You want to help me broaden my horizons, Jack?" she asked in a sultry and clearly playful tone, but it didn't stop a prickle of awareness from dancing up her spine when his breath came out like a quiet growl.

"Badly."

She laughed like he was joking but she wasn't sure he was. "Okay."

She wanted him to show her places. To spend more time

with him. For him to have a reason to stick around. "And for you…" She tipped her head, studying him.

"Me?"

"We'll find your passion."

"While we're fucking about?"

"Inspiration can strike anywhere, that's what Professor Mc-Callister says." Brooke grabbed Jack's hand and straightened his fingers, laid her hand on top of the back of his, gestured for him to add his other hand on top of hers, and completed the stack with her palm on top. "It's a pact."

"Are we in a treehouse in an American movie? Would you like to pinkie promise?" he asked with amusement in his voice.

"You're right, we'd better." She hooked her pinkie through his and dragged their hands up to her mouth. His breath caught while he watched her, and god, she wanted to do this for real.

He brought his lips to his thumb, closing the distance between them. He smelled sweet like watermelon in summer. She imagined him leaning farther and kissing her. Imagined the feel of his hand sliding beneath her hair to pull her in, the soft slide of his tongue.

She was supposed to be making a promise but when she pressed her lips against her thumb, their faces inches apart—so close but so far—she made a wish instead.

NOW

Jack rode in an aging Corolla with Angus—a friendly
B&B owner who prided himself on shuttling hikers to the Skye
Trail—two Bolivian women also setting out for the trailhead
today, and Brooke Sinclair.

He could see the slender curve of her neck through the headrest bars, make out the honey streaks through her hair where
her ponytail caught on the seat. Time hadn't lessened his com-
pulsion to know every little piece of her, but he'd given up the
right a long time ago.

"You'll want to mind the wee bloodthirsty beasties," Angus
said, referring to the midges—the tiny biting flies—that were
notorious in this part of Scotland.

Brooke playfully nudged Angus's shoulder. "That's a terrible send-off."

Catalina zipped her purple windbreaker up as if she could
sense the incoming swarms already. "We bought bug spray in
town," she said, her accent thick and melodic.

"Oh, aye, if you want to add a bit of seasoning for 'em."

The truth in Angus's words was almost enough to pull a chuckle from Jack. He'd spent enough time touring on Skye to know that Portree shops were hawking marked-up bug spray like three-day-old produce at Tesco. "Avon Skin So Soft is the only thing that fends them off."

"Quite right," Angus agreed as the red telephone booth in the middle of nowhere—the official start of the trail—came into view.

"Oddly specific," Natalia said, slipping her hand into Catalina's, quieting her bouncing knee.

Once upon a time, Jack and Brooke could've matched that loving excitement, setting off on a new adventure, but they couldn't be further from it now. The back seat was suddenly suffocating.

As soon as the car came to a rolling stop, Jack snapped at the door handle.

"Och, the child lock's on there," Angus said. He got out of the car and opened the door for Natalia and Catalina. They wriggled in their seats, digging for seat belt buttons, before sliding out.

Brooke got out and closed her door, looked Jack dead in the eye through the window, and walked past without a ghost of a movement toward releasing him. His stomach hardened like she'd turned it to stone with that stare.

He pressed his tongue against his cheek before turning to Catalina. "Hold the—" he said as the car door slammed. Jack dropped his head against the headrest and exhaled through his nose. *Off to a bloody perfect start.*

He hadn't dared to hope for Brooke's forgiveness, but the possibility of her accepting his apology was beginning to feel like absolute delusion.

Angus opened Jack's door. "Come on, then," he said, as if

Jack was the slow walker who couldn't keep up. Which might prove accurate as Brooke had already taken off toward the trail. Natalia and Catalina followed her over the rolling hill obscuring the view of the sea he knew was just on the other side.

Jack grabbed his heavy pack from the boot and slung it over his shoulder. "Thanks, Angus."

When the gray Toyota kicked up dust as it pulled away, Jack raised a hand in farewell. He took a picture of the red phone booth, circling round it to get a rogue sheep in the frame and balance the jewel tones of the green grass and blue sky.

And to give himself a minute to clear his head.

He set off after the women, tapping his palm on the small signpost marking the trail as if it was a start button for a game he wasn't at all confident he could win.

There were no trees in sight, just rolling hills awash in summer green, as they made their way to Rubha Hunish, the northernmost tip of the peninsula. The trail was easy enough to follow here, a dark brown slash cut into the grasses that clung to the earth like moss. The first blush of blooming heather dappled the countryside and their gentle fragrance wafted in the clean sea air. In the distance, the flat blue of the ocean sparkled in the sunlight.

The scenery was soft here, not like the dramatic mountains they'd climb over the next few days, and his photos might've been stunning with the ocean as a background, but the light was too harsh.

A sunny day was so rare on Skye and he couldn't even fully enjoy it. The contrast he needed for a gallery photo was all wrong with light like this. And nothing that'd be suitable for the memoir, either. Jack pushed away those intrusive thoughts that Mhairi should've chosen someone else. That he might not measure up.

Jack jogged to catch up to Brooke, his pack smacking uncomfortably against his back with each step, just in time to hear her ask Catalina and Natalia, "Do you want to hike together awhile?"

"We'd love to," Natalia said.

Jack's heart sank. He didn't mind Catalina and Natalia's company, but he knew what Brooke was doing—building a buffer, keeping her distance—when he wanted to talk. To fix this. To see if there was anything he could do to help her heal.

Brooke looked up when he approached and then straight down at her maroon boots with light orange laces, purple socks pulled up high.

"Are there any specific photos you were hoping for from this stretch of trail?" he asked.

Her cheeks flushed a deep pink and she kept her eyes on her boots. "You read the memoir, right?"

"I did…" And he hadn't felt entitled to the vulnerability of a first draft the way he used to be, even if she'd thrust it into his arms. It'd been a painful one-way connection to Brooke. "I figured since we're walking together, you could show me what you needed."

"Are you taking photographs for something in particular?" Catalina asked, her voice slow and smooth.

Maybe having Catalina and Natalia along wasn't the worst thing—a distraction, at least, from Brooke's hard-edged silence Jack didn't know how to disarm.

"Aye. We're helping my aunt with her memoir. Mhairi McCallister. She founded the trail in the nineties. Brooke's writing and I'm taking photos." He lifted his camera to demonstrate.

Natalia clapped her hands together. "Fantastic! And what is this memoir about?"

Brooke gave Natalia the first genuine smile he'd seen out of her, that glow she always got when she talked about writing settling around her like a halo. "It follows the formation of the trail, how Mhairi and her friends decided on the route, extending and combining centuries-old footpaths that already existed on the island. They found places where it crosses back into civilization so people can day trip each segment and worked with landowners and local governments to make it official..." She trailed off as Catalina grabbed Natalia's arm and pointed to a hawk circling high overhead, her glow fading and flickering out.

Brooke readjusted her ponytail and rolled her neck.

"I'm sorry, what were you saying?" Catalina asked.

Brooke shook her head. "Nothing. What brings you to Skye?"

Cat shrugged her pack and resettled it on her shoulders. "We're backpacking around the world."

"Until we run out of money," Natalia added.

"What an adventure," Jack said, but he couldn't quite relate. He was so focused on earning enough money, to prove to himself and his parents that photography was a worthwhile endeavor. "Are you following the main route?" he asked.

"We'll detour to the Bad Step if I can convince Nat." Catalina shot a hopeful look in her girlfriend's direction.

Natalia hooked her thumbs into the straps of her pack. "This trail seems difficult enough without adding an overwater rock crossing."

"Ah, but Loch Coruisk is the fabled home of the Kelpies—the water horses that are said to pull men down to their watery graves." He recited the story he'd told a hundred times on tours.

"Was that meant to convince me?" Natalia asked with a teasing smile, her accent rolling over the words. "I take it you're crossing the Bad Step?" she asked Jack.

Photographing the aquamarine waters of Loch Coruisk was a bucket list item for him. "I'd love to..." He cast a glance at Brooke.

"We don't have time for detours."

Right. Knowing her—and he was pretty sure he still did—she'd want to finish this trail as quickly as possible because she approached every activity as if it were an Olympic sport, with the added motivation of getting the hell away from him.

Jack gave Catalina a raised eyebrow, well-we-tried look.

"Where were you before this?" he asked.

"We hiked with the llamas on the Colorado Trail." Natalia's eyes went wide with wonder. "My dream is to own a llama farm."

"Really?" Brooke said. "I grew up in Colorado."

They chatted about the mountains and the big summer sky, cementing an immediate kinship. Jack had seen it before on guiding trips, where people shared their stories, found that initial commonality—that love for travel and adventure—and it bound them together.

He couldn't help the rush of envy that Brooke had found that connection so effortlessly with strangers when it felt impossible to rekindle with him.

He took photos as they walked, the small details he knew Mhairi loved, like a half-bloomed purple flower or a sheep with blue spray paint on its rump that farmers used as tags.

About a mile in, they came upon the old Lookout bothy. The rectangular building had no running water or amenities but provided shelter for any hiker passing through, like others scattering the countryside of Scotland. A ladder lay against one side and a mossy green film crept up the walls. The sign under the window read Strictly No Fires Please.

There was something about finding an empty house in the middle of nowhere that made Jack want to look inside. Brooke seemed overcome by the same curiosity as she pushed through the royal blue door. Natalia and Catalina were making their way to the edge of the overlook and Jack followed Brooke up the crumbling cement stairs.

Inside, the walls and ceiling were made of wooden planks. One side was painted in royal blue with a large wooden bench and a bunk bed bolted into the wall. Across the miniature hallway he could barely squeeze through with his pack, the room was whitewashed, a small table and chair taking up most of the space.

Jack snapped a couple of photos of a corner shelf full of seashells, a crystal vase with sprigs of dried heather, beer bottles, and binoculars. A framed poster of whales in this area reflected the sun in white streaks.

Brooke signed her name in the guest book before she crossed to the large wraparound windows overlooking the sea and Jack signed on the same line, some asinine desire to see their names together like they were carving initials into a tree.

She splayed her hands on the glass before they settled on the wide wooden shelf below the window frame. An image flooded his mind of Brooke in the university library, late one night where all she could see was her own reflection, and the way she'd turned to him then, sitting on the ledge, a look in her eye that'd started a series of dominoes he hadn't even tried to stop.

She turned with that same flowing grace and met his gaze, the wide expanse of the ocean through the windowpanes behind her matching the startling blue of her eyes. "What?"

"You look just the same," he said, glancing down at his boots. "Like that night in the library."

He looked up at the pained breath Brooke huffed out, her eyes watery. "I can't do memory lane with you, Jack. I'm having a debilitating go of it all by myself."

"Brooke—" He reached for her as she walked past, but she hugged her waist.

"Please don't." She pushed past him, the wind slapping the door shut with a finality that sounded just like their future. He could boke from the guilt swirling in his gut. *Christ*, he'd been so stupid, so careless, listening to everyone but himself. Everyone but *her*. Jack rubbed the bridge of his nose where his glasses usually sat.

He wasn't sure which was heavier, his pack or his sinking heart.

Claustrophobic, he walked outside and made his way to the edge of the plateau, away from the three women. The land reached into the water to a point, jagged at the ends like an old key. A small island broke the surface of the blue sea, the only discernible horizon with the bright light merging the water and the sky.

He'd never felt so trapped in such a wide, open space. He pulled in a deep breath of the salt-laden air that failed to settle him.

Past the grassy yard near the lookout, the cliff face dropped dramatically to the churning sea below. Jack cut across the field, tall grasses brushing his hands as he walked to the end of the land.

This wasn't part of the official trail, but he could imagine his aunt's excitement standing in this spot, embarking on this journey. He tried to soak in that feeling, to imagine the thrill of adventure in his veins.

Out in the distance, waves crashed against the sides of a large black rock and seabirds chattered and pushed each other into the water.

Jack took out his phone camera, turned it on himself, and hit Record. "Hi, Auntie. I'm at Rubha Hunish, just starting out. I don't know if you've been out this way, but I imagine you have—you always loved a diversion." He flipped the camera around, zooming in on the sea stacks below. "It feels like the end of the earth out here, or maybe going back in time. That's what I always loved about Skye—it distills you down to your essence. Ah, well, before I go and get too poetic, here's another view for you."

He panned across the ocean, the sun shining on the waves like a million broken mirrors, and shut it off. This vlog he'd make for Mhairi wasn't nearly enough but it was the only parting gift he knew how to give.

His heart ached for what was to come. Given the diagnosis of pancreatic cancer, there was no more combatting. The wind ruffled Jack's hair, the sun shone warm on his face, but there was no peace to be had here.

He picked up fallen slabs of rock and balanced the cool, lichen-covered stones one atop the other—an old Celtic custom meant to honor the dead, mark a trail, or as a reminder of things lost.

He wasn't sure of his precise reasons—perhaps all three.

Stacking the stones soothed him like the click of the shutter snap. In a world where every encounter, every risk, every love, was fleeting, the permanence in capturing a moment he could only linger in but never keep was the only thing to bring him any relief.

Jack took his Nikon from the pack at his waist, aimed it at the tan cairn, the green grass in the foreground, the light blue of the water in the distance.

At the edge of the cliff, the ancient rock fractured in large geometric blocks, hanging above the sea. Maybe some desperation drove him to get a shot he knew Mhairi would love when he was failing at everything else, and he crouched on the square ledge, his knees protesting. He winced at the familiar sensation and pushed the doubts of physically finishing this trail from his mind.

Jack braced his front foot out wide, but he'd taken riskier

photos and knew his limits by now. A red boat coasted in the distance and he snapped a photo. Bringing the camera to his eye, he adjusted the lens, zooming in on the birds and the sea spray fanning out from the rocks.

A shimmery gray form breached the surface of the water, leaping up and arching down with a splash. Jack's breath caught and he lowered his camera to watch. A second form coasted along the waves. *Minke whales.*

"Jack!" a voice yelled, sending his heart into overdrive. He whipped around, his weight shifting back. Throwing his arms out, his camera slammed against his chest, but he rocked forward and caught his balance. Standing, he stepped away from the edge of the water, his heart pounding. Brooke stood with a hand to her throat, pink in her cheeks. "Get away from there. Are you serious right now?" She was furious.

A wild emotion swept through him that he immediately tamped down. She cared enough that she didn't want him to die. Which was an extremely low bar.

Jack pointed over his shoulder to the sea. "There're whales."

Her lips tipped up in the faintest smile and her eyes darted to the water. She came closer, stopping next to him.

Spray spouted into the air when their sleek bodies broke the surface. If he listened hard enough, he thought he could hear the rush.

"Whales," Brooke whispered. He turned to her and his breath caught. There was nothing better than the look of awe on Brooke's face. The way her eyes lit and her posture relaxed. His finger itched to capture that look like he'd done so many times before.

She turned to him with a soft smile that reminded him of Sunday mornings they'd spent reading in his bed and it seared through his heart. He'd do anything to keep that happiness on her face.

The only thing that felt safe was Mhairi. The only thing they had in common anymore.

"I stayed with Mhairi on Skye one summer."

"I remember," Brooke said, still looking out at the waves, but it was the first time she'd acknowledged their past and it sent a giddy hope through him.

"Dolphins swam in the wake of the ship we took to see puffins. I remember her saying people are so far from nature now, seeing something wild makes us feel alive."

Brooke hummed, a breathy little sound.

He was addicted to it, needed more. "She said it makes us remember that kind of freedom on a visceral level."

Brooke stiffened instead of softening, turned to him, her eyes dark and serious. "That kind of freedom was dangerous," she said and walked away. Jack closed his eyes against the onslaught of regret.

The freedom they'd shared *had* been dangerous. They'd both been drunk on it, aware of the consequences but not caring because it'd felt so damn good to be reckless.

Jack gave one last lingering glance at the whales before snapping a picture. Capturing that sense of freedom since he hadn't managed to find it for himself again.

He followed Brooke up the steep trail, the tiers of colored rock exposed from ancient times, matching the sea stacks out in the ocean. The past hung in layers all around them—but none so heavy as theirs.

Natalia and Catalina waited for them back by the lookout, lounging on the lawn in front, their faces tipped toward the sun. They tugged their packs on as Brooke approached. "Was it worth it?" Catalina asked.

Brooke glanced over her shoulder, holding his gaze. "No."

Her answer gutted him. He knew what she was really answering and it wasn't about the merits of Rubha Hunish.

She rapped her knuckles on the side of the bothy as she walked past and said, "You should take a picture of this," before setting off to the main trail. She didn't even look at him.

THEN

Brooke stood on the shore of Portobello Beach three days after the night in the library, ready for adventure. Light sand stretched out down the coast, the promenade behind her, and a cement seawall extended forlornly into the ocean like an abandoned pier. Thin-ridged whitecaps interrupted the gray-blue water as it gently rolled toward the shore.

Jack set his kit in the sand next to hers, unpacking his layers of clothes to put on when they finished their wild swim. He wasn't wearing his glasses today and she wanted to study the fan of his eyelashes, inventory the different angles of his face without them. His black wet suit stretched across his broad shoulders, clung to his trim waist, hugged the curve of his muscular thighs. She was going to break her peripheral vision trying to catalog every stretch of that fabric.

Being here with Jack was a charcoal gray area and she knew it. She would've stayed away from him if it hadn't been for that thunderstorm. She was almost certain of it. But now? She couldn't quite summon the reasons not to experience more of what he could show her.

Brooke slipped out of her shoes and even the freezing sand on the bottoms of her feet was a shock to her system, sending goose bumps over her shoulders. The water was going to be torture. "This seemed like a better idea when I was wearing more clothes." She spun her earring and stood with one foot on the top of the other. She didn't like trying things she wasn't good at and it turned out it was uncomfy outside her comfort zone.

Jack looked up at her from where he bent over, his gaze traveling quickly up her body before tossing her a smirk. "You're not backing out on me now, B."

Exhilaration bubbled in her chest at the little nickname, the kind of forbidden excitement that came from sneaking out a bedroom window on a hot summer night—or at least how Brooke imagined that would feel.

But he was right—she wouldn't back out, not when he was looking at her like that.

Not when his face lit up and his eyes crinkled before he made a concerted effort to avoid her gaze during the weekly lecture. It was the opposite of being under a microscope, but she still somehow felt his singular focus.

She'd wanted to know his stories, but now she wanted to know his secrets.

So she was a bit infatuated. What was a little crush between friends anyway? It wasn't like either of them would act on it.

She liked being around him. Liked the promise of adventure. Maybe standing on a beach considering jumping into frigid water a coin's toss from the arctic circle wasn't what she'd had in mind when she agreed to get out of the library, but she couldn't deny the thrill of it.

"Have you considered Olympic swimming as a career choice?" she asked.

"I should. I look great in a swim cap."

"That's nothing to brag about. They just hide big ears."

"Hey, now!" Jack said, cupping his hands over the side of his head and making her laugh.

"Alright, what are we going for here? Time? Distance?" Brooke asked as she pulled the last of her clothes from her bag.

Jack shook his head. "We're trying not to get hypothermia. Since you've never done this before, we're staying in for fifteen minutes."

"Fifteen minutes! It took me longer to get into my wet suit."

Jack grinned. "It's not a contest. It's good for your body, and your breathing. And your stress level."

"I am a high-functioning stressaholic, thank you very much."

"Now *there's* something to brag about." Jack walked down the beach and stopped on the water's edge, turning to find Brooke where he'd left her. "We'll go in together. The trick is to submerge yourself slowly."

"Are you sure? It seems better to jump in." Brooke chewed on her thumbnail as she made her way to the pebbly, wet sand and took one tentative step into the water. She gasped at the freezing shock of it, the cold stealing her breath even though the water was only up to her ankles. "On second thought…"

She had highly underestimated what eleven degrees Celsius felt like.

"Trust me," Jack said and slipped his hand into hers, his palm achingly warm and solid and the only reason she didn't dash back to the beach and her woolly socks.

Jack Sutherland is holding my hand.

Again. And this time, it felt significantly more than comforting. A giddy flutter in Brooke's stomach was drowned out by the alarm bell clanging in her head, but she couldn't focus on either when the cold water burned her feet and calves.

This better level-up her writing.

Jack wrapped one arm around himself against the cold. "Fuck, this is Baltic."

"Say the word and we'll walk away," Brooke said through clenched teeth. She'd give him any out to end this.

Jack caught her eye like he'd noticed the double meaning she hadn't intended, but perhaps should've. Because Jack Sutherland was *still* holding her hand. "We've barely just begun. It'd be a shame not to go a bit further, wouldn't it?" His gaze clung to her and there was no possible way she could stop herself.

Besides, they weren't really doing anything wrong—this couldn't be construed as sexy when her feet stung with pins and needles. She nodded and he squeezed her hand, tugging her forward.

By the time Brooke was up to her waist, every muscle was clenched against the cold. Her stomach was pulled in so tight, her ribs felt like cracking. She couldn't feel her lower body at all.

"I can't do it," she said with a shaky breath. There was an invisible line at her belly button that could absolutely not be crossed.

"I didn't take you for a quitter…"

She'd lost her ability to form coherent thoughts outside of *Freezing… Ow… Why?* but the way Jack widened his eyes in challenge sent a shimmer of heat down her spine.

He slipped below the water, ripples appearing in his wake. He resurfaced with an elated whoop, pushing his hair out of his face and absolutely beaming. Brooke wished she could slow the motion down, to linger in the flex of his bicep under the wet suit, the water droplets clinging to his eyelashes, the curl of his slicked-back hair, the delight in that blown-wide smile.

Jack looked at her expectantly so Brooke scrunched up her face and shoulders and held her breath. Apparently, her desire to impress him outweighed her will to live. Unlocking her knees, she let herself sink as quickly as she could manage. Water flooded her wet suit, the cold boring into her skin and her bones and definitely her vital organs. She pushed back to the surface. "Fuck you, Jack," she yelled, but a rush of exhilaration swept through her, every nerve ending in her body sparking.

He laughed, a loud, booming sound, as relaxed and carefree as she'd ever heard him—the shiniest gold star she'd ever gotten.

A low wave pushed him forward and he rolled toward her, so close she could sense the nearness of his thighs by the way the water rushed faster over hers. He cupped her hip to keep from crashing into her and her body seemed to regain some feeling—at least in the places his fingertips touched.

"We're getting to the good part now," Jack said, eyes flashing before tipping into a wide back float and smiling up into the sky. She couldn't help but read into those words.

Brooke pushed out to where it was deeper, treading water. Her shivers abated and she floated on her back, too, the gentle waves rocking her, her head tight and tingly.

The tension in her body loosened and her mind emptied of to-do lists and her color-coded calendar for papers and studying and bookshop hours. Her attention was completely consumed by the numbing cold making her buoyant, the briny smell of the water, the filtered sunlight on her face.

This was the greatest thing she'd ever done. Better than the high of her valedictorian address or the rush of a new beginning on a flight over the Atlantic.

"I feel free." Like birds disappearing over the horizon.

She heard Jack's quiet hum of agreement over the ripple of the water. Brooke's toes bobbed above the surface, summer red nail polish bright against the deep gray of the water. The sun glinted in strips over the long, rolling waves. Her hair brushed her neck, a floating, gentle caress to balance out the tightness developing in her jaw.

"We should get out," Jack said, his voice muffled.

"Not yet." She wasn't ready to part with this weightlessness. This bliss.

"Can you put your middle finger and thumb together?"

She sat up and tried but her hand felt like a claw. She pushed her fingers together harder and all the adrenaline that'd felt like euphoria shifted straight to blinding panic. "No."

"Time to get out." Jack's voice was tight and it sent more fear through her icy veins. Even her blood felt cold. That could *not* be good.

Brooke trudged through the water, a complete slog to the beach. Her legs felt too heavy, her knees too stiff. Jack looped an arm around her back and helped propel her forward. Her ribs constricted tighter and tighter like a python banding around her. When they broke the hold of the water, her relief was short-lived. The wind was calm, but the air on her wet suit sent a violent shiver through her. She clenched her jaw tight against the agonizing chatter of her teeth.

"Can you unzip your wet suit?"

Brooke reached for the zipper at her throat but didn't have enough strength in her fingers to tug it down. She was never going to get out of this, never going to warm up. As her grasp slipped for the third time, panic zapped through her, a coiling, debilitating thing.

Then Jack's hand was there, tugging the zipper. The wind sliced through her bare skin and she heard herself whine.

"We've got to get you out of everything wet." His hands were on her shoulders, sliding along her arms as he pushed the wet suit down. "Can you take your bathing suit off?"

Brooke could barely get her arm behind her back, it was so heavy, let alone pinch the string on her bikini. She shook her head.

"Turn around. I'll do it."

She followed directions, hugging herself in a death grip against the tremors. Jack pulled the knot of her bikini top and she wished she'd felt it more. Jesus, this was not the way she wanted to get naked in front of Jack for the first time.

He tugged the string around her neck and the ends tumbled

over her shoulders. Before she could protest, he was slipping a shirt over her head. She struggled to release her bikini top and move her arms.

"You got it. Keep moving."

Finally in a shirt, she turned back around and Jack pulled a fleece over her shoulders. As she wrestled with the sleeves, Jack picked up her vest and she noticed how much he was shaking, the blue tinge to his lips. "I'm sorry. I can do it. Take care of yourself."

"I'm okay for another minute."

He tossed the vest around her shoulders and fumbled with the zipper. She wanted to see Jack like this in another setting. Shaky and fumbling, but not from the cold.

"You good?" He looked up at her, his hair slicked back, and she wasn't afraid anymore. He wouldn't let anything bad happen.

Heat flowed back in her core. "I'm good."

Jack unzipped his wet suit, exposing his bare chest. Water droplets clung to his shoulders and pecs. His abs were clenched against the cold and she wanted to drag her fingers over the ridges, down the light trail of hair on his belly. He pulled on a shirt, raising his arms and exposing the swell of his bicep. Then his shirt was over his head, his vest on top, and she kept staring as if she might see more secrets etched in his skin.

"Brooke." He cut through her trance. "You've got to keep adding layers."

"Right," she said, picking up her down jacket from the sand and slipping it on.

"We can both turn around to get joggers on."

"Right," she said again. That was the sensible thing to do. She peeled the wet suit down her legs, which were more or less completely numb, and wrapped a towel around her waist before stripping her bikini bottom off and tugging on sweat pants. She scrubbed the sand off her feet and ankles before sliding on warm socks and boots. Her body still shivered, but a mild heat flowed through her now.

"You alright?" He ran his hands up and down her arms to warm her. Even though she didn't really need it anymore, she let him. She liked his hands on her.

"Yeah."

"You scared me."

"I'm sorry."

"No, I'm sorry." He shook his head like he was chastising himself and yanked a beanie down over his damp hair, the ends curling up around the green wool. "We should have gotten out earlier. Fuck, I should've—"

"Jack—"

"That could've been so dangerous."

"Hey." She stopped him with a hand on his arm. "I'm okay, Captain."

He laughed under his breath. "Can I make it up to you with cake?" he asked, his eyebrows still furrowed with worry, his eyes still searching her face. Like whatever was between them was more than a dare in the dark.

And suddenly, the line they couldn't cross felt like it'd been drawn in the sand, insubstantial and effortless to tread over.

NOW

Brooke knelt by her tent in the diluted rays of the foggy morning, struggling to light her camp stove against the blowing wind. She ran her thumb over the ribbed metal circle on the lighter, the flame sparking before the wind immediately snuffed it out. She closed her eyes against the frustration and hopelessness rising up in her, which was far too large for the number of minutes she'd been awake.

Yesterday, they'd stopped at the Flodigarry hostel for a drink. While Catalina, Natalia, and Jack sipped beers and tipped back on chairs to catch the sunshine, she'd stayed inside. Even the bartender talking bitcoin at her was better than being around Jack.

When Catalina and Natalia had announced they were staying at the hostel with *hours* of daylight still left, an entire war had raged inside Brooke's chest. She couldn't part with the buffer they provided, but she also needed to finish this trail as quickly as possible—for the sake of the memoir and her still-broken heart.

The rest of the day had been a grueling climb until Brooke's feet were throbbing and her shoulders were numb. Every step they took was into an absolute bog. The ground was so saturated, there was no way they could pitch tents. Brooke was all but dropping to her knees in exhaustion and in supplication to whatever old gods might still claim this land. By the time they'd found a campsite that wouldn't swallow them whole, Brooke was starving and bone weary.

Now, she had the start of a blister on her right heel, her shoulders ached from her heavy pack, and the wind sifted through her teal Patagonia with no regard for her mood. She was one inconvenience away from hiking out of here and that included a failure to make a mediocre cup of coffee—dreams be damned.

Meanwhile, Jack was having an absolute field day, wandering around the outskirts of their campsite, taking pictures of the blue sea in the background, the sweeping emerald mountain range, and twigs or something. He'd always loved the liminal light of dawn and Brooke hated that that knowledge was stored in the same part of her brain as the dance moves to the "Macarena"; she couldn't forget, no matter how hard she tried.

She was drowning in memories of him, tossed around by the ones they never got to make, all those wasted nights dreaming about a future that'd never materialized. She was terrified to look him in the eye, to open a connection that had always felt so intimate and inevitable. Afraid she might remember the mornings they'd lain in bed, foreheads pressed together, too close to focus on the autumn brown of his eyes, but still not close enough.

Brooke sucked on the side of her sore thumb, the ridges of the lighter's flint wheel etched into her skin.

Jack circled back to his tent, long legs clad in convertible zip-off cargo hiking pants that should've looked ridiculous, and yet he was somehow channeling an REI catalog model. He tugged on a black puffy vest and zipped it halfway. He was still so insufferably good-looking, so *homey* in morning hiking gear. A gray T-shirt peeked out of the collar of his hunter green sweatshirt and she hated the rumpled look of him. Hated that she used to love it so much.

Jack pulled his camp stove from his pack, squatting down to light it. His tan pants pulled tight over his toned ass and Brooke hastily looked away. *So much for not noticing him.* If she hadn't made the mistake of looking up the original photographer on Instagram and accidentally imprinting the X-ray of his jagged bone pieces onto her brain, she'd leave Jack behind.

She flicked the lighter until her skin was red and raw and still she couldn't keep it lit for the second it took to reach her stove. *Goddammit.*

Jack crossed the expanse between their tents; Brooke had set up her tent as far from his as the boggy soil would allow. "Mine took an age, too. Want some help?"

She cast a look over to his side of camp, where his black stove, shielded by a large boulder, happily boiled water—unlike her disappointment of an outdoor cooking gadget. The only one who hadn't let her down in this wilderness was her left hiking boot.

"I think I've had enough of your help." She was being hostile and immature, but she couldn't deal with Jack being *nice.* Couldn't bear to rely on him, even in this completely insignificant way. Not when she knew how swiftly he could pull the rug out from under her.

She wanted to pick a fight. Wanted to see him affronted just for the excuse to tell him off. Wanted him to suffer like she had. To face some consequence besides leaving a master's program he hadn't even wanted in the first place and following his dreams of being a professional photographer.

"Right," Jack said stiffly, shoving his hands in his pockets.

His chastened retreat back to his tent should've been a triumph, but it made Brooke feel shitty instead. It was so infuriating she could hurl the boots he'd left upturned on the tops of his hiking poles directly into the sea. She had a right to her anger. It was the only punishment he'd gotten.

Brooke moved behind a rock to block the wind and held a hand close enough to the lighter to burn herself, but the flickering flame caught the camp stove and she punched her hand in the air. Victory was hers. And nearly coffee, too.

She boiled water to make her drink, poured the rest in a bag of dehydrated oats, and took a deep breath. She could do this.

After she finished breakfast, Brooke slid the poles out of her tent. As she tossed them on the ground, the tent billowed in the wind. She clutched the fabric to her chest and stepped on the edge as she rolled it up, just in case it blew away. That would be a fucking disaster.

Jack approached, adjusting his pack. Brooke ignored the freckles dusting his cheeks—either darker than she remembered or easier to fixate on without his glasses—and continued stuffing her tent poles inside their bag.

"How do we want to handle navigating today?" he asked.

The Skye Trail was not particularly well marked. It wasn't an official path where rangers came through and cleared the trail, adding wooden steps and footbridges in hard-to-hike places. And today's hike was the most technical section. Eleven grueling hours up and over the imposing Quiraing Mountain Range, which had been created by land slips like glaciers calving, resulting in dramatic cliffs and steep slopes.

Brooke pulled her laminated map from her pack. "I'm on it."

The physicality of the strenuous day and the beginnings of a blister on her heel that she'd expertly bandaged in moleskine were at the top of Brooke's worry list. Navigating was not. They just had to follow the ridgeline.

They set off, climbing hill after hill, her body at a forty-five-degree angle, fighting the steepness and the wind acting like a puppy who couldn't fucking *leave it*. It changed directions, yanking on her pack and trying to knock her off balance.

Next to her, Jack was the walking embodiment of the Calm app. He took pictures of fluttering leaves and rock piles and tiny rivulets along the path. He set up his tripod, backtracked to get footage of himself walking, then looped back to retrieve it.

Into the camera, he said, "Hope you liked that, I had to walk past twice. The first time was set to slow-mo."

She was curious what reason he could possibly have for making this hike longer than it needed to be, but not enough to ask.

Sometimes, being in nature made Brooke feel insignificant in a way that recalibrated her problems so they seemed insubstantial in the greater scheme of things. It gave her perspective. But with Jack around, she was all wrapped up in her head instead of being present in her body. And that was no way to get to the heart of the memoir.

Peace—just another thing he'd stolen from her.

Humming "Wide Open Spaces," Brooke opened herself up to the creativity in the universe. She spread her arms out, the wind tugging at her raincoat sleeves, but she wasn't letting anything hold her back. Not today. She was ready for inspiration to strike, since apparently binge-watching *Lucifer* and *The Great British Bake Off* wasn't cutting it.

She cataloged the scenery for the memoir, recording a voice note. "The range spans out like an unwound ribbon, slipping down to a bowl of the valley littered with pyramidal peaks cupping glassy lakes between them."

She looked for the details she'd missed in her draft. But she'd included the rocky outcroppings covered in white lichen and the fence posts staked into the hillsides and the way the clouds stretched down as if reaching misty fingers to catch the land.

Now that she was here, she'd describe it the exact same way.

She was an A+ researcher. She could make the story more visceral, but it wouldn't be hugely different. Even Catalina and Natalia had immediately lost interest in her description of the trail, distracted by a hawk like her parents near a bird feeder. Details might not be enough.

A spiral of anxiety coiled tightly like a physical knot in her chest and Brooke tumbled into the panic that started at *I've hit a roadblock*, dipped down to *I'm a completely useless human being*, and headed straight on to *The world is ending*. She might fail Mhairi, destroy her legacy.

But Brooke caught herself, taking a deep breath for a count of four, holding it, releasing it. She'd been through this kind of doubt before—the terror of encroaching writer's block when she waited for a shower or a dream or a fucking lightning bolt to unlock the hidden answer. She just had to wait it out.

The sound of quick footsteps reached her and she suppressed a full-body eye roll at the universe's sense of humor. "So, you're still writing?" Jack said as he fell into step behind her.

Not that she wanted to talk about anything else, but she *really* didn't want to get into the details of her work with Jack. He already knew she was cowriting Mhairi's memoir. That was all he needed to know. "Yup."

"Fiction?" he asked.

Jack was a stranger who knew too much. She could crow about all her many achievements, but he was the one person who might see right through her. Who might look at what she'd accomplished, superimpose it over all the dreams she'd shared, and find her wanting.

"Not anymore. What about you? Living the dream?" She gestured at his camera. Their implosion probably did him a favor. Pushed him out of inaction and onto the path he'd always wanted.

He made a noncommittal sound that sounded like *I'm not dignifying the sarcasm with an answer*.

Good. Let him be annoyed with her. Brooke picked up the pace, hoping to lose him.

The wind whipped up clouds from the ocean, a never-ending

cascade billowing over the cliffs like a row of fog machines was installed just out of sight. The ridges of far-off hills became barely-there silhouettes in the distance. The trail narrowed as the slope angled down like a ski run.

Mist swirled around her ankles until it enveloped everything she couldn't reach out and touch. She'd read once that people couldn't sustain a certain level of adrenaline for much more than twenty minutes, but her fight-or-flight reflex was going strong. While her anxiety was primed for creative writing—devising ever more distressing scenarios was her superpower—out here, it was debilitating.

Brooke came to a fork in the trail and stopped, peering into the haziness in both directions. Now she knew why people wrote books about slipping back in time in Scotland; it wasn't at all hard to imagine.

On her first pass through the maps before their trip, she hadn't spent the time she should have in this section. The trail followed the ridgeline. It couldn't get much easier than that. But apparently there were identical-looking offshoots.

She glanced at the map again. Checked the mileage on her watch. Pushed down the rising panic that there was no fork where she thought she was.

She followed one track a few paces until the trail evaporated into trodden grass. It was probably a deer path up another vista. She breathed out a sigh of relief and went back to the main trail. Jack had caught up with her and the stomp of his boots and the swish of his jacket echoed in the all-consuming, almost haunting, fog. A physical embodiment of the ghosts that wouldn't stop nipping at her heels.

Brooke's boot hit a stone and it rolled before dropping out of sight. She took a giant step back, her heartbeat tapping out a violent Morse code, her breathing coming quick and shallow. *Jesus Christ*, she hadn't realized she'd been so close to the edge. Goose bumps spread across her skin and raised the hair on the back of her neck.

Something bumped against her pack, knocking her forward, and she let out a strangled cry before catching herself and whipping around. Jack stood there, hands outstretched. "Sorry."

"Trying to knock me off the cliff?" she asked.

"I didn't want to lose you."

His words cut straight to her heart. She closed her eyes against the sudden stabbing in her chest. She'd longed to hear words like that from him once. But his actions had spoken a lot louder.

"Give me some space," she said, meaning both literally and figuratively, and kept walking.

The trail rounded a high knoll and the wind ceased. This was the landmark she needed. Something she could control. Brooke took a deep breath, trying to settle the pounding in her chest.

She pulled out a laminated map from her pack while Jack passed her. She noted where they were, how the path would head inland for a couple of miles before turning back toward the ridge. She'd revel in the lack of wind while she could.

Following Jack, Brooke cursed her inability to refrain from tracing the slope of his shoulders, noticing the tin mug dangling from his pack, or measuring his assured stride against the tentative boy he'd been.

Jack took off his hat, rubbed the heel of his hand into his eye, and placed the hat on backward. The chorus of Sam Smith's "Unholy" struck up in her brain like a needy pulse that reverberated all the way down to her toes. *Goddammit.*

He crouched down, bringing his camera to his eye and twisting the lens. "Brooke, look at this. It's a lichen native only to Skye."

She slapped at a pinch on her neck. Then her arm. A swarm of midges descended and she waved her hands in the air and let out a strangled cry before running up ahead on the path.

Clearly not faster than the swarm, she dropped her pack to the ground with a wince and tossed out her extra layers, digging for the yellow bottle of bug spray. She misted it all over her head and arms, hoping the tiny piranha flies would drop dead from the sky, but they didn't seem the slightest bit deterred.

One flew straight down her throat and she leaned over, dry heaving, coughing up nothing. "What in the fresh hell?" she rasped, tugging her sleeves down over her knuckles and pulling her hood up to protect her neck.

Jack pulled a bottle from his pack and offered it to her. Avon Skin So Soft stretched across the green label. "It's the only thing that works."

She shot him a scowl and sprayed an additional layer over her shirt. "Because you know what's best for everyone?" she said, being needlessly aggressive-aggressive, but he didn't get to run around making choices on her behalf and acting like he knew better.

"That's not..." He shook his head and a muscle in his cheek jumped before he pulled out a green hat with mesh hanging from the wide brim and replaced his baseball hat. Even once he had it on, he slapped at his neck. "Little blighters," he cursed under his breath.

"You look ridiculous," she said. Like he was trapped inside an oversize bug catcher.

"And not eaten alive." Jack's voice held an edge Brooke hadn't heard before and it made her feel better. It was easier to indulge in her anger than any of the other emotions he stirred in her chest.

The air was completely still now and the thick fog offered no hope for a breeze to blow them off. They were trapped in this hell.

Twenty minutes and an uncountable number of slaps later, Brooke was in pure agony. Her skin burned, and she could feel tiny legs traipsing all over her body—even though they were too small to actually feel.

Jack pulled the Avon Skin So Soft from a side pocket, set it on a rock, and walked in the direction they'd come from, unhooking his tripod as he went.

He never headed backward to set up a shot. He was giving her salvation and a cover so she didn't have to swallow her pride. Or at least not all of it. "Thanks," she mumbled as she popped the top off and pressed the orange nozzle to spray a woodland-and-citrus midge-death all over her.

It might've been a misting fan at a Fourth of July parade for how instantly relieved she felt. The spray was working and she was trying to be magnanimous about it. She really was. She forced herself to wait for Jack.

They pressed on in eerie silence. The lack of other hikers and no signs of civilization were disorienting. Like they were wading through the inside of a cloud.

"This doesn't seem right," Jack said.

It sent another flicker of unease through Brooke's stomach. She didn't need his skepticism making her second-guess herself.

Brooke pulled her paper map out, the one she was so proud of knowing how to read, which was feeling more and more useless with no landmarks to ground her. She tilted her wrist to check their mileage on her watch. "We've been walking for forty minutes since the last time I found a landmark." Brooke pointed to the curve in the path and the high knoll that, in retrospect, had been a portal into Hades. "So that should put us right here."

"Unless we took the wrong ridge," he said gently, his finger skating to a part of the map where they couldn't possibly be.

"I think I know how to read a map."

"I'm not questioning your mountaineering skills, but it's foggy as fuck out here." His voice was laced with frustration and it fueled her. *Finally.*

"I'm surprised you've noticed anything outside of water droplets clinging to the underside of flower petals."

His cheeks turned pink while his eyes narrowed. "Oh, excuse me for paying attention, not charging into the wilderness, so intent on checking off a to-do list."

She just wanted this over with to get away from *him*. "I'm not checking off a to-do list—"

"We're off track," he said in a stern voice she'd never heard from him before. He pulled out his phone and the maps he must've downloaded before the trip and turned on the GPS. The little blue dot lit up right where he'd suggested they were— way up a secondary ridgeline.

Fuck.

"We should turn back," Jack suggested.

"Do whatever you want. You're great at that."

Instead of snapping at her like she wanted, Jack moved in front of her, tipping his chin to catch her eye. "I fucked up. *So* badly. I wish more than anything I could take it back. I know I broke your trust and it's unforgivable." Jack reached for her, held her arms. Brooke nearly twisted out of his grip, but not before she looked up and his eyes were so weary and sad that it sapped all the vengeful wind from her sails.

Maybe seeing the real pain splashed across his face, the real regret, siphoned away some of the resentment she'd carried for so long.

"You don't have to share your life stories or your hopes and dreams, but if we can't trust each other out here, we should end this now. It's too treacherous."

That was the perfect word for being around Jack. Always had been. But he was right. The consequences were too high to fight Jack *and* the elements at the same time. And she needed to keep going for Mhairi.

She would never trust Jack with her heart again, but she could trust the blue dot in his hands.

NOW

Brooke woke in utter darkness to the sound of snapping, like wind whipping a flag. Only the flag was her entire tent.

The wind she'd been pleading for all afternoon to blow off the goddamn midges had arrived in full force, as loud as the roar of the ocean, as if she was sleeping on the beach in the middle of a storm surge. Except she was sleeping in a tent on rocky ground on the lightest air mattress money could buy.

Brooke could've sworn she heard the sound of fabric tearing. Sitting up, she felt along the top and sides looking for a hole, but didn't find anything. As much as the wind sifted through the tent, stealing away the warmth from where her sleeping bag had fallen to her hips, she couldn't find a distinctive draft anywhere, either.

Brooke's feet ached, and her shoulders were probably bruised. Her eyes were scratchy from exhaustion. And every inch of her itched. She reached around in the dark and turned on her headlamp dangling from the arch of her tent to see how many more hours until dawn. *Two in the morning.*

Brooke threw herself back onto the miniature inner tube masquerading as her pillow, clenching her eyes shut as the wind continued to grab and shake her tent. She scratched at her itchy face before realizing what she was doing and curled her hands into fists. She was never going to get any sleep.

Fighting down the hopeless panic spiraling inside her, Brooke pulled out her notebook. Sometimes the only thing that soothed her was getting all her thoughts out on paper. She wrote down Jack's comment about being far from nature and knew exactly where she could slot it into the draft. But she wasn't feeling all that productive as she thought back over the rest of the day.

Now that she'd experienced the trail for herself, she could see how she'd portrayed it like those commercials with a woman traipsing through a meadow, but in reality it was a hellscape of death bugs and duplicitous, boggy soil. If that was the authenticity Mhairi wanted, then consider the job done. Brooke had a lot to fucking say.

Dear Trail Management,
On June 1st, I set off on the Skye Trail. I am writing this letter to bring to your attention that the quality of this trail has left much to be desired. Even a single sign-post along the ridge would do. Surely, others have experienced foggy days on Skye and this should have been rectified by now.

Not to mention the mutant swarms of piranha flies you allow to roam freely, without providing the one-and-only insect repellant they are, in fact, repelled by.

To set matters right, I would like your company to provide me with a portable bug zapper that lights up in a satisfying way at the death of my foes and ensure that my ex must continue to wear his mesh hat that makes him look like an insect trapped in a toy bug catcher.

If you could do something about the wind, that would be great, too.

Sincerely,

Brooke Sinclair

306 Simon Square

Edinburgh, Scotland

Brooke heard something outside, a scuffling that wasn't the wind. She tucked lower into her sleeping bag.

Once she'd gone night hiking with Chels and Kieran up Arthur's Seat and gotten terrified by something lurking in the dark—a mountain lion or a black bear; her biggest fears growing up in Colorado. They'd laughed themselves silly when a rabbit hopped into the glowing sphere of her headlamp and they'd assured her everything ferocious had been wiped off the face of the British Isles centuries ago.

But still. There could be a hairy coo out there. She wouldn't even want to come face-to-face with a fox in the night, if she was being honest.

Brooke's name floated on the wind and a shiver snaked down her spine. Just in case the thought of peeling her own skin off from bug bites wasn't enough to make her cry, the idea of ancient ghosts or water horses seeking her out in the dead of the night was sure to catapult her over the edge.

"Brooooooke."

She sucked in a breath and held it, listening hard through the beat of her own heart and the kerfuffle of the wind in her tent.

"Brooke, it's Jack."

Oh, *fuck*. Brooke blew out a breath and sat up to unzip her tent. "Are you trying to terrorize me?" Because seriously, if it wasn't the debilitating backward hat or the personal attack of looking hot in zip-off hiking pants, he needed to freak her out in the night, too?

Jack stood in the whipping wind—much worse outside the tent—with a headlamp highlighting only the ridges of his perfect face. "I saw your light on. You alright?"

"No. This is awful."

"Here." He reached into the tent, palm up, and Brooke couldn't make out what he offered her.

"What are those? Gummies?" Unclear if that would help her sleep or make her paranoid out of her mind, but it was a risk she was willing to take.

"Earplugs."

She took the highlighter-orange foam from his outstretched hand. And hated that she was aware of the feel of his skin, of those hands that had cradled her face, roamed over her body. Hands that would never touch her again.

Brooke closed her fist around the earplugs, crushing them, but needing something to ground her in the present. "Thank you," she managed to say, looking up into the light of his headlamp.

Jack sucked in a breath on a hiss, loud enough she could hear it over the wind.

"What?"

"Your face looks…painful. I've got some calamine lotion with me. Hold up," he said and jogged off into the darkness. Brooke rolled back from where she'd been sitting on her knees.

It'd been too fortuitous to run into Jack in Mhairi's office when she'd been put together, sparkly eye shadow and all. Of course he'd have to see her now, under a distilled fluorescent light, when she probably looked like she had chicken pox.

The little bubble of light reappeared, closely followed by Jack's shadow. He crouched down at the edge of her tent, the wind ruffling his hair and tugging at his clothes. That gray hoodie had already been ancient when she'd last seen it. Soft and threadbare and just the right amount of cushion when she pressed her cheek into the hollow between his pecs. It probably smelled the same—sweet, like Pink Panther wafers and watermelon.

"Here," he said, handing it to her. "Oh, you don't have a mirror... I can do it."

Kill me now.

She had the wrong bug spray, couldn't actually read a map, hadn't remembered earplugs. She should be able to do this herself. Resentment curled inside Brooke; she hated to rely on Jack of all people. But she'd have chalky pink lotion all over her sleeping bag or miss half her face if she tried to do it alone. "Thanks."

Jack rocked back on his heels from the force of the wind, catching himself with one hand. The glow of the headlamp highlighted his black sweats stretched over his thighs, adding insult to injury.

She did *not* want him in her tent, in her space, but this wouldn't work when the trail was so intent on destroying her. "Um...just come in."

"Right." Jack clicked off his headlamp and tipped his head to crawl into the tent.

Brooke didn't move fast enough, pushing back onto her elbows, and suddenly Jack was above her, hands on either side of her waist, knees bracketing her thighs. She couldn't feel his heat through her sleeping bag, but she imagined it. Could recall the slide of skin on skin so easily.

Her heartbeat pounded like a Wild West steam train and she was sure he could hear it when he looked down at her and froze, only the strings of his hoodie swinging. She had this memory—this impulse—to wrap them around her fist and pull him to her.

Jack cleared his throat, his gaze dropping to his hands as he tried to maneuver in the small space. Brooke rolled to the side, zipped the tent, and pulled her knees to her chest. She mentally added some choice words to her complaint letter to the Skye Trail Management, aka Mhairi, aka the devil.

Brooke's headlamp hung from the loop at the peak of her tent and the light rocked and bobbed with the wind, casting a swaying halo over them. It was somehow too quiet inside, even with the wind, the sound of their breathing too loud.

Jack, kneeling beside her, uncapped the pink bottle and poured out a few drops onto the pad of his pointer finger. He touched spots along her forehead and nose. The bottle gurgled as he poured out more.

When his finger brushed her cheek, she closed her eyes against the ghost of memories that fought to remind her of all the times he'd stroked her jaw, hand slipping to the curve of her neck. He paused, his thumb resting on her chin, and she looked up at him.

"I lost things, too, you know." Jack's voice was faint, whisper soft.

"You were only in grad school because your dad pushed you. You didn't even want it."

"I did by the end. But I'm not talking about getting sacked. I'm talking about *you*. There's a difference between fucking up and screwing someone over. You hurt me, too."

His eyes were black in the dim light, dark pools full of desperation tugging at her.

She'd spent enough hours making eyes at Jack Sutherland. She could interpret what she saw in them with one hundred percent clarity.

It wasn't the look of someone who'd never cared. It was the look of someone who *still* cared.

Brooke didn't know what to do with that information, but she trusted that look more than the thousand times she'd tried to convince herself otherwise. It put a hard revert on all her memories with him she'd overwritten with *one-sided infatuation* and *never cared like you did*.

"I loved you and you disappeared."

Brooke sucked in a breath. She'd felt it back then. Known on some bone-deep level. And the words he hadn't said before settled softly around her heart even though they had no business being there. But she'd loved him, too, once. And maybe that kind of history couldn't be unwritten or plastered over.

"You never told me you loved me."

"I was waiting. I wanted it to be romantic and special. I wanted to do at least that one thing right." Jack's eyes went back to his work as he continued dotting her face. "I'm still trying to do something right. I know I can't undo the past, but I'm trying here."

She wasn't sure if the soothing cold of the lotion was enough to erase the burn of his touch.

Maybe he deserved her anger and it sure as hell felt good to indulge in her rage, but she didn't want to be this bitter person who lashed out just to see him bleed.

They didn't have to be friends—they'd never been good at that anyway—but they could be acquaintances. She didn't need to hold him at the barbed end of a spear.

When he finished, he gave a short nod. "Everything will look better in the morning," he said, and slipped from her tent.

THEN

As Jack ran across the football pitch, the wind plastered his jersey against his chest. Footie always felt like an escape, a hobby with no strings or expectations. He could clear his mind and push his body until he was exhausted. But today, in addition to Jack's parents in the stands—handing out mince pies to Kieran and Chels as usual—Brooke was here.

Outside of class, Jack hadn't seen her in the two weeks since their swim and he was lightheaded from this development, from the giddy rush of finding her attention on him every time he chanced a look over. He could barely even worry about what his parents might be saying to her, he was so aware of his every movement and if Brooke was noticing him.

She wore a navy blue University of Edinburgh hoodie with the white crest on the front and what looked suspiciously like a red University of Edinburgh scarf. No one cared much for football unless it was the Premiership, but she looked straight out of an American movie waving one of his mum's plastic pom-poms.

"After a much-improved display from Glasgow, the points

are shared with nine minutes remaining 'til the half," Kieran called in a booming announcer voice from the bottom bleacher. "Deacon Barr is running boldly through the Glasgow defense as they scramble to defend their goalkeep. Out by Barr to Rohan Kelton. Oh! A near miss, but poorly defended."

Jack stole the ball from a brute of a Glasgow player and passed back to Rohan, who sent the ball flying into the goal.

"It's all the way through!" Kieran yelled. Rohan charged into Jack, lifting him off the ground as Kieran continued shouting, "It's got in! He's done it again. He's superhuman! At only twenty-two years of age, this is Rohan Kelton's fifth goal this season. And Uni takes the lead."

"Listen to that brotherly support," Jack said as he pushed out of Rohan's sweaty embrace.

A familiar high-pitched whistle pulled Jack's attention to the stands where his dad stomped his feet on the bleachers and whistled again with two fingers in his mouth. Gemma whipped a pom-pom above her head. Jack gave Brooke a sheepish smile and a helpless shrug, an apology for his parents. She beamed at him like she'd seen a planet through a telescope for the first time, and his chest filled with fire. His vision went a little blurry at the edges, his head light.

He realized he was lingering at the sideline again while the game rushed on around him. Running back into the fray, the wind chilly where it sifted through his damp hair, Jack dodged a Glasgow player, heading straight for the ball.

"Go, Jack!" Brooke called. She was standing up, hands cupped around her mouth, beautiful, light eyes trained on him.

And then the air was knocked from Jack's lungs, his knee twisted in sharp pain, and he was flat on his back, the thud reverberating over the field.

Jack shifted on the locker room bench, his foot propped up on a plastic chair, and took the ice pack off his knee. The joint throbbed but he couldn't find a towel to buffer the cold and his skin was screaming in protest.

He heard a voice down the hallway. "Jack?"

It was a woman's voice. Not his mother's, who'd already been in here. It was American and sweet and sounded an awful lot like Brooke.

His heart dashed away with the thought, so affected by her that he'd completely forgotten he was in the middle of that field, hadn't even seen the defender rushing him until he was on his back. He'd take the hit again to see Brooke calling out his name, all her attention on him.

He'd known from their initial spark that her presence in his space was more than mere happenstance. Couldn't attribute it only to her love of swimming or cake or a strong addiction to coffee, which explained why she was always at the coffee cart before their lecture. But turning up to his game and charming his parents—if Gemma's knowing glance when she mentioned how *lovely* his friends were was anything to go by. Coming to find him now?

Brooke fancied him right back. And Jack couldn't do a damn thing to act on it.

He wouldn't risk raising conduct concerns because of the nonfraternization policy, or his standing at the university, or her reputation.

She stood in the doorway, concern etched around her blue eyes. "Hey. How're you doing?"

"Better." *Now that you're here*, he wanted to say. He couldn't help the wide grin taking over his face.

"What kind of drugs do they have you on?" she asked, like she could tell his smile was out of the ordinary. Too big. Too fast.

"Adrenaline and victory."

Brooke walked into the room, stepping over gym bags, stray shirts, and a tipped-over shoe. "I'm sorry you got hurt."

"I'll have to work on my focus before my Premiership try-out," he said, brushing it off. But their eyes locked, a heavy moment between them like they both knew exactly why he'd been unfocused.

"Glad to hear this injury hasn't put your dreams out of sight." She trailed a finger over the swollen curve of his knee. "It looks bad."

Jack sucked in a breath as goose bumps broke out across his skin. Brooke looked up and probably noticed the way he'd stopped breathing because her eyes went wide and she snatched her hand back. "Sorry, did that hurt?"

He swallowed past the knot in his throat and shook his head, still not trusting his voice. Her touch didn't hurt but it was certainly torture, her fingertips flirting with the hem of his shorts. "No, the cold feels good."

Brooke laid the backs of her fingers on his swollen knee, her touch pastel soft, their eye contact stealing his breath again.

Jack had memorized the shape of Brooke in his peripheral vision, the curve of her cheek, the sway of her hips, the golden brown tint of her hair piled on top of her head. He was so used to learning the edges of her, one glance at a time, that looking at her now, not worrying if anyone was noticing him staring, was a relief and also somewhat overwhelming.

She pulled her hand away, her chest rising and falling with a deep breath. "Speaking of dreams…"

Jack tried to remember what they'd even been talking about before her touch.

"Making any progress on our pact?"

He had, actually. But he didn't want to get his hopes up, to proclaim it to the world, in case it all turned out to be nothing after all. He gave a half-hearted shrug, hoping the nonchalance disguised his reaction to her touch.

"I nearly *died* in the ocean for you." She threw her hands out as she spoke, her eyebrows shooting up in indignation before a playful smile took over her features.

Watching her was like a lightning storm. No matter where he looked, there was something equally as lovely lighting up just outside his focus.

"Alright." He held up his hands. "I am…sitting in on a photography class." He said it like he was confessing, this thing he couldn't quite claim. "It's not even for credit," he rushed to add, but he wanted Brooke to know he was trying.

Her eyes shone like fairy lights and it was all the reward he'd ever wanted. "That's amazing."

A reckless hope swept through him. And that deep fear he harbored—that he'd find something he loved and not be able to have it—felt a little less daunting with Brooke shining a light on it. Like maybe if he just trusted enough, he wouldn't have to watch it slip through his fingers.

But her attention on him felt like too much. His feelings were too new to articulate. "So you met my parents?" Jack said instead, covering his face with his hands out of potential embarrassment. "Did they tell you endless stories about Scotland? And feed you?" He peeked out between his fingers.

"Both of those things, yes. Did you know the national animal of Scotland is a unicorn?"

Jack groaned but couldn't quite make it believable when Brooke smiled at him like that. "My dad is the *worst*."

"You might consider that not *all* parents would come to a varsity soccer game."

"Intermural football," he corrected quietly because he wasn't quite sure what to do with Brooke's discernment about his parents. He should keep his distance. Shouldn't feel so desperate to share all his deepest fears and hopes for the relief of telling someone who understood.

Brooke sat on the wooden bench and scooted in close. "All I mean is that maybe they aren't so bad."

He replaced the ice pack on his knee with a wince. "They're not bad. I didn't mean to give that impression. They just have such a vision of what my life should look like and it'll break their hearts if I don't follow through."

"Here." Brooke unwound her red scarf and wrapped it around the ice pack. "It seemed to me like they'd support you no matter what. Maybe even photography."

Jack shrugged and took the ice pack from her, settling it on his knee. "Might be."

A random memory floated through his mind and he grinned. "You know, they *did* support my budding photography career early on. We went on a trip when I was five or thereabouts and they'd given me an old camera. I was taking a steady stream of pictures of Loch Oich and dropped the camera straight in the water. While I was blubbering on and on and my parents were busy consoling me, this young guy on his honeymoon ripped off his shirt and jumped into the loch to save it for me. He dove down and reemerged triumphantly with the camera in his hand. Little did he—or I—know, there was no actual film in the camera."

"That's the saddest thing I've ever heard! They didn't even give you film!"

"Eventually they trusted me with it. I never loved guiding and I wasn't naturally outgoing like Logan, so my dad would have me take photos on the trips. It was the only time I felt like a part of the family business and not on the outside with them. It's not their fault. I'm just not exactly what they wanted."

Brooke looked away but her eyes returned to his, soft and unguarded. "I don't see how anyone could feel that way about you."

He clenched his hand into a fist to keep himself from reaching for her but his teammates interrupted the moment before his resolve crumbled, their shouts ringing out down the locker room hallway, and Brooke stood up. "I should probably go."

Jack nodded and cleared his throat. "I'd walk you home, but…" He gestured to his currently prone figure. "Rain check?"

"Dangerous country for those," Brooke said.

He should nod and leave it at that. Let her walk away. Put a stop to whatever hope shone in her gaze. But he couldn't seem to do the right thing. "Sun check, then."

She gave him a blinding smile and disappeared out the door.

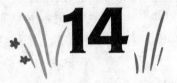

NOW

Brooke woke to the predawn glow, the only proof that she had, in fact, dozed for part of the night. The wind was still feral, her whole tent shaking above her head. She rubbed at her itchy eyes before unzipping her tent to the sun barely rising over the horizon, a blurry pink through the mist blanketing the sky. An instant morale boost.

Jack sat on a boulder, his camp stove between his feet, a coffee mug cradled in his hands. He gazed out at the view, bundled into his burgundy fleece zip-up and a beanie, his dark hair curling out the bottom. His black joggers clung to his thighs and hinted at the muscle underneath.

He'd been right. Things *did* look better in the morning.

Jack caught her staring, a grin spreading across his face. "Ah, this is why you never let me see you without makeup."

Too late, she remembered the calamine lotion all over her face—the chicken-pox look. "It'd serve you right if I was contagious."

"Brooke, scabies are nothing to joke about."

She couldn't help smiling at his overly serious expression. Or the way her stomach hitched at the sound of her name in his lilting accent. "Don't ever say 'scabies' to me again."

His laughter followed her as she headed down the hill for some privacy and to wash the chalky pink lotion off her face. But as her rosy warmth from her sleeping bag faded with the wind, so did that fizzing excitement in her stomach.

Dropping her guard with Jack was too easy, like spring slipping into summer. Brooke might've called a self-imposed cease-fire, but that didn't mean she'd forgotten what he'd done.

They broke camp and headed over the Trotternish Ridge. The day was clear as if they'd passed some test after battling the Quiraing.

By the time afternoon was descending, they closed in on the Storr—the monolithic rock pillars that rose from the slope of the mossy green mountain. The trail had been mostly deserted the past two days, but as they reached the famous landmark, day hikers and tourists abounded. People milled about, shattering the feeling of isolation that had long besieged them, and removed some intensity from the bubble they'd been in.

A trio of pinnacle rock formations pushed ten stories into the sky. Brooke had to crane her neck for a view of the top, imagining being a tiny crab on a beach, staring wearily up at a towering drip sandcastle.

Jack crouched down to snap a shot of the Storr. He moved with an easy grace she didn't remember. More self-assured, like he'd grown into his body, grown into himself.

Brooke couldn't deny she was curious about him. She wondered if he'd worked on other memoirs. If he traveled around taking pictures of extraordinary landscapes. If this was a normal day in his life.

If he still lived in that two-bedroom flat with the bay window he used to share with Rohan. If he still rubbed the heels of his hands into his eyes when he woke up. If he ever thought about her anymore.

That tug she'd always felt with Jack—craving stories, demanding details—returned. But she was older and wiser now, able to recognize an impulse and not chase it down.

"Anything around here would be great for photos," she said, tipping her head toward the craggy pillar. "It's stunning."

"Aye. This entire island is a geological wonder. The high peat content of the soil means it absorbs so much water, making it very prone to landslips. The biggest ones happened nearly three million years ago and we can see thousands of years of exposed layers of sedimentation. The Storr fell some eight thousand years ago, tipped on its head, and has been whittled down into points from the ensuing wind and rain."

Brooke had done her homework and already knew the history, but a grin tugged at her lips and her heart fluttered in recognition at Jack's thoroughness, like the way he'd once told her about the Scott Monument. *Captain* floated through her brain and she bit her lip to stop herself forming the word.

"They call it the Old Man of Storr because from this angle, it looks like the ridges of an old man's face if he was lying down for sleep. Another legend says that he was the last of the giants and when they went to bury him, they ran out of stone, so his thumb still pokes out from the ground. Or…something a bit cruder."

"Jack!"

He cast her a devilish look, his tongue coming out to wet his bottom lip. She couldn't fight the smile on her face or the way her body temperature spiked.

She looked up at the towering rock, shaking her head. "I can never unsee that…"

Jack's laugh rumbled through her and spread out across her skin.

The tourists parted and he jogged down the hill and set up a shot. Someone came up behind him, walked directly into his sight line and took their own picture. Jack glanced over at Brooke with an exasperated eye roll and she grinned in response, like it was an inside joke.

And it felt dangerous, sharing looks like that with Jack. Because Brooke knew exactly where it led. Her heart had always wanted to be in Jack's inner sanctum, to know his secrets. Even if she'd had to be one of them.

But look where that'd gotten her.

Brooke turned away, pulled her attention back to the people around them, back to the present day where she wasn't Jack's secret; she was only his past.

Keeping her eyes off him, she dug her notebook out of her pack and pulled it from the ziplock bag she'd had the forethought to stick it in. She needed a distraction from this humming in her veins. Some reminder to not lose sight of her goal—not a second time.

As she sat on a rocky outcropping, she wrote down the myths Jack had shared. So much of the current draft of the memoir centered around the logistics of the trail development. Maybe adding some legends would soften the narrative, bring some more flavor to the story.

Brooke also wrote details about the Quiraing: the giant craggy pillars, the path that cut through the grass leading to the natural fortress. The glassy lakes down below, cupped in the slope of the land. The faint blue of a mountain range across the water.

Mhairi had said she'd included this landmark because the foot trails were already established in this area. That people were drawn to this iconic and otherworldly site, shrouded in mist and the folklore that came with the unexplainable.

But sitting on the slope of an ancient landslip, a jagged mountain range behind her, didn't feel the same as staring down into the Grand Canyon or gazing up at Half Dome in Yosemite.

The beauty out here, the isolation, made her feel both insignificant and so very vital. So present in her own body. She felt elemental. Minuscule, but essential.

She wondered if that's what Mhairi felt out here, too.

Jack made his way back to her. "Did Mhairi ever tell you about the Skye Bridge?" he asked, not like he was trying to smooth her over, but like he was trying to help.

"No."

"They built the bridge in '95 to connect Skye and the mainland, mostly to support tourism and make it easier to reach without a ferry. But as soon as the bridge was built, they started charging a toll. Well, the islanders didn't appreciate that very much and some refused to pay. They were ticketed and to add to it, the government set the court on the mainland so they'd be in double offense once they arrived."

Jack stood with one leg straight and the other bent to accommodate the hill. He cupped the lens of his camera even though it hung from the red-and-black strap around his neck. The memory of that first night in his room popped into her mind, soft and rosy. When he'd been some irresistible mixture of brooding and shy and she'd wanted to know his heart.

"But there was a loophole in the law about the tolls that exempted farmers or anyone with livestock. So Mhairi and her friends went round and talked to the landowners. The ones closest to the bridge agreed to build a wee corral on each side, so if you were ever needing to cross the bridge, you'd pick up a sheep on one side and drop it off on the other. Of course, Mhairi would opt to bring a sheep round with her to do the shopping."

Brooke smiled at the image of Mhairi chatting with a sheep while she loaded her bags into the truck. "I can see that. Naming it Lambert or Peabody."

"Or Ewe Jackman."

Brooke laughed, that easiness settling between them. "She never told me that." But it tracked, Mhairi's streak of defiance that came out when faculty members murmured about her pop-up critique groups in the lobby coffee shop or the way she let her mail pile up an extra week after the office manager told her to clear it out. She knew Mhairi. She'd literally heard her life story. But the image Jack painted was a bit different than the Mhairi Brooke had written into the memoir. A little more fun. A little more audacious.

The heartbeat of a story was never beautiful scenery or folklore footnotes. It was always character. *Was this what Charlotte thought was missing? The heartbeat?*

Brooke scribbled flowers in the margins of her journal. Wrote "Mhairi Characterization??" and underlined it. A tendril of anxiety twisted through Brooke's chest. She'd nailed Professor McCallister's voice, but was this story about Trail Mhairi instead?

When the crowds thickened and Jack gave up on photos, they made their way down the steep hill, past the parking lot stuffed with cars and tour buses, and crossed to the other side where the trail picked back up and led toward Portree.

"Did you know *The BFG* was filmed here?"

"Well, there's a fun fact. You could've made a great guide."

"I would hope so. I did it for six years after…" He gestured between them.

"What?" The word was out of Brooke's mouth before she could even process it. "But you hated it." She knew how much grad school had felt like a lifeline to Jack. Or a reset button. He'd been right there with her, chafing against expectations, wanting more for himself. It would've cost him dearly to go back to his family's business.

She'd assumed he'd gotten everything he'd ever wanted after they'd imploded. He was *here*—photographing a prestigious memoir. The idea that Jack had gone back to his family's business when she knew how crushing their expectations had been didn't compute.

He walked with tight shoulders and hard lines around his mouth. "I was a little delayed developing a spine, wasn't I?"

"Jack."

The regret on his face was almost enough to make her reach for him. Brooke assumed he hadn't faced any backlash because it'd suited her anger. He might be the villain in her story, but he'd been knocked down, too.

"I left The Heart last year. I have you to thank."

"We haven't talked in years."

"No, but back then, you made me question what I really wanted. It just took a bit for me to sort it out."

Brooke had been so full of herself, so sure of her path and wanting Jack to feel the same way. She'd been such an asshole, pushing him like that when it had cost her nothing—but it could've cost Jack his family. She wanted to apologize, but it didn't seem like the right thing to say. He seemed happier now.

Brooke studied his profile. The hard slope of his nose. The curve of his cheekbones. The roundness of his lips that she'd once fantasized about tasting and then knew like her own mind.

The way he gazed out at the land in front of them—greens and purples and blues—was still the look of a dreamer, but grounded now. Steady.

She knew exactly how hard it was to make a change after choosing the safe thing.

Pride swelled in her chest for him, but it also buzzed with unfriendly spikes. She wondered what he thought of her; the one who'd challenged him hadn't achieved any of her dreams. Wasn't even fighting for them anymore.

15

THEN

Brooke's boots crunched along the snowy, frozen ground. The night was sparkling. She'd grown up with her fair share of snow, but it never lost its magic. Especially when a once-in-a-lifetime storm blew through. Fat flakes came down while she followed Kieran and Chels hauling a full-size kayak up the side of Arthur's Seat—the steepest sledding hill next to Mount Rainier. Rohan and Jack led the way.

While the idea belonged to Chels, the kayak belonged to Rohan. And wherever Rohan went these days, Jack went. Jack struck Brooke as a person with common sense and a survival instinct, not someone who frequently entertained the idea of careening down a sporadically rocky hill under patchy snow cover. Her chest radiated heat at the thought of why he'd agreed to this completely bonkers activity.

She knew why *she* was here. Being around Jack was addictive. As was the rush she'd found blowing off studying and trying something new. Her writing felt amazing lately, like she'd leveled up or tapped into a higher energy source. She felt inspired and buzzy.

"You're doing great." Rohan swung his arms as he walked beside Kieran struggling with the kayak grip. "Quite impressive."

"Oh, fuck off," Kieran said, dropping the kayak to flip Rohan off and earning a disgruntled "Could you be any more *useless*?" from Chels.

Jack laughed under his breath, his arm brushing against Brooke's as they trekked upward into the darkness. He'd lent Brooke and Chels headlamps, and the golden light cast bobbing halos at their feet.

It was probably unsafe to choose footing based on the proximity to Jack's body instead of other, better things, like stability and lack of loose gravel. Maybe that made her a bit desperate, but this longing to see him had morphed from silly and fun into something heavy and insistent. Being around him was exhilarating. Swimming in freezing water had left her with a thirst for adventure she'd never felt before. And also an unquenchable ache for Jack. She wanted to major in the furrow of his eyebrows, the crinkle of his eyes, and the low roll of his accent.

She loved that he was vulnerable. That he shared about the pressure of expectations and the feelings of being lost. Loved that he'd told her about the Scott Monument instead of laughing at her when she'd exposed what a nerd she really was for coming to Edinburgh for the literary history. He didn't think less of her and her failed attempt at wild swimming.

She felt safe telling him things. She wanted to impress him but she didn't feel like she had to, and that was remarkably special in her world.

"This is the spot," Rohan declared from somewhere above them. Even without supporting the kayak, Brooke's ragged breaths came out in white puffs, illuminated by the headlamps. Her winter jacket was no match for the damp cold of the air this close to the sea, but she was flushed from the exertion. By the time she made it to the flat shelf, her thighs burned from the climb.

Kieran and Chels hauled the kayak over the lip and both collapsed in a sprawl, like they might make snow angels the second their strength returned. Rohan made a move toward the front seat but Kieran wrapped his arms around Rohan's leg. "I'm going first if it's the last thing I fucking do," Kieran said, punctuating his words with gasping breaths.

"It's *my* kayak."

"Irrelevant." Kieran hoisted himself up and steadied the boat, hooking a leg over the open side.

Chels put a hand on his chest to stop him. "I'm taking the front. This was my idea."

"And I did the bulk of the heavy lifting."

"You absolutely did not." Chels slipped into the front seat and Kieran moved to the back, grumbling, and they fisted their gloved hands in the snow, rocking back and forth.

"On my count—"

"No, on my count," Chels said.

"One—"

"One, two—"

Rohan adjusted his black hat with soft red and orange spikes, and Brooke winced before he yelled, "Three!" and dived in behind Kieran, sending them all bombing down the hill.

Chels's high-pitched scream and Kieran's broken curses reached them like smoke billowing behind a steam train.

Brooke held her breath as she stared into the darkness below, the hiss of sliding along snow interrupted by thuds and bangs as her friends hit rocks on the way down.

Maybe she wasn't feeling *that* adventurous after all. She wasn't ready to get a concussion and end the night early, especially when she was up here—*all alone*—with Jack.

She turned to find him watching her, lit in the dusty tones of the snow-filled sky, a shy smile on his lips. It made her bite her own, her heart twirling in her chest like the snowflakes all around them, a delicious dance of anticipation.

A crash sounded, followed by a cheer erupting from somewhere far away.

Jack shook his head with a huff of laughter and unzipped his backpack, pulling out three bottles of red wine.

"What do we have here?"

"Mulled wine. Or, it will be." He rummaged in his bag, retrieving a small camp stove, igniting it with a lighter he slipped from his pocket. The purple flames glowed bright in the night, sending shadows dancing along the snow.

"Oh, so you're *outdoorsy*." Brooke liked a man confident enough in himself to bring a camp stove to uni. She hadn't been camping since she moved here, but she could totally see herself getting back into it, especially if Jack was the one sharing her tent.

He flashed her a grin, white teeth and rosy cheeks illuminated by the flame. "I don't know my way around a filleting knife, so I suppose it's all relative." That awareness between them bloomed, like he was collecting her details—tiny, immaterial things—and cataloging them as if they intrigued him.

"Roll that out, would you?" Jack tipped his chin to a yoga mat hooked on the bottom of his pack and Brooke laid it out the best she could, sitting down and trying to keep as much snow off it as possible.

Jack hooked a loose-leaf tea strainer to the edge of the camp stove, the smell of cloves mingling with the fresh, snowy scent of the night.

"Have any oranges for that?" Brooke teased. He was adorably committed to this and while she sat on his yoga mat and he tossed cinnamon sticks into the pot, she wondered if he'd planned this just for her.

"Orange *juice*." Jack pulled a pint-size container from his bag. "What do you take me for?"

"A certified sommelier."

"Ah, then you would be correct." He handed her an open bag of Pink Panther wafers. "A sous chef, too."

She pretended to roll her eyes. "What an overachiever."

He joined her on the mat while the wine heated up, sitting cross-legged, his knee resting atop hers, and the touch that had felt innocent and comforting in the library felt charged here. Made her count her own heartbeats and the minutes before their friends returned.

"How'd the paper turn out?" The heat from his leg seeped through her jeans.

Brooke took a bite of the vanilla wafer, crumbs falling into her lap. "So great. Mhairi said she was going to stop grading for the night but got pulled into my story." Her chest flushed relaying the praise. Wild swimming, stealing secret glances at a soccer game, and now night hiking in the snow had given her this feeling of drafting grandiosity—and if she kept this up, kept going on excursions with Jack, there was no way she wasn't getting into Mhairi's fellowship.

"Did you frame that?" he asked with a lopsided grin.

She nodded. "Obviously. Big gilded one. Sparkles in the light."

"Just had that lying around?"

"A whole set. I've got big dreams, Jack."

He snatched the wafer from her fingers and ate it. "I know. I like that about you."

Brooke's heart went oddly melty. Jack was like the snow, absorbing all the noise in her brain, making her feel cozy and peaceful.

He leaned back on his hand, his shoulder slipping behind hers, his face close enough she could make out the faint flush of his cheeks. His knit hat bowed out where his glasses rested and his hair curled out from underneath the fold. Jack's eyes dropped to her lips and she was sure the air had crystalized between them the way it shimmered.

"*You* do it, then!" Chels shouted, and the crunch of snow beneath boots infiltrated the little bubble of firelight she and Jack had gotten wrapped up in. Brooke's heart beat like she was about to be discovered breaking into a safe with a stethoscope and a ninja costume.

Jack cleared his throat and stood, blowing heat into his hands as he went to check on the wine. Brooke's disappointment lingered as Rohan and Chels reappeared and Jack fished honest-to-god wineglasses—albeit plastic ones—from his backpack. He ladled one full for Brooke.

"You sure know how to woo a girl." Brooke smiled.

"I'm trying as hard as I can." Jack didn't inject even a bit of sarcasm in his voice and Brooke's heart sped up at the confirmation that he *had* planned this all for her.

Chels picked up an empty glass, holding it out to Jack. "I want to be wooed, too," she said.

Realizing she'd been overheard, Brooke took a gulp of wine, scalding her entire mouth and letting out a pained cry.

"It's hot," Jack said with a wince.

Brooke scooped up a handful of snow with her mittened hand and placed it directly on her tongue. "Gathered that."

Rohan tutted. "Schoolboy error," he said and Brooke laughed at the expression.

"We call it a rookie mistake."

"Oy, we invented the language. Play by the fucking rules. And you!" Rohan shouted, as Kieran emerged victorious from the slope, pushing the kayak over the lip, snow covering his hair and the left side of his face. "Could you take any longer?"

"Maybe if I hadn't been abandoned!"

Kieran and Rohan scuffled in the snow before they settled into a rock-paper-scissors system for turn-taking. Either all the hollering into the night was infectious or the mulled wine was working overtime because hurtling down a mountain in a water vehicle started to sound exciting to Brooke, too. Like a capture-the-flag kind of wholesome fun.

Brooke circumvented the brothers and Jack was suddenly there. "Need a hand?" he asked, reaching for her waist as she climbed into the back. His touch and the low tone of his voice went straight to Brooke's head, more potent than the mulled wine, making her feel light and effervescent.

"Mind the boulder halfway down on the right," Chels said from somewhere far away, too far away to really register the warning when Jack was nudging Kieran aside and hopping in the front.

"Oy," Kieran objected, but Jack rocked at the top of the ledge and pushed off and then they were careening down the slope.

Rocks scraped the bottom of the kayak and the blows sent shockwaves reverberating through Brooke's bones. The wind they created blew across her face and whipped her hair backward. Jack's silhouette was dark against the twinkling city lights before them.

The freedom of flying coursed through Brooke as they slid along a stretch that must've been straight mud. She would've thrown her arms out wide if she didn't have a death grip on the rim of the boat.

The kayak shifted and tilted, then slammed against the side of a boulder.

She was weightless for a breathless moment, then rolling, snow in her face, hands grabbing for purchase.

Brooke knocked into Jack's body, her momentum sending her sprawling on top of him. She braced herself with hands by his shoulders, snow soaking through her jeans at the knees where she straddled his waist.

In the glow of the moonlight, she could see his eyes locked on her mouth, could feel his fingers splayed across her hips, could sense that he wasn't shifting her away. Her breath came in heavy pants, mingling with the white puffs of his.

Her heartbeat kicked a bass drum in her chest to the beat of *want, want, want*. There was a long list of reasons she absolutely should not make out with Jack Sutherland on the side of a snowy mountain at night, but something about the darkness and the adrenaline made her forget every last one of them.

"Jack," she said and her voice sounded husky in the darkness. Her hair hung around his face, snow caught in the dark strands.

"Don't say my name like that," he said, his voice gravelly.

Her pulse pounded in her temples—in her fingertips, between her legs—with the knowledge of the ledge they were straddling. Of how easy it would be to tip over the side. "Jack," she said again.

His fingers flexed, gripping her hips, and a low growl fell from his lips. Lips she couldn't resist for a second longer.

She leaned down and kissed him. Pressed hard against the softness of his mouth. Jack's hands immediately moved, one sliding to her lower back, the other slipping beneath her hair, both pulling her closer. His mouth slanted against hers and she met every tangle of his tongue, hot and insistent, excitement pulsing in her veins like starlight.

The cold tip of Jack's nose brushed her cheek as he changed the angle of the kiss, the pressure of his fingers in her hair tightening. She moaned into his mouth and his arm banded across her waist, pulling her tighter. She rolled her hips against the hardness she felt between her legs and his hand fell to her thigh, squeezing. Jack groaned, the vibration buzzing across her lips, and she kissed him deeper, her tongue sliding against his.

Kieran called from up in the dark, "Oy! Did you two die?"

Brooke sat up, heart pounding, as if Kieran could see them all the way down here in the dark. Jack's hands fell from her body and cold flooded the warm handprint he'd left on her leg.

His attention still trained on Brooke, his breath came in

heavy pants. "We're coming," he shouted. To her, he whispered, "We can't do this," and even though his voice was breathy and light, it slammed into her all the same.

She scrambled off him as swirling black mortification snuffed out the starlight.

They took an endless number of trips down the hill, but Jack's retreat had completely wiped out the fun, turning Brooke's buzz to a pounding headache. She'd been delusional to think kissing Jack was okay.

As soon as Kieran got to the top and threw himself on his back in exhaustion, Jack packed up his backpack and Brooke grabbed the front of the kayak to help carry it down the hill. She was ready to get out of here, away from the way he avoided her gaze and not in a secretly seductive way.

"Are you mental? We're riding it down!" Rohan shouted.

Kieran and Chels clambered in and Rohan took a running leap onto the back, shunting them down the hill. *Their* buzz was still fully intact.

After a chorus of bumps and bangs, followed by cheers and hollers, Brooke could barely make out the shapes of Rohan, Kieran, and Chels at the bottom of the hill. *Damn.* She hoped they hadn't been able to see her draped across Jack earlier, even in shadow.

Her friends raised the kayak above them as they rushed down to the sidewalk ringing Arthur's Seat, looking like rats absconding with a footlong sub.

The crunch of Jack's boots reminded her that they were alone in the dark. The air so still and quiet, she could hear her own heart beating. Brooke took wild steps down the hill, needing to put space between them, to get away from the silence between them that no longer felt like charged anticipation but suffocating tension.

She shouldn't have kissed him. She considered apologizing,

except that was beyond disingenuous. She didn't feel sorry. Especially not after Jack had kissed her back the way he had. But she didn't know where they went from here, how they found their way back to the easy companionship they'd found. If she'd wrecked it all.

At the bottom, they crossed to the sidewalk, the path looking sleepy from the golden streetlights muted by the fog. Romantic, under different circumstances.

She wanted to ask if he regretted it. If once that magical spell in the snow snapped, and reality had come rushing back in, if all the consequences outweighed that moment. But she didn't really want to hear the answer if he did.

Brooke rolled her shoulders, her anxiety taking up too much space inside her chest. Jack walked beside her, hands shoved into his pockets, eyes straight ahead.

"You know why, right?" he asked.

Embarrassment flushed through her. Of course she knew why they should never have crossed the line. Why *she* shouldn't have. "Yeah."

"It's against university policy. It's a huge conflict of interest. Even though I'm not your TA, since we're friends with Rohan, it could look like he was being pressured to give you special treatment. It's possible I could lose my job, or there could be consequences for you. We can't."

"Oh my god, you really don't have to lay it out. I get it." She adjusted her hat over her forehead. This was worse than him freezing under her in the snow. She didn't need him to chastise her like she was in the principal's office. She'd gone way too far on this quest for adventure, gotten reckless and greedy from the rush of it.

"I'm trying to be responsible."

Brooke wanted to take a darkened side street detour just to get away from this. She wanted to bury herself in her coat or jump down a manhole. "Seriously. It's fine—"

He caught her wrist, his finger slipping inside the cuff, brushing against the soft skin of her wrist. Her eyes fluttered closed at the chill and the heat dancing across her skin simultaneously. She turned toward him.

"Please don't confuse this with indifference," he said, his face golden in the streetlight, deep grooves shadowed between his brows. "I don't want to jeopardize what either of us has going on."

"Yeah." She twisted her wrist and Jack released her.

"Brooke," he called but she kept walking. She needed to lick her wounds out of his sight.

NOW

Jack studied the map on his GPS and calculated their walking speed based on the amount of fussing Brooke was doing with her backpack, alternating between slipping her hands under the straps and cushioning her lower back.

As much as he'd been dreaming of the campsite in town with a shower, his knee throbbed and he was shaky with hunger.

They weren't going to make it into Portree before the sun set.

Up on the next high vista, he pressed his heel into the ground to check for the boggy squish he'd grown accustomed to, but the ground was solid. A small burn trickled by to refill water. "Let's stop here."

"Oh, thank god," Brooke said, her pack hitting the ground before she finished speaking.

Jack dropped his own pack, but before he could rummage for a freeze-dried pouch, the view caught his eye. The deep cobalt sea in the foreground contrasted with the dusty blue of the Isle of Raasay in the distance. The lighting was the perfect golden glow that airbrushed away all the imperfections of real life. His finger twitched to capture it.

Jack pulled out his tripod and Nikon from his pouch, his stomach protesting the idea of anything coming before supper. But the lighting was soft and hazy and the whole shot looked sleepy and serene. He had to capture it before the sun sank any lower.

As he snapped the tripod out and framed the shot, Jack's stomach growled again. His camera felt heavier than it was, his arms weak.

He heard the click and whoosh of Brooke's camp stove while he paced back and forth along the cliff edge, trying to find the exact right spot. He took a few pictures and checked them on the display. It was almost time. When the sun dropped a bit lower, the clouds would go cotton candy pink and he'd be ready.

Jack pulled out his phone while he waited, flipped it toward him, and hit Record. "Hi, Auntie," he said. "We found the perfect campsite tonight. Look at this." He turned the phone around to scan the water below the dramatic cliff, Raasay muted in the background. He panned to the side, to where Brooke was setting up her tent—right next to where he'd dropped his pack. His breath caught at how much closer she'd moved since the first night and he forgot to keep moving the camera.

Brooke looked up and waved with an indulgent smile. "Hi, Mhairi."

Jack turned the phone back to his face. "My stomach's eating itself, but I've got to get this shot. I think it's the one." Not the one that got him into the galleries, that made people notice him, that made it all worth it. But the one Mhairi would love best.

He waved goodbye and put the phone away as the sun dipped below the horizon. He stepped behind the tripod and snapped. The image popped up on the display and adrenaline coursed through him.

The saturated blues and light pinks complemented each other perfectly, and the shadows in the distance created texture and depth. It reminded him of Mhairi: soft and nuanced and welcoming.

"Here you go," Brooke said at his shoulder, and he turned to find her holding out a bag of freeze-dried food, steam rippling into the air. "Hope you still like curry."

He wasn't sure which stood up faster, his stomach or his heart. For the woman who'd blasted him with ice three days ago, making him dinner was a clear olive branch. Even better that it was hot and smelled spicy and heady.

He took the bag from her. "Thank you."

This trip had been nothing like he'd hoped. He'd gotten enough good shots he wouldn't have to rehike the first segments, but the lighting had been terrible the first day, the scenery shrouded in mist after that—not that he'd had any spare attention for taking photos with his whole being consumed by regret. But this gesture from Brooke, the way she'd softened to him today, and the beauty around them tonight, felt like a sign from the universe to keep going.

Brooke waved at the camera equipment while he shoveled food into his mouth. "Photography turned out to be the thing, huh?"

In a family where he was so often overlooked, where his dreams had been minimized, even by himself, she'd always seen right to the heart of him. It made him glow on the inside like the last sunbeams hanging on the red-orange clouds.

"It did," he said around a bite.

She turned the full force of her gaze back on him and where he'd shrunk in the face of it that first day, he seemed to grow because of it now. "I'm proud of you."

Jack's heart expanded uncomfortably in his chest. He hadn't realized how much he longed to hear those words, for some confirmation that he wasn't selfish in leaving the family business, that his dreams mattered.

"Sorry, that's probably a really weird thing for me to say,"

Brooke said, her head tipping down as she picked at invisible lint on her leggings.

"Not at all. It means a lot." It meant *everything*. Logan had been furious with him for so long, at the boundary he'd created, but The Heart of the Highlands had been an alluring safety net and he'd had to cut free from it to really move forward with what he wanted. No more hedging, no more hiding.

"But there's not much to be proud of. Honestly, I'm not getting loads of traction. Galleries either want some very specific type of high-contrast black-and-white photo I can't seem to perfect, or a big platform. People manage to start these vlogs and have a million viewers and I don't know how to do that. I'm not personable that way."

"You're just so serious in those videos."

A warm grin spread across his face. "You watched my YouTube channel?" He'd assumed Brooke had walked away and never looked back. The fact that she'd checked up on him went straight to his head. His mind flitted over all the videos he'd taken on hikes and excursions, documenting the landscapes and the folklore and probably too many birds. He wanted to know every thought she'd had about them.

She rolled her eyes but her cheeks turned a delicious shade of pink. "Tell me you haven't internet stalked me."

He held up three fingers for scout's honor but she narrowed her eyes.

He laughed, giving in. Of course he'd searched for her. "But I couldn't find anything."

"That's because I'm a ghost." The teasing words didn't disguise the edge of something in her voice he couldn't quite place. "My point is, what if you make videos like the ones you're doing for Mhairi?"

"You need to be serious to be taken seriously." He repeated the comment his dad had made a thousand times.

"I'm sorry, have you met the internet?" she asked. "I get

wanting to hide behind the most professional version of your-self, I really do, but you have to be *authentic*. Like you are with Mhairi."

Brooke's belief in him was so unwarranted, but he wanted to be worthy of it. Wanted to be worthy of her again.

Jack finished his meal and crumpled up the bag, stuffing it into his rubbish sack. From his pack, he grabbed the half-crushed Pink Panther wafers. "Want some?"

Brooke hesitated and her eyes met his before she gave him a soft smile and took a stack of pink wafers from the bag. "I haven't had these in forever," she said before stuffing one into her mouth and settling on the boulder next to him. She crossed one of her long legs over the other, her hiking boot bumping into his, then shifting away. He wished she'd sat next to him so he could slide in closer, feel the muscle of her leg through the thin fabric of her leggings.

"As good as I remember," she said.

She was as stunning as she'd ever been, sparkling and perfect. "Agreed."

Brooke turned to look at him, probably from the seriousness of his tone, the way he hadn't quite meant to reference their past, but it was hard when he'd never really let it go.

Instead of pulling away like he feared, her eyes shuttering, she flashed him a genuine smile and stuffed another wafer into her mouth, crumbs collecting at the corner and a groan falling from her lips. "These always remind me of you."

His heart warmed imagining her thinking of him in the time they were apart, but he wanted to be more than a collection of memories. He'd started this trip wanting to support her, want-ing her forgiveness. But it'd morphed into wanting her atten-tion, the easy companionship they'd once shared. And if he let himself get carried away…more than that, too.

He'd always wanted more with Brooke.

THEN

Jack left his office in the dim twilight, crossing the pud-dled streets on campus and passing by the library. He glanced up at the windows glowing in the misty night, the yellow light dancing across the glossy cobblestones. Brooke was probably up on the fourth floor, sitting at the same table, twisting her earring as she highlighted pages.

He clenched his jaw against the impulse to see her, talk to her, touch her. He'd told himself a thousand times she was bloody off-limits. She was a *student*. Except that felt like refer-ring to his brothers as his colleagues; it wasn't remotely ade-quate to describe their connection.

He craved her on a fundamental level—this vibration in his chest he couldn't settle when he was away from her.

Each of the last four nights since Brooke had kissed him in the snow, he'd managed to tip his head down from the beck-oning light of the upstairs window and carry on home. He had coursework to grade, photos to take. But tonight, this desper-ation that consumed him—this need to know what she was doing, what she was wearing, how she was feeling—propelled him through the turnstiles and up the elevator.

Sure enough, Brooke sat at the same table, books and papers spread out all around her, hair tied up in a messy topknot.

"Hullo," he said, his voice caught somewhere between a whisper and a plea.

Brooke looked up and her eyes went guarded, her slender brows pulling together like it pained her to see him. "Hi."

He sat on the edge of the table, not quite sure he trusted his legs to support him.

She twisted her necklace around her finger. "What are you doing here?" She watched him as he failed to come up with any suitable words, waiting for the honest ones to settle. *I missed you. I hate this. I'd take back every word I said for you to smile at me again.*

"I've got an assignment to finish for my photography class. I was wondering if you could help."

"Jack," she said, and it was nothing like the way his name had sounded in the snow. It was imploring and melancholy and excruciating. He never wanted to hear her say it that way again.

"We can still do this, right? Get out of the library?"

She bit the corner of her lip, like she was holding back the word *no*, and he rushed to say, "We had a pact. I vividly remember a pinkie promise," before she could get it out.

Little dimples appeared in her cheeks where she held in a smile. "I *am* great at homework."

His breath expanded in his chest, a heady rush of excitement pulsing through him. "Then come on an adventure with me."

Jack headed up the Royal Mile, the lights from the flats above him incandescent in the darkening twilight. The library had been neutral ground but there was no good reason for them to be out in the city center together and Brooke must've felt it, too, since she walked ten paces behind. He cast a surreptitious look over his shoulder and she gave him a secret smile that sent a flare of heat through his chest, the exact temperature of the burn of her fingertips against his cheeks in the snow.

He made it to the opening of Dunbar's Close and slipped into the tunnel-like alley leading to one of the places he wanted to bring her tonight, his heart beating in an unnecessary flutter of anticipation.

Brooke walked out of the halo of the streetlight and he reached for her hand, tugging her into the little pocket of darkness inside the tunnel. She stumbled into him, her boots lined up with his, her breath coming out in a warm puff against his cheek.

He stole two seconds to drink her in—the shadow of a smile line bracketing her lips, the strands of her silky hair playing in the breeze from under her yellow knit hat, the nearness of her body that sent his blood pounding. He conjured the huskiness of her voice saying his name that night before clearing his throat.

"This way," he said, heading down the wide cobblestone close, trailing his hand over the ivy leaves clinging to the stone walls to keep from reaching for her.

Tucked between the red-painted storefront of the Christmas Shoppe and a souvenir outlet that lured the tourists past the entrance, the tunnel opened into a pocket garden that was still a bit of a hidden gem.

Row houses with dark, slanted roofs cast beams of light from their windows, illuminating the tall trees in a gradient of gold and bronze. The flower boxes ringed in low shrubberies had gone dormant, but sculpted pine trees in teardrop shapes stood proudly in the centers. They walked along the gravel pathways, the damp fallen leaves muffling their footsteps like a silent getaway car.

"This close was named after David Dunbar—a writer—who owned tenements here in the 1700s. It's also rumored that Robert Burns has visited this garden—he was quite fond of an oyster cellar nearby."

Brooke gave him a wide smile before moving farther into the garden, turning in a circle and lifting her face to the night sky, which still held the dusty sapphire tones of twilight. He wanted to capture that look to keep forever, but she'd hear the shutter snap of his camera. She'd know what he was on about.

"This is like a whole other world," she said.

And it was with her here. One full of possibility, heavy with anticipation arcing in the air.

"That's what I love about night photography. My assignment is to capture something overlooked. All these familiar places show a different side of themselves at night. It's when the light matters most of all."

"Oh, you're *into* this," Brooke said but her tone wasn't full of mockery; it held something like approval. Like she sensed this passion and didn't ask him to tuck it away. The acknowledgment made him want to tell her more, to make it real, to hold this feeling close.

"People act like it's some bastardization of black and white, but instead of the high contrast there, night photography deals in the shades and increments. It's more subtle and sullen in a way black and white seldom is." He could capture the dark alleys and the ribbons of light over glistening cobblestones and it could be dark and imperfect.

"Maybe a bit brooding?" She bit her lip but failed to hold back a smile, clearly talking about him.

"Are you teasing me?" he asked, a lightness in his stomach from the relief that she wasn't closing him out anymore.

She headed down another path, reaching her hand out to brush the tidy evergreen tree and grinning over her shoulder. "I would never."

The chill in the air stood no chance against the spark in his chest. The night held a sense of enchantment, an unbridled recklessness Jack wanted to get swept up in. Maybe he already had, as he imagined following Brooke deeper into the garden, tugging her under the briarwood trellis, kissing her breathless. Hands in her hair, thumbs stroking over the soft curve of her cheek, lips pressing secrets against hers. No one would see; no one would know.

But if he kissed her again, he wouldn't want to stop.

"Look over there. You can see the Burns Monument lit up on the hill."

Brooke turned so quickly, he nearly bumped into her. "Jack Sutherland, are you taking me on a writer's tour?" She tipped her face up to his, a flicker of a question—*Are you actually this smitten?*—mixed in with the mirth dancing in her eyes like the stars.

He took a step back, his heart racing, and followed a different gravel path. "There are simply a fuck-ton of Scottish authors—the weather is such shit, there's nothing left to do but sit round drinking or writing. I prefer the former, myself." He set his camera on a wooden fence to stabilize it, centered the view on a shadowed park bench under the tree, a single golden leaf trailing from the reaching branch, and pressed the shutter.

Brooke stopped behind him, looking over his shoulder, and said, "Mmm-hmm," the disbelieving sound skating over the back of his neck.

He held his breath, shutting off oxygen to his thundering heart before turning to her. "I have more to show you."

They emerged from the secret garden onto the bustling High Street, the noise and the people a shock to his system he should've expected. Trailing behind him once again, Brooke felt suddenly out of reach, his heart beating in a reckless chant to have her to himself again.

He took a detour from his original aim, headed up the Royal Mile a few more blocks until they arrived at the steps of St. Giles' Cathedral. The centuries-old church presided over the square. The intricate architecture and beautiful crown dome begged to be photographed.

"Is it even open?" she asked from beside him and he wanted to step closer, to tug her jacket until she fell against him.

"It's a church."

"But they're not open all night." She twisted her scarf in her hands as if she was nervous and he found he liked pushing her out of her comfort zone. Liked that she felt safe enough to do something brave with him.

"Might as well check." Jack tugged the large vertical brass pull and the door swung open, music spilling out. Brooke's smile and the citrus scent of her hair as she brushed past him and inside felt like a new beginning, like an adventure. He followed her into the dusty warmth of the sanctuary awash in shadows and the sliding sounds of mournful fiddle strings.

They rounded the main atrium, the arched ceiling lit in blue-and-red light. Propping his arm on the back of a wooden pew, Jack took a snapshot of the deep colors staining the brickwork, the multitudes of gray shadows clinging to the edges. The cathedral always held a moving grandiosity, but the concert he hadn't expected added a layer of magic to the night.

The folk trio played on a small stage in the center of the room, the singer's melancholy voice carrying and echoing in the expansive church over the soft tones of the accordion and guitar. A small gathering listened from wooden chairs.

Brooke had made her way farther into the sanctuary and leaned against a stone pillar, one foot hooked around the opposite ankle, watching. She looked captivated, her eyes wide, the slope of her shoulders relaxed, her lips parted.

He longed for her, not just for her touch, but to be the one to witness that kind of awe on her face. To make these adventures exactly what she wanted, so she might keep coming back to him.

All moments were fleeting, but some left their mark more than others. And Jack knew this one would live on for him. He raised his camera and zoomed in to capture the look of wonder on Brooke's face, lit in glowing blue.

He went to stand by her, his shoulder brushing hers, and she turned full eyes on him. Unable to stop himself, he slipped his fingers along her palm and between her fingers. Her lips parted on a breath before she gave him a chastising sort of look, full of *You told me we can't do this*, but she curled her fingers tightly around his anyway.

Jack held his breath as her thumb slid slowly over the back of his hand. As he listened to the staccato rhythm of the guitar, the swelling crescendo of the strings, the singer's words about missing his love rang out in the cavernous room and made Jack miss something he'd never even had, but now knew enough to long for.

He felt an inevitability with Brooke, like the changing of the seasons. Like no matter how hard he fought it, he couldn't change the outcome. He couldn't seem to walk away.

When the concert ended and the crowd dispersed, Brooke slipped away with wistful eyes and Jack tracked her movements through the sanctuary, the light way she trailed her hand along the brickwork, the tilt of her chin as she admired the organs and chandeliers.

He wasn't sure how much time had passed when a man in all black and a driving cap approached him. "We're closin' up."

"Thanks," Jack said. He could've stayed in the stillness of the sanctuary all night, basked in the peace and the hope he felt there, the tiny, stolen moment he didn't want to give up. He meandered his way to the exit, so aware of Brooke, he could sense her behind him.

Outside, the night air held a stronger bite, the sky a darker black, the streetlights a golden yellow. She stood on the church steps, face tilted up to his. He'd been planning to walk her home, but couldn't bear to part with her just yet. "I don't want the night to end. Can I show you one last place?"

He wanted to show her this piece of himself because he wanted all of hers.

"I'd love that."

They crossed the Royal Mile, which had settled for the evening, and he waited at the opening of Advocate's Close. Brooke gave him a pirate's salute. He huffed out a laugh as she made her way toward him. He shouldn't love all these little secrets, shouldn't stash them away as if preparing for winter, to return to on cold nights.

"Captain," she said as she passed by him, close enough to touch, before they took the stairs down Advocate's Close and crossed Waverley Bridge. The darkened Gothic spire of the Scott Monument reached up into the night. They crossed the manicured lawn and when Brooke saw where they were headed, she turned to him, her lips rolled inside, her eyes crinkling. There was no denying it—they were absolutely on a writer's tour and he was absolutely this smitten.

He raised his camera to his eye to shield his flaming cheeks and snapped a photo of Sir Walter himself. Carved from marble and lofty ideals, the writer and philosopher perched on a pedestal beneath the four legs of the monument. Jack walked round the base to the tollbooth and grabbed hold of the lockbox.

"Can I get deported for breaking and entering?" Brooke asked, shifting her weight from foot to foot, either from cold or nerves.

"We're not breaking in. I have the code."

She didn't look convinced, hands shoved deep in her pockets. "And how did you acquire this code?"

"What's the most nefarious option you're cooking up over there?"

She narrowed her eyes.

"From guiding. Old Marty gave it to me. He can't remember a key to save his life and they had to replace the locks so many times, they finally gave up." He gestured to the lockbox he'd just sprung open.

"And Old Marty doesn't mind you stopping by after hours?"

"Och, he'd give us a right proper scolding. But he's long since abed."

Jack opened the door and pushed it open to the writer's museum. Brooke hesitated on the threshold, peering into the dimly lit space.

"You're living, remember? A big, exciting life," he said.

She looked up at him, took a deep breath, and stepped inside. He followed her into the crisp, still air.

"Okay, this is so cool," Brooke said in an excited whisper, bouncing on her toes beside him. "I never do anything like this. Like, I never even made out under the bleachers in high school."

"That's shocking," he deadpanned, but he liked that. Didn't want to imagine Brooke's lips against anyone's but his.

She moved in front of the large stained-glass window. "Whoa." It wasn't as impressive as it might've been during the day, sunlight splashing colors on the stone floor, but there was enough light from the city to illuminate the royal blues, light greens, and deep reds of the cloaked figure of Saint Andrew.

Jack raised his camera, resting an elbow against the wall to keep as still as possible.

"A charming guy at a party told me he knew a secret about the Scott Monument, but I never expected this," Brooke said in a hushed voice.

"You don't have to whisper, you know. There's no one here," he was pretty sure he said, but his brain was stuck on the word *charming*.

"I know, but it makes it more fun, doesn't it?"

He could hear the smile in her voice. Jack shook his head but he loved this side of her, loved being the one to give her this experience she wouldn't forget. Wherever the winds took her in her writing career, when she remembered Scotland, he wanted her to think of nights roaming the city with him. Of exploration. Of freedom.

"There's more," he said and they climbed the spiral stone staircase, the metal railing cold under his hand. He took pictures of the stairs for the contrast and the interesting lines and also as an excuse to take a break from the pain tightening in on his knee. But he'd fight through worse to show Brooke this place he loved.

"Logan and I used to come up here when we were first in uni, wild after a Hibs win and too much ale, but I come up here alone now. A place to think, to get above the noise of the city."

She stalled and turned, tilting her head to study him, her hands gripping the fleur-de-lis cutouts of the keyhole windows. He couldn't help imagining pinning her against the curved wall, kissing her until her breath went ragged. Or simply looping his arms around her waist and holding her close.

"Your sanctuary?"

"Aye."

"Thanks for bringing me here," she said, reverent.

When they made it to the viewing platform, the chill of the night breeze welcomed them. Brooke hugged the railing, staring down into the darkened gardens below.

"Jack, this is incredible," she said in a rush, all amped up like they'd just robbed a bank, had plans to flee the country and live out their days on a white sandy beach.

He loved how excited she was, that she was getting something out of being with him, that this silly pact was starting to feel more and more important. Like they were on the cusp of greatness.

The city sounds wafted to them in the crisp air, the low rumble of engines, the slam of car doors. But they were removed from the bustle in the intimate quiet.

He leaned against the railing next to her. "I come up here for the reminder that there's a world out there with lots of people with much bigger problems than mine. When my life feels out of my control, when the expectations feel like too much." Like a camera, up here he zoomed out and the perspective shifted, bringing different details into focus.

Graffiti and etchings covered the walls, uncovering the original tan color of the stone from its aged black. He took a picture of the glittering city, the silhouette of the castle against the dark sky, the low-lit pillars of the museum, the wisps of Brooke's hair swaying in the wind. *Click*.

She turned at the sound of the shutter snap. "You know you can tell me whatever. I'll listen."

Jack took a deep breath, startled and deeply comforted by this open invitation to share when he didn't feel welcomed that way with the people who mattered most to him.

"I've tried so hard to be like my brothers, especially Logan. I have the same pride in my country, in the land and the history. But where my family enchants people from all over the world with our stories, I feel self-conscious and...performative maybe. I've been waiting for guiding or grad school—anything, really—to feel right. But I don't want to get on tour buses or run spreadsheets for the business, no matter how disappointed my dad and brothers might be."

"So what *do* you want, Jack?" She looked at him like they both already knew the answer. Like she was challenging him to name it. To stop hedging.

And that, right there, was why he knew this was more than some passing fancy for a beautiful woman. She saw to the heart of him. Understood and supported him.

He raised the camera to the jagged silhouette of the rooftops, the pearly face of the Balmoral clock tower. "This—connecting people through my photography, showing them the sweeping landscapes and the tiny details that provide a different perspective." That felt like *him*. Like the extra piece of the puzzle that made him not quite fit might actually be a beautiful possibility.

"You know what I like about us?" she asked. "I tell stories with words and you tell them with pictures." She turned back to look at him with her ocean eyes, her dark hair spinning out in a wave. *Click.*

The shutter snap reverberated all the way down to his soul.

Jack looked down at the picture he'd just taken, the side of the camera smooth against his hand. The display glowed with the blurred movement of Brooke's hair, the rosy tint to her cheeks, the city lights sparkling like static electricity behind her. And that smile. That smile that made him believe he could do anything—*be anything*—with her by his side. An image he'd treasure forever.

He wanted more than these fleeting moments with Brooke. He didn't want this to be fleeting at all. Because if he was being honest, he'd felt that click of certainty the first time she'd placed a hand in the center of his chest and looked up at him with those striking blue eyes.

NOW

Brooke was making coffee on her stove when Jack emerged from his tent, rubbing the sleep from his eyes with the heels of his hands, and her stomach hitched at the familiarity of it.

"Morning, Brooke."

Was she imagining him saying her name more, or just hung up on the roll of the *r* in his accent? "Morning," she said.

Something had shifted last night, eating wafers she hadn't touched since *then*. The quiet between them this morning felt almost shy. Charged. And she wasn't ready to leave it, to set off and start the day.

The wind picked up, clouds rolling in. Brooke tucked strands of hair behind her ears where the breeze blew it out of her ponytail and wrapped her arms around herself against the chill. When her coffee finished brewing, she tucked back into her tent and her sleeping bag, rolling to lie on her stomach, head out the front of the tent, her notebook at the ready.

That anxiety around the memoir and the book's heartbeat and what she was doing with her life couldn't be subdued by fresh air. She wrote notes about birdsongs and the light of the morning and the descent coming off the Quiraing. But none of it quieted her restlessness, because none of it felt quite right.

She peered to the side to find Jack watching her, tucked into his tent like she was, five feet away. He raised his coffee cup to her in a salute and she returned the gesture, a tiny thrill in her chest at the connection and the reminder to slow down.

Jack had always treated time like he had enough to spare where Brooke had always thought of it as a nonrenewable resource, in terms of efficiency and productivity, something not to be squandered. She'd forgotten how nice it was to follow his lead, to watch a sunrise without calculating an opportunity cost. Not only did he make her slow down enough to appreciate what was right in front of her, but he'd also always made her feel like there was nothing more important than spending his time on her.

She was still mad at him, of course. The consequences of his betrayal were not easy to forgive or accept. But being with Jack these past few days had also brought back the good memories. And aside from their disastrous end, things had always been so good with Jack.

Brooke could still remember the comfort of climbing in his lap, interlocking her fingers behind his neck and burying her face against his shoulder, breathing him in. And the way he'd slide his big hands up her thighs, her hips, her spine, and back again. How her mind had quieted down and her heartbeat mellowed and she felt so present in her body and not like she was living three weeks in the future—always anticipating, strategizing, contingency planning.

Looking over at him now, his hair ruffling in the wind, she could almost feel that calm, that relief at turning over her worries to him. Couldn't help imagining climbing into his tent now, the way his eyes might go wide before his arms locked around her, feeling that serenity she hadn't felt in so long.

She couldn't help wondering if this was what life would've been like. If things hadn't exploded. If she'd finished school and he'd finished his master's. If they would've broken up somewhere along the way anyway, or if they would've stayed in love. Spent weekends hiking and camping, or cuddled up in a bookshop somewhere, Jack reading some science fiction novel he couldn't wait to tell her about when she closed her notebook.

It was a useless—but well trodden—path to wander down. But typically, when she let herself think about Jack, it was with some mixture of anger and disappointment. Not this urgency to tuck against his skin to see if he smelled the same. Or this anguish pooling in her chest that they might've had the real thing and broken it beyond repair.

They watched the dawn break in pinks and purples across the water. When the sun crept over the Isle of Raasay across the sound and day was upon them, they emerged from their tents and made breakfast.

"Do you still live in the same flat?" Brooke asked.

"I do, actually. I rent out the spare room. I've had some characters through there."

"I'm sure."

"What about you?"

"Out in Northfield with Chels. We had a little break when she moved in with a girlfriend a few years back, but we've recommitted." Brooke got a pang in her chest wondering if Jack had ever lived with a girlfriend. She thought he might be the reason she couldn't commit to anyone outside of Chels; she'd given Jack too much of herself and never gotten it back.

The wind gathered intensity, knocking over Brooke's camp stove and ripping away her empty oatmeal packet. Jack chased after it, stomping on top to stop it from blowing off the cliff.

"Thanks." She took the bag from him and he held it a moment too long. Standing in front of her, so close, the wind danced through Jack's hair, that shadow under his lip pronounced in the morning light. Another gust blew and he stepped back. Brooke stuffed the oatmeal package into her trash bag. "This really came out of nowhere," she all but shouted, gesturing to the wind whipping through their tents like it had gnarled claws and the intention to destroy.

A grin crept over Jack's face. "You've lived here a minute, aye?"

He was right; she shouldn't have been surprised. There wasn't much Brooke could count on in this life, but shit weather in Scotland was one of them.

She rolled up her sleeping bag, decompressed the mattress, and repacked all her gear, which kept slipping away in the wind while she tried to stuff it back.

A snap caught her attention from where she crouched by her pack. Jack had his tent unstaked, holding on to one end as he attempted to roll it up. The wind yanked the gray material, like those old parachutes from gym class where a good flick of the wrist could send balls soaring in the air.

Brooke's hood blew off and she pulled it back up, cinching down the elastic, while her hair fluttered in her eyes.

Crack.

She looked up and Jack's gaze was already on her, his eyes soft. His tent snapped again, the material yanked from his hands.

Loose, it twisted in the air, higher and higher. Jack jumped to reach it, chased after it as far as the edge of the cliff, coming to a skidding stop at the edge while Brooke called out, "Jack!" terrified, once again, that he would drop to his death, or a very broken leg or two.

Her heart thudded in her chest as she watched the tent contort itself in the air. Surely it would come down. Would twist back their way and Jack could catch it. But the material was caught in some stray jet stream, rippling and floating farther and farther away. They stood on the green ridge and watched as the tent got smaller and smaller, a gray wisp on a direct path to the sea.

Jack turned, locking his hands behind his head, his elbows jutting out.

A laugh bubbled out of Brooke. It was so absurd, so highly *unsurprising* based on how this trip had been going. Jack's laughter joined hers and she remembered the exhilaration of making Jack throw his head back like that. Tears leaked out of her eyes and she wanted to trace the smile lines on Jack's face. God, he was handsome like this, unrestrained and free.

A wave of giddiness flowed through her until Jack's shoulders stopped shaking and his smile slipped away, his eyes going to her tent.

Her brain was slower on the uptake, belatedly catching up to the implication.

They now had only one tent.

Jack's hands fell to his sides. "Well, fuck."

NOW

Jack and Brooke headed toward the village of Portree.
The sky was an absolute weapon slicing down on them and didn't look like it was letting up anytime soon.

The rain pelted them, the water freezing and angry. "Do we feel cursed to you, because we feel cursed to me," Brooke shouted over the pounding rain. She walked so close to Jack, her arm brushed his. All the distance between them had evaporated, first between their tents and now with her touch. Raindrops clung to her eyelashes, her smile dancing like it always had back then, and Jack *did* feel cursed—for wanting this woman he couldn't have.

He couldn't believe he'd let himself get distracted enough by the quiet breakfast he'd shared with Brooke and the faraway look in her eyes that he hadn't kept a tighter grip on the tent. He also couldn't believe the wind would be so treacherous as to whisk it away in the first place.

Or fortuitous.

A small thrill went through Jack as he thought about Brooke offering to share her tent, but there was absolutely no reason to do that, to push whatever quiet peace they'd found last night into something charged and fraught.

The road rounded a bend on a hill and from over the stone wall, the harbor full of tethered boats came into view. The iconic row houses painted in pastel yellow, pink, and sky blue hugged the pier. Behind them sat an old stone church and a forested hill blanketed in summer green. Raindrops pooled and fell off Jack's hood as he and Brooke walked into the city center.

Portree was the capital of the island and this area was known for its wilderness; surely he could find a replacement tent. But before they could tuck into one of the outdoor gear shops on the main road through town, Brooke grabbed his arm. "Do you smell that?"

Jack sniffed the air, the greasy smell of fried fish reaching him.

"We need fish and chips immediately."

That sounded astoundingly good after days of freeze-dried food, but he'd follow Brooke anywhere when she got that look in her eye. They rounded the corner and found a fish and chips shop overlooking the harbor. Red tents covered worn picnic tables in front of the walk-up window.

Brooke towed Jack along to the counter. The man inside welcomed them with a broad smile.

"Hi. How are you?" Brooke asked. Even after living in Scotland for nearly a decade, that adorable Americanism hadn't faded.

The man in the black hat ignored the question. "What can I get you?"

"Fish and chips, please." She turned to Jack and gestured for him to step up to the counter. "I'm buying."

It was so small and stupid, but the acknowledgment of that night at the vending machine, that inconsequential moment that'd ended up being the greatest beginning of his life, made hope swell in his chest. "I'll have fish and chips, too. And a Coke, please."

"Ooh, yes, one for me, too."

Brooke rummaged around in the side pocket of her pack for her wallet and Jack stepped underneath a tent, doing his best to shake off the rain before sitting down.

When Brooke joined him, she straddled the bench seat and her knee bumped against his, lingering there while she pulled her hair into a messy topknot. As much as his stomach rumbled, he was still vexed when their order was up and he had to move to grab their take-away containers.

They returned to the shelter of the tent and opened the aluminum foil surrounding the paper basket. The fish was fried to golden perfection, the greasy smell billowing out, and Jack's mouth started watering immediately. He bit into one of the chips and let out a groan.

"This is the best idea I've ever had," Brooke said.

"You usually think that when food is involved."

Jack had always thought if Brooke had only been beautiful, he'd have managed to keep his distance. But the playful side of her had always called to him, so unguarded and unselfconscious.

Her eyelashes fluttered as she ate fried fish and she winced after drinking Coke too fast like all the bubbles had caught up to her. When he laughed, the smile she gave him sent a wave of hope through him, like it always had before. For a brighter future. For more.

When they'd eaten far more than they needed to, and Brooke was wallowing in discomfort, they grabbed their packs and returned to the window. "Hey, mate, can you point us in the direction of an outdoor gear shop?"

Jack had been to Portree more times than he could count, but he usually waited with the driver by the coach in case anyone needed something from their luggage. If he wandered about, it was through the tourist shops in the main stretch of downtown.

The chippy worker wiped his hands on his apron. "What're you lookin' for?"

"A new tent."

His lips pulled into an apologetic line and a wave of panic went through Jack. They absolutely had to find another tent. "You can try the shop down the street here." He gestured behind them. "But it's more jackets for tourists who didn't check the weather forecast."

Brooke's eyes had gone wary and she followed him without a word.

The first shop they tried only had outdoor gear, boots, and postcards. The owner suggested another two blocks down, but they were met with more apologies and a slight glimmer of don't-you-know-this-is-a-tourist-town looks. Most residents went to the mainland for nonessentials.

On their way to the last shop that *might* have a tent, Brooke tugged Jack into a tourist shop. She picked up a miniature hairy coo stuffed animal, all orange and furry. She made big eyes at Jack. "Can we keep him?" she said with a smile.

Christ, he loved her like this. Playful and exuberant. He'd started to worry that she'd lost that carefree excitement along the way. That it'd been his fault.

She checked the tag and balked. "Seventeen pounds?" She set the coo back into the basket with its brothers and sisters and wandered farther into the shop, running her fingertips along the spines of hiking books the way she used to run her fingers over the ridges of his ribs. Jack scrubbed a hand over his face. They could not share her tent tonight.

He swiped a stuffie from the basket and headed for the cash register. "Do you know of a place we could buy a tent?"

The shop keep rang him up while listing the places they'd already been.

"We've tried those."

The man scratched his chin through his bushy red beard.

"Inside Out on the Green might have one. Besides there, I'm afraid I don't know."

Jack thanked him and slipped the coo into his pack, then trailed Brooke to where she browsed silver Celtic knot necklaces and earrings.

He knew her details, but only the secret ones—she stood with one foot balanced on top of the other while she brushed her teeth, she slept in fuzzy socks, she had terrible taste in pizza toppings—but not the ones in the real world, like the way she investigated long drip candles as if she might actually buy them. There was so much he still wanted to know about her.

Jack's phone buzzed in his pocket with a weather alert. The red warning banner on the screen was not comforting. A thunderstorm was predicted to roll through late in the night. He didn't want to alarm Brooke, especially since weather reports skewed more *guess* and less *science* in the Highlands, but they'd have to find a hotel or Airbnb. He didn't want her in a tent under those circumstances.

He found Brooke flipping through a V-shaped crate of photo prints. "It's not looking good for a new tent," he said. "What if we take a zero day and try to find a hotel, especially with this weather?" Jack's knee was throbbing again. He wasn't opposed to a rest day.

"That actually sounds really good." She pulled out a plastic-covered print of the Storr. "Have you thought of getting your work in places like this?"

Jack shrugged. "Och, I'm still chasing the prestige of the galleries." He longed for someone to tell him he was good enough, that he'd *made it*, that the choice to leave his family's business had been justified by a smashing success elsewhere. Instead, it'd been a lot of investment in expensive gear and very few sales on a less-than-stellar website he'd built himself.

Brooke pursed her lips. "Yeah, I get that," she said and flipped to the next print of the Storr. "Don't take this the wrong way, but it seemed like the part of guiding you *did* like was sharing the beauty of Scotland. And I get all the reasons why that wasn't the way you wanted to do it. But what if you had prints in a place like this, so people can take your work home and remember their time here?"

Jack felt a bit dizzy. For a brief moment he let himself imagine his pink sky shot in the rack. Brooke had so easily mapped out a future that fit him perhaps better than the one he was charting.

She still understood him.

And he was hit with the gripping fear that even now, he might be chasing someone else's definition of a dream.

He ran his fingers through his hair. "I don't know. Calendars feel a wee bit like selling out." He breathed through his nose, through the pain of wanting Brooke to be a part of his future—for her wisdom and sincerity and challenge and support—and not knowing if these moments were all they had.

"I love a good calendar," she said. She reached past him for a shrink-wrapped package of stationery, but misjudging her intention, he stepped in front of her instead of shifting away. Her hand brushed his waist and she looked up, stilling, as close to him as she'd been, pink spreading across her cheeks.

He wanted to know if she was feeling the same pull, the physical pain of not touching. If she remembered it from before. Remembered how it felt when the tension had finally snapped.

Brooke swallowed hard before grabbing note cards with a watercolor map of Scotland splashed on the front and turning on her heel for the register.

Jack ran a hand over his face. *For fuck's sake.* His heart pumped uncomfortably and she hadn't even touched him. They absolutely had to find somewhere else to sleep tonight. And it needed to have two rooms.

NOW

The bookshop café overlooked the harbor of the tiny
fishing village of Portree. Brooke didn't actually know if it was
a fishing village—the town might've been a Condé Nast set—
but little boats bobbed in the water out the window. Brooke
had tea and a cozy armchair surrounded by books, and she was
utterly charmed.

Jack sat across from her at the round bistro table, already on
the phone with a hotel in town.

As much as a teeny, tiny, insignificant part of her had flushed
at the thought of sleeping next to Jack again, obviously the situation was terrible. Horrible. Inconceivable that the capital of
Skye would have exactly three outdoors shops and not a one
would carry tents, only touristy pullovers for the wayward trav-
elers who thought summer meant warm, even this far north.

Jack scrunched his eyes shut and rolled his neck in circles.
He seemed stressed enough for the both of them and Brooke
pushed away the pinch in her heart at his deep dedication to
finding alternate accommodations.

She took a large sip of her tea, plugged in her phone, and sank back into the cushy muted pink chair with a sigh. Her body hummed with relief at the thought of not getting back on the trail today. They'd been pushing so hard through terrible conditions. She'd been pushing so hard against *him*, and it felt nice to soak up the smell of books and coffee and the comfort of a plush chair and let it all go.

The barista dropped off the warmed-up scone Brooke had ordered and she thanked them eagerly. It hadn't even been that many days, but rehydrated food in a bag had nothing on clotted cream. Brooke rubbed her hands together just to see Jack's smile.

He held his phone to his ear but his grin and the lightness in his eye made her go all mushy.

"Thanks for checking," Jack said into the phone before setting it down with a heavy sigh. "They didn't come right out and call me an eejit but the subtext was quite clear."

From her research, she knew the population of Portree was less than the number of people cruise ships often dropped off for the day. The chance that they'd find a room without a reservation from eight months ago was slim. "You've guided here a minute, aye?" she asked.

Instead of laughing at her teasing, he said, "We'll find something," like he could will it into being with a good attitude. Brooke had long since given up that kind of optimism about the world.

While she inhaled her scone, Jack made more calls that all ended in "Thanks anyway." Not to be completely outdone, she turned on her phone and looked through Airbnb. Nothing showed up within walking or cab distance, as she'd expected.

Jack scrolled through his phone. "I'll reach out to some old friends from guiding, but beyond that, I'm out of ideas." He ran his fingers through his hair and fisted the roots like he was downright despondent.

"You're really committed to not sleeping in a tent with me tonight." She did a terrible job keeping the defensiveness out of her voice.

A thought that should've occurred to her earlier clanged around her brain. It wasn't her business and it had absolutely no bearing on anything whatsoever, but the words slipped free anyway. "You have a girlfriend or something?"

Jack watched her a little too intently before shaking his head. "No."

Brooke shoved the last bite of scone in her mouth and tried to bury the butterflies in her stomach lest they spread their good cheer to her cheeks and give her away. She didn't want to look too closely at the fact that, in her mind, Jack had always been a little bit *hers*.

"Have you checked the weather report? I didn't want you to have to be out in that."

"Oh." So he was doing all this for her.

"I don't mind sharing a tent, if you'll have me."

"I'll have you." Maybe she was imagining his eyes darkening.

"Alright. Then we'll wild camp and it'll be a long fucking night."

Those words lit up her whole body—chest flushing, blood pounding—even though that was the last thing he meant. "Sounds good." Brooke's voice came out squeaky.

Jack's cheeks flared pink like he'd noted his words, and he stood up. "I've sent some texts, so we'll wait to hear back. Maybe we'll get lucky," he said as he made his way to the wall of bookshelves.

Anticipation zinged through Brooke's veins. She wasn't rooting against Jack's efforts, but she couldn't claim home team status, either.

She pulled out her notebook as Jack perused the spines. "Will I find you here? Sanders, Scott, Sinclair…"

Shame draped around Brooke's shoulders and dragged her down. She never used to feel like that. She wasn't sure if it was because it was Jack asking or if that day at the book signing had uncovered some discontent she hadn't successfully reburied, but she hated that she couldn't explain her work with one thousand percent confidence and conviction. "You won't. I'm a ghostwriter."

"That makes sense."

Brooke bristled, her chest flushing hot and red. She'd expected his pity, maybe, that her dreams had veered so far off course, but *expecting* that of her was a low blow. "What's that supposed to mean?"

"Last night, you said you were a ghost."

"Oh." She'd meant more than the writing. Her whole life felt empty, like she was stuck in a purgatory that looked an awful lot like her white laminate writing desk.

"I can see you being great at that. The manuscript sounds just like Mhairi. You perfectly captured her voice: humble and matter-of-fact. Which isn't at *all* how you talk about her."

Brooke tossed her pen at him and he held up his hands in self-defense and gave her a playful smirk.

But Jack was right. If she was writing a biography, she'd write it differently. She'd let Mhairi be larger than life, wouldn't box her in to a fraction of her real impact. And maybe that was the problem.

"Can I ask you something?"

Jack knew Mhairi in a way no editor could. She wanted his opinion even if it meant revealing her shortcomings. But he never judged her or measured her against her accomplishments, even when she'd wanted him to. "I feel like I'm missing an important piece of this narrative."

"Alright…"

"What do you think makes Mhairi so special?"

"That she asks flowers permission before picking them."

"I'm serious."

"I am, too."

Brooke gave him a flat look.

Jack tipped a book off the shelf before scooping the pen off the floor. He tucked it behind his ear and sank into the armchair at their table. "I think Mhairi sees…not the best in people, but the truth to them. Until you came along, she was the only one who really saw I wasn't happy. Maybe even more than I did. She has a way of encouraging people to meet their potential, maybe."

Brooke felt the same way. Seen. Understood. Challenged. Mhairi's sense of wonder and curiosity inspired people to be greater than they were; Brooke was a better writer and person for knowing her.

"I've been so focused on capturing the details of what Mhairi's most proud of—the trail development and the impact it's had on the land and tourism, but when we were talking to Cat and Nat, even though they chose to hike *this* particular trail, they didn't care much about how it got here, but they *would be* interested in Mhairi."

"Can you blame them?"

Brooke had made the trail the main character, but that wasn't right at all. This story wasn't about the impact of the trail; it was about Mhairi's impact on the world. Brooke laid her head on the table. "I feel like I'm fucking this all up."

"Sometimes we have to fuck it all up to know how to do it right." Jack touched her forearm, the pads of his fingers gentle against her skin. "She trusts you to tell her story. She chose you. And I have every faith you can do this."

Brooke looked up at the earnestness on Jack's face, that encouragement in his dark eyes she hadn't realized she'd missed so much.

Jack used to tell her she was clever or perfect and she'd glow under the praise like those words were the biggest compliments she could ever receive. But they were nothing compared to this. "Thank you," she said a bit breathlessly.

Mhairi had encouraged her to live more boldly, but Jack had taught her how. She'd done the best writing of her life with him by her side. Because he made her feel safe enough to take risks.

She felt that support now. That blooming creativity welling up inside her. "I think I have an idea."

Brooke pulled out her notebook and busied herself taking notes on how she'd revise the book. She'd include more of Mhairi's stories, more of Jack's stories. The ones that showed Mhairi's zest for life, her creativity, her love of livestock as shopping companions.

Brooke filled pages of her notebook, crossing things out, writing in the margins, handwriting so sloppy she might not be able to read it later, but she needed to get all the ideas out of her head before she lost them. She hadn't felt that rush of a story pouring out of her in so long.

Brain swirling, she stared at the bookshelf while she thought of where these new pieces slotted into the draft.

Jack shifted in his chair, blinked with tired eyes. He set his book on the table, dug around in his pack, grabbed a toiletry bag and headed to the bathroom.

Brooke went back to her notebook, writing down a story Mhairi had told her over tea in her kitchen last winter about the Troublesome Trio, three brothers she grew up with on Skye.

The vine-painted door swung open and Jack stepped out— wearing his glasses. The gold-and-brown-speckled frames accentuated those irresponsibly long eyelashes, rested against the light freckles dusting his cheekbones. After four days of not shaving, thick stubble covered his chin and jaw. He pushed his dark hair—curly on top from the rain—away from his forehead with a casual sweep of his fingers. Brooke's heart beat with a heavy echo in her chest.

"Captain."

The word came out breathless instead of teasing. Jack's head snapped up and his stride hitched, but the smile that bloomed across his face was the full version where his straight teeth showed and his eyes crinkled—heartbreakingly tentative and hopeful.

It'd be so easy to fall for Jack again. She could trip right back into it if she wasn't careful.

He crouched to get into his bag and his knee popped so loudly it made Brooke grimace. "Are you a hundred years old?" she asked.

"Some of us have football injuries, thank you."

Brooke studied his face. The teasing was there, but he also wasn't joking. "Wait, from me?"

"Well, from Johnny Kendrick, but yes, that game."

That game. "That was the first time I was sure you liked me."

Jack tipped his head down, his tongue coming out to wet his bottom lip. "Och, I was in over my head long before that."

His eyes met hers and Brooke's stomach fluttered from the grin tugging at the corners of his mouth. On second thought, this was a terrible thing to talk about before snuggling up in a tent together.

His phone rang, buzzing on the table.

"This is Jack Sutherland." He moved the phone to his other ear. "You do? Yes. We'll take it. Can I pay you over the phone?" He dug into his pack for an old leather wallet Brooke recognized and mouthed "I'm buying" before reading out his credit card information. "Thanks, mate." Jack hung up and turned a broad grin her way. "It's not a hotel, but you're still going to be excited."

Brooke took a fortifying sip of her tea, hiding her grin behind her cup. "Tell me."

"The Portree campsite has a spot. And...they have showers."

She pretended to swoon over the arm of her chair. "That's the sexiest thing you've ever said to me."

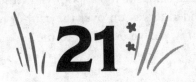

THEN

In nothing but their alcohol jackets to fend off the wind, Brooke, Chels, and Kieran ventured across town. The Caves was a club off the Cowgate, a low road through the touristy part of Edinburgh that was once the path to bring cattle to market. All that remained of that illustrious history was the back half of a cow sculpture mounted on the outside of the building facing the street and the front half sticking out down the alley.

As that seemed like a clear indicator of their destination, Brooke followed Chels and Kieran to the door with a metal placard reading, "He who is without mathematics shall not enter."

"Decidedly not what we're here for..." Kieran said scornfully.

Brooke wasn't, either. She was here to see Jack. She could admit to herself that she shouldn't be going out of her way to see him and that she was absolutely going to anyway.

Past the bouncer, they descended into the Caves. The tomb-like space should've been claustrophobic, but with the music bouncing off the stone walls, the shadowed alcoves promised secrets and stolen moments. Lights embedded in the wall cast hazy purples and blues over the rounded bricks and rippled like they were underwater. It made the night surreal, an alternate reality.

They made their way to the bar under a low stone archway—the obvious place to find Rohan.

Sure enough, he was there shouting to the bartender, but Brooke's attention snagged on Jack, elbows resting on the bar, eyes on her.

Her heart fluttered, a smile exploding on her face. She took in his dark jeans and the way they clung to his thighs before trailing her gaze up to the white T-shirt that hugged his chest and shoulders, the lights from the stage painting it pink and teal.

Jack shook his head at her perusal and took a deep pull from his beer, casting his eyes to the ceiling. Brooke's heart pounded in time with the beat of the song, a helpless *want, want, want.*

She'd been so sure he'd kiss her at the top of the Scott Monument. They'd had a moment before he'd retreated, saying they didn't actually want to find out what Old Marty would say about their trespassing.

This thing between her and Jack felt a bit like a contest of who would break first. And she was tired of being smart. Of playing by the rules.

Chels and Kieran got to the bar first. Kieran swiped Rohan's drink and started a brawl between brothers, but Jack never took his eyes off her, his gaze lingering on the scoop neck of her black top, on the curl of her hair over her shoulder.

She stepped into his space, her toes lined up with his, and looked up at him. "Captain," she said with a flirty quirk of her lips. The blue-and-purple lights flickered over him like a mirage. She wanted to reach out and touch him, drag her thumb over his lips, just to make sure he was real. Wanted to feel the weight of him and the slide of his tongue and his hands on her body, and compare it to the way he'd touched her in the snow.

He clenched his hands into fists. "Brooke," he said with a warning in his voice that only wound her up.

Brooke turned to the bar, standing on tiptoes and leaning over the top to get the bartender's attention. She moved her hair over one shoulder and when she looked back, Jack's gaze was tracing the ridges of her spine exposed by her halter top. He ran a hand over his face, pushing his glasses up and resettling them, and she bit her lip against the smile she couldn't hold back.

Brooke paid for her drink and turned around, sliding into the space between Jack and the bar. If he so much as leaned, their legs would be touching. She twirled the straw in her drink before closing her mouth around it. Jack stepped toward her, his hips brushing hers, and leaned down to her ear. "Are you trying to tempt me?"

She looked up under her eyelashes. "I would never."

He growled and she grinned.

Chels appeared and yelled, "Let's dance!" over the volume of the music. She tugged Brooke away, Kieran in tow. Brooke looked over her shoulder and her gaze hooked on Jack's.

He didn't strike her as someone who liked dancing, but he followed anyway.

On the dance floor, Chels and Kieran did an excellent impression of jumping jacks. Most things were a joke to them, and dancing especially must not be taken seriously. Rohan nodded along with the band, his shoulder bumping into Jack's every so often.

The thumping beat filled Brooke's ears, casting a spell over her that made her feel heavy and light at the same time. The humid heat pressed in on her, and she wondered if Jack was noticing the sway of her hips.

The song changed to one Rohan must've known because he jumped forward to hook an arm around Kieran's neck, knocking into Brooke. She stepped back, directly into Jack, her ass pressed against him. His hand went to her waist to steady her and then lingered. She closed her eyes, consumed by the heat of his hand against her bare skin between her top and jeans.

The lights scanned across the crowd from the stage, leaving the room in foggy darkness most of the time. It made the dance floor feel anonymous. All their friends were in front of them, facing the stage. No one could see them; no one could tell.

Before Jack could drop his hand, Brooke covered it with her own, her touch soft, her fingers slipping between his.

Jack lowered his head by her ear, his heavy exhale brushing her temple, and chills broke out across her skin. She rolled her hips gently to the beat and Jack dug his fingers into her hip, sending sparks through her.

This was a bad idea and they both knew it, but damn, she felt powerless to stop. The sexy pulse of the music, the press of bodies around them, the darkness—it had all gone to her head.

Jack slid his hand flat across her belly, drawing her tighter against him. Her stomach pulled in with a hitched breath as he kept his palm pressed tight against the sway of her movements.

Brooke reached behind her for his other hand, linking their fingers together. Lightheaded, she tipped her head back, rested her temple against his jaw, zeroed in on the soft brush of his breath against her skin.

He slid his pinkie finger along the top of her waistband, back and forth, and Brooke fisted his jeans. Her heart beat between her legs, screaming at the injustice of being so close but with so many barriers between them.

The light from the stage scanned the room, flashing into her eyes—a wake-up call that doused the spell around them.

They were in the middle of a room of people with their hands all over each other.

Jack stepped back and when Brooke turned to face him, he

raised and dropped his hands. Shook his head. Looked like he was about to leave.

She wrapped her fingers around his wrist. He paused, let out a helpless breath, and then said, "Come here," though she wasn't sure she heard it.

She followed him through the crowd, just like that night at his flat, keeping close behind before people pressed back in on her.

Past the bar, he turned, looked over her shoulder, and gently pushed her into an alcove. The pulse of the music was quieter here, the overwhelming noise of it all dampened by the wall Brooke leaned back against.

Jack ran a hand over his jaw. Stepping into the cradle of her hips, he rested his forearm against the stone by her head, blocking them from view. Her heart raced from the feel of him pressed against her, at the promise in the way he caged her in.

"You're destroying me, Brooke," he said into her ear. "I'm desperate to touch you."

She was desperate to touch him, too, and flattened her palm against his stomach, trailed her hand up and over his pec. He stopped breathing. "So do it," she said.

He leaned in closer, his temple against hers, and she breathed in his fresh scent.

"I can't touch you in a fraction of the ways I want to." He tilted his head, placing soft kisses along her jaw. "We shouldn't."

The corner of his lips brushed the corner of hers. Not a kiss, not a real one, not anything that counted. Just the tiniest step over the line, negligible.

But her heart had never beat faster.

His bottom lip tugged on her top lip as he breathed against her and she slid her fingers into his hair, holding him there. The tenderness and tentativeness in his barely-there kiss broke her heart open.

"Jack," she whispered. "What do you want?"

"You." There was no hesitation in his voice and she'd never loved a word more.

She brought her lips to his ear. "Then no one has to know."

NOW

Brooke rolled out her sleeping bag over the mattress pad overlapping Jack's and tried not to bump into him. *Again.* Rain pelted down on her tent like they were directly beneath a waterfall, bowing the thin orange material and making the space feel even smaller than it was.

She sat cross-legged at the far side of the tent while Jack unrolled his yellow-and-teal sleeping bag on hands and knees. She wasn't sure if it was his gray T-shirt stretching over the rounded muscles of his shoulders and hugging the tops of his triceps or the thunder rumbling ominously in the air that sent a shiver down her spine.

The anticipation of sleeping next to Jack buzzed in her veins and mixed with the memory of his deep voice rumbling over the words, *I was in over my head long before that…* Her brain went completely haywire.

If the thunder and lightning didn't destroy her composure first, she'd spend the entire night overanalyzing those words.

Maybe, against her better judgment, she was hoping something would happen between them tonight. *But is he hoping that, too?*

Brooke longed for the days when she didn't examine the consequences of her reckless actions but was old enough to know that following that line of thinking to its logical conclusion was more treacherous than crossing the Quiraing.

Brooke rubbed at her sore shoulder, trying to loosen the muscles and the chokehold the thought of Jack's lips had on her.

"Do you want me to…?" Jack asked. He gestured to her hand clamped on her neck.

Brooke's eyes flashed to his. *Do I want you to…trail your fingers over my skin, kiss up my neck?* "Rub my shoulders?"

Under the light of the headlamps, Jack's cheeks darkened and she wanted to run her thumbs over the blush. "I didn't mean like that." He tipped his chin down, his damp, wavy hair falling forward and sending a wave of his tea tree shampoo to invade her senses. "You look uncomfortable."

If he meant uncomfortable from this longing to sink her fingers into his hair and breathe in the familiar smell that conjured the feeling of being young and free, roaming the streets of Edinburgh, and stealing kisses in clubs and alleys, then yes. She was uncomfortable.

"I'm fine."

Jack dug a flask from his pack and took a deep sip before passing it to her. She took it, pressing her mouth against the metal warmed by his lips. She didn't mean to hold his gaze. He watched her swallow, his eyes clinging too long to her mouth, and a fire spread out in her chest that wasn't from the burn of the whisky.

Thunder ripped across the night, raising the hair on the back of her arms, and she took another pull from the flask. Maybe she should be grateful for the storm—it couldn't be worse than this will-they-or-won't-they she was engaged in in her own damn mind.

Lying down next to Jack was a fraught activity, but so was sitting here, ogling the cut of his arms. Brooke slipped into her sleeping bag and zipped it up.

Jack lay down beside her and she shifted away, bumping into the wet wall of the tent and having to scoot toward him again. The rain fell so hard it sounded like a rushing river. Brooke tried to remember how diligent she'd been reapplying the seam sealant. Skye was nearly a rainforest for how much precipitation fell, but had she been thorough enough to turn this thing into a canoe? Because that seemed like where the night was going.

Jack shifted against her thigh, seemingly making the same calculation that closer together was better than absorbing the dampness from the side of the tent. "Sorry," he mumbled.

"It's fine."

He rolled onto one elbow and propped his cheek in his hand. His bicep flexed in that position and Brooke struggled to pull her gaze from his golden skin and that space against his shoulder where she used to rest her head. He reached above them and clicked off the headlamp, plunging them into darkness. "I mean about the tent." His voice was sharing-secrets-in-the-dark low and suddenly the satiny nylon of her sleeping bag felt like a deliriously weak boundary between them. "That was stupid of me."

"Hmm? Oh, it wasn't your fault. It was the wind—which I plan to make the villain of Mhairi's story."

Jack's deep chuckle flitted across her skin.

Lightning flashed, illuminating the tent, and Brooke tensed, counting *one, one thousand…two, one thousand* before the boom rumbled through the ground.

A primal surge of adrenaline shot through her, an instinct to take shelter, especially when her normal definition included four walls and a sturdy roof. Brooke readjusted her pillow and cinched her sleeping bag under her chin. She hated that she was still so affected by storms but at least Jack already knew and she didn't have to pretend to be brave.

If she'd been alone, she would've curled into a nice little ball, but there was barely enough space for her and Jack in here, their mattress rolls overlapping under her. *Maybe they can serve as rafts.*

She shoved the thought of their tent being flooded down the hill out of her mind. They were in a campground. If it got too terrible, they could hide out in the bathroom.

Thunder clapped again and Brooke pinched her eyes shut. Her body was responding as if an emergency alert was coming over the radio when the greenish hue of the sky conveyed *Fuck around and find out.* Her heart practically vibrated. She took a deep breath in through her nose, held it for a count of four, released it.

Heeding some instinct to not turn her back on the storm, Brooke rolled over. In the darkness, the hazy outline of the orange material rippled from the rain beating against it.

She couldn't calm her racing heart. Couldn't stop the barrage of memories.

Brooke could still feel the numbing rain above tree line soaking through her shirt, seeping beneath her backpack, goose bumps breaking out across chilled skin. She stared into the dark sheets of rain, a never-ending deluge obscuring even the closest peaks. Her dad yelled over the noise of the rain from too far away like they were getting swept apart in a riptide. "Crouch down, Brooke! Only touch the ground with your shoes!" She squatted, tucking her arms against her chest.

The thunder boomed and she clapped her hands over her ears, tensing against the possibility that the next lightning strike would sear right through her. Her hair stood on end from the electricity in the air, buzzing with a physical weight. Rivulets of water, bubbly white, rushed by her hiking boots. Adrenaline pumped through her heart but she was frozen in place.

Jack touched her arm and Brooke flinched, but it brought

her back to her body. She clenched the material of her sleeping bag in her fists to remind herself where she was. Jack had always had a gentleness about him—a quiet strength that felt like a refuge drawing her in—but especially out here where she'd give anything to fall into his arms and let him weaken her fear for a bit.

Lightning flashed twice, so bright she could make it out through the nylon above her, shooting in diverging directions. Brooke whimpered, her breathing quick and shallow. "Will you hold me?" she asked.

"Of course."

Jack unzipped Brooke's sleeping bag like an evening gown, sending shivers skittering over her skin. They were so close he barely had to shift to bring his body next to hers. His fresh, earthy scent enveloped her and the heat of his chest immediately seeped into her muscles like a soothing balm. He slid his hand inside her sleeping bag, hesitating for a moment like he wasn't sure where to touch her, before his hand wrapped around her forearm, warm and reassuring.

She suddenly felt more grounded, and she blew out a long breath.

Lightning splintered over the roof of the tent again. *One, one thou—*

Thunder cracked directly above them, the ground trembling, and Brooke turned into Jack's arms, burrowing her face against his neck. She balled up the material of his shirt against his chest in one fist and slipped her other arm around his back. He cupped her head and held her tightly against his shoulder.

She tensed when the thunder rolled again and Jack readjusted, sliding an arm under her. "I've got you." A ghost of a kiss brushed her temple and her heart stirred.

The storm raged, a never-ending dance of light and sound. Brooke focused on the rhythmic caress of Jack's hand up and down her back. She matched her breath to the motion, slow and deep, soaked in his heat. This wasn't as terrifying as being all alone. He always made her feel stronger and braver than she was.

The next clap of thunder was farther away and Brooke pictured the storm moving fast, taking its ferocious energy elsewhere. She listened to the steady *thump-thump thump-thump* of Jack's heartbeat under her ear until hers slowed to a normal pace. He'd always had this calming effect on her—the feel of his arms around her a refuge that quieted her anxious brain.

Brooke relaxed a bit, releasing the clench of her shoulder muscles. She wanted to thank Jack, to tell him she didn't need him anymore, but she couldn't quite form the words.

The lightning faded to flickers, the thunder only a grumble in the distance. Brooke's muscles loosened, and Jack's hand stilled in the middle of her back, but she couldn't move away.

They fit the same way, her head into the slope of his shoulder, her hand to the curve of his chest. She'd been exerting so much effort fighting the bond between them, the invisible bands that always pulled them back together, and it felt so good to give in, to let herself snap back into place.

Even as the rain faded to a dull pitter-patter above their heads, Jack didn't move away. She might've thought he was sleeping with how still he held himself, but as she let go of his shirt, smoothing it over the hard muscles of his chest—so slowly she wasn't sure he'd notice—his arms tightened around her.

"How do you still make me feel so damn safe?" she whispered, tipping her face up and accidentally grazing his nose with hers.

His exhale fanned her cheek and his hand slipped from the back of her head to her neck. "Because I care about you."

He pressed the gentlest kiss to the corner of her mouth, lips soft and tentative. It didn't feel like an invitation or a move. It felt like a pinkie promise.

Tears welled in Brooke's eyes at the intimacy of the touch,

at that familiar spinning sensation she'd had the first time she'd fallen so fast and effortlessly.

It turned out telling herself she didn't want Jack didn't make it true. But she wasn't sure she trusted either of them enough to begin again.

23

THEN

Brooke and Jack left the pulsing music of the Caves,
all but running through the streets, stopping to tug each other
into darkened doorsteps for stolen kisses until they were in his
stairwell, unlocking the door, stumbling through the shadowed
hallway of Jack's flat, kissing and bumping against the walls.

She didn't need the light; Brooke could map him in her mind
from the countless hours she'd spent cataloging the wide set of
his cheekbones, the span of his stride.

She was tired of only looking; she wanted to touch him.

They made it to the end of the hall and into Jack's room,
where he closed the door and fumbled with the lock behind
him as he kept kissing her, the soothing press of his lips catching her up. The taste of the malty, dark beer he'd been drinking infiltrated her senses like a contact high.

Jack unzipped her jacket with ruthless efficiency, pushing it
off and trailing his hands over her shoulders. It was everything
Brooke remembered from the day on the beach, only warmed
up and slowed down, the same sense of urgency but no panic
so she could savor his grip sliding down her arms until he cap-

tured her wrists and her coat slipped to the floor. Chills rippled up her spine.

Jack laced their fingers together, his mouth sinking against the exposed slope of her breasts above her black halter top, his tongue hot on her skin. She arched into his touch. "I would've worn this weeks ago if I'd known you'd react this way."

Jack lifted his head and cupped Brooke's neck, his grip rough. "Like you weren't tormenting me enough," he said on a low growl before crashing his lips against hers. She smiled against his mouth as the pads of his fingers curved behind her jaw, then sank into her hair, hot pressure points against her scalp that made her knees weak.

She *had* been taunting him, desperate to see him snap. Nothing had ever felt as good as watching his eyes darken to a dangerous black in the Caves, simmering with dirty promises. He hedged every touch, every word, under the guise of plausible deniability, but not tonight. Tonight he was unrestrained, uninhibited.

"Wait." She pulled back. "You're not drunk, are you?" *Please don't be drunk.* Her heart hammered a death march, incapable of surviving the disappointment if he was.

Jack shook his head, his hands stilling on the curve of her neck. "No, are you?" he asked, his breath coming short and heavy.

"No."

"Thank fuck." He tipped her head back with one hand, trailed hot kisses along the side of her throat while his other hand popped the button on her jeans and pulled down the fly. Brooke's eyelids fluttered closed, her multitasking abilities completely failing her, all wound up in the wet press of his lips and his fingers flirting with the open top of her jeans.

She reached for the smooth buttons on his pea coat, pressing them through and sliding the jacket from his shoulders. She needed to feel all of him. Her hands went to his waist, to the hot skin under his shirt, and pushed it up his flat stomach, the ridges of his abs and the curve of his pecs. He groaned in her ear, reaching behind his neck and tugging his shirt clean off.

"Damn," she said, her voice breathy. She liked him buttoned up and polished, but she liked him even better like this. This side of him only she got to see.

Jack discarded his shirt before divesting Brooke of hers, pressing kisses between her breasts as he tugged down her jeans.

They crashed together again, the heat of his abs against her belly, her arms wrapped around his shoulders, hands tangled in his hair. An unbridled relief swept through her to be skin to skin, to finally be this close to him. For this admission that he felt the same way she did, swept away by this thing more potent than reason or consequences.

Jack walked her backward, arms locked around her waist, until she bumped into the edge of the bed. He laid her down on the rumpled blankets, cool against her back, and kissed her deeply before standing up to yank off his jeans.

He was beautiful. Propped up on her elbows, she took in the trim cut of his waist, the slope of his pecs, the strength in his shoulders. If she was writing him, she'd detail the sweep of his black hair over his forehead, the little crease between his brows as he struggled to kick off his jeans, his full bottom lip she wanted back against hers. She'd write about the way he made her feel noticed and important, rebellious and daring. And also safe.

He slid off his boxers and his erection sprung free. Brooke made a whimpering noise and his eyes snapped to hers, a fire she couldn't exactly make out in the glow of the streetlight shining through the window, but felt all the same. Jack hooked his thumbs into the sides of her panties, sliding them down, his knuckles brushing along her thighs, her knees, her calves.

He discarded his glasses on the nightstand—a flick of the wrist, a click of plastic on metal as they knocked against his lamp—illuminated by the red numbers of his alarm clock. Brooke had been daydreaming about the glasses toss to the point of distraction, but she hadn't pictured the hot look in Jack's eyes turning her molten, the rumpled look of him, his hair mussed from her fingers. Hadn't pictured his skin bathed in the lamplight from outside, shadows of the windowpane playing across the curve of his shoulder.

He kissed back up her inner thigh and her legs shook with every brush of his lips against her sensitive skin, his fingers following their path.

And just when she thought his mouth would land where she ached for him, he stopped. "Is this too fast? Shit, we can slow down," he said, his hands spread wide across her thighs.

"It's not too fast, Jack. I've been fantasizing about this since the first time I came in your room."

He paused over her. "I'm going to need to know the *minute* details of those fantasies."

"This is better," she said, breathless. "And I have a *great* imagination." Her fantasies hadn't come close to the real thing, the heat coming off his skin or the tea tree smell of his sheets.

Jack kissed the inside of her knee and then rested his cheek there. "Show me," he said, his breathing loud in the darkness. "What you like."

Another wave of lust washed through Brooke at his words, his desire to know her, to make her feel good. And it was enough to override any insecurity or vulnerability she might not show someone else.

Brooke slipped her fingers between her legs. "Circles," she said, having never talked about this with anyone before. "Slow at first, and then faster."

Jack made a deep sound and nipped the soft skin by her knee while he watched her, his fingers gripping her thighs. "Fuck, Brooke. This is so hot."

He made her feel confident and bold and sexy. She reached

for his hand, brought him to where she wanted his touch, moved their hands together where she ached for him. When he followed her rhythm, she dropped her hand, fell back against the bed, sank into the sensation of his fingers and his tongue trailing swirling kisses up her leg.

This need built inside her, swelling until she was about to fall over the edge, but she wanted more of him, to feel his weight on her, his skin against hers.

She moved up the bed until she sank into the plush pillows, Jack following on his hands and knees.

"Was that okay?" he asked at her retreat and she pulled his mouth to hers.

"It was perfect." She kissed along his jaw and reveled in the rush of breath he released. "But I need you."

His mouth met hers again in a frenzy as he reached behind her to unhook her bra. The clasp popped and he dragged the straps off her shoulders, tossing it to the floor. Jack's fingers caressed the curve of her breasts, teasing her as her nipples tightened into hard peaks. Brooke arched into his touch, clinging to his shoulders, until he circled her nipples with his thumb, pinched them until she moaned.

She kissed Jack, rushed and sloppy and breathless while he reached blindly for a condom in the drawer. He rolled it on and settled his weight over her. She shifted underneath him to line them up better, to bring him against the ache between her legs. To finally have a reprieve from all this yearning.

He cupped her face and kissed her deeply while he nudged at her entrance. She rolled her hips up to meet him, welcoming the pressure, needing the release from the insane buildup over the past weeks.

His hand skated along her thigh, guided her knee to hook around his waist while he pushed into her, clenching his jaw and breathing out with a low groan. Brooke clung to Jack's shoulders, wrapped her legs around him, arched into him as he thrust, his lips coming back to claim hers.

She rocked against him, pushing the tempo faster, delirious from the friction between them. Needing to trace the muscles bunching in his shoulders, the dip of his triceps, to wrap herself up in him like this could be forever.

His lips met her throat and kissed up her flushed skin. "I won't last like this, B. You're driving me out of my mind."

"We'll go slow next time," she said and tugged his face back to hers. He groaned against her lips when she arched, grinding against him, needing more.

"Touch me again?" she asked and Jack braced his weight on one arm while his other hand slipped between her legs and he drew tight circles with his thumb. Brooke whimpered as she rocked against him, clung to his neck, tracked her hand down his chest.

"Fuck. Yes," she said as pressure swelled inside her, fueled by his fingers and his thrusts deep inside her.

Jack dropped his head to the crook of her shoulder. "Christ, I love the sounds you make," he said on a low breath.

She felt out of control and needy, too big for her body, expanding into a painful peak, like she might flame out any minute. She gripped Jack's wrist. "Lighter," she breathed and he applied the perfect pressure.

"Like that?"

"Mmm-hmm," she managed to say, barely able to focus on anything but the ache deep in her core, the slide of Jack's skin against hers. "I'm so close. Keep doing that."

He brushed kisses along her lips, kept the pace steady, just what she needed. She tightened around him and he groaned deep and low, sending tingles across her skin. Another roll of his hips and Brooke fell over the edge, waves of pleasure ricocheting through her. Jack let out a deep groan and thrust faster.

She pushed his hand away when the sensation became too

much, riding out the waves as he orgasmed. He dropped to both forearms above her head and she kissed his neck, the curve of his jaw, the soft center of his cheek, as he shook above her.

Brooke breathed through her nose, fast and shallow, with no hope of ever recovering her breath or coming back down to earth.

Jack rolled her to her side, cradling her against him, his nose in her hair.

"I guess we found something else you're good at," she said and Jack's loud laugh filled the room, rumbling through her.

"What can I say? You bring out the best in me, B." He nuzzled against her ear, and an overwhelming peace wrapped around her, as snug as his arms. She sank into the feeling, the overarching rightness of being with him.

"Jackie!" Rohan called and Jack jolted up as Brooke squeaked and pulled the blankets up and over her head. Rohan jiggled the doorknob and the knock sounded again, three sharp raps on the wooden door that matched the intensity of Brooke's pounding heart. "Why's the door locked?"

Brooke blew out a breath. Thank god Jack had remembered.

Jack grunted. "Piss off, Rohan."

"Who's in there with you?"

"No one."

Brooke stiffened at the words. Jack reached under the blanket, found her hand where she gripped them above her head, squeezed like he was comforting her. Like he didn't mean them.

"Go away," Jack ground out. "I'm sleeping."

"Wanker," Rohan called out, and they waited for his footsteps to fade down the hall. Brooke took a deep breath, trying to slow her heartbeat, but it wasn't going to even out, not with reality crashing in around them.

Jack lifted the edge of the blanket and slipped down under it, holding it above their heads like a tent, like they could stay in their little world just awhile longer. "I shouldn't have said 'no one.' Brooke, you're everything," he whispered. He placed a kiss against her lips, soft and gentle.

She hummed against him and kissed him deeper, the sheet brushing against the top of her forehead as they moved. "You are, too," she said, but she couldn't disguise the worry in her voice. What would've happened if Rohan had walked in? Would he freak out? Would he say something?

"Hey." Jack cupped her cheek. "Are you regretting this?"

"No." Even though she hated the heaviness settling around her at the idea of getting caught, she didn't regret it. She wanted Jack and she'd make the same choice again. She shifted, her hand flat against his chest, and tucked in under his chin, hiding her face while she asked, "Are you?"

"Not at all." Jack wrapped his arm around her tighter, kissed her hair. "We'll be safer. It'll be okay."

Brooke pressed kisses along his collarbone, nodded against his shoulder. "I trust you."

NOW

Brooke's vision filled with the slope of Jack's cheek-bones, the curve of his jaw, the soft fan of his eyelashes against his cheeks while he slept. Still tucked into her sleeping bag, warm and pressed close, she felt her heart call for him. She wanted to curl into his embrace with an intensity she tensed her muscles against. She could wake him with kisses, run her fingers through his hair, tell him everything was forgiven and forgotten, watch his eyes darken with want.

She breathed out against the yearning curled in her chest. She might be able to forgive him one day, but she didn't know how to forget.

It was scary imagining a future with Jack now that she knew what it was like to lose him. It'd been effortless to love him openly and freely the first time—without any perspective, without knowing what heartbreak and betrayal felt like.

But now he made her feel vulnerable and unsettled. He was old and new at the same time and she couldn't reconcile the two.

Brooke extricated herself from the sleeping bag as quietly as she could and slipped on her sandals, grabbing her pack and heading for the bathrooms. The day was dawning clear and bright like it always did after a big storm. Like the world was refreshed and had purged all the dark feelings. She wished it was that easy.

She took another shower just because she could. The campsite showers were janky, running hot and cold and hot again, but it was worth it to stall, to put some space between her and Jack just for a few more minutes.

After Brooke was dressed and brushing her wet hair, Catalina walked in. "Brooke! Hi!"

A powerful relief swept through Brooke. She hadn't pushed Cat and Nat to hike with them since they'd had a hostel reservation in Flodigarry, but she sure as hell would today. "Hi! I wasn't sure if we'd see you again."

Cat wrapped her up in a hug and Brooke melted into it like she would with Chels, her feelings too close to the surface this morning, willing to take whatever comfort she could find.

"We barely made it into Portree last night. The weather was such shit."

"Yeah, it was." A chill ran across Brooke's arms. "Are you heading back out today?"

"As soon as I get a shower. I let Natalia sleep."

"Do you want to walk together when she's up?" Brooke needed a buffer from Jack this morning while she sorted out what to do with the way he'd touched her last night, the way she'd responded, and how she could hold herself back from the incessant tug she'd always felt toward him.

"Definitely. What campsite are you in? I can meet you when I'm packed up."

"Perfect. We're in fourteen."

Catalina headed for the showers and Brooke finished drying her hair as best she could with the hand dryer. She made it back to the campsite to find Jack awake and boiling water for breakfast. Brooke wasn't quite brave enough to meet his gaze.

"I ran into Catalina and invited them to hike with us this morning."

Jack ran his tongue over his bottom lip. "Alright," he said, his searching gaze roaming over her features. She turned away from his scrutiny, from that flare of disappointment in his eyes at the distance she'd created. But it'd always been all or nothing with them.

She didn't know how to be his friend.

After a quiet breakfast, they met up with Catalina and Natalia. The trail today was mostly along the paved road out of Portree. Still scenic with croft houses and tall grasses, but nothing like the views they'd grown accustomed to.

The lack of varied terrain on the paved road made it hard on joints, stepping the exact same way every time. Her knees were holding up okay but she worried about Jack. She checked his face for signs of wincing but couldn't make out his expression behind his black sunglasses.

Cat and Nat told stories about hitchhiking the Ring Road in Iceland. Brooke envied the places they'd been, the people they'd met, the things they'd experienced. She wanted to see geysers and volcanoes and backpack through Prague. Cat and Nat linked hands, walked in lockstep, and their easiness made Brooke straight-up jealous as her gaze drifted to Jack for the thousandth time.

By the time the midday sun was glaring down, Jack's jaw was clenched and he leaned forward onto his hiking poles more than normal. A brook trickled into a jungle of ferns along the side of the road. "Let's see if we can refill water here," she suggested.

"The wee burn may lead us straight to the sea." Jack's accent sent a tingle up her spine. She wanted to feel it against her skin.

Cat followed her into the foliage. "Oh, good thought. We almost ran out on the Quiraing and now I'm terrified."

"We were never in any danger," Nat said.

Brooke pushed through the thin branches until the foliage

cleared and opened onto a rocky beach. The place was secluded, boulders bracketing the stream as it made its way to the ocean. The water was calm here, the bay probably shallow.

Jack dropped his pack and sank onto a neighboring boulder with a wince and a heavy sigh.

"Let's take a break here, this is lovely," Brooke said.

Jack glanced up, gave her a suspicious tilt of the head with a small smile playing on his lips, like he realized she might've suggested the diversion for him. That heartwarming grin only made her restless. She wasn't sure she could leave the past behind. She'd been stuck there for so long.

"Lovely," Catalina repeated, her boots already off and her feet in the shallow water meandering past.

Brooke found another rock to settle on and tipped her face up to the wispy clouds drifting lazily overhead, the sun warm against her cheeks. *Hello, old friend.* She should really get away from her desk more often; sunshine was good.

Jack pulled off his boots and socks and rolled up his pants before sinking his feet into the water. He took his camera out of his pack and turned it toward his face. "Hi, Auntie. We're leaving Portree today, heading to Sligachan. The tarmac is killer on my knees." His eyes trailed to Brooke's, an acknowledgment, but maybe a bit of a challenge, like she couldn't pretend she didn't care about him when she so clearly did. "You couldn't find any paths through here to help a nephew out?" he said with a teasing grin.

"Oh, I want to say hi, too!" Catalina called. Jack handed over the camera. "Hi, Aunt Mhairi! I'm Catalina! We're a little off your trail here, but you'd love it. Look at this beach." She tilted Jack's camera to the side. "Hashtag goals, right?"

Cat and Jack told Mhairi stories as Natalia walked gingerly to Brooke, her red toenail polish bright against the gray stones. "Are you finding inspiration for your book?"

"Mhairi's book," Brooke said. Because it wasn't hers, even

if her name would be on the cover. "But, yes, this has been incredible to see firsthand."

"You doing alright?"

Brooke looked up into warm brown eyes. She stretched her neck to one side and then the other. "I feel a bit lost out here."

"Not everyone who goes into the woods finds themselves," Nat said with a wry smile.

"False advertising." Instead of butterflies and sunshine, there'd been bugs, blisters, and freeze-dried food. A tingle of fear curled in Brooke's heart that there might not be any clarity at the end for her.

Natalia laughed and pulled at tall wisps of grass. "Catalina is fearless. She decided to conquer the world, so she will. I'm not like that."

It was one thing to be fearless, but another to move forward when you weren't. "And yet, here you are. Don't diminish what you've already accomplished."

Natalia wove the thick grass into a small circlet before her kind eyes lifted to Brooke's. "Likewise."

While Brooke dug out a granola bar from her pack, Natalia made her way carefully over the rocks toward Catalina, standing behind her and dropping her chin to Cat's shoulder to fit in the frame. "Hi, Mhairi!" She waved. "We've been on trails all over the world and yours is our favorite. I can see why you wanted to write about it."

Brooke smiled. Mhairi would love that.

Her words from all those years ago came back to Brooke on the breeze, her hair gently dancing against her cheek: *Live a life worth writing about.*

Cat and Nat were doing that, running toward adventure, but Brooke had been standing still.

Jack had moved on from the commandeered vlog to his regular camera, bare feet tenderly stepping over rocks, crouching down to snap a picture of a leaf caught in the gentle flow of the stream, bobbing to the surface and under again. Brooke wanted more of that in her life. Noticing the details. Not diminishing the little wins as foregone conclusions. Trying something new.

She was here, on the adventure of a lifetime, looking out into a sea few people visited, a sky that was always changing, and she still felt stuck. Was there a shelf life on that old dream, passing her by while she'd thrown herself into other people's stories?

It wasn't now or never, but if it wasn't now, would she ever?

NOW

Brooke woke late that night to the faint sounds of creaking plastic. She bolted upright, her heart in her throat, and crept toward the zipper of her tent, tugging so slowly her arm shook. Crouched over her crossed legs, she peered through the opening she'd created through her tent and rain fly, her eyes still scratchy with sleep.

The figure of a man stood at the edge of their campsite, a shadowy silhouette compared to the dark black of the mountains in the distance and the inky blue sky. As he moved to a small sack on the ground, the nylon swipe of hiking pants brushing together reached her. He fiddled with something that looked like…a tripod.

Brooke exhaled through her nose. "Jack?" she whispered to not wake up Cat and Nat in their tent nearby. At the same time she reached for the place he'd been sleeping and found it empty.

The man whipped around and froze. "I'm sorry I woke you," that familiar voice said.

Brooke let out a heavy breath. "What are you doing?"

"Taking a time-lapse of the Milky Way."

She smiled. "So you still love night photography?" She used to imagine him prowling the city, forlorn and lonesome—and maybe he had been—but she could see the beauty in following his passion, too. Of seeking out something magical while the rest of the world slept on.

"Aye. If you're up, the stars are incredible tonight."

"Give me a sec." Brooke disentangled herself from her sleeping bag. She came out zipping her fleece against the chill of the night and wrapped her arms around herself. She peered at the sky. "Wow."

The sun went down after ten this early in the summer, but the island was so far north it hadn't gotten completely dark while she'd been awake. Even late into the night, there was a glow to the sky. But now a deep, velvety black spanned above them and the stars sparkled like sun-kissed ripples on the sea.

Jack stood in silhouette, his tripod in front of him, the camera display shining a faint light against his chest. Brooke wanted to move behind him, slip her arms around him, press her cheek against his back, soak up the love he had that used to extend to her.

"Are you sleeping out here?"

"I couldn't quite maneuver my gear out of the tent without waking you, sprawled across both mattress pads—"

"They overlap," she said but couldn't quite muster a defensiveness. She'd gotten more comfortable being close to Jack. She might've been tucked in close.

He hummed a little laugh. "But there's nothing better than sleeping under the stars—when you're at least halfway assured you won't wake up in a downpour."

There were no guarantees of calm nights on Skye but she didn't want her fears holding her back. Sleeping out here sounded incredibly freeing.

"So, let's do it." Brooke pulled their sleeping bags and mattress pads out of the tent and spread them out on the grass. She slipped off her sandals and tucked back into her still-warm sleeping bag, the lingering heat soaking through her leggings and socks and sending a delicious shiver up her spine.

Jack fiddled with the tripod while Brooke lay on her back, hands propped under her head. The stars were as bright as she'd ever seen them and she could believe the stories from all sorts of ancient societies trying to explain their existence. How they were first sprinkled across the heavens.

Jack crawled into his sleeping bag and turned to face her, propping his head in his hand.

She had this desire to be closer to him, to whisper "Hi," all breathy and hopeful, the way he used to when he brought his face so close to hers she couldn't focus on his eyes but didn't need to. She could feel him all around her.

"You seemed pensive today."

Brooke rolled onto her side, matching his pose, breathing through the yearning clouding her chest. "That's a good word."

"Care to share with the class?"

Brooke huffed out a laugh and toyed with the zipper on her sleeping bag. The reminder of being in school with him didn't summon the angst it used to. Something had changed between them—this version of Jack felt safer somehow. But he still felt like the old Jack. The one who knew all her dreams and fears.

"Talk to me, B."

It made her think of the night when he'd put calamine lotion all over her face. The hurt in his voice that she'd walked away, that she hadn't at least *talked* to him.

Brooke ran her tongue along the inside of her cheek, summoning the strength it took to be vulnerable. Especially with him. "I was listening to Cat's and Nat's stories today and when I think back on the last seven years, there's nothing of note. I haven't experienced anything worth writing about. I feel no further along than I was when I started."

"I'm sure that's not true."

"I haven't written my own stories…in a long time."

Jack hung his head, his exhale loud in the darkness, like he could mark the exact day when she'd stopped, just like she could.

She had a bookshelf of stories that weren't hers and a career she was torn between loving and resenting. She didn't feel that different about the man in front of her. "I'm a ghost. This faded version of myself."

"You're still so bright to me."

Jack had known her when she'd been optimistic and romantic, driven and vibrant. That he still saw that in her, that it might still exist, took the shattered and sharp pieces of her heart and began slotting them back together. A work in progress.

"I haven't felt inspired since that fall. And I know we both got punished for that, but you seem to have moved forward. You're doing what you always wanted. Chasing your dream. I want to feel like that again."

"So, where do we start?"

A hopefulness bloomed in Brooke, loving that Jack was still there to support her, whatever it entailed.

Even thinking the words made her heart race. But she wanted to do something daring. Something wild. Something for herself. "I want to cross the Bad Step tomorrow." The crossing was notoriously challenging, and it would add more time and they'd skip the main section between Sligachan and Elgol. But Mhairi wouldn't mind. This had never been about detailing her exact steps on the trail; it'd been about telling a story. And Brooke wanted to be able to do that again one day.

Jack took her hand, flattening it and laying it on top of his, stacking his other on top, his skin warming her on both sides. Brooke's heart skipped and she laughed, a giddy, unrestrained thing as memories of that night under the library table came back to her. The start of a heady adventure she could feel bubbling in her veins.

Jack had always had a way of making time stand still. And making her feel like the boldest version of herself.

She used to think of them as star-crossed, and maybe it was all the same in the end, but under the heavy blanket of night, she thought they might be destined.

Brooke placed her other hand on the top of Jack's.

A pact.

"Should we pinkie promise, too?" he asked, his voice low and serious.

She repeated the words she'd said all those years ago, "We'd better," and brought their linked hands to her lips.

THEN

Jack pressed a kiss against Brooke's temple as she settled herself more snugly against his chest in his bed, her pen scratching against her notebook, her books spread out on the blankets. It'd been three weeks of sneaking into her room or sneaking her into his, kissing her in deserted stairwells on campus and springing apart when doors on other floors opened, sharing longing stares from across the coffee line or lecture hall. Reading on opposite sides of bookshops, running through the Meadows at night.

He'd wondered if the high of pretending they didn't know each other when he knew what every inch of her skin tasted like would wear off, but if anything, it had only gotten stronger—more addicting. He was enthralled and obsessed and so fucking smitten—he'd shown up to her flat the night before with a bouquet of highlighters just to see her smile.

"I think, after Christmas," she said, putting her notebook on the nightstand and snuggling against him, "we should make a coffee shop bucket list of all the best places in Edinburgh where you can read and I'll write."

"Will we use special pens to make this list?"

"I'm not sure *your* handwriting is going to be involved but if by *we* you mean *me*, then yes. And the pen will be purple."

"Oh, well, if it's purple, I'm in."

She laughed. "Maybe we could sneak away to Inverness after finals."

"If you're looking for a checklist, I'll take you on the Heilan Coo Trail. The city has hairy coo statues all about town painted by local artists."

"No, they don't."

"It's like a scavenger hunt. You'll love it."

It was only a few more weeks of classes but it felt like forever, the way the end of the semester always did. Like there was too much to do, but time still managed to crawl by. Especially waiting for this future Brooke dreamed up.

Jack loved everything about her big dreams and he was starting to understand it now, too. Since the night they went up the Scott Monument, he'd stopped connecting his lessons to The Heart and instead applied them to his future photography business. How to market a product, how to build a simple profit-and-loss statement, how to navigate business taxes. All the components he'd need to be successful if he ever struck out on his own.

Maybe he was still biding his time, in a way—delaying telling his family he was serious about photography because he didn't want to suffer the consequences, to deal with the fallout that was sure to happen. The thought of telling his dad, telling Reid and Logan—especially Logan—sent a shock wave of fear through him. But Jack had finally found something that felt right.

For maybe the first time in his life, he really *wanted* something. Something that was *his*.

"Can I show you something?" he asked.

"Mmm-hmm." Brooke twisted the strings of Jack's hoodie around her fingers.

He grabbed his phone and navigated to BBC news. He felt like a kid showing Brooke treasures sometimes, wanting her to see all the pieces of him, feeling so assured that she would never diminish or dismiss the things he cared about.

He scrolled to a picture in Dunbar's Close, the park bench under bronze-leafed trees, the golden lights of windows behind it. A small black banner in the corner of the picture framed the words "Photo Credit: Jack Sutherland."

Brooke bolted up and grabbed his phone. "Jack! That's your name! That's your picture!"

He chuckled. "Aye. They didn't pay me for it or anything. But it exists out in the world."

She stared at the picture a bit longer, zooming in on the leaf with two fingers, before handing the phone back to him. "Mhairi always says that about a first draft. It just has to exist. The starting is the hardest part."

"Wise woman."

Brooke climbed into his lap, wrapped her arms around his shoulders and kissed him a hundred times, all over his face. He laughed at the onslaught until she tipped her forehead against his. "I'm proud of you," she said, the words ringing in his ears as if he'd never heard them before, slotting into a space in his heart he hadn't realized was empty. Surely his parents had told him those words, but maybe he'd never quite believed them.

But he believed Brooke.

Three sharp raps sounded on the wooden door. "Oh, Jackie," Rohan called as he jiggled the doorknob. The door flew open before Jack or Brooke could even react.

Rohan froze, as still as Jack had ever seen him. Brooke scrambled off his lap and he thanked his lucky stars that they were still fully clothed. Although maybe that would've made Rohan immediately retreat instead of standing there staring at them.

"Are you two serious right now?" he asked.

Brooke looked at Jack, her eyes wide, her mouth open like she was going to say something.

"This isn't what it looks like," Jack said, guilt sitting heavy in his stomach at lying to his friend.

"Great, because what this looks like—besides you two *in bed together*—is you giving Brooke extra help…" He waved his hand at the books scattered all over.

"I'm not helping her," Jack said.

Brooke stood up, zipping her hoodie. "This isn't even for our class. I'm just studying here."

Jack climbed out of bed as Rohan shook his head, his raised-eyebrow gaze on the ceiling, like he couldn't believe what he was hearing.

There was no sense in trying to deny to Rohan what he could so blatantly see. "We were trying to wait for the end of term to get involved—"

Rohan held his hands up. "I do *not* want the details."

"We know the optics aren't good…" Brooke fiddled with the zipper pull on her hoodie.

Rohan pinched the bridge of his nose in the exact way Jack's mum did when she was beyond exasperated. "There is a clear policy and I don't know if I'm implicated by this. There could be all sorts of questions raised about bribery and manufacturing grades. Brooke, you have the highest marks in my recitation. We've been friends for years. I live with *you*." Rohan emphasized the word with a disparaging glance in Jack's direction that made Jack's stomach sink even lower than it already had. "This is well beyond bad optics. I have no idea what kind of consequences there could be if real accusations started flying around."

Jack had avoiding articulating the risks quite so clearly to himself, knowing if he didn't, he could tell himself that he and Brooke were outside the rules, that surely something that felt this good couldn't be wrong, that no one would get hurt.

"You have to end this," Rohan said and Jack could barely process the words over the relentless pounding of his heart.

"Until the term is over…or, so no one gets suspicious, maybe until the *next* term is over."

Brooke's head snapped up. "That's so long from now…" She trailed off at Rohan's dark look and chewed on the edge of her lip. She looked downright chastened and Jack wanted to comfort her, to pull her into his arms. He knew it would make everything worse, and maybe it was a small blessing that he felt so frozen in fear he couldn't have moved to her if he'd tried. He couldn't give Brooke up.

"I pray to god you've been careful enough that no one else knows about this." Rohan opened his hands wide in a gesture of frustration before striding from the room. "Wankers!" he yelled from down the hall.

As oxygen seemed to reenter the room and Jack's heartrate came down from its frenzy, he closed the door and reached for Brooke, massaging her upper arms, casting about for anything to say to make this better. She didn't melt against him, her hand rubbing against her chest in small circles as she stared over Jack's shoulder at the door. "How much do we trust him not to say anything?"

"Hey." Jack pulled Brooke into a hug. "I trust him."

"I do, too," she said quickly. "Like…ninety-nine percent," she said, her body still stiff against Jack's. "Ninety-two. Eighty-four."

Jack wasn't one hundred percent certain, either—he knew how much grad school meant to Rohan. They'd put him in a terrible position questioning if even a small part of his future and aspirations hung in the balance.

Brooke pulled back, her eyes wide and guarded. "Is he right? Do we need to stop seeing each other?"

Jack's stomach clenched hard. "That's the last thing I want."

He cupped her cheek, ran his thumb over her bottom lip. "Is that what you want?" He held his breath.

She shook her head. "I don't think I even could."

Jack kissed her, a hard press of lips, and Brooke slid her hand to the back of his neck, holding him tightly against her. He gentled his touch, kissing along her bottom lip, her breath warm against him, her lips soft.

Brooke snuggled into his arms, wrapped hers tightly around his waist, and buried her face against Jack's chest with a heavy sigh. Resting his head against the top of hers, Jack ran his hands up and down Brooke's back. He breathed in her shampoo, let the orange notes soothe him like they always did.

They could be more careful, but his flat was no longer a safe place to be together and they'd always considered Kieran and Chels dramatically more perceptive than Rohan.

They could see each other less. But it was never enough as it was. Jack wanted to be with Brooke constantly, cherished the peace he felt whenever they were together, found himself texting her while he biked home from campus—desperate to know her favorite sandwich or what song she was listening to while she studied or what story she was dreaming up that day.

"We could disclose this to the administration. Get ahead of it," he suggested.

Brooke pulled out of his arms. "Absolutely not."

"I don't want to stop seeing you. And I don't want to implicate Rohan."

"People will fist bump you for sleeping with your student, but they'll accuse me of sleeping my way to the top. It's not the same for you," she said, tugging at the cuffs of her hoodie and tucking her hands inside.

Jack could see the truth in her words and the stubborn straightness of her spine. "I get that. I do. But there's so much at stake here." He pushed his glasses up and rubbed his eyes.

At the start of term, he would've walked away from this

master's over nearly any inconsequential obstacle. But now it felt like the key to his future. The way to prove to his family that he wasn't chasing down another whim, that he was serious this time. He didn't see any other way to keep this hope and to keep Brooke, too.

"You're not even *my* TA. I know why the policy exists but I don't think we'd really get punished. We'll be more careful—and trust that Rohan is our friend and wouldn't hurt us. Please keep this a secret."

Jack blew out a long sigh. It was a terrible plan—a dangerous plan—but the alternatives were no better.

NOW

Jack and Brooke set out from their campsite toward the
Sligachan Hotel with its whitewashed walls and slate gray tur-
reted roofline. Jack had been to this part of Skye with a thousand tour groups and he pointed Cat and Nat in the direction
of coffee, but he went on ahead. He wasn't in the mood for a
pick-me-up this morning. He didn't deserve one.

Brooke's admission that she hadn't written her own stories
since everything fell apart hung heavy around his shoulders.
He'd fucked up so very much back then, so unsure of his direction, of who knew what was best for him. He'd listened to
so many voices, but never his own. And she'd lost her voice as
a consequence.

The soft morning light lit up the famous Sligachan Bridge,
casting the three arches in shadow and turning the rocks in
the river a matte bronze. The water mirrored the light blue
sky. In the background, the Cuillin Mountains rose from the
valley floor to formidable peaks, the tops shrouded in wispy
white clouds.

Jack walked across the mottled stone bridge and leaned

over the edge on his forearms. The first time he'd come here had been that summer with Mhairi. They'd hiked and bird-watched. He hadn't even given in to his teenage surliness pretending to hate it because he'd been here with Mhairi and no one could sulk with Mhairi about. It'd been the best summer of his life, a break from his parents and their expectations.

He was already nursing a dark mood this morning, and thoughts of Mhairi tugged him deeper. His heart ached wondering if that'd been the last time they'd be here together. If they could find time to fit in another trip.

It was one thing to live each day like it might be the last— he didn't have to suffer the consequences of his own absence. But living like it might be someone else's last day was excruciating. Hoarding the time and the memories, knowing he'd need them later.

He tipped his head down until his forehead pressed against the cold, smooth stone of the bridge.

How many more tattie dinners did they have, watching the Hibs play footie on the telly? How many more Saturday family lunches? How many more phone calls and hugs and *I love you*s?

A hand wrapped around his forearm and he raised his head to find Brooke slotted up against him, her eyes full of concern. "What's wrong?"

Jack wanted to tell her the depth of what he was feeling. They could hold on to their memories together; Brooke could shoulder his grief and he could shoulder hers. They'd get through it together.

But there was time for that later; he wouldn't break Mhairi's confidence or destroy this optimistic glow Brooke had had around her since last night. Like she was reclaiming what he'd stolen from her all those years ago. They'd be back in Edinburgh in another three days and Mhairi could tell Brooke in her own way. "I'm fine."

"This is Mhairi's favorite place and even *I* know the lighting is fantastic this morning. You'd be double fisting cameras if you were fine."

Jack blew out a long breath; he never wanted to hide his feelings from Brooke. So he told her the true parts he could share. "Mhairi brought me to Sligachan that summer I spent on Skye. We stood right here and she told me about the igneous rocks of the Black Cuillin and the granite of the Red, the folklore of the archers." Jack rolled his neck. "And then she was almost tentative in this way that made me really listen. She said, 'It's alright to not know what you want, but when you do, don't let it go. Give it everything you have, or you won't stand a chance of ever being happy.'"

Mhairi had known even then that Jack didn't quite fit in with the family. That he wanted so badly to be something he wasn't. But he wondered now if she'd been talking about having the courage to follow an entirely different path. Maybe he'd misunderstood her wisdom and thrown himself into guiding and then grad school instead. Into this pursuit of gallery recognition.

Brooke hummed in agreement, turned her searching eyes on him. "She's told me some variation of that, too."

He hated that Brooke had ever needed that advice. She'd been the most driven person he'd ever known. Even now, even if she couldn't see it anymore, she still was. She was out here taking chances—sharing her secrets and vulnerabilities and about to cross the Bad Step—even though he knew it scared her. It felt more important than ever to support her. To help her reclaim that fearless side of herself she thought she'd lost but he could still see so clearly.

He stared down at the glassy water rippling below the bridge.

"I've been thinking about what you said in that tourist shop with the prints. And wondering if I'm still hedging. If I'm still wrapped up in some idea of grandeur—" If he was still listening to everyone else but himself.

"Jack, I didn't mean to question you. I think it's amazing you're following your dream."

"But is it the right one? The real one? I've been so focused on getting into galleries, so intent on justifying this to my family." He wrapped his fingers around the curved, cool stone.

"So, what do *you* want?" There was that question she'd asked him before, that cut right to the heart of him.

You.

It'd always been Brooke. Jack had never felt surer of anything, back then and now. And all he could do was support her on this trail—encourage her, tell her stories about Mhairi, listen.

A couple crossed the bridge behind them and pulled Brooke's attention. Whatever he'd been about to say out loud, he swallowed down.

He scratched at the grout between the rocks, the sandy feel of it rough on his fingers. "I don't know." He still didn't know. He'd been so sure that he'd grown up, that he'd finally found what he wanted and gone after it. "I want to capture magical moments and share them with people who understand, who see the beauty in a darkened cobblestone lane or—" he waved his hand "—a leaf in the wind."

Brooke laughed and his lips tipped up.

He wanted to share Scotland with anyone who loved the landscapes of the moors and the hills and the particular green he was sure couldn't be replicated anywhere else on earth. "I want to create something that marks that I was here. That I existed. Something lasting. Something *mine*."

The lighting *was* perfect this morning. It cast Brooke's smile in a golden glow. "It sounds like you *do* know what you want, then."

She unzipped the pouch at Jack's waist and pulled out his camera, holding it out to him. He just had to be brave enough to reach for it.

He gripped the lens, feeling its weight. Brooke looped the

strap over his neck, flattening it against his chest with both palms. The look in her eyes was nurturing and soft. "Come on, then."

He followed her across the bridge and down the square-cut boulders holding back the riverbank.

Jack took pictures of the shallow water, the tumbled rocks, and the pyramidal mountain in the distance. He settled into the assurance he always felt with a camera in his hands. He could capture life right now. Hold on to it. He could still share it with Mhairi.

Brooke hopped across the tan rocks to get closer to the water and the arch of the bridge. Jack raised his camera to his eye. The top of the bridge was a straight line balancing the blue of the sky and the gray of the stones. Through the bridge, the river was a reflective white, the far bank a deep green. Brooke was framed perfectly inside the stone arch, the orange of her jacket bright against the natural tones of the river.

"Brooke," he called.

Balanced on two wide rocks, she turned to the sound of his voice. When she noticed his camera, she gave him a smile that stretched across her whole face. It was the same bright-eyed one as that first picture he'd taken of her on a dark and magical night, the sparkling city lights behind her, when he hadn't wholly understood that yearning he'd felt in his chest.

For the feel of a camera in his hands. For the love of a woman who made him feel like he mattered.

And a hope he hadn't dared reach for stirred in his heart.

NOW

At the end of Loch Coruisk, they came to a pool of water, sheltered like a crater. On one side of the oval loch, a hard slab of rock rose steeply from the water, covered in lime-green lichen. The beach, if Brooke could call it that, was tumbled stones the size of her fist. A massive boulder bracketed the other side of the pool, and the last side opened to the sea.

The water was as turquoise as the Maldives, but she was sure the temperature would disabuse her of that notion in a milli-second. Even so, the water called to her.

Nat and Cat came around the ledge, Jack on their heels. "Stay there," Jack called, jogging down to the beach.

He pointed his camera at the three women and Cat looped her arms around Brooke and Nat, yelling, *"¡Queso!"* in Brooke's ear.

Jack pulled the camera away from his eye to look at the pre-view. He frowned at what he saw and dropped into a crouch like the lighting was wrong, bringing a hand up to block the direct light.

Cat pulled at the corners of her mouth with her pinkie fingers and Nat stuck her tongue out. With a laugh, Brooke went cross-eyed for the picture.

"Stunners, the lot of you," Jack said. Brooke squeezed Cat as they laughed and the shutter snapped again. "That's what I was looking for."

They found a place to drop their packs, everyone ready for lunch. As they ate and lounged in the sun, Jack made a vlog for Mhairi and Brooke chatted with Nat about the proper way to shear a llama.

From down on the beach, Jack asked, "Who wants to go swimming?"

Cat responded with a swift "Absolutely not," and Nat crinkled her nose.

"What about you?" he asked Brooke, and she was about to decline, citing the hassle of wet underclothes, not to mention the temperature of the water, until she met Jack's gaze. It held that quiet challenge that her heart always responded to. That call to adventure she'd never been able to resist.

She crumpled up her trash from lunch and made her way to the rocky beach.

Jack grinned and reached behind his head. He grabbed the collar of his shirt and slowly tugged it up and off, revealing the waves of the muscles along his ribs, the curve of his pecs, the deep divots around his collarbone. His tongue touched the corner of his mouth and she nearly expired on the spot.

She'd caught glimpses of him on the trail, tugging off a top layer and revealing a sliver of his stomach, lifting the bottom of his shirt to wipe sweat from his face. But she hadn't seen him bared to her like this since back then. He'd filled out, his shoulders broader, his chest wider, the dip between his pecs more pronounced.

He'd been irresistible to her back then, and time hadn't diminished that pull, that need coursing through her to touch him, to feel him against her.

Humor danced in his eyes when she met them and she cleared her throat as if that would disguise her blatant perusal and her shaky breathing. "As long as you don't get hypothermia on me," he said.

She grinned at the reminder of that first time they'd gone to Portobello. "I kept swimming actually." Kept searching for that feeling she used to get from being with Jack.

"Really? I thought I scarred you."

"No. You made me feel alive." She hadn't meant to say the words out loud, but it was the truth. Jack always pushed her to reach further, showed her how to be free.

She pulled her shirt over her head and tossed it on the rocks. She thought about being self-conscious of her trusty sports bra for one single second before his eyes met hers and what she saw there heated every inch of her body.

Dropping to one knee, she unlaced one boot and then the other before unbuttoning her hiking pants and slipping them off her hips, hyperaware of Jack's attention on her like a caress.

"Let's do this, then," Jack said, his voice rough, and they waded into the turquoise water. She sucked in a breath as the frigid chill stole through her and heard Jack's gasp next to her.

Brooke sank under the water, holding her breath as her veins seemed to fill with a heavy cold, and brought her hands up over her face and hair as she broke the surface.

Jack growled low and deep before turning and floating on his back, his toes, thighs, chest, and face breaking the surface. Brooke tore her gaze away, breathed out, and floated, too, letting the water hold her up.

Something grabbed her ankle, tugging her down below the surface. She sucked in a breath before she was dragged under, kicking wildly to free herself. She came up spluttering, blinking water out of her eyes, her heart racing, her skin crawling, and curled her legs up to her chest, away from whatever had touched her.

As she scanned the water, she noticed Jack, his hands held up in front of him. "It was the Kelpie!" he said, the mythical water horse who dragged people to the depths of this loch.

Brooke narrowed her eyes, charging him with a splash, and he yelped, but she was faster and more determined. She launched herself at him and tried to push his head underwater, but he held her in the air, arms banded tight around her waist. She pushed against the hard muscles of his shoulders and squirmed in his grip but he held fast.

"A Kelpie wouldn't let go so easily," he said. The words sounded light and teasing, but his tone wasn't. She stopped resisting and he brought her lower so her face was level with his. "Not this time." She risked looking into his eyes and they were dark as the bottom of the loch.

She hadn't realized how much she needed to hear that assurance that *if* she was brave enough, *if* she could trust him again, that he'd be there. She'd walked away before, and it hadn't been right, but he'd let her go.

The warmth of his chest against her stomach made her ache. Made her want more. She wrapped her legs around him and his lips formed an O on a heavy breath. Her stomach hitched and she spread her fingers out, pressing her palms into the taut curve of his shoulders.

"Come on, you two. The rain's coming in," Cat called.

Brooke dropped out of Jack's hold and he released her, but his gaze didn't. Like this wasn't over at all.

THEN

Brooke sat in the front row of Mhairi's class as she handed back essays with red marks on the top. Brooke could never quite quell the anxiety that raced through her when grades were delivered, especially when it was Mhairi's judgment coming down the line. But since the first paper, a rush of excitement seemed to inflate Brooke's lungs. She wanted to impress Mhairi—she was living for her praise.

The past three months had been the best of her life. Exploring the city, getting out of her comfort zone, taking risks. She felt like she'd come into her own. She understood now when people talked about finding themselves in college. Her grades had slipped a bit in her other classes, but it'd felt so good to not be tethered to the library, to be really *living* for the first time, and she knew her creative writing grade would more than make up for it.

Brooke really understood now what it meant to write from a place of big emotions, to describe something she'd experienced instead of something she'd only imagined.

Brooke held her breath as Mhairi slid her paper onto the

desk. Brooke flipped up the corner, hopeful butterflies in her stomach. The red mark was sharp, the C slipping out of focus as Brooke's body flushed and her hands went numb. She could feel splotches breaking out on her chest and heat collecting on the back of her neck.

She'd never gotten a C in her life. She discreetly covered the mark, checking over her shoulder that no one else had seen, but everyone else was focused on their own papers or rushing to tuck them into backpacks.

Brooke never understood people who could wait to check their grade. She flipped through the comments in the margins, so fast she could barely take in the notes about missing conflict, not immersing the reader enough, not ringing true to life, while Mhairi said something in the background.

There was no way she could get into Mhairi's fellowship with this kind of feedback. Mhairi wouldn't want her. And without it, Brooke would never have the skills to write a novel or the credibility to be a published author.

Her eyes filled with tears and she sucked in a deep breath through her nose, blinking furiously. She was not going to cry.

Brooke only realized Mhairi had released the class when someone's backpack swung into her face. She dodged out of the way and headed for Mhairi's desk.

"Brooke with an e," Mhairi said with a teasing lilt, but Brooke couldn't even appreciate it or bask in the familiarity of the greeting.

"I was hoping you could tell me more about this grade."

"I thought you might," Mhairi said with a patient smile.

Well, that was humiliating.

"Stories are such a magical thing, aren't they? Whether it's an essay or a book or a song. We step into another life and try it on for size. We let them hijack our minds. And the reason we do that is conflict. We want to see how characters handle impossible situations. It doesn't have to be dark, but it has to have tension, a push and a pull. Feeling split between good and evil or torn between want and need."

Brooke could understand *that* feeling very well.

"This paper skimmed the surface. Did you write more than one draft?"

Embarrassment burned up Brooke's throat like acid and she considered lying for a split second. But maybe that was even worse for Mhairi to think she'd put in her best effort for a mediocre story. "No." Her paper could've been more—*would've* been more—if she hadn't been gallivanting around town with Jack, spending all her nights and weekends in his bed. She'd completely lost sight of what really mattered, all wound up in the feeling of being wanted by someone.

"Did you have a classmate critique it?"

Brooke shook her head and bit the inside of her cheek to keep from crying.

"Your story was lovely but it felt rushed. Like it could've been more."

Shame, hot and thick, spiraled inside Brooke and curdled in her stomach. She should have listened to Mhairi's other words, too. The ones about the magic of revisions. Should have swapped papers with someone, should have put in the time to incorporate feedback. Should have cared more and worked harder.

"There's still one paper left this term. No need to fret." Mhairi's reassuring smile didn't reassure Brooke at all.

An urgent need to redeem herself made Brooke's knees weak. "Could I rewrite this?"

"It's not fair to the other students if I regrade a new paper, but I'd be happy to read a new version if you'd like to write it. I think it would be a good challenge for you."

Brooke nodded, not trusting herself to keep the tears back. "Thanks."

She deliberately kept her stride even as she made it to the

doorway of the classroom, then flew down the hallway and stairs of Appleton Tower, tears threatening to overflow before she was away from all these people. Her cheeks pulsed with the shame flushing through her.

It'd been so easy to convince herself that swimming and prowling the city at night was living and that spending her nights in Jack's bed was the kind of risk Mhairi had been talking about. Brooke had been fooling herself—all the way into a C. Jeopardizing everything she'd been working toward for years.

Jack stepped in her path in the lobby, both hands going to her arms, his eyes crinkled with worry. "What's wrong?"

Brooke shrugged out of his grasp. She might be distraught enough to throw herself into Jack's arms, but she had enough wherewithal to realize this was not the place for it.

She must look terrible if he'd forgotten he couldn't touch her like that in public.

"Nothing." Brooke pushed past him and headed for the Meadows. The metal bar on the door was cool as she shoved against it and fled into the fresh air. She needed to clear her head. To keep the crushing disappointment and self-loathing from spilling over in tears.

Brooke sped along the sun–dappled sidewalk and through the tightly packed buildings until she made it to the park. She followed the path that cut through the fields, under the cherry blossom trees that were nothing of their former glory, scraggly and leafless now. The branches reached for each other, knotted together above her head.

She found a park bench and let her bag slip from her shoulder. Sitting down, she hugged her knees to her chest, burying her face.

"Brooke."

She looked up and Jack was there, hand outstretched like he wanted to touch her. "What happened?"

Brooke's stomach squeezed at the thought of Jack knowing

how badly she'd messed up. To know she was so very mediocre. He tugged the paper she still clutched in her hand, looking at the letter on top before she could stop him. She held her breath while he scanned the comments, flipping through the pages. When his eyes reached hers, he looked hopeless, confused. But not disappointed.

"You don't have to say anything."

"I do feel as though nothing I say right now would be correct," he said cautiously.

Brooke huffed out a humorless laugh. "Yeah."

"Come here," he said, opening his arms and sliding across the bench to her.

There was hardly anyone in the Meadows in the fading daylight, the December chill stealing the warmth from the classroom, but it wasn't worth the risk.

"No." She shot him a look that was maybe too harsh. It wasn't Jack's fault that she'd gotten this grade. But the absolute last thing she needed was for him to make this worse.

Jack sighed and sat on the far side of the bench.

She hated the defeated slump of his shoulders, but there was too much on the line. "I'm already at risk of not getting into Mhairi's fellowship with this." She took the cursed paper back from Jack and stuffed it in her backpack, her eyes welling up against her will. "And if I don't, my academic career is over, and I'll never write again, and the world will end."

Jack's lips tipped up at the corners. "The world won't end," he said soothingly.

"It *will*."

"I could talk to Mhairi."

Brooke sat up straight. "You absolutely *cannot*."

"You're right. I'm sorry. I just…" Jack rested his elbows on his knees, dragged a hand down his face. "I want to help."

"The only help I need is apparently to study. I don't know

what I was thinking just blowing off school this term like it didn't matter. Like I could afford the distraction."

Jack leaned back against the park bench like she'd pushed him. His lips pressed together and his eyebrows pinched as he nodded. His hurt settled around her shoulders.

"Come on. I didn't mean it like that."

"Yes, you did."

Brooke tipped her head back over the bench, face turned to the dreary gray sky. Jack wasn't *only* a distraction, but he *had* been one. She'd completely reprioritized her life and it revolved around the time she could spend with him. "I just need to re-focus through finals."

He ran his hand over his jaw.

"It's not that long," she said. "And I'm not going home for winter break. We can take a train somewhere no one knows us. You'll have me all to yourself. I promise."

"Alright," he said, but he didn't sound convinced at all.

NOW

In the shadow of the Black Cuillin Mountains, the Bad Step was infamous—a rounded stone slab hovering over the turbulent green waters of Loch Coruisk. The giant crack that split through the rock provided a path of sorts—if Brooke took the same creative license with the word as all the guidebook authors had. The crack was nothing more than a ledge, the width of a single stair, angled up and over the side of the rock so they couldn't see how far it extended on the other side.

The white light sparkling over the water made her dizzy and she held up a hand to block the afternoon sun. A rocky shore wasn't an apt description of the edge of this sea loch. The rocks were boulders, tumbling down to the water's edge and disappearing into the dark depths of the cerulean sea. She had no question why the stories of earth giants had arisen in a place like this.

Cat and Nat tipped their heads like they were contemplating the climb.

"I don't think I can do it," Nat said.

Brooke was likewise questioning her rash decision to embark

on this particular adventure. Standing on the side of the rock, it looked so much higher than it had in the pictures online.

"There's a boat that ferries across this loch," Jack said, ever the expert on touristy things. "We could try to grab that instead."

A boat was an appealing idea—they could skip this death trap and also, *how quaint*. It would make an excellent premise for a story.

The wind had come up hours ago but hadn't felt quite so dire when it was only whipping her hair around. Up on that ledge, it'd be playing with her pack, too, her center of gravity already completely off. Worst case, she would fall in the loch with all her gear and drown.

"We can go back and loop around," Cat said, holding Nat's hand. Brooke knew how much Cat wanted to cross this—it was basically the first thing she'd said when they met. But Brooke could tell Cat wouldn't push Nat—or any of them—if they really wanted to walk away and head back to the official trail.

If they did, they'd lose half a day they couldn't really afford after picking this detour.

"No. I want to do it," Nat said.

Jack nudged Brooke's shoulder. "What do you think?"

She looked into his eyes, shadowed by the brim of his hat. She'd survived a raging storm without a full-blown panic attack because of Jack. She could do this, too. Needed to know she could still take chances. "I'll go first."

"You sure?" Jack asked. Brooke nodded, not quite trusting her voice to come out anything but strangled.

"I'll follow you, then."

Brooke walked down the stepping staircase of fractured boulders, Jack behind her, then Nat and Cat. Brooke gripped the grass growing in pockets between the smooth rock. When she was overwhelmed, Chels often told her to go outside and feel the grass, but this advice seemed laughable now. The grass couldn't do a single thing to keep her from falling off this ledge.

Sliding her fingers into a long horizontal crack, Brooke shuffled across the incline, her body pressed against the cool rock to counteract the pull of her pack and her fear of falling. She wondered, not for the first time, how rock climbers did this, how they trusted the sheer strength of their fingers to keep them safe. She envied that kind of conviction about literally anything.

The ledge narrowed and Brooke's heart pumped uncomfortably in her chest as her jacket scraped against the rock.

"This is worse than I thought," Natalia whined. "I can't see my feet."

Brooke took shallow breaths, sliding her hands around the flat rock, searching for some sort of grip.

"Take your time," Jack said to Brooke, his voice distant. "Don't move until you see the path forward."

Brooke nodded, then shook the divot she'd found to make sure it was sturdy before shifting her weight.

She couldn't see her feet, either, and it sent a panic through her like driving at night in the fog. Like one wrong turn and you could crash over a ledge to your demise. She'd add this to her list of nightmares to revisit.

The water was directly below them now, the sun's reflection a blinding circle, sparkling and marking the spot where they'd drop into the water. Rocks lay in a jumble on the edge of the lake like they'd fallen and splintered. More boulders were probably just below the surface. If anyone in their group fell, it would mean getting airlifted out of here.

"You've got this," Jack said, his voice calm and firm like his conviction might seep into her.

Brooke pulled her attention back to the rock, smooth from the elements of millions of years and climbers rubbing their hands along it, searching for purchase.

Her breath was coming out in pants and gasps, audible over

Natalia's swearing. "I can't fucking see my fucking feet. Shit, that's a long way to fall. Why is this rock so goddamn slick?"

The rock bowed away from the water, making it too hard to grip. Brooke felt like she was teetering on the ledge now. She crept along the side of the rock, keeping her hands splayed wide. The wind whipped her hair into her eyes and she twisted her head into the brunt of the breeze to blow it out.

The roiling green of the water below distracted her, the tiny whitecaps making her seasick. Was it a twenty-foot drop? Two hundred? All sense of spatial skills was lost to the sea below.

"Brooke," Jack said, his voice commanding. Without realizing, she'd frozen. "Take it slow. Breathe."

Her anxiety was getting the best of her, the calculating, the playing out routes and next steps and worst-case scenarios.

"Look at me."

She shook her head, a tiny movement so as to not upset her center of gravity.

"Do you trust me?"

She traced the gray cracks in the rock with her eyes. Trusting Jack had nearly destroyed her. But he'd also pushed her to take risks and if she looked back on her life, the times she felt free and whole and fulfilled had been because of him. Brooke gripped the rock tighter, turning her head to look at Jack. She nodded.

He took exaggerated deep breaths and she followed them. In and out. Her heart rate returned to light-jogging levels instead of top-of-a-roller-coaster realm.

"I believe you can do this," he said. "Do you trust yourself?"

Jack wasn't swooping in to rescue her—he'd always believed she could do it on her own. And it'd always made her believe in herself. His reminder was the buoy she needed. She didn't want to lose these moments to her fear. She wanted to live them fully.

"Yeah."

"Good. Because you're already doing it."

Brooke took in the details around her. When she wrote this, she'd describe the deep cerulean of the water and the triangular island in the middle of the loch. The light blue shadows of mountains in the distance, fluffy clouds banding above them. The wind toying with the tabs on Jack's backpack straps. The slope of his jaw, the curve of his smile. That proud look he had in his dark brown eyes, his fearlessness against the steep slope of the rock, the flutter of her heart that they were doing this together.

After so much had passed between them, it felt like they were right where they were meant to be.

On a cliff hanging over the ocean, Brooke felt safe with Jack again.

"I'm good." Brooke pressed on. The split in the stone widened, deepened to a cut where they could grab both sides and jump down onto a flat slab, splintered into geometric patterns below her feet, the water trapped in the grooves sparkling like gemstones. Brooke grabbed on to a cracked dome of a rock and slid through a cave-like opening and passed through to solid ground.

She'd done it.

Looking back, the Bad Step didn't look so daunting. It looked conquered.

She held her hand out to Jack and he took it, jumping down.

He wrapped her up in his arms and she could feel his heart beating under her ear. She let that familiar serenity seep into her. Jack cupped her cheek and tilted her face up to his, searching her eyes, searching for signs of terror. But she didn't feel afraid anymore.

Something akin to survivor's lust flared through Brooke's veins. She wanted him to kiss her, to feel his lips crashing against hers. To feel even more alive. And she'd kiss him back. Feel the slight rasp of Jack's stubble, trace the seam of his lips with her tongue, moan when he licked into her mouth. Adrenaline still coursed through her, compounded by the memory of his touch, his hands in her hair.

The wind brushed her cheeks, and the possibility that'd been snuffed out so many years ago seemed to burst into flame before her. Brooke reached up onto tiptoes, some magnetic pull to be closer to Jack. His eyes darkened and his lips parted, his arms tightening around her, like he felt this need, too.

The smash of boots hitting rock sounded behind them, followed by Cat's holler. "We fucking made it! That was fucking fantastic!"

A wry smile played on Jack's lips and he loosened his hold on her. Brooke stepped back, but that pull hadn't faded in the least.

31

NOW

Stony peaks in the distance became bright green, reaching the valley floor and stretching out toward the lazy sea. The simple stone bothy stood alone in the windswept glen of Camasunary Bay, a solitary white building capped with slate gray shingles.

As Brooke and Jack followed the path, their arms brushing, electricity zinging in her veins, she let herself imagine, just for a minute, that Cat and Nat were more than ten minutes behind them. That she and Jack had crossed the Bad Step, trekked across the glen, and found themselves in this isolated bothy—a roof over their heads, somewhere dry. With room to maneuver.

Brooke opened the door and the impassioned conversation inside paused, replaced with a raucous cacophony of welcomes. Five people sat around the two wooden community tables, topographical maps pinned to the white drywall behind them. Gear was spread out on every surface, packs tipped against corners, boxers hanging from the one framed picture.

There was no reason for the disappointment cratering through Brooke. But she'd wanted those ten minutes alone with Jack before Cat and Nat arrived. Wanted the feel of his weight as he backed her against the wall, the relief of the press of his lips, the flick of his tongue.

Jack raised a hand in greeting. "Hello."

"Join us," said a man with an Irish accent, graying hair and bright blue eyes as he waved them over.

"We'd love to. We'll just settle in first." Jack put a hand on Brooke's hip and steered her toward the sleeping room to claim a bed. *Good thinking.*

Bunks were built into the wall of the sleeping room, wooden planks suspended with two by fours, but it looked heavenly to Brooke. Benches ringed the other walls—wide enough to sleep but narrow enough to make it precarious. Shirts and long johns hung over the railing to dry and sleeping bags were spread out on the bunks.

"Does this work?" Jack asked, gesturing to the empty bottom bunk. If Cat and Nat took the unoccupied top, there was no other space unless Brooke wanted to cuddle up next to a stranger.

"Yeah." The thought of snuggling with Jack sent a flutter through her belly.

He placed his pack on the ground and pulled out his sleeping bag, laying it out and smoothing his hands over the blue material, probably checking for wet spots.

While he pulled out damp clothes and hung them from the hooks on the wall, Brooke climbed into the bunk and spread her orange sleeping bag out next to Jack's.

When she climbed out, Jack stepped in front of her. He reached one arm out to block her path, his hand catching the top bunk by her head with a faint thud. Brooke sucked in a breath at the possessive move, at the thrill of being caged by his arm.

Jack's hair curled at the top, wavy from the wind, his cheeks pink, his jaw stubbled. He dragged the flats of his fingers across his jaw looking at her with fire in his eyes that warmed her whole body.

"You almost kissed me back there," he said, the low intensity in his words pinning her in place. Jack was almost never like this—confident, forward. It made Brooke weak-kneed and lightheaded.

She'd wanted to kiss him then, and she wanted to kiss him now. "I did."

His other hand cupped her hip and they both watched his fingers spreading out slowly over her waist. Brooke's pulse picked up like it could race across her body to meet Jack's touch. His tongue rolled across his bottom lip, snagging all her attention.

"Caught up in the moment?" he asked, his voice gravelly.

She looked up into his dark eyes, full of barely leashed desire. He used to look at her with a distant longing, but this was more potent, more forceful. She shook her head. "The hard part was always *not* kissing you, Jack."

He stepped closer, his thigh slipping between hers, their hips flush. The wooden bunk pressed against her shoulders and her calves, and her heart beat in time with a heavy echo between her legs.

"And now?" he asked.

"Nearly impossible," she whispered, looking over Jack's shoulder. "But there's a room full of people out there."

Jack made a low sound of disappointment as Cat and Nat bustled into the room. He dropped his hand and Brooke's body tensed with the strain of not falling into him as he stepped back.

"Oh, this is cozy," Nat said, and Brooke didn't have enough brain space available to tell if she was being suggestive or liked the bunks.

Cat and Nat tossed down packs and stripped off layers but Jack's eyes clung to Brooke's as he shook his head and mouthed, "For fuck's sake," at their interruption.

A grin tugged at Brooke's lips, quieting her racing heart. She'd waited this long for Jack; she could be patient. Probably.

They finished organizing their things while there was still daylight before settling at the community table. Nat started her camp stove boiling and Cat snuggled in next to a black-and-white border collie.

"Her name's Willa," a young Scottish man with a tuft of ginger beard on his chin said. "And I'm Oliver."

"I'm Anya." A woman in an orange thermal and pigtail braids waved. "And my husband, Duncan." She leaned back against his chest. "We're from Australia."

"Murray," the Irish guy said, opening a tin of Heroes the size of a hat box, and pushing it into the middle of the table.

Brooke grabbed a Dairy Milk Caramel from the purple tin. "Ooh, thank you."

Her accent must've given her away because Duncan leaned over his forearm and said, "Are you American? Fucking Los Angeles. Worst place I've ever been."

"Won't argue with that. I'm an expat," Brooke said with a laugh.

Anya grinned and shook her head. "Can't go to a hostel in Europe without encountering Australians rolling cigarettes and talking shit about Americans. Especially if you bring this one." She hooked a thumb in her husband's direction.

"Well, he's not wrong," Brooke said.

The group settled into more small talk while Jack boiled water for coffee, mouthing, "Want some?" from across the table. Brooke nodded. The bothy was warm and cozy but the air still held a chill from the incoming rain.

"I thought I was going into Loch Coruisk today," Nat said. "If Jack hadn't scared me about the Kelpies, I might have found it a more enjoyable way to get to the other side."

The group chuckled and Murray launched into a story about the last time he'd hiked this trail with his late wife and the pilgrimage he was on to remember and to let go. "We crossed the Bad Step and I didn't know my wife knew so *very* many curses, let alone that she could say them with such vigor." He smiled at the memory and chuckled when Jack hooked a thumb in Nat's direction and shot his eyebrows up.

Nat shoved Jack's shoulder and he held up his hands. "I was impressed." He turned those smiling eyes on Brooke and that little flutter she used to feel in the lecture hall flickered under her breastbone.

Willa let out a yawn and settled her face on the table. Oliver made kissing faces at her. "Willa hurt her paw yesterday. I couldn't just fucking carry on with her limping and hopping along on three legs so I managed to get her and her pack strapped to mine."

"Did you come over the Bad Step?" Anya asked, her eyebrows up to her hairline.

"Och, no, we came in from the South. I did her up draped over my shoulders, but then all the extra weight was fucking unstable. Fairly destroyed my back." Murray pulled the collar of his shirt to the side to show off where the straps had cut into him, purple bruises rimming his shoulders. "So I had to put everything in the pack and rig up my fleece like a baby harness to carry on the front. She's like fifteen kilos."

Brooke cupped her hands around the coffee mug Jack passed her, heat seeping into her fingers. The bothy was full of good vibes and the friendly effervescence of being with kindred spirits. Everyone bonded effortlessly over their love for the outdoors and the trials of the trail, like high-speed summer camp connections she rarely encountered as an adult.

The plaque on one wall read, "Remembering a lost brother, Neil. We enter as strangers, we leave as friends," and Brooke could see that magic stitching them together just the same.

This was what Mhairi had meant all those years ago when she'd told the class they might find inspiration anywhere, even in a pub. As Brooke listened to the hikers' stories—stories she never would've encountered without every step that led to this moment—that creative glow warmed Brooke from the inside.

She itched to write down every detail of Murray's bright, crinkly smile and Oliver's wispy ginger beard. The gentle way Cat stroked her thumb over Natalia's neck, leaned in to kiss her on the temple. Jack's booming laugh and the way his eyes kept coming back to meet hers.

The inspiration to write flooded Brooke's senses from the overwhelming contentment and camaraderie in the air.

Anya asked, "What's your story, Brooke?"

Brooke was used to being the one asking that question; it felt good to be on the other end of it. She leaned forward on her elbows. She always answered, *I'm a ghostwriter*, but this time she said, "I'm an author."

Across the table, Jack's eyes sparkled, his smile as wide as she'd ever seen.

That pride on his face made her heart brim over and made her realize she was proud of herself. She was doing this.

"What are you working on?"

Brooke could kiss Anya for the question instead of asking, "Anything I've heard of?"

"We're helping Mhairi McCallister finish her memoir about founding the Skye Trail. I'm writing. Jack's taking pictures."

Anya said, "That's incredible. What an honor."

"Mhairi McCallister!" Murray shouted in surprise, his palm coming down on the table while he leaned back.

"Do you know her?" Jack asked. "She's my aunt."

"She picked us up hitchhiking on a trip through Skye near on thirty years ago. She told us if we tried anything funny she had a knife in her boot and knew how to use it. And then she taught us the song 'Roamin' in the Gloaming.'" He started in on the chorus with an upbeat old-timey vibe and Jack joined in with a low harmony, overrolling his *r*'s and drumming his fingers on the table.

Brooke laughed and met Jack's eyes, a happy buzz passing between them.

"We've been making a vlog for her," Jack said, pulling his video camera out of his small hip bag. "Care to say hullo?"

Murray shoved across the bench seat, squishing the people in his way. "Damn right, I do."

"Hi, Auntie. There are some people here who want to meet you."

The group took turns sliding across the bench to be in front of the camera, to tell Mhairi a story about their journey or their appreciation that this magical place existed, away from civilization.

It hit Brooke all at once that Mhairi's impact was even bigger than she'd realized. And her story was more than the beauty of the land and the sense of achievement that came from finishing the trail. It was about struggles and setbacks, persistence and courage. About people coming together in support of something that mattered to them.

Murray talked about the transformation he'd felt on the trail. Brooke felt it, too, freer. Like the raw power of nature Mhairi had talked about had been hard at work on Brooke's soul. She felt like her old self, adventurous and bold, but also different. Brand-new.

She'd blamed Jack for where her career had ended up. But that wasn't fair. She'd made a lot of decisions along the way to hold back, to not risk putting her work out there in case it wasn't good enough. She'd gotten slapped down and she hadn't wanted to feel that desolation again. It'd been hard enough trying to pick herself up once.

But how long was she going to hold on to the past? How long would she let it affect her? How much did it get to define her?

Natalia gave Jack a discreet nod and he leaned back, pulling the video camera with him and flipping it toward her. Brooke felt a flutter of anticipation at the secret signal.

"Catalina," Nat said, her eyes already starting to well up.

Even though Brooke wasn't exactly sure what was coming, her eyes welled up, too, hoping.

"You are fearless. And you make me fearless, too. I know our life will be full of adventure and I'd follow you anywhere, even across the Bad Step again. Although, please do not make me," she said through her tears while the group chuckled. Nat pulled the grass ring she'd woven by the beach yesterday morning from her pocket and tears leaked from Brooke's eyes.

"Catalina, will you marry me?"

Cat was full-on bawling, wrapping Natalia in an embrace and saying *"Si"* over and over through kisses. The bothy erupted in clapping and hoots that echoed off the walls. In a simple structure far from civilization, these were the moments that defined a life well-lived.

Brooke looked across the table and found Jack's camera on Cat and Nat but his gaze locked on her. Heat zinged through her at the open *want* on his face—like they could have a happy ending one day, too. A matching yearning bubbled up inside Brooke and she was sure her heart shone out of her eyes.

After the tea and biscuits ran out and the stories turned straight to tall tales, the hikers started dispersing to their nightly routines and claiming sleeping places.

After a hilarious romp through the rain to pee with Cat, Nat, and Anya, Brooke came back into the bothy, laughing and hanging up her rain jacket on the hooks, scrunching the water out of her hair.

Everyone got ready for bed, but Brooke wasn't tired. The night was still awash in a rosy glow inside her, expanding with a need to come out in words.

She pulled her notebook from her pack and turned into Jack's beaming smile.

"I know that look," he said with so much pride in his eyes, she felt downright giddy. Like that girl who couldn't go to bed because she wasn't done with her story, Jack asleep next to her while she wrote by a book light. Inspired and creative and free.

He brushed his thumb across her neck with a little squeeze before disappearing into the sleeping room. "Happy writing."

Brooke sat at the community table with a small lantern and her pen for company. She wrote about the feelings of being on this trail. Of how it could change someone fundamentally. How Mhairi would have wanted people to experience it. Brooke took notes on where she'd make changes, new outlines with Jack's stories and Murray's memory and her own details.

Everyone shuffled around in the other room, until Anya called, "Lights out," and the shaft of light disappeared. Willa made a whining noise and her nails clicked on the wooden floor until she jumped up.

"Oof," Oliver grunted.

The room eventually fell quiet, but Brooke wouldn't have noticed either way. Somewhere, she'd turned a page and the story was no longer Mhairi's—it was Brooke's. She wrote in a way she hadn't in years. About the Bad Step and the friends she'd made, about the bothies in Scotland and the way Highland hospitality still reigned.

Brooke had long ago lost feeling in her right leg from sitting in a cramped position on the hard wooden bench. She shifted, sitting cross-legged and rolling her shoulders. She kept going.

Writing again, even if no one would ever read it, even if it was only for her, made Brooke feel alive. She didn't want to hold back out of fear anymore.

When her eyes ached from writing in the low light and no amount of flexing her hand could tug out the cramps, Brooke crept into the sleeping room. Jack lay on his back, arm flung over her sleeping bag.

She rested one hand and one knee on the plywood and tried

to move over him. He startled, making a strangled sound before whispering, "Brooke?"

"Sorry." She climbed up and slid into her open sleeping bag.

"Don't be." He rolled toward her.

"Something magical is happening here."

"They *are* inspiring bunk beds."

She smiled in the dark. "I started writing something new. Something for *me*."

"That's incredible."

That warmth in her chest swelled to an unmanageable heat like sitting too close to an open fire. "I feel like I found my voice again."

Jack cupped her head, his thumb slotting into that sensitive spot behind her ear. "I never doubted you, B."

His assurance cradled her heart. She doubted herself all the time—but not now. Not anymore. Not about this.

Brooke scooted closer to Jack, her sleeping bag falling open around her hips. She didn't want to hold back with Jack anymore, either.

She wet her lips, her heart fluttering. She slid her fingers over the curve of his chest and tipped her head, her mouth close to his. "Is this okay?"

"There's a room full of people," he whispered, repeating her concern from earlier.

"I can never seem to follow the rules when it comes to you."

With a low hum, his hand went to her hair and he brought their mouths together, a soft press of his lips, a slow slide of his tongue. A familiarity that felt like a homecoming and a brand-new adventure all rolled into one.

Fused with heat and need, Jack rolled them until she was on top. Brooke made a small sound and he pulled back, touched the tip of his nose against hers and shook his head in a warning at the noise.

He kissed her again, his hand slipping below her shirt, sliding up her back, fingers spread wide like he wanted to touch as much of her skin as possible.

If the bothy had been empty, if the weather hadn't been too wet to justify a tent, Brooke wouldn't have stopped this time.

NOW

Brooke sat at the community table in the bothy in the early hours of the morning, writing by headlamp. Even the cold and dark morning, coupled with Jack asleep beside her, wasn't enough to keep her tucked into her warm sleeping bag—the pull of the words inside her was stronger.

Oliver emerged from the sleeping room and gave her a nod, clearly not up for conversation this early. His camp stove was already on the wooden picnic table and he pulled out his lighter, the click and hiss sounding as he lit it.

Brooke kept writing, the details of the trail pouring from her, the stories she remembered from Mhairi's interviews and her own research bubbling to the surface, also wanting to make it onto the page.

Jack walked in, pulling a hoodie over his head. His hair fell over his forehead and his stubble had grown in dark along his jawline. He smiled when he saw her, a tentative, raw look. "Morning."

"Morning," she breathed. Brooke felt almost shy around him after last night, the energy charged between them.

He lit his camp stove, setting the lighter down on the table with a clatter and stretching his arms above his head, a sliver of skin peeking out at his waist.

Oliver dug out a satellite internet console, distracting Brooke. She didn't care too much about being off the grid, but also, she was a millennial. "You have internet? I want internet."

He grinned at her and ran his hand over the wispy beard along his chin. "When I'm done, you're welcome to it."

"Thank you."

By now the other hikers were awake, setting up camping stoves with morning voices and disheveled hair, rummaging through packs.

"Morning," Murray said. He picked up the tin from the night before and settled into a meal of chocolate.

"Breakfast of champions," Brooke said.

He toasted her with a raised candy wrapper.

Anya opened jars of peanut butter and salsa, left on the shelf by earlier hikers, and sniffed them. She recapped the peanut butter but brought the salsa with her to the picnic table. Oliver studied the bursting bulletin board before rearranging the flyers on top with a blue push pin.

Brooke tucked her notebook away and filled her stove with water to boil. While she made coffee and oatmeal, she chatted with Cat and Nat, who were still beside themselves, discussing fantastic destination wedding locations even though Nat insisted they were getting married in her parents' backyard.

When Oliver was finished, Brooke connected to his internet and pulled up her email.

To: Brooke Sinclair
From: Charlotte Lane
Subject: Exciting Opportunity! Call me!
Hi Brooke,
We just landed the memoir for Jennifer Aniston and I put your

name forward as her ghostwriter. This opportunity is going to go fast! I should mention it would require being in LA for a few months, starting this fall. I know you're out on the trail, but give me a ring as soon as you're back in range.

xo Charlotte

Brooke took a deep breath in through her nose and held it. *Jennifer Fucking Aniston.* Brooke's brain swirled with images of *Friends* and her favorite rom-coms. Of the absolute *uproar* that would happen over this book. Instead of conducting interviews in the publisher's conference room, she might do them... *ohmygod...in Jennifer's house.* They would be on a first-name basis. She might call her *Jen.*

Having this book on her list of credentials would mean Brooke could get any job she wanted after this. To be part of a project with this much name recognition was *the* literal dream.

But...*whose* dream?

Her excitement wilted. She'd been on big projects before and they were all-consuming; this one would be even more so. The amount of research, the sheer amount of source materials, would be staggering. Brooke wouldn't have time to sleep, let alone work on her own manuscript.

Even though it didn't have a shape yet, wasn't *anything*, her heart ached at the idea of putting this off again. Of going back to writing someone else's story in place of her own. Brooke knew the exact cost of renouncing a dream. She'd been paying it with ennui and restlessness for seven years.

She crossed to the window. Outside, the sky was a misty blue and the craggy hill blanketed in green rose from the water. The vibrant grass waved in the wind, green and yellow rippling under the shadows of clouds rolling above, but she couldn't find any comfort in the idyllic setting.

Jack met her at the window, resting a hand on the countertop and effectively creating a little bubble from the rest of the group. "You alright?"

She wanted to tell him the news. Wanted to shout it from the roof of the bothy. And she also wished she'd never checked her email. "I got a ghostwriting opportunity. Like bigger than anything I'll ever do again in my career."

That little crease appeared between his eyebrows.

"It would be a ton of money and huge for me professionally."

"But you don't look happy."

Brooke sighed and ran her thumb back and forth over the handle of her mug. "I'd have to be in LA for a few months. It'd be around-the-clock work. I wouldn't have time to write my own stories."

"Ah."

"But my own stuff—it's a couple chapters. It's literally nothing."

He ran his hands up her arms and squeezed, a comfort and encouragement all in one. "That's not how you felt last night."

She looked up into his dark gaze, the light from the window casting a shadow of his frames across his cheek. She chewed on her lip. He was right. It'd felt damn good writing again. Simultaneously cathartic and freeing.

"Brooke." Jack wrapped an arm around her waist. "I'm not just saying this because I want you to stay here, even though I do." He moved his other hand to her back, sliding up, his thumb brushing the curve of her neck. "Take a chance on yourself. Trust that the thing you love will take you where you need to be."

Jack had always cared for her in a way she didn't recognize: without expectations or requirements. Encouraged her in a way that made her feel like he believed in her, not like he was running ahead, ready to move the goalposts.

That kind of love had been so comfortable. Not boring, but

a safe place to recharge. Where she didn't have to be perfect—she just had to be herself.

"Trust that the story you want to tell is just as important as theirs."

She scoffed. "No one's as important as she is."

"Yes," he said, his eyes locked on hers. "*You* are."

33

THEN

Jack finished buttoning up his shirt while Brooke stud-ied his new pictures hanging on the wall, her hands clasped behind her back. He felt like putting on a tie, just to mark the importance of the day.

He was bringing her home to meet his parents.

He almost wanted to cancel, to lay her back on his bed instead. Since she'd gotten low marks on her last paper, she'd rekindled her love affair with the library. A place where he could no longer join her.

He wouldn't tell her, but he was chafing against their secret. If they disclosed their relationship, he'd work in the library next to her, take her out for coffee when she needed a break. Jack missed waking up with Brooke, missed the adventures she didn't have time for until after exams.

And some of the distance made him wonder, when his texts went unanswered or she worked late and didn't come over after all, if it was only about her studies or if maybe she'd been around for the excitement and didn't need it—didn't need *him*—anymore.

So he'd done the only logical thing and invited her to meet his parents. As his girlfriend. Perhaps it was some desperate play for reassurance, but he genuinely wanted his family to meet Brooke, for her to know them. And to have a space out in the world where they didn't need to hide.

Jack straightened his collar and Brooke circled in front of him.

"You're nervous," she said, a flash of amusement in her eyes. "I'm great at meeting parents. And I've already met yours."

"I know. I want it to go well, is all."

"It will." She stood on tiptoes to kiss him.

Jack wrapped his arms around her and held her tight, fighting away the feeling that she was slipping away when she was right here.

"And, well…" He didn't want to hide his feelings from her. "It's a big deal to introduce you. I've never brought someone home before."

Brooke tipped her head back, her expression serious, and traced the curve of his jaw with her thumb. Then she pulled from his embrace, turned toward the printer and tugged one sheet of paper from the stack.

"What are you doing?" he asked as she ripped the paper in half with a tearing sound and handed him one piece.

"We're on the same page, Jack."

His heart expanded in his chest, bursting with the words *I love you*, knowing they were too big, too soon. But maybe not so far away, either. "God, I like you," he said instead, reaching for her. She melted against him, met his kiss with a sweet one of her own. He slipped his fingers under her necklaces, traced the curve of her neck.

"Come on, let's go," she said, tugging his hand.

Jack folded the paper and tucked it into his wallet.

They took the bus to Fife and walked down the lane in the

December sunshine until they reached his parents' brick house, ivy climbing all the way to the chimney.

"Do you think Gemma will show me baby pictures?" Brooke asked as they climbed the front steps. "Actually middle school would be better."

He couldn't handle the nerves and the embarrassment of *that*. He turned around and headed for the street. "Actually, you're uninvited."

"Too late, I'm going in. Your mom's a fantastic cook."

Jack jogged up the steps and reached Brooke before she could knock, wrapped his arms around her and lifted her from the ground. She ran her palms over his jaw and kissed him on the nose.

"Let's do this, then," he said. Releasing her, he opened the red front door, yelling, "Mum, we're home."

Gemma accosted them in the foyer, smoothing his hair back, and for the first time, Jack didn't mind. He especially didn't mind the way she bundled Brooke up in a hug, too, not even waiting for a proper introduction.

"And this is Brooke," Jack said.

"Aww, you're making me miss my mom." Brooke squeezed Gemma back, her eyes a little misty when she met Jack's.

His eyes got a bit misty, too. Some weight settling around him like this was a moment worth capturing, one he'd commit to memory. That unbearable rightness.

"I know, dear. We met at the footie," Gemma said, patting Brooke on the arm. "Come in, come in."

They followed Gemma to the kitchen but Jack didn't miss the way Brooke tracked the garland wound up the banister or the framed school photos on the walls. She made her way straight for the Christmas tree in the corner of the kitchen, immediately zeroing in on the ornaments with pictures of them as kids. "Oh my god, look at this. Your teeth!"

"Yes, he really has grown into them, hasn't he?" Gemma said with a laugh.

"For fuck's sake," Jack said under his breath. "I'm standing right here." But he couldn't keep the smile off his face. This was exactly what he'd hoped for—everyone at ease, like Brooke could fit seamlessly into this weekly tradition he thought he'd rather enjoy with her by his side.

"I'm here, I'm here," Neil said, striding into the kitchen and clapping Jack on the shoulder. "Pleasure to see you again, Brooke." He gave her an enthusiastic clasped handshake and she beamed at him as Reid came pounding down the stairs and into the kitchen, lanky in the way Jack had been at seventeen, too.

"Hi. I'm Reid." He gave Brooke a sheepish smile, and immediately ducked his head, his sandy blond hair falling forward.

"Brooke," she said and cast a look at Jack, clearly holding back a smile. His youngest brother was adorably tall and apparently flustered by beautiful women.

She turned her attention back to Neil while Gemma fussed with the tea. "You know what I learned recently? That the Tay is the best river in the world for salmon fishing."

Neil let out a delighted cry. "Quite right, my dear. I once caught an old bloke—thirty pounds he was." He pulled out a kitchen chair, the legs scraping against the wood floor, and sat down.

Brooke had done her homework like she wanted to impress them. Jack's heart felt like it was trying to escape his chest.

Gemma set mugs on the island counter, their handles clinking together, in front of where Reid slouched against the countertop.

"Found the way straight to Pops's heart," Reid said to Brooke with a grin, and Jack felt a matching one on his lips.

"Oh, we bonded over unicorns at the game, so…" She gave a little shoulder shrug as if this was a completely normal occurrence and also explained a deep connection. Jack was rather

ALEXANDRA KILEY

smitten with this playful family dynamic, the way she took the pressure off him.

"Fast friends," Neil said.

Jack pulled out a chair for Brooke at the head of the table and she covered his hand with hers as she moved to sit down, smiling up at him as if to say, *See how well it's going?*

And it was. His family was warm and welcoming to strangers from all over the world. Jack had never been particularly worried about this meeting, but he hadn't expected a view of a future rolling out in front of him, one where he could imagine Brooke joining these Saturday lunches and charming his family, making these gatherings as lovely for him as he suspected they were for everyone else.

Reid passed a steaming mug to Jack, tipping it until the angled plane of brown liquid met the rim. Jack's hands flew up to catch the scalding liquid and he winced against a burn that never came.

Reid righted the mug at the last minute. "Dinna fash," he said with a devious smile and handed the mug steadily to Brooke.

She laughed, caught the annoyed look on Jack's face, and immediately turned it into an unconvincing cough that set off Neil's booming laughter.

"Ye wee bawbag," Jack said to his brother.

Gemma settled in her seat with the mauve pink cushion, her hands curled around her mug, looking completely unfazed after a life of raising three boys. "So, Brooke. What are your plans after graduation?"

Brooke sat up straighter, her hands clasped together in her lap. "I want to be a writer. I have a million ideas and so many half-started projects."

A sting of fear hit Jack in the chest—that his parents might dismiss her ambition or call her passion a hobby. "She's a fantastic writer," he said, sending his parents behave-yourselves looks, warning them not to undermine Brooke's confidence or excitement. But they were looking at her how he did, with full attention and adoration.

"It's my dream to visit my book in a bookshop one day. Walking into Waterstones and seeing 'Brooke Sinclair' on the cover." She fanned her hand out in front of her as if she was imagining it.

Neil made a quiet snapping sound with his fingers, gazing into the corner of the room, thinking. "Who's the literary agent we just met on that Highland tour…?"

"Ah, Marty Hendricks?" Reid answered.

"Aye. We'd be happy to connect you."

"Really?" Brooke damn near bounced in her chair. "That'd be amazing. Thank you."

Jack squeezed her knee under the table, loving that his parents were being so supportive.

"And how're classes going for you?" Neil asked Jack.

His instinct was to give as little detail as possible, to skate over the high points until talk turned to something else. But their reaction to Brooke's dreams made Jack wonder if he'd overexaggerated their perceptions or maybe, like she'd said on that day in the locker room, they'd support his dreams, too.

Perhaps it was the high of this day going even better than he'd imagined, of being here with Brooke as she slipped her hand into his, but suddenly he felt brave enough to tell them the truth.

"Fantastic. And I've made some decisions about the spring. I'm planning to pursue photography."

Brooke squeezed Jack's hand as Neil's face split into a grin, and a joy Jack hadn't dared to wish for rocketed through him.

"That's wonderful," Neil said. "We need more photos for the website. The Facebook is really taking off. You could take photos on the tours…"

Jack clenched his eyes against the frustration welling inside him. He wanted to accept the praise, to take it to heart. But it only mattered to his dad as it related to the business. His skill and passion only mattered if it served the greater good. "No, not for The Heart. For *me*. As my job."

Neil's face fell, a look of exhaustion flickering across his features. It was a look so familiar to Jack, but still had the power to knock his feet out from under him. Neil took a long drink of tea, his mustache disappearing inside the cup. The table went silent and Jack's heart beat like a moth trapped under glass.

"Jack, you belong at The Heart. Ideally as a guide—"

"I don't want to be a guide." Maybe he'd never come right out and said it before, but they should've *known* by now. They should've *seen* him.

Reid cleared his throat like he was uncomfortable. *Christ*, what had Jack been thinking bringing this up? This wasn't what this day was about; he was wrecking a perfectly pleasant afternoon. He wanted to call back the words, let his mom tell embarrassing stories from childhood that made Brooke laugh, not sit stiffly in her chair like she was trying to figure out the best escape route from the room.

Gemma leaned across the table and placed her hand on Jack's arm. "Then in some other role."

Neil looked between Jack and Gemma, his eyebrows furrowed. "This is the entire reason you went to business school." He had the decency not to mention who was funding said degree. Jack's heart hammered in his ears. "For stability for you *and* The Heart. There's no security in photography."

Gemma leaned back in her seat, her thumbnail tapping against the ceramic handle of her mug. "We only want what's best for you, dear."

Jack swallowed past the thickness in his throat. He should end this conversation. Tell them they'd talk later or agree to their visions for his future, but he needed them to listen. Needed them to *hear* him. "*This* is best for me."

He longed for the reassurance of Brooke's smile but was too afraid to find pity or disappointment on her face instead.

Neil ran his fingers over his mustache. "Why is this different from the other times? When you wanted to skip uni to start a rock band or do a farm-stay in Brazil?"

Embarrassment flared through Jack, heat rising through his chest and cheeks. Not only for the lack of faith his dad had in him, and his clearly low opinion of Jack's decision-making skills—his seriousness—but also that he'd brought Brooke here to witness it. To see his parents' disappointment firsthand. To hear those hard truths laid bare.

His dad wasn't wrong about Jack in the past, but he'd changed. He *knew* now.

"Brooke," Reid interrupted in an overly loud voice. "Do you want a tour of the house?" Jack was shocked at Reid's ability to read the room, but profoundly grateful. "Fairly certain I still know where Jack's box of trinkets he'd never want you to see is hidden," he said. "Lots of embarrassing secrets."

That was right here, Jack thought. *Laid out on the kitchen table.*

When Brooke's eyes cut to Jack, asking if she wanted him to stay or go, he gestured for her to follow Reid and listened to their footsteps heading up the stairs, louder than his heartbeat in his ears.

"I didn't want to mention this…especially in front of your brothers…" Neil's eyes cut to Gemma and she gave him an encouraging nod. "The Heart is in a wee bit of a downturn—that damn McRobbie's and their hairy coo van…" Neil let out a weary sigh. "You're clever with the books and damn creative. We need you to work your magic on the accounting side, on the *internet*."

Shite. That was the last thing Jack wanted to hear. If his family needed him, if the business was in trouble, could he really walk away? Could he really be that selfish?

Neil ran a hand over his mustache. "Whatever happened to good old word of mouth?" he muttered. "I despise the internet."

Gemma patted his arm.

"Take your photos, Jack. No one's saying you can't. But do them for The Heart and for a hobby. The path is so clear. The Heart is where you fit. We need you."

He'd longed to hear those words for so long, but he knew they weren't true. He didn't fit here at all.

The doorbell rang and Jack let out a sigh of relief that Logan had arrived to steal the attention and lighten the mood. Maybe his mum would pack him and Brooke a take-away lunch and they could escape this hell he'd plunged them into.

Footsteps sounded down the hallway, and Jack froze when it wasn't Logan who walked into the kitchen.

It was Mhairi.

She couldn't know Brooke was here. But he couldn't exactly rush upstairs and hide her in his childhood room, either. *Fuck*.

Mhairi wrapped Gemma in a hug, her pale purple sleeves enveloping her sister, and then she was there, reaching for Jack. Over her shoulder, Reid appeared and Jack's vision went a little blurry as Brooke trailed in behind him.

Mhairi pulled back and must've caught his look because she turned around to see who he was staring at—Brooke, gone completely white, her eyes wild.

"Hello, Brooke," she said evenly before turning around to give Jack a hard look that shriveled his stomach.

"How do you two know each other?" Gemma asked, sounding more confused than delighted, as if she knew her sister well enough to read into Mhairi's neutral tone.

When Brooke stood there without blinking, Mhairi said, "Brooke is in my creative writing class."

"Oh…" Gemma said, her eyes skating to Jack. His mum always told him when Mhairi was joining. He hadn't even considered the risk. He could tell she wanted to pry. Wanted to question how they knew each other, ask what exactly was happening here.

His breathing went sideways. "Shall we sit?" Jack said, pulling out a chair for Brooke.

They settled in around the table and he tried to catch Brooke's eye, but she was looking away from him like her life depended on it. He didn't want her to feel like she was on her own here. He reached for her hand under the table but she pulled away, sitting up even straighter.

Jack's mind thrashed around, not sure what to even do right now or how they could exit immediately. Not that it would matter; the damage was done.

The idea of having it out with Neil was suddenly the least of Jack's worries.

The lunch passed in an uncomfortably stilted conversation. The second his dad put his fork down, Jack was there, clearing plates. Mhairi followed him into the kitchen and he filled the sink, slipping his hands into the soapy water as she leaned against the counter. He chanced looking at her and her gaze was sharp.

"Is she your student?"

"She's in the main class, but I'm not her TA."

Mhairi breathed out heavily. "Still. Have you disclosed your relationship?"

"No."

"I'm assuming you know, but this creates a great deal of trouble for everyone."

Jack let out a heavy breath, some mix of guilt and relief that one person in his professional life knew and wouldn't hurt them with the knowledge. "I do know. But she doesn't want to. There's so much stigma associated with this relationship." He sank his hands back into the water, warming the chill he felt across his whole body.

Mhairi nodded. "The world is still unfair. But regardless,

you're endangering both your futures carrying on like this. You're in a position of power. You need to protect yourself."

"Not at her expense. I wouldn't do that to her."

"Then do it *for* her. She's on the short list for my fellowship. I can't in good conscience select her knowing you two have a relationship the administration isn't aware of." Her voice was hard, brooked no discussion.

They stood in silence as Jack scrubbed a plate to a pristine shine, soap sliding between his fingers. He couldn't endanger Brooke's dreams—not for the selfish need to be with her. But he couldn't walk away, either. They hadn't even made it through this term yet. The idea of another six months without touching Brooke—especially knowing how it felt to be with her—would be impossible. Telling the administration—it was just a note in a folder in an office somewhere. They didn't need to go out in public together. He didn't need to sit with her in the library or wrap his arms around her in the coffee line.

Mhairi sighed and rested a hand on his shoulder. "This wasn't what I meant when I told you to go after what you wanted."

Jack snorted without humor. "Believe me, it was not in the plan."

"These things never are." She squeezed his shoulder. "Do the right thing, Jack. I can give you two weeks, and then I'm ethically bound to disclose this."

34

NOW

Jack pushed a jade green fern out of his way, turning and holding it back so it wouldn't snap into Brooke's face. She reached for it, her fingers warm where she touched his hand, her eyes locked on his. "Thanks."

He should be taking photos, but he couldn't concentrate on composition when his head was so full of Brooke. She'd been looking at him like that all day. He knew that look—it used to pass between them all the time.

He could remember the exact temperature his body would heat to in the middle of class when she'd turn those sky-blue eyes his way, darkened to the hazy gray of a storm on the horizon. And he knew exactly what that storm meant. It meant Brooke laid out on his bed, his mouth on every inch of her skin. Somewhere along the trail her fuck-you eyes had turned to fuck-me eyes and *Christ* he wanted to oblige.

Jack whipped back around, his heartbeat wild, and kept walking toward the secluded cabin his friend had offered when they'd been in search of accommodations the night of the storm. No Nat and Cat, no Australian backpackers. They'd left everyone with big goodbye hugs and exchanged emails as they each planned to finish the trail on separate routes.

And now he and Brooke were alone, and he had no idea how he was going to handle the night with her looking at him like that. He couldn't do a trail hookup, couldn't survive touching her only to lose her again.

Although, Jack was beginning to think that was only the half of it—that he couldn't survive her walking away at the end of the trail no matter what passed between them. But the way she'd kissed him in the bothy gave him all sorts of ideas about exactly what that could mean.

He wanted her, of course, had been burning up with her so close yet just out of his reach. But it wasn't only the physical release he craved; it was what it would mean: forgiveness, a path forward. A future. His hopes were rampant, but he could tell Brooke needed time and he wouldn't do anything to make her feel pressured.

The pace was too fast, his knee was throbbing, but he couldn't stand the anticipation. Jack trudged down the narrow dirt path, trying to notice the twittering birdsong or the dimming daylight or the low clouds heralding rain.

The cabin came into view, tucked into trees on the rise of a hill like a hideaway. When Jack reached it and opened the door, he cursed under his breath. Inside was even more romantic than he'd pictured. A bookshelf towered against the back wall, round lanterns on the top. A small pine table and low chairs with blankets thrown over the backs sat in the corner, an old fireplace with a black stovepipe behind them.

In the front of the room was an enormous white bathtub on a raised platform, looking out the picture window to the rolling green hills and the small blue loch below.

But Jack barely took in these details, because all his attention was on the king bed tucked under the enormous skylight. The white comforter was covered with a pearly blanket at the foot and a mountain of pillows at the head. He pictured walking Brooke backward, swiping away the pillows, laying her down.

There might as well have been rose petals and towels folded into swans on the bed. Jack scrubbed a hand over his face. He could not be having thoughts like that. So what if there was only one bed here? It was significantly larger than the bothy and certainly bigger than Brooke's tent. They'd feel like they were a continent apart.

But it wouldn't matter. He'd still feel every shift as she slept, every sigh, every breath.

If the bed didn't look so damn delightful and his bones didn't ache so much, he'd consider taking her tent and sleeping outside, away from this torture.

Brooke dropped her pack with a groan and leaned it against the exposed log wall. "Do you mind if I rinse off?" she asked. Jack took in the glass shower. *Christ.* There couldn't even be a shower curtain? Forget all-inclusive couples retreats in Mallorca; this place screamed intimacy and he struggled to drown out the call.

"I'll get the fire going," he said, crossing the room and crouching in front of the wicker basket of wood, his knees popping like fucking glow sticks. "And then I might use the tub to soak my knee. We'll just… We'll face away from each other." His voice was more than a little coarse. Jesus, he wasn't going to make it through the night.

"Okay," Brooke said, a lightness in her tone that sounded an awful lot like amusement.

Jack got the fire roaring in the old fireplace, the reflection of the flames licking up the sides of the glass windows. Outside, the daylight was fading into the muted glow he'd gotten used to. The clouds turned shades of tangerine and candy-floss pink and cast a matching stain across the light pine floorboards and the white of the bed.

The steam of Brooke's shower was already floating in the air but he didn't need anything more than the sound of running water to confirm her whereabouts. Keeping his eyes resolutely on the ground, he crossed to the tub and turned the water on.

Christ, must it really be a glass shower? Brooke would be turned away from him—he knew that—but the idea of undressing for the bath with her eyes on him made him unbearably hard. He tugged his shirt and undershirt off in one go, feeling a prickle of her attention as if it clung to the stretch of his back muscles. He pulled off his socks and then unbuttoned his hiking trousers, letting them fall from his hips before tugging down his boxer briefs, picturing her in the shower, water flowing across her skin, watching him strip naked before her.

He climbed into the bath, hissing at the heat and sinking in slowly. The tub was easily big enough for two and Jack shut out the mental image of Brooke joining him. When he looked out the window into the valley below the house, the swaying grasses, the heather, and the loch at the bottom of the hill, he could make out a blurry outline of Brooke's movements in the reflection. Even though he shouldn't, it didn't stop him from pleading with the sky to darken, to turn the window opaque.

Jack ran his hands over his face, the hot water soothing. He tipped backward, his shoulders hitting the cool porcelain, and he slipped below the surface of the water. When he came back up, he pushed his hair out of his face and rested his elbows on the edges of the tub.

The shower shut off and Jack stopped breathing. The door creaked as it opened and closed and he pictured Brooke wrapping herself in a towel. He tracked the pad of her footsteps, sure the sound was getting closer and also sure that was only his hopes carrying him away.

But then Brooke stood in front of him, water skimming down her calves, the material of the white towel hitting at midthigh, cinched at the top around the round slope of her breasts, hair dripping. The setting sunlight clung to her skin. She fairly glowed.

Jack looked up into Brooke's eyes and her pupils were blown wide.

"Are you still offering that shoulder massage?"

35

NOW

Brooke's skin cooled from the shower while she stood at the side of the tub, dripping wet. Jack had frozen at her question, his strong fingers gripping the edge of the tub. As if shaking himself, he moved. "Of course," he said as he lifted from the bath, triceps flexing, water skimming over his chest and down the triangular rift below his pecs.

But she didn't want him to get out. She wanted to go all-in.

She'd held him at arm's length to protect herself, but there was a cost to keeping safe, to not experiencing life, to holding back. And it felt too high now.

She dropped her towel and Jack sank back into the water on a heavy breath, water rolling to the sides and back again.

"Brooke," he whispered. Her heartbeat fluttered wildly as he drank his fill of her, his gaze lingering on her hips and breasts before meeting her eyes. "You're even more beautiful than I remember."

Brooke took the compliment, buried it like a piece of stolen treasure. Jack had always made her feel cherished in a way no one else ever could. She was done holding back, done hiding.

He took her hand and held her waist as she stepped into the tub, his rough palm spanning her hip, his heat flowing into her skin. She turned her back to him and sank into the water. His legs bracketed hers, coarse hair against her outer thighs, water lapping at her breasts, an ache flaring deep in her core.

Jack's strong fingers moved to her shoulders, kneading her sore muscles. But more than soothing backpack fatigue, a deep relief swept through her at the feel of his hands on her again—intentional and purposeful. Her body came alive, lighting up in all the places he touched. Chills danced across Brooke's shoulders and down her arms, disappearing into the heat of the water. With a finger, he swept her wet hair over one shoulder, his thumbs traveling up her neck.

Brooke let out a whimper and Jack groaned in response. "Those sounds haunt my dreams."

She'd dreamed of him, too. So many times. Woke reaching for him, still feeling his caress—gentle like a winter daybreak, a tingle across her skin. She could never shake his memory on those days, the missing, the wondering what he was doing now.

"I know a thing or two about that." Brooke ran her palms over his thighs and Jack's fingers stilled a moment before they resumed their movements, his breath brushing against her shoulder. She wanted him to nuzzle against her the way he used to, find that spot below her ear that'd always felt like assurance and refuge.

His fingertips reached her collarbone and she willed his hands to slip below the water, the ache between her legs intensifying. The need for him to touch her everywhere overwhelmed her senses, but he kept his caress gentle.

The firelight flickered across the room and Brooke slipped her feet to the end of the tub, leaning back against him. His dick was hard between them, his chest hair tickling her back. But instead of pulling her tight, his hands moved to her arms, sliding up and down, the backs of his fingers barely brushing the curve of her breasts.

Brooke dropped her head to Jack's shoulder, arching her back so her breasts crested the top of the water, her nipples hard peaks in the fading pink daylight. Jack sucked in a breath next to her ear, but the whisper of his hands didn't move to where she wanted him. Like he was taking her request for a massage literally. Like stepping naked into his bath wasn't a clear enough indicator for what she wanted.

Like he was still holding back until she made it clear she wasn't anymore.

She tilted her face to see him. His wet hair was slicked back, his jaw clenched, his eyes the dark brown of autumn's last leaves. The heat in his gaze chased away the chill of the air not yet warmed by the fire.

She cupped his jaw, the grown-in stubble rasping against her palm, and he cradled her face, his thumb stroking her cheek. He tipped his face down, barely brushing his bottom lip against hers. He kissed the edge of her mouth and she breathed out in a rush. The first time he'd kissed her like this in a dark club had been tentative. But this gentle stroke of his tongue, this barely-there caress, was a reminder of all the love and desire they'd felt back then, a promise in the subtle press of lips.

She wasn't changing her mind or pulling away. She could let the past go if it meant a chance for a future she'd never stopped wanting.

A light rain pitter-pattered above them on the glass ceiling, the hazy light caressing her skin the way Jack's hands did. They skimmed up her side, traced the curve of her breasts until she ached for him.

With his cheek pressed against her temple, the rasp of his stubble against her ear, they both watched as he cupped her breasts, finally rolling her nipples between his fingers. She whimpered again and Jack's groan rumbled through her and then his mouth was on her neck. She reached behind her to slip her fingers into his hair to keep him there.

One large hand slipped below the water, skimmed across her belly, dipped between her legs. Jack massaged circles on her inner thigh, so close to where she wanted him, but not close enough.

"*Please,*" she whined, arching her back.

She grabbed the side of the tub and tried to twist in his arms, but Jack's other hand closed over hers, pinning her fingers against the rim. "Not yet." He squeezed his hand over hers in a silent command to stay. "Isn't the anticipation the best part?"

"No." It'd been seven years since she'd felt this kind of connection with someone. "I'm tired of waiting."

He laughed under his breath and his hand dropped from the edge of the tub, banding against her rib cage and pulling her back against his dick. "Always so impatient," he whispered before gently biting her earlobe and squeezing her thigh. Jack had never been fumbling, but he was more in control of his movements now—more in control of her—and the small shift in power drove her wild.

She rocked her hips against him, and he moved his thumb to draw circles against her.

"God, that's perfect."

"I remember," Jack said against her shoulder. "All of it." She remembered, too. The rush, the exhilaration, her hair blowing in the wind, that carefree smile, the freedom that'd been so damn alluring, uninhibited and real.

"You're fucking mesmerizing," he said as he kissed up her neck. "And enticing." He pressed his lips to that spot below her ear he used to tuck his nose against when they fell asleep and it sent shock waves through her—a fluttery echo around her heart and an insistent pulse between her legs. "And excruciating."

"Excruciating?"

Jack rolled his hips, his dick pushing against her back. "Excruciating," he whispered in her ear. "Walking behind you…" He hooked a hand under her knee and pulled it up, slid his palm down her thigh. "Watching your hips sway…" He gripped her hip and tugged her tighter against him. Her legs fell open and his skilled fingers dipped inside. "You've been driving me out of my mind, Brooke."

Jack increased the pace, his fingers sliding deeper, and Brooke gripped the hard muscles of his thigh on a moan.

Her entire body was on fire, from the hot water and the heat of Jack behind her, to the intensity building between her legs. She chased her orgasm, feeling the pressure build and build inside her. She almost didn't want to reach for it, didn't want this to end.

Jack slipped his nose behind her ear, hummed against her skin, and she nearly lost it from the familiarity and the comfort, the relief at returning to this place she'd worried couldn't exist for them anymore.

As much as her view was stunning—the orange glow of the fireplace flickering over the bookshelf, the blue twilight, the rain trickling over the windows and glass roof and blurring the outside world—the view of Jack's smile was always better.

She needed to see him, to hold him, to press their foreheads together. "I need you."

Brooke sat up, grabbing the edge of the tub to turn to face Jack, but her fingers slipped on the slick surface and she fell, water sloshing over the edge. Her hands plunged under the water to brace herself, one landing high on Jack's thigh. He hissed, his knees coming up beside her, and grabbed her waist to stop her from wrecking the mood completely.

She laughed self-consciously as she turned to face him. "So much for being sexy."

Jack's lips tipped up on one side, that little smile line appearing in his cheek. His hands circled her waist and drew her closer, helping her balance while she moved to straddle him.

He shifted under her, bringing his legs up at the same time his hands slid to her knees and tugged. She fell forward, water sloshing, the cut of his hips pressing against her inner thighs. She sucked in a breath at the feel of his dick pressed against where she ached for him.

"Still very sexy," he said on a quiet breath. His eyes were like the fairy pools, vast and endlessly deep. Like if she fell into them, she'd never come out again—and she was very ready to fall.

"Hi," she said.

Jack's eyes turned even softer as he tipped his forehead against hers, going out of focus. "Hi," he said against her lips.

His hands skated from her knees to her hips, and his touch felt soft and silky against her water-warmed skin. Brooke sank her fingers into his wet hair and rocked her hips against him. One large hand settled on her lower back, stilling her.

"Fuck," he said, his head dropping to her shoulder. "I don't have a condom."

"I have an IUD and I got tested recently. All negative."

"I've been tested, too. I can show you the results—"

"I trust you."

Jack tipped his mouth against her neck, a quiet *mmm* falling from his lips before he was pressing them to hers, like maybe that's all he'd wanted to hear from her. Something that had been so hard to give him felt effortless now.

Brooke ran her hands over his shoulders, down over the slope of his pecs. She rose up on her knees to take him, sinking slowly, watching the way Jack's head tipped back against the edge of the tub, throat working, eyelids heavy. His lips parted, fingers tightening on her hips.

Jack growled in the back of his throat as Brooke rolled her hips to take more of him. He cupped her jaw, brought her mouth down to his, kissed and licked and hummed against her lips.

"I missed you, B," he said. "Not just like this."

"I missed you, too." She'd spent so many lonely nights hating him, loving him, regretting him, but most of all, longing for what they'd had. What they'd somehow managed to recover.

They made love slowly, the water rolling in quiet waves around them, the rain pattering on the glass above. She banded her arms around his shoulders, clung to him, rocked against him as the pressure built inside her.

Brooke came apart, stars behind her eyes, and Jack followed, his hand twisting into her hair and he shuddered below her. She snuggled against his chest, never wanting to leave the intimacy of this moment. Jack brushed her hair away from her shoulders, ran the pads of his fingers lightly over her back, squeezed her tight.

They stayed there, twined together until the water turned cold and goose bumps pebbled her arms. Jack kissed along her jaw and shifted beneath her. "Let's go to bed."

They climbed from the water and Jack bundled her in a plush white towel before wrapping another around his waist. "I'd carry you to bed if it weren't for my knee."

Brooke buried her smile against his throat, placed kisses along his hot skin. "We're taking enough risks on this trip."

36

NOW

Jack sprawled across the big white bed in the cabin, like he could sink into it and never get up. After Brooke had found dried mix and made something resembling pancakes, she sat cross-legged in the oversize bed, clutching her notebook to her chest. "Want to read my story?"

Jack's heart nearly tumbled from his chest. "Badly." He sat up and mirrored her pose, their knees touching. He took the notebook from her gently, knowing this was a precious and delicate thing. Not only was he infinitely proud of her for writing her own stories again, but he was also honored that she'd trust him with her words after everything that'd happened. It was a gesture he didn't take lightly.

"I remember this loopy handwriting," he said with a wide grin, remembering the way it felt to be privy to her innermost thoughts, to be the first one to read her work.

He started reading, immediately distracted by the intensity of her gaze on him. She pulled the sleeves of her teal fleece over her knuckles and tipped her chin into the collar while she watched his face for any sign of reaction.

"Stop it, you're making me nervous."

"Read faster, you're making *me* nervous."

"Shush," he told her and went back to her notebook.

He slipped a finger underneath the pages before he was ready to turn them, his thumb absentmindedly flexing over the blue lines along the edge. When he did turn pages, he did it reverently, slipping each one carefully around the spiral binding.

He smiled at the description of the wind as a circus—riding around on a unicycle, honking horns, and generally making a ruckus about nothing at all—and Brooke leaned over to see what he was reading. He gave her a look meant for a naughty child and pulled the notebook away.

Brooke took a deep breath and held it in puffed cheeks. By the time Jack finished and laid the notebook on his knee, she let out the breath in a rush and fell back onto the pillows. "Okay, tell me. But don't hit me while I'm down."

"For the record, you knocked your own self down."

She sat up with a smile and then bounced in place, impatient for him to continue.

"It's amazing. The setting is stunning, but the main character… I can feel her pain and longing. It's wonderfully drawn," he said truthfully. Brooke was incredibly talented. Even this new chapter had so much more movement and depth than the stories he'd read of hers in uni.

"It's just a start."

"Don't diminish it. Starting is the hardest part. And starting *again*…even harder." He hadn't meant to repeat the words she'd told him when he first had a photo credit, but Brooke's eyes turned soft.

"Yeah. It is," she agreed, and that look made him think she meant about starting things with him, too. It tugged the breath from his chest.

He wanted her to know how much he cherished her words,

wanted to mark this occasion. Since he didn't have chocolate cake or champagne, he did the next best thing.

He got out of bed and found his camera, coming back and tugging off the lens cap. He stood at the edge of the bed and zoomed in on her notebook.

"Gonna put that up on your refrigerator with a little ABC magnet?"

He captured Brooke's teasing smile and the little eye roll when she noticed his change in subject. "It's art. I'm putting it in a gilded frame. I remember your big dreams." Would do anything to help her reach them.

He met her eye over the top of the viewfinder and watched hers go wide and weepy. He clicked the button to capture that, too, as Brooke tugged at his boxer briefs and yanked him back onto the bed. "Careful of the equipment," he teased, setting his camera on the nightstand with his good knee braced on the mattress.

Brooke's hair curved around her face, falling from her messy bun. Shorts capped her strong thighs where she sat cross-legged and her wooly white socks were pulled halfway up her calves. She held herself still, her back straight, and drew in a deep breath. "You make me feel so good about myself. Like you genuinely believe in me—"

"I do." She was the most creative and driven and thoughtful person he'd ever known.

Brooke ran the backs of her fingers against the stubble on Jack's cheeks. "It makes me believe in me, too. When we get back to town, I'm going to turn down the ghostwriting job. I want to give my own work a chance."

Jack sank onto the bed, his heart swelling at her courage. At the bet she was placing on herself.

"And I want to give *this* a chance, too," she said, sliding her hand into his.

Dizzying relief flooded Jack's head. "That's good news because I've been planning to date the hell out of you. It's been on my bucket list for nearly a decade. See the northern lights. Photograph the Grand Canyon. Date Brooke Sinclair."

Her eyes lit up like a summer sky. "You wanna go steady? I've still got my letterman jacket. You'd look great in navy blue."

"I want to be your lover and your partner and your best friend."

Her eyes went misty when they reached his and she cupped his jaw, ran her thumb over his bottom lip. "Deal."

He pulled Brooke into his lap and she wrapped her arms around his neck. Kissing her felt brand-new and just the same and so bloody perfect. Their lips pressed together and held. He breathed her in, clung to the stillness and peace he felt in her embrace.

He slid his hands up and down her thighs and then rubbed circles into the arch of her foot. She moaned a deep and satisfied sound.

"Seriously? You did *not* make that sound last night. I'm offended."

Brooke bit her lip but didn't restrain her smile in the least. "You're going to have to try harder to please me."

He tickled the bottom of her foot and she yelped and pushed backward off him, landing on her back. Pinning her flailing ankle, Jack leaned over her, kissed across her stomach, over her chest, and up the column of her throat. "I will dedicate my life to it."

Her hands slid into his hair, tipping him back to look at her, her eyes serious. "It's off to a good start."

37

THEN

Brooke sat in the hallway of the centuries-old dean of English building. She didn't actually know how old it was, but the draftiness sure fit the Victorian era she conjured. Or maybe all the blood had simply exited her extremities, taking up residence in her stomach to give herself an ulcer. Good thing she wasn't going into medicine—that was probably not how things worked.

Brooke hugged herself tighter, crossing her legs and generally trying to shrink as much as possible. She'd never been called into a principal's office before, and had feared that fate more than most things. On second thought, her high school principal was a kind old man who ended every morning announcement with, "Make it a great day or not, the choice is yours," which everyone mockingly quoted to each other throughout the day.

Why was she even thinking of that? Probably because it was an easier thing for her brain to fixate on besides the reason she *had* been called in here. Her grades had absolutely dipped this term, but it wasn't like she was failing anything, even though that C from Mhairi had felt just as bad. The only possibility was because someone had told them about Jack.

Chels would take that information to her grave. Kieran was reliably oblivious. But Rohan…they'd put him in a terrible position. He might've felt like he'd had to. And Mhairi? Brooke hadn't seen her since lunch at the Sutherland's the previous weekend, but their parting hadn't been exactly warm. Mhairi was a professor; she absolutely could've been compelled to notify the administration.

Brooke hated the uncertainty swirling in her stomach. She pulled out her phone and texted Jack, her fingers shaky.

Brooke: Got called into the dean's office. Freaking out.

She pushed some of the stray strands of hair that'd fallen from her ponytail back behind her ears. She could barely breathe, anxiety sending out tendrils of frost through her chest. Maybe she would only get a slap on the wrist, but it might be like a bee sting allergy—you didn't know if it was deadly until it happened.

The door to the dean's office opened and she about jumped out of her chair, but froze when Jack emerged. He barely had time to send her a pleading look before Dean Campbell ushered him down another hallway and turned to her. His red sweater vest was wrinkled, his wire glasses perched low on his nose as he said, "Ms. Sinclair," with a stern clip. Brooke's stomach curled in farther toward her spine.

She stepped into his office, cluttered with books and dust, and took the seat he pointed to. Dean Campbell closed the door firmly behind her and resettled in the chair behind his sprawling mahogany desk.

"We understand you've engaged in a relationship outside the boundaries of the code of conduct."

Brooke tensed, not knowing if she should confirm or deny

it. Jack had just been in here, so they clearly knew something. Was this the moment to plead the Fifth and call a lawyer? Her brain supplied the completely unnecessary information that she was in the UK and therefore there was no Fifth to plead.

"Uh…" she said stupidly, eyes darting around the room to the books in the shelves and the framed diplomas behind the desk, all while her chest threatened to rupture.

Rohan or Mhairi might have divulged their secret. But it could've been so many other people. God, she and Jack had been so irresponsible. So *conspicuous*. She had not refrained from making eyes at him in class one single time. She always lingered as the students filed out. Brooke and Jack had run all over Edinburgh that night taking pictures and had basically hooked up on the dance floor of the Caves. She mentally groaned as her list grew longer by the second. They'd been so fucking reckless.

"Jack came forward—"

"He *what*?" Her voice came out two octaves too high while her stomach sank even lower. *Jack.* Jack had told them—even when he'd promised her he wouldn't.

Her mind spun with *How could he?*, but it wasn't a leap at all.

Of course he had. Jack had his own ass to cover. He cared about this job and finishing his master's, and he was jeopardizing that by having a secret affair with a student. She was such a fool.

"We need you to make an official statement about the nature of this relationship. If you feel more comfortable telling a woman, I completely understand. If this was in any way *untoward*…" the dean trailed off, his eyes flicking around the room. This stoic boulder of an ancient man was exceedingly uncomfortable. It made her want to giggle. Or throw up. She was distinctly lightheaded.

Brooke took a deep breath and tried to focus. "No, there was nothing untoward. It was completely consensual. In fact, I pursued him." She wasn't entirely sure why she was defending

Jack in this moment when she was so fucking pissed at him, but he'd never set a foot out of line, had never taken advantage.

The dean visibly relaxed, his shoulders dropping.

Oh. This was all about image. About a harassment suit she wouldn't be filing. The anxious energy drained out of her.

Of course that's what the school would care about. She could make a statement, they'd have it all on record, and everyone could go on with their business.

"I'm glad to hear that."

"So, are we good here?" Brooke asked, already grabbing the strap of her bag, ready to get the hell out of this stodgy old room.

"Unfortunately not." Brooke sank back into the chair, fear clawing its way to the surface again. "There remains the issue of bias."

"Bias?" The angry look on Rohan's face the day he'd caught Brooke and Jack together flashed through her mind.

"On Mr. Sutherland's part."

Her relief that they hadn't implicated Rohan was short-lived. "Jack's not even my TA."

"Be that as it may, we cannot condone this type of relationship for the very reason that it is impossible to parse. You have the highest marks in the class, which is not condemning in and of itself, but it certainly raises questions."

Brooke felt heat rise in her chest. "Is there some reason it would be shocking for me to have the highest grade in the class?"

She could tell she was going off the rails. That the best course of action in this meeting was to remain calm, to tell the truth and stop casting doubt on the relationship. Defensiveness wasn't the way to go, but damn him, calling her intentions into question and insinuating she needed to sleep her way to the top. It got her all riled up.

The dean shifted in his seat. "Of course not, Ms. Sinclair, but there is no way for the administration to uncover how much extra aid you received outside of recitations and office hours, or how much information was provided to you before examinations that your peers did not receive."

She raised her hands, palms out. "That's not what happened here. Jack and I never talked about class. We just…" *Fell in love* was the end of that sentence, but it didn't seem right for the dean of English Department to be the first one to hear of it. "We care about each other. There were no ulterior motives."

"I am not intending to make accusations. I cannot prove our concerns one way or another." Dean Campbell settled his hands over his belly. "As such, you will be required to retake the class. We will allow you to drop it without the usual penalties because of the extenuating circumstances."

The world shrunk to the size of the dean's bald, round head and the immovable expression she found there.

"Then I won't have enough credits to graduate on time. I'm a candidate for a very prestigious writing fellowship this summer. I may never get an opportunity like that again."

"I'm afraid that part is out of my hands. The course will be available again next fall."

Brooke shook her head, her lips dry, her breath coming too fast. "I'm on a scholarship. If I drop a class, I won't be a full-time student and I'll lose my financial aid."

"I do apologize for that, Ms. Sinclair, but we must maintain the integrity of the university."

38

NOW

The last day on the trail was an easy walk through val-
leys and along long slips of lakes. Brooke scrambled down a
rocky outcropping to meet the black rocks ringing the shore
alongside a steep mountain. They crossed the washed-out path,
hopping along the rocks, and she threw her arms out for balance. She heard the shutter snap and turned to glare at Jack over
her shoulder. Brooke was met with his black camera blocking
out his face, only his wide smile visible beneath. When she
flipped him off, the shutter snapped again.

Ruins dotted the countryside as they went up the pass. Water
still trickled down in rivulets from the rain the night before.
Mud clumped up on her boots, but even with her heavy pack,
she felt light.

As they made it over the pass, a wide valley stretched below
them with three peaks standing tall and rounded on the far side.
Sheep grazed along the path and tiny white flowers bloomed
across the land. In the distance, the white houses of civilization dotted the hills, following the thin gray line of the road
into Broadford.

The end of the trail.

A weathered wooden sign, gray and splintering, marked the distance they had left: 2.2 km. Jack took her hand and tugged, pulling her against him and wrapping her up in a hug, mountains and the jewel-toned green of the landscape spreading out in a panorama.

"We made it," he said, his voice heavy with the double meaning and light with hope.

Against all odds, they had.

Brooke felt like a different person on this side of the trail. Forged by wind and rain, despair and courage, hope and love. And she also felt brave and fearless like she had back then. Like she was getting her happy ending after all.

Jack lifted his camera, but instead of turning it to the gray slope of the mountains and the dusty blue of the sky, he turned it around, looping his arm under her pack. "Let's mark the occasion, aye?"

She slipped into the crook of his shoulder, taking comfort in his solidness, and tilted her smile to the lens.

They'd found their way back.

The gentle path into Broadford was a flat and grassy walk over what used to be a railway line servicing the marble quarries. They crossed through a gate onto the paved street, and back into town.

The sheer commotion and noise of the cars driving past, even in a relatively small town, was startling. It'd been so quiet lately, just the two of them, that even the street traffic felt intrusive.

Jack held his hands above his head and clapped hers like they'd finished a soccer match. "This is kind of anticlimactic."

"There should've been balloons."

"Och, should've commissioned you a trophy," he said with a smirk.

She shook her head. "Such an oversight."

A truck rushed by, drowning out her words and stirring up dried leaves, mixing into the air with the smell of diesel.

Maybe she'd pictured a statue marking the end of the trail, or at the very least a welcoming party. Instead, they were met with a crossroads—one way back to Portree and one way forward, over the Skye Bridge to the mainland.

What lay ahead was exhilarating and terrifying—unknown. It was one thing to put her own story into a notebook. Another to take it seriously. To find the time and the courage to turn it into something real. But she wanted it in a way she'd been scared she'd never feel again.

Mhairi's book needed so much work in a short amount of time and Brooke could feel the anxiety spinning back up inside her. But also this excitement to call Mhairi, to tell her all about the trail and her ideas. To hear that Mhairi was proud of her for taking this chance, for finally understanding the heart of her story.

And after that, Brooke could share new pages with Mhairi like she had in uni, only this time it wouldn't be for a grade; it would be one step closer to her dream.

"I should check in at home," Jack said.

"Okay. I'm going to call Mhairi." Brooke dropped her pack, rummaging for her phone. She turned it on and tapped Mhairi's contact while Jack meandered into the small park by the side of the road.

The ringing tone trilled and trilled before Mhairi's loud voice instructed Brooke to leave a message Mhairi probably wouldn't return. Brooke hung up.

Jack was across the park, his posture rigid, rubbing one shoulder as he talked. His body seemed to curl in on itself, his arm braced tight across his chest, his head bowed, and she was at his side before she realized she'd moved.

He reached for her, his eyes locked on hers like a lifeline as he nodded at whatever the person on the other end of the phone said. "Alright. Bye, Mum I love you, too."

"What's wrong?" Brooke asked when he hung up.

Jack swallowed hard and wet his lips without saying anything. Her stomach rioted, a pinwheel of flurries she was helpless to dim.

"Mhairi's sick." He said the last word with a heaviness. A finality.

"How sick?" Brooke's mind flashed to the last time she'd seen Mhairi, when she'd wondered at the frail set of her shoulders. She shook off the worry. Surely Jack meant a very bad cold. The flu. A completely treatable autoimmune disease. But as Jack's expression remained stormy, his mouth in a tight line, Brooke's heartbeat grew louder in her ears.

"Pancreatic cancer."

The bottom of the world slipped out from beneath Brooke. "No." Her knees buckled and Jack reached out to steady her, pulled her against his chest.

"It's aggressive and late-stage," he said, his breath ruffling the stray hairs by her temple, as he ran his hands up and down her back. "The doctors gave her six months about nine months ago." His voice was low and soothing but did little to calm the heartache spreading out in waves inside her.

"That was when we started this project." Brooke's mind hooked onto the completely inconsequential detail to avoid thinking of the biggest one. *Mhairi was sick.*

Grief scrunched down around Brooke, suffocating.

Mhairi wasn't going to be here anymore. She wouldn't blow into the yellow coffee shop on Buccleuch Street, a colorful butterfly drinking an endless stream of tea and shredding the paper tag on the string.

She wouldn't regale Brooke with stories of her students or her childhood on Skye. Wouldn't detail every second of the

Fringe, acting out the stand-up comedy routines with animated hand gestures.

They wouldn't spend sunny days hiking the hills around the city, inventing stories about the locks left by couples on a chain near the summit.

This was so fucking unfair. Tears spilled down Brooke's cheeks but she didn't bother wiping them away. They leaked into Jack's shirt as he stroked her hair.

This shouldn't happen to anyone, but *especially* not to Mhairi. Not someone who still had so much to give to the world. God, Mhairi must be so scared, grappling with this all alone. She was strong and independent, but having to face an uncertain future, not relying on the people who loved her most to support her, absolutely destroyed Brooke's heart. She would've taken Mhairi to appointments, brought her dinners, found some way to bring even the slightest ray of happiness to an impossibly dark time.

Jack pressed a kiss to the top of her head. "I know it's a lot to take in."

Brooke pulled back to look at his face. Where she expected to see grief etched along his eyes was only concern for her and this tendril of suspicion twisted up her spine. "Did your mom tell you *all* of this on the phone?"

Jack opened and shut his mouth. Rolled his bottom lip inside. "Mhairi told us in March."

A hollowness opened inside Brooke and she blinked against the shock of it. "You knew?" she whispered, her voice hoarse.

He dragged a hand over his face. "Mhairi asked me not to share. She was going to tell you when we got back—"

Maybe. Or maybe Brooke wasn't important enough to know. Wasn't actually in Mhairi's inner circle.

And apparently not in Jack's, either.

He'd let her struggle through the trail, through chafed shoulders, burning muscles, blistered feet, freeze-dried food, and terrible sleep. Let her struggle through the physical pain and the fear that she wouldn't understand the narrative for the memoir, when he'd had so many more answers than she'd had.

Like, why Mhairi had wanted a cowriter instead of writing the memoir herself. Why she'd insisted Brooke and Jack hike together. Why she'd wanted to write this story in the first place. Because Mhairi was running out of time. Trying to capture this life in something that would outlive her. Her *legacy*.

Brooke hadn't known how important this project was, how far off the mark she'd been. How much was riding on finishing it.

"You should have told me." Anger spread out in deep waves through her.

Jack gripped her upper arms but she stepped back. He let his hands drop before shoving them into his pockets and rocking back on his heels. "At first, it seemed like there was no reason to. The hike is only a week and—" He looked desolate, but not as desolate as Brooke felt. "I know you and I have history. And I never wanted to have a secret between us again. I wanted to tell you so we could carry the weight of this together."

But Jack had deprived her of the chance to share those memories, to find her own peace on this journey, to grieve with him. For all his talk of trusting him and trusting herself, he hadn't trusted her enough with this, hadn't wanted to face this together. "But you didn't."

"It wasn't my secret to tell, Brooke."

She met his dark and somber gaze, saw the pain and hurt reflected there. Her anger seeped from her and left her shaky. As much as she wanted to blame him, to blame anyone, to lash out just to get these too-big feelings out, she knew he was right. She closed her eyes and took a deep breath through her nose. "*Mhairi* should've told me."

"Aye. But she didn't want you grieving out here. She wanted you living." Jack tucked a stand of hair behind Brooke's ear, his voice soft. "She was going to tell you."

Brooke swallowed against the thickness in her throat. Ran her palms over his cheeks and jaw, his beard soft under her hands. Tried to calm herself. Tried to believe him. "I get it."

She tucked against him and Jack exhaled a quick breath before drawing in a new one, releasing it like an ocean wave, his arms tightening around her.

He was hurting, too. Brooke closed her eyes against the fresh surge of grief, this time for him. For all he'd lose.

"I'm sorry you carried that all alone."

Jack shuddered against her and she pulled back, wiping the tears from his cheeks with her thumbs. "You were saying goodbye to her out there, weren't you? With the videos and the pictures of tiny flowers?"

"Yes." He kissed the top of her head. "And the stories. They were for you, but they were for me, too. So I don't forget. So she lives on in your writing."

Brooke's tears came like the rain and she squeezed Jack, pressing her face harder against his chest.

Living in stories would never be enough. Brooke would never be ready to say goodbye to Mhairi, never be ready to watch her walk the path set in front of her.

"And I wanted to give her something. She's given me so much."

"Me, too," Brooke whispered. She needed to finish the memoir. To make it perfect and worthy of Mhairi.

Jack must've noticed the dampness seeping into his shirt because he pulled back, cupping her face, wiping tears from her cheeks and kissing her wobbly bottom lip.

They linked their hands together and Brooke kissed each of Jack's knuckles before pulling his hand in close to her chest.

They stayed clasped together like that, crying until the tears faded to hiccuping breaths.

NOW

The journey back to Edinburgh required approximately forty-seven modes of transportation. Brooke had kept it together relatively well on the bus from Broadford to Portree, but she and Jack sulked by the harbor, eating fries they had to tuck inside their rain jackets to keep away from greedy seagulls.

The sky was a dark gray that matched the color of the water and Brooke's mood. Even the pastel-painted waterfront shops couldn't save her from herself and this brewing grief that seemed to knock into her heart like waves.

She'd wondered before if knowing death was coming was better than the shock of it, but the knowledge was its own kind of torture, creating a war inside her between wanting to commission a private jet to get to Mhairi's side as quickly as possible and the desire to pretend it wasn't real if she didn't have to see it with her own eyes.

They took another bus to Inverness, the capital of the Highlands, but the last train back to Edinburgh had already departed. After they checked into a hotel for the night, Brooke got in the shower and sobbed under the hot spray, trying to purge enough of her grief so she could be strong for Jack.

They shared a mince pie but only managed to eat half before climbing into bed and holding each other. Jack wrapped his arms around Brooke and it made tears well up in her eyes even though his touch was all she wanted. She pressed her nose into that spot in the center of his chest that always felt like an assurance that things would be okay, even though she wasn't sure they would ever be okay again. She breathed in his scent—fresh soap and safety.

When Jack started to shake with held-in grief, she slid up the bed and tucked an arm under him. He didn't resist, resting his head over her heart and pulling her closer. Wet tears fell against her chest and she hooked her leg over him, trying to wrap him up, shelter him from the pain.

"I can't fathom a world where she's not in it," he said, his voice cracking.

Brooke's heart broke entirely and she clung to him, tunneled her fingers into his hair. He tipped his head up, pressed his lips to hers in soft, sweet, salty kisses.

He settled back over her heart and she ran her fingers through his hair, under the sleeve of his T-shirt, over his shoulders. And when his breathing settled, heavy and deep, his eyelashes quiet against his cheeks, she cried for herself.

Brooke's mind couldn't quiet, couldn't stop running through memories of her and Mhairi hiking Arthur's Seat, or brainstorming on the quad where Brooke had first taken her class, or the nights they'd stayed up drinking tea with papers spread out all around them. As gently as she could, she extricated herself from Jack's sleeping form.

The only thing to do was to write down her thoughts and empty her brain or she'd never sleep, just continue down and down into this spiral.

Brooke pulled her notebook out of her pack and went into the bathroom, sitting on the floor in the light from the shower. The tile was hard and cold, but it felt good to have her body feel some fraction of the pain her heart did.

She wrote everything swirling in her mind, things she might want to include in the memoir, ways to honor Mhairi's memory now that Brooke knew what was really at stake. How important this story was.

She wrote about landscapes that felt so vast they made her feel larger than life, too. People so authentically themselves it was impossible not to forge an immediate and deep connection. Self-rediscovery, of being distilled down to her essence by the wind and the rain, perseverance and inspiration. Recapturing her voice. And for a flicker of a moment, the confidence to pursue her dreams again.

Brooke suddenly felt lightheaded, like she needed to sit down, even though she already was. She yanked the hair tie out of her bun and twisted it back up, pulling her hair out of her face, trying to work off the shaky energy coursing through her, the fear that she wasn't on the trail anymore; she was back to real life and real stakes, and everything was out of her control. What if she couldn't live up to Mhairi's expectations, couldn't do this story justice? Especially not if she had to do this alone.

And writing for herself again? She absolutely couldn't do that now. Not when Mhairi wouldn't be there to spitball ideas to jump-start Brooke's brain. Wouldn't be there to read Brooke's drafts or encourage her or challenge her. How could she write in a colorless world without this woman who brought so much adventure and excitement to hers?

Brooke crept back into the room and found her phone on the bedside table. Jack breathed deeply, lying on his back, one arm thrown over his face. She pushed down the worry that he'd be disappointed in her, that he'd stop believing in her. But she couldn't do this on her own.

Pulling up her email, Brooke typed out a message to Charlotte—the only safe path forward.

THEN

Jack waited down the hall from the dean's office for
Brooke, the minutes absolutely slugging along. His knee
bounced and his heart raced.

Sacked. He'd never been sacked before; perhaps those were
the perks of nepotism. His stomach clenched at the thought of
returning to the family business, but what other choice did he
have? His dad needed him. Neil shouldn't have to hire some
fancy MBA when he'd already financed one that Jack had set
on fire. Jack had irreparably humiliated himself.

He steepled his fingers together and pressed them against
his mouth. His parents were going to be shocked. Mhairi was
going to be so disappointed.

A small part of Jack wanted to blame his aunt for this—he
wouldn't have disclosed his and Brooke's relationship if it hadn't
been for her prodding. But if he was honest with himself, he'd
been looking for any reason, so desperate to love Brooke out
loud and in the open, that he'd barely thought this through.

His heart had been halfway in the right place—never wanting to stand in the way of Brooke's fellowship—and halfway bloody fucking selfish.

What a fool he'd been, not even talking to Brooke about this first, not giving her any warning. He'd jumped on his white horse like some gallant knight she didn't need. She was in that office getting blindsided right now.

The dean had refused to discuss Brooke. As far as he could tell, they were worried about sexual harassment and seeing as how that wasn't the case and Jack had been terminated from his program, Brooke shouldn't face any consequences. It'd been Jack's fault, his lack of restraint. He was the one in a position of power. Or he *had* been.

But a small part of him worried that the dean's long-winded recounting of a sexual harassment case from the previous year meant they were coming down on this hard, and that it wasn't out of the question that Brooke would face some repercussions. Jack blew out a long breath through his nose.

Footsteps echoed along the hall and Brooke turned the corner in a flurry. Jack stood, stopping her with his hands on her arms. She shrugged him off, tears spilling out of her eyes. "What the *hell*, Jack?"

His heart pounded hard with regret and guilt, a steady staccato of *you absolute wanker.*

"I'm sorry. I'm so sorr—"

"Why would you do that?" Brooke said on a desperate breath, her eyes pinning him in place.

"For you. For the fellowship."

"Forget the fellowship, I'm not even graduating," she said with a decisive scoff.

His pulse whirred in his ears. "What, why?"

"I have to retake the class."

It would add to her workload next term, but she'd already learned everything. It didn't mean she couldn't graduate. She was so clever, she'd be able to make it work. He'd do whatever he could to help her—obviously not the coursework, *Jesus*, but make her dinners or carry her books to and from classes. He'd find a way to fix this. "That seems punitive, but doable." And much better than the worst-case scenario that'd been rumbling around in his mind.

"I'm here on a scholarship." She looked at him like he was an absolute child, not understanding what was at play.

The light flickered above him like the lightbulb that should've been going off in his brain.

"To keep that scholarship," she said slowly, enunciating every word, "I have to be a full-time student. Which I no longer will be since I'm being forced to drop this class. Thanks to you."

Jack felt like sinking to the floor, his joints going loose, his head light. A shout from a student a long way off echoed through the empty corridor. A door slammed in the distance. "Brooke, I never meant—" He'd been trying to do the right thing. Not destroy everything. "I can help you pay for it." He'd make decent money at The Heart. He could move home, get an extra job—

"I think you've done enough, don't you?" Those blue eyes were the shade of the deep sea, dangerous with fury.

"I was trying to protect you," he said on a desperate plea as she pulled away from him with a look of icy indifference he'd never seen before.

"You were protecting *you*." She stabbed a finger in his direction. "You betrayed me. You finally figured out what you wanted and fucked up my life to get it."

Christ, he *had* fucked this all up, but she had it wrong. It'd never been about him. He would give it all back to fix this. "It was never like that—"

"I lost *everything* because of you." Her voice was harsh and ragged.

Panic burst through him at the errant thought—or maybe premonition—that this was the end. Cheeks flushed, loose tendrils of hair curving over her shoulder, necklace straining against the deep V of her throat where she sucked in angry breaths.

"Brooke—" He reached out to touch her, to pull her back, to grasp what he felt vanishing from his life.

She knocked his hand away before he touched her shoulder.

"I never want to see you again."

NOW

Brooke rode next to Jack on the train back to Edinburgh, hands clasped and quiet.

"You probably don't remember," Jack said, "but we'd planned to come up to Inverness one day."

"No one forgets the Heilan Coo Trail."

He hummed out a sigh. "I thought about waking you up this morning to take you out before we left. But it didn't feel like the right time to enjoy it and be playful."

"No. I just needed to be held this morning."

Jack unzipped his pack and pulled out a little orange hairy coo plushie. The same one she'd picked up in the shop in Portree.

"Jack." She tucked the stuffie against her chest and nuzzled against Jack's neck. "Thank you. We'll come back another time."

"I'll take you up the riverwalk when it's dark and the string lights glow under the trees."

"I love dreaming with you."

Jack pressed a kiss against her temple and she watched the

distant horizon flash outside the train, interrupted by shrubberies and trees, their reflection hazy in the window. As much as her heart was breaking for Mhairi, anxiety a constant hum in her chest, she also felt calm here with Jack, tucked up against him. Like she always had.

"You want to know something?" Brooke pulled her wallet from her jacket pocket. She slipped the ripped piece of printer paper from the sleeve and unfolded it. "I could never quite part with this."

Jack's biggest smile spread across his face before he pressed a hard kiss against her forehead. "You want to know something?" He adjusted his hold on her, reached for his wallet in his front pocket, and Brooke's breath hitched.

"Really?" she asked as he pulled out the other half, unfolded it, matched it up to hers like a love locket.

"I could never part with it, either."

Tears welled up in Brooke's eyes. "That was the cheesiest thing I've ever done," she said as they put the paper pieces away.

"Well, I loved it. And you."

Brooke's pulse raced. At the words he almost said. At how much her heart wanted to hear them and say them back. She wasn't sure how to tell Jack about the ghostwriting job and how she'd put it off this morning because the timing didn't feel right. But she wanted him to come with her. To never stop feeling this way.

"So, the ghostwriting job. It's for Jennifer Aniston."

"Jennifer Aniston. Wow."

"You have to wipe that from your brain now." She wouldn't have told him, but she trusted him and she needed him to know what a huge opportunity it was.

"It's nearly deleted."

"I told my editor I'd take the job last night." She took a stabilizing breath. This thing with Jack was old but it was also so new. She wanted him to be with her, to keep seeing what a future could hold. "Will you come to LA with me?"

His chin dipped down and he rested his hand above her knee. "Brooke," he said, his voice pitched low, but not how she'd expected it. Not with a softness like he was thrilled she'd asked. Her stomach pulled in at the hesitation, at the way it sounded like he was about to let her down easy. "You're still going to ghostwrite?"

She didn't like the hint of disappointment, maybe even judgment, in his words. She sat up straighter. "Taking this job gives me so much stability and choice going forward."

"I know this is scary, and Mhairi being sick makes everything feel unsettled."

"Yeah, it does. Life is short and unpredictable." She breathed through the defensiveness welling up in her at his lack of enthusiasm. She'd been thinking about this for days and she'd sprung it on him. He just needed a minute. "I don't want to leave you. This feels fragile still and, god, I've spent so much time in the last seven years missing you. I don't want to miss you anymore." She looped her fingers around his wrist. "Come with me."

Jack's eyebrows furrowed. He opened and closed his mouth and her heart felt too big for her chest. "LA is on the other side of the world."

Their reconnection had felt so certain until this moment. Before it looked like Jack never missed her back. When the possibility entered her mind that this rekindling might've meant less to him than it did to her. Not a vacation hookup but maybe not forever, either.

Brooke pulled her hand away, tucked her feet up on the seat. "I know. But it's a short gig and we wouldn't leave for a few months."

"I'm a Scottish landscape photographer. I can't do that from somewhere else. Especially not when I finally feel like I know what I'm meant to be doing." Jack squeezed her knee as if this would convince her it was better to spend months apart. Her dreams were important and his were, too, but she thought being together was just as high on that list.

"There are interesting landscapes in California. You could diversify your portfolio. We can go hiking on the weekends in the hills. I could take you out to Catalina Island. I went once in high school, it's beautiful."

"Brooke, you'll be working." His voice was so soft. So *placating*. "What did you tell me? 'Around the clock'?"

This was spiraling out of control. She'd asked him to come with her as a next step, as the start of a future together that was disintegrating in front of her eyes. Brooke turned in her seat, rested her knee over Jack's thigh, and wrapped an arm around his waist. "I would make time for you." She'd be busy, but all she wanted right now was to be in Jack's arms. To explore together. To give this a real shot.

Jack cupped the back of her head, ran his fingers through her hair, traced her jaw. She sank into the comfort, lifted her chin when he nudged it with his thumb, met his eyes, all soft and pleading. "If this was your real dream, I would be there in a heartbeat."

"Are you serious right now? Just say you don't want to come."

He sucked in a long breath and let it out, resistance in his posture, regret etched around his mouth. "You know what it feels like to put this on hold, to not be sure if you'll come back to it. You know what you're asking me to do here. I can't sacrifice my dream that I only just started to chase because you're scared."

Brooke wasn't sure when she'd stopped breathing. She was already feeling insanely vulnerable and then to hear Jack tell her she was running?

She pulled her chin out of his grip, straightened in her seat. "I'm not scared. I'm being practical." How dare he always remind her that she wasn't chasing her childish dream. That dream didn't pay the bills. "Writing my own stories is all risk and no guarantees."

"Brooke," Jack said as he tried to catch her eye, squeezing her knee. "It's okay to be afraid. I believe in you."

"Why is everyone always pushing me? Maybe all this *potential* isn't real. Maybe I can't do it. Maybe I'm not good enough."

Not without Mhairi. Not when everything was spinning out of control like it had back then. Like she could be left with nothing.

"I understand that fear. Believe me, I do. But this isn't the life I want, where we make ourselves smaller because we're scared. I'm tired of living that way, and I can't watch you do it, either."

Brooke flushed hot all over and then cold. It was just like Jack to try to pick her life for her.

"I think you still need to figure out what's most important to you."

Brooke twisted her rings, tried to unclench her jaw. "I know what's important to me. My writing. My career." The things she could control. "Back then in secret, and now on the trail, you made me believe I could have everything, but it never pans out that way."

"That's not fair. What happened in uni has nothing to do with now."

"It has everything to do with now. You encouraged me to turn down a huge opportunity *knowing* Mhairi was sick. Both times, you had more information and you didn't talk to me. And I should've remembered that. Maybe this trip was the closure we needed. This—" she gestured between them "—never seems to work in the real world, does it?"

"It doesn't if you go to LA and ignore your dreams. I lived that way for so long, and you did, too. Some people are happy that way, but you and I aren't. We're made for bigger things. For telling stories and sharing them with the world. You'll end up sad and jaded if you don't follow your heart. I know you."

"Or maybe you just always think you know what's best for me." Brooke stood up and yanked on her pack wedged in the overhead rack, trying not to notice Jack's clenched jaw, the etchings of frustration around his lips.

"Then go to LA," he said in a voice so soft it hurt. "Pay the bills and live Jennifer Aniston's story since you're too afraid to live your own."

Hot tears pooled in Brooke's eyes as her pack came free and the weight crashed against her chest. She *would* go to LA. Go back to being a ghost. It hurt a hell of a lot less.

She moved to a vacant seat at the front of the train, her heart pounding hard enough to shatter. Jack always managed to leave her that way. She never should've opened herself up to this pain again—she'd barely survived it back then.

And now? They'd hurt each other enough for two lifetimes.

42

NOW

Jack got off the train from Inverness late that night, as Brooke headed in the opposite direction and climbed a double flight of stairs. They'd agreed he'd go see Mhairi first, because they were now like divorced parents negotiating custody.

Her ponytail swung as she climbed, her backpack obscuring half of her face, her feelings and her heart out of his reach. He'd watched Brooke walk away once before and it had nearly broken him. He wasn't sure he was breathing now. He was only sure his heart hadn't stopped because it hurt so fucking much when Brooke slipped out of sight.

Jack stepped around wrappers and old newspapers overflowing from the bin as he made his way through the deserted station. When he and Logan were kids, they'd loved it here. Jack always thought the trains represented freedom for Logan, but for Jack, it meant returning, coming home. But there was no solace in that notion now.

Logan sat on a bench outside Café Nero, looking at his phone, probably texting Addie. The thought sent a dagger through Jack's heart—not that he begrudged his brother's happiness, but because Jack had been *so close* to being someone who grinned stupidly at a text message from someone he loved.

"Hi, ye wee bawbag," Jack said and Logan looked up with a smile, slipping his phone into his pocket as he stood. In a moment of weakness and need, Jack wrapped his arms around Logan instead of tripping or backslapping him.

Reaching around his pack, Logan awkwardly hugged him back, and when he let go, his eyes were etched with concern. "You alright, then?"

Jack drew in a deep breath and let it out. He'd taken all manner of transportation to get home and he still hadn't been able to wrap his head around the past twelve hours. The reality of Mhairi's illness. The anger in Brooke's words. The finality of her retreating form. The numbness that consumed him. "Not really."

Logan took Jack's rucksack and swung it onto his own back. "Christ, no wonder," he said with a wince and Jack was profoundly grateful for a brother who knew what he needed without asking. Right now, that was a small bit of ribbing, space, and a ride to his aunt's.

"How's Mhairi?" Jack asked as they crossed the empty station.

"She's out of hospital. A right pain in the arse she was, too. She banished mum from the house for *fluttering*." He put the last word in air quotes. "She seems intent on getting her affairs in order. Addie and I dropped by to bring her supper last night and she barely looked up from her desk." Logan adjusted the pack, the lines around his mouth sharp. "She looked well enough, but..."

Jack closed his eyes against that future. Mhairi had told them not to join walks and fundraisers. That they could do that after she was gone. For now, she didn't want it to be the focal point, the only thing people asked her about; she still had more living to do. But at some point they were all going to have to contend with this disease. And it seemed that point was now.

"She used to tell me she'd live to be a hundred." Jack pushed his glasses up and rubbed his eyes, watery and dry at the same time. "I think I believed her."

Logan gripped his shoulder but the comfort couldn't pierce the ache in Jack's chest. Mhairi's diagnosis felt deeply real for the first time and he hated thinking about how little time she had left, about how impossible it would be to say goodbye to her.

They climbed the stairs up to the street and Jack felt mildly guilty that Logan huffed and puffed with his pack, but mostly grateful. He wanted to be coddled right now.

Past the restaurant lining the entrance, the Scott Monument stood proud against the night. A tower of secrets and memories.

"Can we make a stop?" Jack asked. He was in the mood to suffer.

He followed the pavement and crossed the street to the grassy lawn of the monument. He didn't know if the code on the door was the same from all those years ago, but he headed for the kiosk at the foot of the structure and punched in the numbers. Red flashed at him and his chest constricted with irrational fury.

"Och," Logan said from behind him, slightly out of breath. "Old Marty changed it two years ago." He nudged Jack aside to unlock the door and didn't even take the opportunity to dig an elbow into Jack's ribs—that's how pitiful he must've seemed. "I'm not carrying this upstairs," he warned.

Logan could leave the pack outside for all Jack cared. He didn't want anything in there. He couldn't see how camping, hiking, or the general outdoors could ever be a solace now. He felt like he might never see the beauty in anything ever again.

Logan grabbed his arm, turning Jack toward him. "What happened?" he asked in a softened voice.

"Christ, I don't even know where to start," Jack said, by-passing the museum and the stained-glass windows and grabbing hold of the smooth black railing curving its way up three flights of stairs.

"That bad?" Logan asked.

"Everything's all fucked up with Brooke. Fate seems particularly cruel to have brought her back into my life when we still can't seem to sort it out."

"I need a wee bit more detail," Logan said from behind him.

Pockets of light from the fleur-de-lis windows covered the stairs and Jack stomped on them. "The trail felt like a second chance and then maybe a future. She asked me to go to LA with her for a job."

"Hmm, I seem to remember someone asking me, 'Why aren't you on a plane right now?' when Addie left."

"Whoever said that sounds like a right bawbag."

Logan's laughter and footsteps echoed in the spiral stairwell before he said, "Aye."

When they made it to the viewing platform, Jack gripped the tall railing on curved posts bowing toward them and looked out. Princes Street Gardens was a dark scratch separating him from the towering city. The tan-and-gray buildings were lit with golden streetlights casting deep shadows up their sides.

"Why aren't you going, then?" Logan asked.

"I think I finally understand you."

Logan tipped his head, not following the non sequitur.

Jack scratched at the soft stone of the railing. "I get why you care so much about The Heart. What it means to have a passion. But you failed to mention that it's absolutely wretched."

"Och, aye," Logan said. "Bloody miserable." He gripped Jack's shoulder and squeezed.

NOW

Jack walked into Mhairi's house with a quiet emptiness unfurling inside him, a billowing need to lay his grief at her feet. But when he and Logan found her at her desk, the yellow lamp the only holdout against the night, all Jack could feel was despair. Her face was pale against the floral print of her blouse, her shoulders curled in a way that made her look frail. Like she'd somehow shrunk in the time he'd been away.

He found himself mimicking the stature, not strong enough to hold himself up to full size.

Mhairi looked up, took in his expression, and shook her head at him in warning. He could hear the unsaid words. *No weeping.*

"Logan, I need you to wash the dishes," she said, her eyes on Jack.

"Abusing me *all day*," Logan complained, but headed for the kitchen, giving them privacy.

Mhairi stood, bracing her hands on the arms of her chair, and Jack crossed the room in two strides. He reached for her and ignored the way she waved him off, wrapping her in a hug that maybe she didn't want but he needed.

Her head rested against his shoulder and she smelled the same, like dusty books and the promise of adventure. He closed his eyes to better soak it in, to file it away with his memories of exploring Calton Hill in the rain, the bread she made on particularly cold February days and the sound of her shouting at the TV when the Hibs played like rubbish. He wanted to squeeze her like he could keep her with him that way, but he forced himself to keep a loose hold.

"It's not so bad as when you were fourteen," she said, patting him on the back. "But you reek, dear."

He huffed out a laugh, but he wasn't ready to let go. He kept a hand on her arm while she settled back in her chair and gave him a disapproving look, but didn't brush him off. Like she might need the support.

Christ, what she must be going through. Jack couldn't even imagine having to stare a diagnosis like this in the face. To contend with the time you had left and how to spend it.

"How did the photos turn out?" she asked.

"Do you really want to talk about the memoir right now?"

"Yes." Mhairi straightened some papers on her desk and Jack rubbed a hand over his chin.

"Alright. I took some of my favorite photos of my life. The lighting was terrible at the start, but then moody and foggy and we had a perfect day at the Storr. I took photos I thought you'd love and they ended up being better than ones I tried to take to be compositionally correct or some shite."

Mhairi laughed and Jack latched onto it. Held it against his heart.

"And how is Brooke?"

"She struggled, and then I think she found what it was she was looking for. She'll write an incredible story for you, I have no doubt."

"I don't, either. But I mean, how *is* she...knowing about me?"

Jack looked down at the ground. "Devastated. Hurt, I think, that you didn't tell her."

"I didn't know how. This matters to her in a way that perhaps only you and I can understand." Mhairi steepled her fingers together under her chin and looked past the darkened windows. Her eyes misted and so did Jack's as he sank into a crouch before her. He took her hand and she patted the top of his.

"And the two of you?" she asked.

He stared at his boots, shook his head, tried to stop the panicked beat of his heart that he'd lost her again. "We can't seem to get it right."

Mhairi squeezed his hand, but he stood quickly, breathed in deeply. "How are you holding up?" he asked.

"Frankly, I'm disgruntled. Everyone stopping by and tiptoeing around me—" Her eyes cut across the room. "I can hear you, Logan."

"I'm a rather poor tiptoe-er," he said, popping his head into the doorway. "You're going to need to accept some help, Auntie. It's being offered genuinely."

"No, I don't think I will," she said with a defiant air. "But I do know what I want—I sorted this out in the hospital while my roommates droned on about their wee bairns sixteen hours a day. I'd like a life celebration ceremony."

"Veering into the morbid, I see," Jack said, even though the time had come for that. To talk about *after*. He just wasn't ready for it.

"No, I want it while I'm still here. Why have a celebration I can't attend?"

Jack looked over to Logan and they shared a grin. She'd always been the life of the party—of course she wouldn't want to miss one in her honor. It lit some spark of hope in Jack's chest. He knew the ending, but he'd hold on to the chance of something to look forward to without dread. Something good in all this.

"It doesn't have to be fancy," she said. "But it does have to be big."

Logan leaned against the doorframe, drying a cup with a hairy coo dish towel. "Whatever you want, Auntie."

"I want it on Skye."

The thought of going back there sent knives through Jack's stomach. It was too fresh, too bloody devastating to return to a place that had always held so much peace for him and now felt like shattered glass in his heart. But he'd do anything for Mhairi—even this.

NOW

Brooke knocked on Mhairi's plum-purple door—the one that contained so many stories, so much *life* behind it, but one day, very soon, there would be nothing for Brooke on the other side.

Mhairi opened the door in her highlighter-pink-and-red caftan, a cheery facade that didn't hide the fragile slope of her shoulders or her washed-out complexion.

Brooke immediately stepped in for a hug, clinging to Mhairi. When she pulled back, she tried to keep her expression neutral, her eyes free of tears, to stay strong for Mhairi.

"Come in, dear," Mhairi said, her face unreadable, and gestured for Brooke to make her way into the sun-soaked kitchen.

The large windows framed the garden out back, the trees in their peak-of-summer laziness, the vines on the trellis reaching for the light. Brooke had spent some of her happiest afternoons at Mhairi's round wooden table, the top bleached and scratched from use, staring at the blooms bobbing in the breeze outside as her mind turned over new ideas and fresh words.

But the Pyrex dishes covered in silvery aluminum foil lining

Mhairi's countertops seemed to siphon off the creative energy that usually flowed here.

"That's a lot of shepherd's pie," Brooke said.

"Aye, there's been an awful lot of fussing over me," Mhairi said in a dry tone. Brooke knew not to press, not to ask how she was. "You're welcome to take one home. I don't particularly like stew."

Mhairi filled and started the kettle and Brooke grabbed two mugs from where they hung under the sage green cabinets like she always did; she'd stopped being a guest here a long time ago.

"I want to hear all about the trail," Mhairi said as they waited for the water to boil.

She'd known Mhairi wouldn't want to discuss her hospital stay or what came next, but Brooke didn't particularly want to talk about the trail, either.

She tried to think of the oversaturated green of the hills and the slope of the peaks, the stories about Cat and Nat, Murray and Oliver and Anya. But the memories that jostled their way to the top were all Jack. Raising his tin campfire mug in a toast in the pink blush of dawn. The fan of his eyelashes. The sparkle of the stars they'd slept beneath. The way he'd pieced her back together only to shatter her once again.

Brooke blew out a breath. "I'm sure you know how hard it is to describe."

The kettle clicked off and Mhairi poured steaming water into the mugs. "It *is* otherworldly."

Brooke took her tea from Mhairi, twisting the white string of the tea bag around her index finger, and sitting stiffly in her usual seat at the worn kitchen table like they had so many times before—poring over printed pages of academic publications, red-lining and arguing and brainstorming. A deep fear drove through Brooke that they wouldn't be able to do that much longer. That she'd be left without this woman who inspired her, who felt like home and a safe place to land.

Her eyes must've misted up enough for Mhairi to notice because she let out a sigh, heavy with regret. "I should've told you."

"I understand why you didn't. I'm not family," Brooke said into her tea.

She hadn't earned that place, hadn't managed to see to the heart of Mhairi's impact even though she'd experienced it firsthand.

When Brooke set down her mug, Mhairi folded her hands in her lap. "I didn't keep this a secret because I couldn't trust you with it. I didn't want to be…diminished in your eyes. I wanted you to have the freedom and discovery in the writing without knowing the ending. Without sorrow seeping into the narrative."

A tear slipped down Brooke's cheek and she wiped it away. "It's okay. But, Mhairi, I don't think I can do this without you." Her words came out in a rush, all her fears and insecurities pouring out. "I'm not good enough. I think you picked the wrong person. I can't live up to what you need—to be responsible for your legacy."

Mhairi reached for her hand. "This memoir is not my legacy, Brooke. *You* are."

Brooke's throat went tight, Mhairi's form blurring through her tears.

"You will carry on with my teachings and do amazing things and I will live on through your adventures and your stories."

Her words wrapped Brooke's heart in bubble wrap, tenderly, carefully; they soothed something deep inside her.

"I asked you to write this with me because you notice details that bring a setting to life and find the most beautiful words to explain deep emotions. But I also saw an opportunity for you. I wanted to give you the push you needed to regain your confidence and reclaim your path. You're a fantastic writer." She squeezed Brooke's hand like she was making sure she had her full attention. "And you've been hiding."

Brooke cast her eyes down to her lap. If Mhairi had said that two weeks ago, she would've argued—cited all the amazing projects she'd worked on, the accolades she'd earned.

But if the trail had taught her anything, it was that a list of accomplishments did not add up to a life. Brooke sniffled and nodded.

Mhairi had always pushed Brooke to be better, to reach higher, but she'd never loved her any less when she stumbled. The ache of knowing Mhairi wouldn't be here to see her achievements and her setbacks was an unrelenting vise around her rib cage—but there was hope pushing back, too. A surety that Brooke would find her way and she'd know Mhairi was proud of her no matter what.

"When you suggested going to Skye... Well, I wanted that for you. I wanted you to experience all the beauty and wonder my homeland holds and for it to open you back up. I want you to live your life, Brooke. To reach all your dreams. I'm sorry we don't have more time for this one."

Mhairi's eyes held a soft gleam, an encouragement. "But when you're finished with my story...it's time for you to write *yours*."

45

NOW

Jack strode through his parents' house, carrying his easels on one arm and his prints under the other. Mhairi had not exaggerated about Gemma taking the lead on organizing the event—she didn't even greet him at the door.

His mum's coping mechanism had turned from fretting to planning every detail of the life celebration. Their living room was piled with everyone's contributions, ready to be transported to Skye tomorrow. Two teal flowerpots full of purple geraniums sank deep into the plush carpet. Jack couldn't venture a guess as to where that podium had come from.

The reality he'd been avoiding—hiding behind his computer, editing his video for Mhairi—struck him all at once, a knife to the ribs. There was a day, and soon, when his world would contain a gaping hole. He wanted to wrest back her time, physically fight whoever was responsible. But all he could do was show some pictures at a ceremony he wished they didn't need to hold. It left him feeling beyond helpless.

The table Gemma used for entertaining was out, covered in old photographs. Jack set his prints and easels against the wall and pored over them, his finger nudging the softened edges to uncover another layer of shiny pictures. Mhairi as a baby who'd look indistinguishable from Reid if it weren't for the black-and-white photography. Mhairi in pigtails while a young Gemma held the handlebars of a tricycle. Mhairi holding Jack and his brothers as newborns.

Each photo resurfaced a memory of his childhood. The smell of soil and new leaves while Mhairi took them grasshopper hunting in her garden with an absurdly large net. The taste of buttercream frosting on birthday cupcakes in the garage. The rifling of the breeze through his hair on the boat off of Skye, the life jacket cinched high and tight across his chest. He'd always felt such a thrill of adventure around Mhairi, that sunny outlook that anything could happen.

Gemma walked into the room and without so much as a greeting, gestured toward his prints. "You have four, correct?" She didn't even go in to adjust his collar.

Guilt wrapped around him for all the times he'd taken his mother for granted. He'd needed distance sometimes from a family that was so close, but it didn't excuse all the times he'd swatted her away, rebuffed her fussing. He would even welcome it at the moment. And surely Gemma needed to be fussed over sometimes, too.

Jack stilled her with a hand on her arm and pulled her into a hug.

Gemma stiffened as if surprised and then melted against him. "Och, Jack," she said against his shoulder. Warm wet spots seeped through his shirt. A matching grief welled up in him, caught in his throat, pushed at the backs of his eyes.

Gemma pulled away, her eyes puffy, and waved a hand in front of her face. She headed in the direction of her room and his chest ached for all of them. He felt completely unmoored, completely useless. And he couldn't ask the only two people who always made things better to comfort him.

Jack crossed his arms on the back of the couch and rested his head on top. He wanted to curl up and sleep, to fast-forward to when this didn't feel like endless sadness sprawling down the road of his future.

His phone dinged in his pocket and he straightened, pulling it out. A notification popped up with an email from the gallery in Leith. His overtaxed heart gave a whimper, the slightest stirring of that damnable hope that never let him quit.

Opening the email, Jack braced himself for the inevitable rejection he'd hardened himself against, even though it always managed to slip in like a paper cut.

Dear Mr. Sutherland,
We are pleased to inform you your photograph "First Blush" has been selected for inclusion in our next gallery exhibition. Congratulations!

The selection committee was impressed by the creativity, technical skill, and unique perspective demonstrated in your work.

Details regarding the exhibition dates, opening reception, and any additional requirements will be provided in a follow-up email. In the meantime, please ensure that your artwork is ready for display, and feel free to contact us if you have any questions or require further information.
Best Regards,
Susan Landis
Curatorial Director, Portside Arts

The cut never came. Jack reread the email, not absorbing the words. *Congratulations.* They'd accepted him. He had a gallery spot.

"What is it?" Neil said, suddenly beside him.

Startled, Jack looked up from his phone. This was the moment he'd been waiting for. To tell his dad. To make all the fights and disappointments worthwhile.

"I got accepted to a gallery in Leith." He could barely believe the words leaving his mouth, and understood even less that the photo to make it was not a black-and-white composition he'd been working so hard to perfect, but the one that he'd taken for Mhairi on a night where he and Brooke had felt that first blush of reconnection.

It had the depth and light and life that he wanted to capture. Clouds so soft you could feel the vastness of a summer night, resurface the smell of the briny sea air and the caress of the wind off the water. It might even elicit the musings of another life in another century or ignite the curiosity for the communities nearby.

Neil's hand landed heavily on Jack's shoulder. "Jack, that's brilliant. Well done." He looked Jack straight in the eye, said the words earnestly with genuine pride on his face.

It was all Jack had wanted. Not the gallery spot, but the credibility. The justification. But it didn't feel at all like he'd imagined, like a balm to erase the past. The right words were there, but the euphoria he'd dreamed of was missing. Instead, there was something like resentment that he'd felt the need to justify himself at all. That he'd needed this validation.

Maybe he was too old to need his parents' approval, but he was still their child, still hurt by their expectations he could never quite reach.

Jack hadn't slept in days. Everything hurt and he wanted to make it worse.

"You know that's all I ever wanted to hear from you."

Neil's eyebrows furrowed. "I've always told you you're talented."

"No, you said, 'These would be great for The Heart's website' or, 'Those will grab attention on The Heart's social media.' It was always about business. Never about *me*."

The rational part of Jack's brain was aware that this was the kind of moment people told stories about when a loved one passed away and everyone lost their minds, stealing inheritances or speaking ill of the dead. Everyone's emotions ran high and between losing Brooke and imminently, Mhairi—the only two people who had ever really seen him—Jack's emotions were higher than he could tame.

"You pushed me into something I was ill-suited for and acted like it was the best choice for me. You had to have known it wasn't." *You had to have seen me better than that.*

Neil gave that long-suffering sigh like he knew where Jack was headed with this conversation and the fatigue only fueled Jack's anguish.

"We knew you didn't love guiding. But, Jack, you were so lost. We were trying to give you a direction."

"You were holding up a mirror in the exact shape and size of Logan."

Neil grimaced and his mustache bunched above his lip. "Logan is just like me—he was easier to parent because of that. He was easier for me to understand. But it never meant I loved you any less." Neil slipped a hand to the curve of Jack's shoulder and squeezed. "You never said what it was that you *did* want. You never *committed* to anything."

"I did, once."

The accusation hung heavy around them, the ghosts of that afternoon in this house still here, still lingering, when his parents hadn't believed in him or supported him, but pushed him back on the path they'd forged without asking.

"Son, you'll forgive us if the one time it was real we didn't recognize it. We were trying to give you a purpose. The Heart had given us so much satisfaction and joy. We only wanted the same for you."

"I've found it now." And shockingly, it wasn't Neil's approval that Jack had been chasing for years. It wasn't even the gallery spot.

Both those things were incredible, but they were nothing

compared to the feeling of taking a photo that captured a moment that meant something to him. Jack knew the cost of not following a dream, the physical pain of leaving it tethered inside. "I'm going to start a vlog and sell photos in tourist shops in Portree. And make postcards. And maybe a fucking calendar."

Neil beamed at him, a slight question in his eye like he might never fully understand, but he cared anyway. "I'm proud of you for naming your dream. Go after what you want." He gave Jack one last squeeze and headed back to the kitchen.

Like everything these days, Neil's words made Jack think about Brooke.

He'd never chased after what he wanted with her, either.

Back then, Jack had been in a position of power he never wanted to abuse. He'd been trying to be responsible. And on the trail, he'd known he'd hurt her. He hadn't wanted to press.

But that'd been awfully fucking convenient to never have to put himself out there, to always be assured of her interest in him without having to take a risk.

He'd let her walk out of his life twice now and he'd be a damn fool if he didn't at least tell her how he felt.

46

NOW

Brooke stood at the back of the community garden, surrounded by low stone walls holding back cascading blooms and ringed by spherical trees, leafed out in their midsummer glory. In the center of the garden, wooden folding chairs were lined up in the gravel around an aisle. At the front, a podium and potted flowers made a small stage.

A projector screen was set up on one side and on the other, four pictures rested on easels. Brooke could guess whose photographs they were. She scanned the crowd of Mhairi's friends and family for him as she curled the program in her hands.

Kieran, Rohan, and Chels had come as moral support and they chatted in the back row with Jack's brother Logan—his arm around a pretty blonde woman dressed in a chic black dress. The other young man beside them looked familiar with his unkempt sandy blond hair and broad shoulders—Reid. And wow, had he had a glow-up since high school. He'd filled out, stood with a confident stance, his arms clasped behind his back.

Brooke spotted Jack across the garden talking to his parents, and her heart slammed against her chest like it could reach him if it only pounded hard enough. She wanted to hightail it through the gravel parking lot as fast as her too-high heels would take her. And simultaneously go to him—throw her arms around his waist, rest her cheek against his chest, feel his chin tip down as he wrapped her up. Take comfort in his soothing embrace, face the day and what came next, together.

If she'd thought the book signing stirred up a chaos of emotions, it had nothing on this.

Brooke took deliberate breaths in through her nose but couldn't seem to tear her eyes from him. Jack's white button-up stretched across his broad shoulders and tapered at his waist. He wore a kilt meant for special occasions, the navy-blue-and-forest-green fabric swishing around his knees, and tartan flashes peeked out from the cuff of his tall black socks like bookmarks.

Jack in a kilt—*damn, didn't know that was on my bucket list.*

She let out a loud breath right as Mhairi appeared at her side. Brooke's eyes immediately began to water and she didn't see the use in trying to hold it back. "I'm going to cry today."

Mhairi patted her hand and Brooke turned hers to hold it. "So am I, dear."

They stood beneath the poplar tree, watching the buzz of the gathering, clasped together in a stolen moment—one of so few left.

They'd spent afternoons in Mhairi's kitchen when she was feeling up to it. Brooke treasured every laugh, every piece of advice, every moment of Mhairi's time. Brooke was writing faster than she ever had before, changing the narrative to deepen Mhairi's impact and her joy. Turning over words to find the perfect ones. And some nights, when she was feeling brave, and especially when she was feeling scared, Brooke kept writing the story she'd started on the trail. Her story.

"I've been writing," Brooke told Mhairi, like a promise.

Even if no one ever read it, even if it was terrible, now that she'd started, there was no way she could stop. She would tell her story and even though Mhairi wouldn't be there to read it, to see what she'd created, she would live on in Brooke's pages.

Mhairi squeezed Brooke's hand and held on tight. "I have every faith in you."

A tear leaked out of Brooke's eye for Mhairi's trust. For how much further those words would have to carry her.

Gemma moved to the podium and tapped the microphone, sending static into the air. "Let's all take our seats," she said, squinting into the sun.

Brooke resettled Mhairi's hand on her arm and walked her down the aisle like a bride, but she wasn't sure who was giving who away. Brooke's eyes filled until the colorful gathering swam before her and when they reached the front row, Mhairi squeezed Brooke's hand and nodded like they both had to walk their own paths from here on out.

Brooke took the empty seat behind Mhairi and caught Jack's gaze from the front row. His look felt like a lingering kiss to the forehead. His lips twisted in their shared pain and Brooke pulled a tissue from her purse, dabbing at the corners of her eyes as she sniffed back tears.

Gemma adjusted the microphone again. "Thank you all for joining us and what a lovely day to come together and celebrate my sister, Mhairi McCallister. For all our lives, Mhairi has been the adventurer, the risk-taker, the one looking toward the future and the impact she can make. One thing I've always loved about you, sister, is your sureness in yourself. So many of us spend our time trying to understand ourselves, to figure out what we want from this life." Gemma wiped away a tear.

"But from the moment you were born, you've seemed to know exactly who you are and what you want in life. You forge communities wherever you go." Gemma gestured to the audience. "This gathering is a testament to that. You see needs and fill them. You founded a hiking trail that thousands of people visit every year, many drawn to our island because of it. And you've taught countless students, shaped them into better writers and better people. Written stories that've moved people, the world over."

Gemma's mouth pinched at the sides, and she blinked quickly. Brooke held back her tears, too—both for herself and for Gemma's pain. For what they would all miss in this incredible woman.

"But more than all those crowning achievements, you are open and generous with your love and your time. You are an absolute light in this world and we love you so much."

A tear trickled down Brooke's cheek and she brushed it away.

Gemma returned to her seat, smiling at Brooke as she made her way past Mhairi. Gemma had always made Brooke feel welcome and taken care of, even now.

A middle-aged man in a red-and-black kilt and faded jacket took Gemma's place behind the podium. He fiddled with the bow tie that looked out of place with his unruly beard. "I knew Mhairi when we both lived on Skye."

"And who are ye?" a shout rang out from behind Brooke.

The man at the podium shielded his eyes from the glare of the sun as if the driving cap offered little relief and said, "Och, your own brother, ye daftie. But for the rest of you, I'm Callum."

Mhairi turned in her seat to whisper-shout to Brooke, "Part of the Troublesome Trio."

"Now, if you're from here, and of a certain age, you'll recall the addition of the Skye Bridge and that damnable tax to pass to and fro across it."

This earned a booing kind of grumble from a contingent in the back and "A right scam!" from Callum's brother.

Callum told a story about Mhairi arriving at a pub one night with a brown paper bag of 1p coins she'd gotten at the bank so they could pay the fee in the most obnoxious way possible, about her uncanny ability to create joy where there was none.

"Don't forget the best part!" Mhairi called out.

"Och, quite right." Callum scratched his chin through his thick beard, a smile blooming on his face. Mhairi turned in her seat to smile devilishly at her childhood friends. "Mhairi goes, 'We might be leavin' out one or two, to make the countin' worthwhile.'"

Mhairi's friends whooped, cheering for their fearless leader, and Brooke laughed despite herself. She caught Jack's eye again, the smile on his face stealing her breath. Callum took off his black cap and held it against his heart. "You'll be missed, my dear."

Brooke blinked fast, her relief from a humorous story short-lived.

Reid bounded up from his seat to the podium with a stack of note cards he fanned out and back like playing cards. "Hello, everyone. For those who don't know me, I'm Reid, Mhairi's favorite nephew."

Logan called out a loud "Oy!" and everyone laughed at Reid's devil-may-care grin. Mhairi turned to blow Logan a kiss but Brooke didn't miss the way her eyes landed on Jack as she turned back around, the soft smile she had just for him, the way his eyes crinkled in response. It somehow warmed and broke her heart at the same time, seeing that love and affection on his face, wanting it turned in her direction again.

"When I was a kid, maybe five, Aunt Mhairi had just gotten a butterfly tattoo. She showed it to me—" He tapped his inner forearm to demonstrate. "Oh, shit, is this public knowledge? Sorry, Grandma." His wide eyes cut to Mhairi, who rocked back in her chair with laughter, as a devious smile spread across Reid's lips.

"Anyway," he said, pulling the attention back. "She showed me her tattoo and said, 'Don't tell anyone.'" He rested his forearm on the podium and leaned over it. "Now, we all know you don't ask kids to keep secrets anymore." He shook his head in

Mhairi's direction with a little tut-tut and another ripple of laughter went through the gathering; Reid had grown into a natural charmer.

Reid laid down the note cards he hadn't been using anyway and curled his fingers around the edges of the podium, straightening. "But being included in this secret made me feel special. And seen—like I was worth confiding in. And I think Mhairi makes a lot of people feel that way. I've never met a better listener. Or someone who can so clearly see through to the heart of a problem or to the heart of a person."

Mhairi had always made Brooke feel the same way. Tears leaked out of Brooke's eyes and she blotted them with the tissue she'd wrapped around her index finger at the touching and true sentiment.

Mhairi's friends and family took the stage one at a time, each sharing anecdotes and embarrassing stories, and the warmth radiating from Mhairi's joy seeped into Brooke.

Jack walked toward the podium, a remote in his hand. He fussed with the projector, dropping to one knee, and his kilt swished while he twisted the lens to bring it into focus. Brooke couldn't help watching his every moment, yearning for him to look at her, to make this easier, to calm her mind and her heart.

When he got the video playing, a dim version from all the sunlight, he stepped out of the way. A stunning image of the Storr filled the screen. "I don't know if you heard, but my aunt helped found the Skye Trail," Jack said into the mic.

"We know!" Reid shouted and the ripple of laughter sounded again. Brooke wanted to join in but her heart was still in her throat.

"Brooke Sinclair and I—" his eyes found hers and her breath caught "—just got back and we met amazing people along the way who wanted to share their love."

The video of Cat at the beach outside Portree played. "Hi, Aunt Mhairi! I'm Catalina! We're a little off your trail here, but you'd love it. Look at this beach," Cat said from the screen, the beach coming into view with the tilt of her camera.

Jack pressed his palms flat on the podium top. "You've impacted the lives of countless people. People who've never even met you."

Oliver and Murray, then Anya and Duncan, filled the screen, all saying their hellos and best wishes.

"You inspire people, you're a part of their stories."

Natalia and Catalina were back, smiles shining in the dim light of the bothy, and Brooke's stomach swooped with the anticipation of the moment, even though she'd been there, even though she'd known the answer the minute she'd met them.

"Catalina, will you marry me?"

"You've been a part of the most important moments of our lives."

Jack's eyes were back on Brooke and she couldn't breathe. Mhairi had altered the course of Brooke's life so many times. She might not have crossed the ocean or that room at a house party. Might not have crossed the Bad Step or the lines she'd drawn with Jack before she'd let him back into her heart.

He turned his attention back to Mhairi. "But to me, you're Auntie. This larger-than-life person I've always idolized. You draw people to you. It's something that's never come naturally to me—"

"Oh, posh," Mhairi said from the front row.

"I was never very good with words. Or saying what I wanted…" His eyes cut to Brooke. "Or how I was feeling." Jack gestured to the screen, the picture he took that night over the Isle of Raasay when things first started feeling hopeful between them. Still images faded in and out: the pastel harbor in Portree, the gray stone bridge in Sligachan, the white bothy against the blue sea.

"I hope my pictures can show you the profound impact you've had on my life," he said. "The profound impact you've had on people you've never even met, but especially on each and every person gathered here today."

When Jack finished, Brooke summoned her courage and made her way to the front for her turn to speak, wobbling through the gravel, still unused to wearing shoes like this after the hike. Her throat ached from holding back tears and anxiety fluttered under her breastbone, unsure how she was going to get through what she wanted to say.

As Jack drew close on his way back to his seat, Brooke's ankle gave out and she stumbled. He caught her arm and steadied her and her racing heart reached for him. She looked up into his dark eyes, full of such warmth and love. "You can do this," he said under his breath.

She nodded back. He always made her feel like she could do anything she put her mind to.

When she made it to the podium and turned to face the group assembled in front of her, she said, "Whew. That was a dicey trek."

Friendly laughter floated to her, but the weight of Jack's gaze eclipsed it. Soothed her, grounded her, gave her the push to go on.

"I'm Brooke," she said. "I'm one of Mhairi's former students and I've been writing with her over the last seven years. Because of that, I naively thought it would be easier to put Mhairi's impact on my life into words. But I could actually write a whole book about her."

She and Mhairi shared a smile and like the other speakers, Brooke laid her palms on the podium, the sun-warmed wood a calming force.

"My admiration for Mhairi stretches back before I even met her. I read *Black Currents* in high school and it was filled with such adventure and promise that I chose to study at the University of Edinburgh, to experience Scotland for myself." She looked at Mhairi. "It was everything you wrote about and more."

Brooke swallowed and flipped to her next note card, the black ink swimming. "Then I took Mhairi's class, and talk about a fangirl. I may or may not have asked her to sign my book on the first day."

"We've all been there, lass," Callum called from the audience.

Brooke laughed and cleared her throat, rubbing a hand against the tightness in her chest. Her heart swelled with the knowledge that Mhairi's stories would live on. This group of people would share Mhairi with those they loved. This wouldn't be the end.

"I remember Mhairi talked about experiencing the world to become a better writer. She encouraged us to live a life worth writing about. To take chances and step out of our comfort zones, to love fearlessly." Brooke couldn't keep her gaze from traveling to the first row. Jack's hair lay in gentle waves, his white shirt rolled to his elbows, his mere presence calming her racing heart.

Brooke wet her lips and brushed away tears with the heel of her hand and looked back to Mhairi. "Thank you for investing in me and sharing your wisdom. I am so grateful for all the stories we've worked on together, and all the ones that are still to come. You had to force me out on a *formidable* hike—but I think I finally learned your lesson."

When Brooke's eyes settled on Jack's, he was looking at her like she was the whole world.

She'd been chasing the wrong second chance.

NOW

At the end of the speeches, Gemma retook the stage, explaining about the new garden boxes and the flowers that were available for planting in Mhairi's honor. Mhairi's echoing advice for everyone to get their hands dirty rang out in the clear afternoon air.

But all Jack's attention was focused on Brooke seated in the second row, her eyes red, Mhairi turned around and squeezing her hand and Brooke nodding back, like they had some secret language between them. His heart pumped madly in his chest, never planning to settle after the way she'd looked at him and filled him with wild hope.

When Brooke glanced his way, her light eyes landed on him like a gentle, soothing wave. Her gaze cut to the cherry blossom tree and back like a question. He gave her a pirate's salute like she'd done all those years ago at Advocate's Close and her answering smile sent a starburst of hope through him. Maybe they still had a secret language, too.

As he walked past, Mhairi gave Jack an encouraging and simultaneously cheeky smile. "Auntie," he said with a warning in his voice that only made her chuckle.

As Brooke gingerly walked through the gravel, Jack crossed the distance between them in long strides, offering her his arm.

She looked up at him through her eyelashes. "Captain."

The nickname lit him up, sending all his well-planned words into chaos, worse when she looped her hand through the crook of his arm, her fingertips sending five points of heat into his skin.

"That was quite the slideshow."

Jack led Brooke along a gravel path rimmed with cut green grass toward the towering trees at the edge of the property. He wanted to blurt out all the thoughts consuming his mind and forced himself to slow down, to get it right, but the battering of his heart had other ideas, urging him on, needing to know what she'd say.

They stopped below a tree leafed out in early summer glory and he turned to look at her. Salty tracks ran over her cheeks, and her eyes were the beautiful blue of his favorite photo of Loch Oich. Suddenly all the words he'd rehearsed were gone. He was a hammering heart and an echo of fear.

"You were right," Brooke said, and the words restarted Jack's breathing. "I've been so focused on the memoir and my career, and the things I could do to prove to myself and the world that I was worthwhile." She gazed up into the white blooms above them. "And I have never been good at taking chances that might end in failure."

She turned her sky blue eyes on him and pressed her hand over his heart. "I shouldn't have asked you to sacrifice your dreams. I just didn't want to lose you."

Jack slipped his hand over hers, holding her there. "I know."

"I don't know why it took so long for me to realize, except that I was afraid. Afraid of our past and trusting you again and what it would mean to me if things didn't work out. But you were right that I can't keep living other people's stories." She took a breath, stepped in a little closer. "I turned down the ghostwriting job."

Brooke must've been able to feel Jack's heart under her palm, it beat so fast. He bit back his questions—if this meant she was writing again...if this meant she was staying.

"I've been working on my story."

"I'm so proud of you."

"I was scared—I'm still scared—but I don't want to hide anymore. You have always made me feel safe enough to live a big life."

Brooke had always encouraged him, too. Made him feel like he could have the world if only he was brave enough to reach for it. "You make me feel like that, too."

"And while I was writing, I realized that I haven't been chasing the things that make a story, that make a life worth living."

Jack wanted to wrap his arms around her, wanted the comfort of her embrace, the promise in her touch, but he backed up. He couldn't let Brooke bear the responsibility for the words just because she was better at them.

"I need to say something, too," he said.

Brooke nodded quickly, her wary eyes locked on Jack's. "Okay."

"I was genuinely trying to protect you back then, to make sure you'd be eligible for Mhairi's fellowship, that you could have everything you ever wanted."

"I should've realized."

He looked at his shoes before dragging his eyes up to hers again. "I should have *talked* to you."

Brooke nodded.

"What I regret even more is letting you walk away. I was utterly charmed the first moment you tripped into me." Like adjusting the lens of a camera and the whole world coming into focus. "I was transfixed by your ambition and passion and

I wanted to be a part of it. You made me feel like I mattered. You lit up my whole life. I've spent too much time trying to make other people happy, but the time I was happiest was when I was with you."

The breeze whispered through the leaves and twirled the orange tie at Brooke's waist, blowing a strand of her hair against her lips. With the pad of his finger, he tucked it back behind her ear.

"Those old feelings never went away for me. I should've told you I was falling in love with you again. I should've told you what I wanted."

Her breath caught, and he wanted to pull her to him.

"So...what *do* you want, Jack?" she asked with a quirk of her lips, that old question he could never quite answer, could never quite bring himself to say out loud. But he could now.

"I want you. I want a whole life, full of you. To share a flat in Portobello overlooking the water. I want to swim in the mornings and warm you up with coffee and cake." His hand cupped her cheek, his thumb stroking back and forth. "I want to explore Glencoe and walk the West Highland Way, take you on the damn Heiland Coo Trail. I want to read all your stories and I want to be a part of them. I have your history, Brooke. I want your future, too."

Brooke sank her fingers into his hair and he cupped her cheek, tipping her head back and kissing her long and deep.

"I love you," she said on a whisper and pushed his hair out of his eyes. "I always have."

A single tear leaked out of her eye and Jack brushed it away with the pad of his thumb. "I never stopped."

✦ EPILOGUE ✦

NOW

Two years later…

Brooke and Jack climbed the flight of stairs to their apartment. It didn't have an ocean view—because what were they, aristocrats?—but they did live in Portobello. Brooke pushed her wet hair off her shoulders where it was dripping into her hoodie as they came up the last flight of stairs, gym bags with soggy bathing suits and towels rolled up inside, the smell of the sea still on their skin.

A rectangular brown box sat on their Nice Package doormat and while Jack bent down to pick it up, Brooke checked out his ass.

He turned, pushing his damp hair off his forehead. "Brooke Sinclair," he said with a huge grin crinkling his eyes behind his glasses.

Brooke's stomach swooped like a gull over the ocean. "My books?"

Jack tilted the box and shook. "I think it's a dishwasher."

"Don't hurt them," she said, making grabby hands and taking the box from him. She held the box close to her chest while Jack dug in his pocket for the keys and unlocked the door. He held it open for her and she headed straight for their kitchen. Setting the box down on the bistro table, she passed Jack's calendar hanging on the side of the fridge open to a shot of the Storr. As she rummaged through the junk drawer looking for a pair of scissors, Jack wrapped his towel around the bottom of her wet hair. "Trying to wreck them straight off?"

She grabbed the scissors with a triumphant "Aha," and Jack shook his head.

"Apparently you are," he said under his breath, grabbing the small box cutter and trading her for the scissors. "Do you want me to film this?"

"Look at me right now," she said, pointing to her general dishevelment. She didn't have time to make herself presentable and the overwhelming feelings of pride and happiness and relief in her chest were too big to share. She shook her head. "This is just for us."

She sliced through the tape and ripped at the edges where the flaps held. Inside was a flat lay of perfection, an extension of her soul outside her body. She gazed at the pastel purple covers, neatly packed together, before running her hand along the smooth finish. Jack stood across from her, one arm crossed under the other, one hand cupping his elbow, and watched her with watery eyes.

It made the moment even more surreal. From the first time she'd met him, she'd had this dream and the hard work and tears and joy were all somehow organized into a story she could now hold in her hands.

Her novel was a heart book. A story that had poured out of her, borrowing little pieces of her real life. She'd been so scared she couldn't do this without Mhairi, but Brooke had felt her presence, her encouragement, her faith, in every word she wrote.

Brooke picked up one book and flipped through the pages,

the tiny Scottish thistles on the chapter headings making her smile so hard her cheeks hurt.

Jack gave her an amused grin. "Go on, then."

Tipping her head down, she breathed in the smell, like dust and ink and love. Brooke let the scent settle on her heart. "It reminds me of Mhairi."

Brooke still missed her, but it didn't hurt as much these days. She felt Mhairi's spirit in their old coffee shop, when strangers shredded tea tags, in unruly gusts of wind, and in unexpected bursts of inspiration.

"I can't wait," Jack said, stepping away and tipping his head toward the living room. Brooke followed him to the bay window, the low morning light filtering in on the bookshelf he'd built to house all their favorite books. "Another one for the Brooke Shelf," he said.

Signed copies of every one of Mhairi's books were on the top shelf, tucked next to Mhairi's collection of all the books Brooke had ghostwritten. The last addition was Mhairi's memoir with Jack's soft pink picture of the Isle of Raasay on the cover. Her favorite story.

Sometimes when she reread it, parts felt like a fever dream that she barely remembered writing, they'd flowed so effortlessly out of her.

But the moment Mhairi had read the final draft was distilled in Brooke's mind. The happiness shining in Mhairi's eyes. The warmth of her hand as she reached for Brooke's. The way she'd said, "Thank you for bringing my story to life," with pride in her voice.

Jack wrapped his arms around Brooke's waist and rested his cheek against her temple. "How does it feel?" he asked, nuzzling her ear, that soft spot that always felt like home.

"Like everything I ever wanted." Brooke reached up to cup his cheek, to bask in the future she'd always dreamed of that'd become her present.

Maybe it wasn't so easy to edit in real life, to delete and revise and correct, but she was so grateful for the grace to fail and make mistakes and still find a happy ending. Brooke twisted to kiss Jack, his lips soft and warm and comforting as he squeezed her shoulders, his thumbs pressing gently into the slope of her neck.

And then she turned back to the beginning of her book. To the name that mattered most—not the one on the cover, but the one tucked safely inside:

To Mhairi,
For giving us our second chance.

★ ★ ★ ★ ★

ACKNOWLEDGMENTS

Where *Kilt Trip* was my love letter to Scotland, *Scot and Bothered* is my love letter to the people finding their authentic selves. And… still to Scotland because I just love it there so much!

Writing the dual timeline in this story was, let me just say, a *challenge*. Jack was a character who has been with me from before I wrote *Kilt Trip* and I have always envisioned his story including a university timeline. I pulled so much from my own study abroad experience to include in Jack's and Brooke's college days. I wanted to capture that youthful exuberance for exploration and the feelings of freedom and possibility when we don't know much about the real world yet. The places they visit in uni are some of my favorite spots in Edinburgh and I hope I captured the magic I feel every time I'm there.

When I was first daydreaming about *Scot and Bothered* and how it would relate to *Kilt Trip*, I felt a bit daunted about how to showcase Scotland in a different way because I had put so many places in that book that were so personal to me. Jack and

Brooke's story really came to life when I decided to set it on Skye. I have never been to a more mystical place.

The Skye Trail is a real trail on the island and it is as rugged as the story suggests. Mhairi is a fictional character, but inspired by Cameron McNeish and the group of hikers in the '90s who set about developing this trail that is now one of the most popular in Scotland.

During the summer when I was first drafting this book, I convinced my friend Adrian to hop a plane from where she was staying with her family in Denmark and come join me for a week of "research." We visited my favorite places in Edinburgh and then ventured up to Skye to scope out some landmarks along the trail (because I am in no way outdoorsy enough to do the full trek). It was as magical as I remembered and it was a delight finding old and new places on the island.

Adrian, I will always treasure walking miles and miles with you, eating gelato for dinner, and fending off jetlag with middle-of-the-night ramen and Cocoa Puffs parties. Thank you for coming on a book trip with me and for all the enthusiasm and joy you bring to my life.

To Lynn Raposo, my fantastic editor, thank you for coming along on this journey with me that started when I pitched a—hopefully more eloquent—version of "I think…exes reunite and have to hike a grueling trail on Skye and there's probably only one tent." You were foundational in shaping this story, brainstorming with me, and not getting upset when I turned in a nearly finished draft with an additional 4000 words you weren't expecting. Thank you for your wisdom and encouragement and for always knowing how to make my stories better. You're truly a delight to work with.

And to my fabulous agent, Jill Marr—it will forever be my goal in life to make you cry on an airplane while reading. Thank you for loving my stories, for your support, and for your emails that always brighten my day. I couldn't have asked for a better advocate!

Maggie North and Sarah Brenton, you are both so integral to the way I write and I truly could not do it without you. Thank you for the endless brainstorming sessions, the group chat draping, and all the commiserating and laughter along the way. I admire you both so much as writers and am so lucky to get to go through every step of the drafting process with you. You are my rocks!

Kym Summers and Suzanne Junered, you two made every Tuesday morning coffee writing session the highlight of my week. Thank you for all the support and cheerleading and drinking copious amounts of tea with me. While we didn't always do *the most* writing when we were together, I felt so inspired by your energy and enthusiasm for all of our stories. You're the best friends a girl could ask for.

Livy Hart, Hannah Olsen, Aurora Palit, and Emily Matheis, thank you for reading an early draft and helping me figure out what story I was even trying to tell. You are all so creative and thoughtful (and hilarious in the margins!). This book is so much stronger because of your wisdom.

Amanda Elliot, Jessica Joyce, Sarah T Dubb, Tarah DeWitt, Shaylin Gandhi, Neely Tubati Alexander, and Falon Ballard, (along with Maggie North, Livy Hart, and Aurora Palit), thank you for reading and lending your beautiful words and names to my story with your blurbs. I admire your writing so very much and value your friendship even more.

Thank you to my family for all your encouragement and support in letting me follow my dreams. And to Kara and Riley—who won't read these books until they are *much* older—thank you for being my biggest fans, getting as excited as I do when we can unbox new books, and for telling everyone I'm your favorite author. I am so honored to be your mom.

And to my readers. Meeting you and sharing my stories has

been the most incredible and unexpected gift in all of this. Thank you for DMing me about *Outlander* and hairy coos, for helping to spread the word through cover reveals and release days, and for sharing your stories and the ways mine have touched your hearts.